PENGUIN BOOKS

A SHOOTING STAR

Wallace Stegner (1909–1993) was the author of, among other novels, *Remembering Laughter*, 1937; *The Big Rock Candy Mountain*, 1943; *Joe Hill*, 1950; *All the Little Live Things*, 1967 (Commonwealth Club Gold Medal); *A Shooting Star*, 1961; *Angle of Repose*, 1971 (Pulitzer Prize); *The Spectator Bird*, 1976 (National Book Award, 1977); *Recapitulation*, 1979; and *Crossing to Safety*, 1987. His nonfiction includes *Beyond the Hundredth Meridian*, 1954; *Wolf Willow*, 1963; *The Sound of Mountain Water* (essays), 1969; *The Uneasy Chair: A Biography of Bernard DeVoto*, 1974; and *Where the Bluebird Sings to the Lemonade Springs: Living and Writing in the West*, 1992. Three of his short stories have won O. Henry prizes, and in 1980 he received the Robert Kirsch Award from the *Los Angeles Times* for his lifetime achievements. His *Collected Stories* was published in 1990.

Wallace Stegner

* * *

A
SHOOTING
STAR

Penguin Books

PENGUIN BOOKS

Published by the Penguin Group
Penguin Books USA Inc., 375 Hudson Street,
New York, New York 10014, U.S.A.
Penguin Books Ltd, 27 Wrights Lane, London W8 5TZ, England
Penguin Books Australia Ltd, Ringwood, Victoria, Australia
Penguin Books Canada Ltd, 10 Alcorn Avenue,
Toronto, Ontario, Canada M4V 3B2
Penguin Books (N.Z.) Ltd, 182–190 Wairau Road,
Auckland 10, New Zealand

Penguin Books Ltd, Registered Offices: Harmondsworth, Middlesex, England

First published in the United States of America
by The Viking Press, Inc. 1961
Published in Penguin Books 1996

7 9 10 8 6

Chapter 13 first appeared in *Contact*.

Library of Congress Catalog Card Number: 61–7037
ISBN 0 14 02.5241 X (pbk.)

Printed in the United States of America
Set in Goudy Old Style

For Mary

A SHOOTING STAR

CHAPTER 1

E XCEPT for an occasional dry question, he left the talking to her, waiting while she fought out the difficult words. It was as if he applied a pump: she could feel the contents of her insides, discolored and poisonous, being exposed to his laboratory scrutiny. If he had said anything—anything!—to indicate that he felt as a wronged husband should feel. But that controlled suspension of judgment, that look not critical but only clinical, as if the gross symptoms of treachery were to be gathered together objectively like the symptoms of peptic ulcers. Any distress before or after eating? Any blood in the stools?

In the middle of it the telephone rang. He excused himself and left her—it felt like being left in an obstetrical chair—and when he returned he said in his dry and level voice that they would have to postpone it, he had to go out on a call.

She could not believe she had heard him right. *"Now?"* she said. "Right when we— Oh, Burke, isn't this one time—"

"I'm sorry, I'm afraid I have to."

His forehead, smooth and high under the thinning front hair, shone in the light from the hall. With a terrible, complicated feeling of pity, shame, and protectiveness she recognized in her very hands how his forehead felt, its smoothness and bareness, at times when she touched

3

it testing for fever, or put her palm there to flatten out wrinkles of fatigue or strain. Yet she was still glaring at him, unable to control the warping of her mouth. "Somebody's stomach ache?"

"Probably somebody's appendicitis, yes."

"Are you the only doctor in Pasadena?"

"She's my patient."

"I should think your wife might matter as much as . . ."

An indescribable grimace tightened in his face. He seemed to squint against a bad light. "*Are* you my wife?"

"Oh!" she cried. "If you go out at a time like this!"

For a second he seemed to weigh things in his mind. He made her feel the difference between his probity and her disreputable collapse. His jaws looked narrow and severe, and under the compressed lips she could see the bulge of his teeth. His gray eyes forced her toward a shameful self-judgment. "Other people's emergencies won't always wait on ours," he said. "We can go on with ours in a half hour."

Anger went through her as paralyzingly as if she had laid her hand on an electric fence. Her eyes felt scalded. For one long instant she stared into his gray glance, and then she spun away. She escaped into motion without thinking where she would go.

In the drive, her lights exploded against the porte-cochere with its clot of purple bougainvillaea, the motor awoke under her foot, her backing lights flared on lawn and flowerbed and the smooth boles of royal palms until she cramped into the turning circle. As she shifted the automatic drive lever she glanced furiously back at the entry. Dark. He had not followed her to the door.

Then, as an alternative to being consumed by her feelings, she willed herself to be as much a part of the car as the fuel pump. She became a photoelectric eye that responded to red and green and amber light, a switch that blinked back at an irritable blinking, a foot that forced jets of fuel through the carburetor, a pair of hands that spun smoothly the power-driven wheel. It was a night warmer than usual, a summer-shirtsleeve night. The eddying air was city-smelling, flavored by watered lawns, exhaust, flowers. Through it for quite a long time she drove as if at her own volition, capable of stoppings, turnings, and returnings. Yet she went as mindlessly as a plane on automatic pilot, and through a traffic pattern as compulsive as the structure of atoms. Her mind was clenched like a fist.

Later, a half hour or an hour, her street spun into a concrete whirlpool, and she was swept into a swift reach of freeway. On both sides, the service roads dazzled and winked their roadside businesses. Light gleamed off the beetle backs of cars, flooded from windows where mannequins had come out to inspect the crowds, rained against façades of glass and stucco, bored upward from moving searchlight lenses. Pausing for a red light while a trucker next door stared down at her from his high cab, she emerged from her automatism long enough to despise the cheap and frantic glitter of everything, and she tasted in her throat the poisonous carbon compounds of automotive waste.

She flickered her eyes off the trucker's admiring glance, knowing exactly how she appeared to him—a good looking woman in a late-model convertible, something out of a motor ad, a cliché of desirability, absolutely at home on this main street of Vanity Fair. Then the stain of red light on the trucker's face went amber, he lunged to his gears, she put her foot down and drew smoothly ahead.

Traffic thickened and began to stack up. She was smothered in trucks, buses, cars, big square trailers belted with lights, jalopies that crippled along limp-fendered and wobble-wheeled, showing quilts and cartons on their roofs and Negro or white or Mexican faces at their windows and feet over the tops of doors. An impatient car ducking out of its lane to squeeze through brought Sabrina's foot down hard on the brake pedal. In the mirror she watched the lights behind her surge up big and ominous, and hunched her shoulders against the crash that did not quite come.

The even lanes of cars broke up around flares and standing men, the flashing red light of a police car, a pickup slewed sideways and a sports car on its side like a squashed bug. The wreck held her attention only while she was easing past it. Then the delayed traffic leaped out, but not fast enough to free her. Cruising behind a car that refused to speed up or move over, Sabrina edged over the double line. An opposing driver rode his horn, lights glared, horn howled and was gone, leaving her chased back into the dazzled dark of her own lane. "Toad," she said. She might have admitted the justice of his protest, but she despised people who used their horns.

Again she sneaked over the double line, this time saw room, and whipped out to pass. More lights were coming, the driver she was passing increased his speed, risking a wreck to teach her a lesson. But her foot was down on more than three hundred horses. She lifted and poured by, cutting the passed car short to teach *him* a lesson. The hollow night filled with the whish and thud of the passing projectile. Sabrina lightened her foot, and, with her lane clear for two hundred yards ahead, settled back down to seventy.

She was coming onto the Grapevine, or what had been called the Grapevine in her childhood. Now it looped through the hills six lanes wide, its curves softened and its grades evened out, and only trucks or buses recognized it at all. They were already getting over into the slow lane, beginning to labor, shifting down: one, and then another, and then another, a succession of concussions of collapsed air. The white-lined highway curved away under planed cuts, above the shadows of filled ravines; she was winked at by the constant eyes of the crash fence. The horizon humped up into hills, and the stars gathered and came closer. Into her cockpit the wind eddied the sudden smell of dust and dry weeds, and it was that, with its suggestion of aromatic desert—that and the new openness and nearness of the sky —that turned loose her mind again.

The picture came without warning, cameo-sharp and small: the hot butte of Monte Alban, and the two of them locked together in an exposed, sun-soaked tableau. Neither ten days of that romantic-novel insanity, nor anything that had happened tonight, had lessened her incredulity at herself in that context. Disbelief, as much as honesty, had made her tell Burke. She had had almost the feeling that he could waken her and talk her out of the dream.

She whispered the word "lover" to herself, and closed her eyes an involuntary moment and felt a nervous spasm tingle outward from under her ribs and pebble her skin with gooseflesh. She saw them kissing under the big open sky among temples and courts and the unexcavated mounds of ruins. Whoever was supposed to look after the

6

place had crawled into the shade to sleep. There were only the two of them, watched by a burro who waggled flies out of his ears.

Mainly she remembered the intense searching of eyes that went on between kisses, as if they really were the windows of the soul and you could discover another person that way. She had traced all around his eye-sockets with her finger—why? To know him all through, even to his skull and skeleton? (Why else should her hand remember the cool smoothness of Burke's forehead?) What made the excitement of knowing and being known? Men and women born incomplete and mad to be made whole? Then the most private act of life was a throwing away of everything the self meant. A woman with no one to give herself to might covet even the sterile intimacies of her analyst or her gynecologist. The profound touch, the unqualified permission . . .

A sob as unexpected as a hiccup jumped in her throat, and she drove with her face hardened and her teeth gritted and her eyes blurrily fixed on the white line unreeling past her left front wheel. Her chest was tight, her eyes stung, she pounded her hand on the wheel. The nature of what she had been coughing up into Burke's clinical sight overwhelmed her, and obliterated the brief shiver of desire. For it was dirty, it had all been dirty and treacherous, and she hated herself, Bernard, the circumstances that had thrown them together in that Oaxaca hotel, the hypocrisy of their accidental meetings in the zocalo, the unadmitted conspiracy that had first created and then enlarged opportunity. How little for so much to turn on—a decision to go together, at hot midday and without a guide, up onto Monte Alban. All that pretense of relaxed friendliness with which a man on a buying trip treated a woman traveling without her husband. But he had known what he was suggesting when he wondered if she would like to go, and she had known what she was accepting. They had gone almost holding their breath, though they talked of Mixtec history.

And why did it have to turn out deserted as they both hoped it would? A dry plateau that whispered of a fantastic life now quiet: human sacrifices, ball games to the death, burials that heaped the dead with jewels, victory ceremonies around the temple whose every upside-down figure represented the chief of a conquered town. Why did it have to catch the throat with its desert valley spread below in miniature villages, white strings of roads, lines of trees and cactus fences, patches of milpas on the hillsides high up? All that beauty, and all that dry history whispering, See how it passes? How much has already passed? Their blood was clogged, their talk was like talk overheard, not spoken to be shared, and their mouths were dry with what was unsaid, barely hinted—until a moment when they turned toward one another and it was as if electricity leaped the gap.

That day they read no more.

And yet it was all so damnably Freudian and obscene, the two of them kissing among the ghosts in that place of tombs, helpless love and cureless treachery and inescapable consequences all combined in the first act of a wretched modern *Liebestod*. It occurred to her that there might be tragedy in it and in herself, the dignity of human passion and pain, but she could not retain that literary and schoolgirl idea. Knowing as much as a modern woman was supposed to know, who could be Iseult and believe in potions? Having knowledge of the endocrines, who could be Francesca and keep from laughing?

In her mind she inspected the two of them again, staged and brittle, like *Vogue* models posed in sports clothes against the ruined columns of Luxor or Baalbek, and she hated it, hated it. A little while ago, telling Burke, she might have managed to say how little she had wanted or expected this—how little, actually, she believed in it. She had said all the wrong things and failed to say the right ones; she had never made him understand in the slightest how it was.

It isn't as if I'd wanted to, she said, framing the words carefully as if speaking them aloud. It isn't as if I'd gone there with anything like that in my mind, some vulgar little cruise-ship affair. Yes, I was fed up. Yes, I was sick of seeing you a slave to the office—haven't I been for ten years? I was sick of the life I led. We'd had that quarrel once too often. But it wasn't anything deliberate, believe me. I went down there to get over it and come back rested. We might have lived happily ever after. I'm not the unfaithful type, darling, in spite of everything. I missed you down there, I was lonesome and restless and it just . . . happened. You'd never predict him as a person I'd fall in love with. He's no younger than you, he's nobody glamorous, just a buyer for a department store. I suppose it was his voice—he's got a rich warm caressing sort of voice. But that shouldn't be enough. He's got three children and he drinks too much and he's miserably tied. But darling . . . oh, damn.

The road crested and swept curving down. She saw the crawling lights of cars ahead and below, and far away the glow of towns. The night air here was soft and sweet. She found a cigarette in the glove compartment and pushed in the lighter and drove leaning forward, one hand out to catch the lighter when it popped. For the second or two of the act there was again a complete suspension of her mind. But when she held the red circle against the cigarette and drew in, the glow lighted her forehead and nose and the dark smooth wings of her hair. She watched her reflection in the windshield, drawing on the cigarette to brighten the image, exhaling to let it fade. It reassured her, in a way. It gave her an object to resist. She found it easier to think with her own faintly suggested face suspended before her. She always thought better in conversation than when she sat down by herself to muddle something out. The sense of an audience stimulated her; alone, she went in circles. Now she acknowledged the image in the windshield, barely a shadow of movement as the cigarette darkened, to be a dark division of herself, and she tried in an objective way, giving evidence, to explain to it.

Not to make an excuse of the fact that I've felt trapped, she said. I knew when I married him what a doctor's life was. I knew he was ten years older than I was. I knew he was ambitious and proud. I agreed when he wanted to do it himself, without leaning on my money or connections. How could I blame him? I respected him for it. And God knows I wasn't forced to marry him. I fell into his arms, and I swear I was a loyal wife, even after it got so tiresome and he organized the clinic and was always off at meetings or on calls. I did my duty. I kept his house and kept myself available and entertained myself as I could, and tried to be gay, and tried was it my fault I couldn't?—to bear his children. I was a good wife, I was, I was.

And yet when that happened down there, and it was clear what we were up to, did I feel terrified or ashamed? Oh, no. I felt the wildest sort of excitement, as if I had escaped. It isn't fair to Burke, but that's exactly how I felt. I went into it without a qualm. You would have thought I'd been waiting around all my life for the opportunity.

As if there weren't always a million opportunities, as if you didn't avoid opportunities the way you look both ways before crossing a street. Why *this* opportunity?

So it wasn't, she said, watching her shadowy face glow and fade again—it wasn't only hormones, it wasn't the ugly sort of thing you hear some women talking about, who's better in bed, who *satisfies* most. You'd think men were chocolates, and you could go through the box pushing a thumb through the bottoms or biting off a corner to see if they're the kind you like, and putting them back if they're not. Spitbacks, Barbara used to call them. But it wasn't that. Keep it honest. I could have closed my eyes and it could have been Burke. And yet all the time I was feeling that exultation, as if at last I was free, and *wanted,* in ways I never had been before. There was something in it for me stronger than guilt or fastidiousness or anything else. I wasn't swept off my feet; I swept myself off them.

She started to stub out the cigarette, automatically responsive to a lifetime of warnings about throwing out matches and cigarettes in a country where even the soil will burn, and then her lips hardened and she flipped it back over her head in a shower of sparks. A car slammed by; she was surprised that she remembered none for some time, though she must have been meeting them constantly. Behind the brief brightening to sudden glare, the even more sudden dark closed around her hurtling cockpit. Dry desert smells filled her head.

Miserable and yet at the same time alertly wondering, thinking with narrowed eyes, driving carelessly with the speedometer between seventy-five and eighty, she gripped the live wheel, thinking, Burke, oh, Burke, you might as well know, what I couldn't tell you. It hasn't been that way with us except when we were first married. Once it happened I was insatiable, I wanted him all the time. Why? I don't think just for the pleasure. Something else. The way a criminal must feel when he's got away with it and put it over on everyone. Is that the way I am? Have I had things like that festering in me? Have I resented it that much? It isn't hormones, hormones are just a vulgar itch. Something else. Pride. *Pride?*

She had a picture of herself slipping through that Oaxaca hotel corridor and into a door. Pride? What a wonderfully original way to be yourself.

Nevertheless it did not seem to her, no matter how much she might will it, that she could ever again go through all the pretenses and postponements of being Burke's wife. Into her mind, the moment she began to formulate the possibility, crept an angry irritability, and remembering the scene she had run from, and Burke's face (like an actor, like a bloody British actor registering self-control in a crisis!) she stirred in the seat, and stretched her stiffened ankle, and kicked off her shoe and drove with the corrugated rubber throttle rough under her stockinged sole. Why couldn't he have been really magnanimous? She had half hoped and half expected that he would—and yet there were those questions, so dry, so edged to wound, so honed on hurt vanity. Did he have to know how many times, where, when? Did he have to say that about the letters ("I remember your letters. I kept thinking how much good the trip was doing you. When did you write them, just before, or just after? Maybe you wrote some of them in his room.")

She felt like lifting her face into the blast of cool air and screaming, I *told* you I was sick over it, I told you how it happened, how I never . . . Do you think I'm made of iron? I'm still raw, can you realize that? I'm raw and sick, I've been raw and sick since it happened. Must you have every sluttish act out on a slide with a cover glass over it?

Screams, screams.

I don't know, she said half aloud to her image lurking barely seen in the glass. I don't know, I don't know.

The highway leveled off into the great valley, reaching north toward Bakersfield, Fresno, Stockton, Sacramento. The traffic now was mainly trucks and trailers that crashed past with concussions that rattled her teeth. Then ahead, on the shoulder, white signs glared. With her foot lifted above the throttle she rolled down to fifty, to forty, trying to read. Some said Bakersfield, Merced, Fresno. Others, pointing left, said Taft, Coalinga, U.S. 33. She cramped the wheel and slammed her foot down again and shot off down the secondary road to Taft.

She had no desire to drive through the brightness of a big town. Even at this late hour there would be people, and she felt and probably looked like the Witch of Endor. She wanted the dark of cotton fields and wasteland.

It was then, as she bored down the black road westward, that she first asked herself where she was going. Driving, yes, but hardly aimlessly. From the time she came out of her own driveway she had pushed the car as if bound for a critical appointment. If she had only intended to drive around a while and then go back, it was time to turn. She examined that possibility—to come in after four or five in the morning, fagged and pale, and face Burke's controlled and coldly furious eyes, and be reconciled, cry, beg his forgiveness and accept it. At least at that hour he shouldn't be called out. But even while she imagined it and yearned for it, it had the look of something spurious: the B-movie heroine after her standard few days of frenzy bidding a lingering good-by to the trench-coated wanderer lover, and returning shivering, contrite, soaked with rain and grief, to her kindly pipe-smoking husband and the tenderness of a little golden head in a crib.

Ugh! She thanked God, or nearly, that there was no tousled head to pull her back for the wrong reasons. And as for Burke, would he play the understanding role that the script called for? The way he had taken her confession made her wonder.

As if she had looked up at him across a room, she could see his still, long-cheeked face, and his gray eyes that kept their watchfulness, and his compressed mouth. More and more he wore what she thought of as his crisis mouth. When they were married he was just back from the Pacific, delayed in his career by four years of service, and he was cocked like a gun, determined to establish himself quickly, solidly, profitably. As part of his program of making a place for himself in Pasadena he used to play in an occasional club golf tournament. She had seen his mouth when he came up onto the edge of the green to study the lie of a putt: he could not do anything without doing it to win and without being aware of the effect it would have, on himself and others. Now she wondered if he had been suffering at all as he listened to her story, or if he had only been living up to what might have been expected of a good competitor.

Ah, if he'd only shown an emotion! He didn't have to cry or rage. Just any apparent feeling.

So where was she going? To Bernard? Walk up his walk and ring his bell and have his wife or one of his children answer the door?

I'm going to Hillsborough, she thought. At least nothing there is messy. I'm going back to Mother's for a while and try to think.

And call San Francisco?

She ran a distracted hand back over the coolness of her hair, and her mind was full of their agonized parting in the lost and gray-jade city of Oaxaca, only—my God!—that morning.

How she had swung away from him, the whole world dissolving, her knuckled hands to both eyes and her grief so great that she didn't care about the steward on the steps, the passengers loading, the pilot looking down from the Plexiglas nose. Even her memory of seeing them there was distorted and magnified by her tears. So was her memory of his face. They had agreed it could not go on, they had encouraged one another to think of their obligations elsewhere, they had been tender of those they had deceived, they had deliberately not taken the same plane home, they had parted as if parting were a death.

But here she went racing up the valley toward her mother's house, and Hillsborough was only twenty dangerous minutes from San Francisco, where Bernard worked, or from Stonestown, where he lived.

It was nearly three by the cowl clock, and cool. She did not have even a scarf to tie over her head, much less a topcoat. She struggled into the cardigan that until now she had worn shawled across her shoulders; waggled her stiffened foot; yawned, but not sleepily; turned up the cowl lights experimentally. Their greenish glow made the shadow of herself, steadily watching in the curved windshield, look like a skull with eyes.

Unfaithful, she said to herself, watching the reflection for a reaction. She saw none. Adultery, she said. The skull watched her.

Adultery. What a ridiculous Old Testament notion, and how vile that after resenting her mother's New England–Victorian notions all her life, she should find herself netted in a New England conscience of her own. When practically every woman she knew had had, or now had, or would have, a lover or many lovers; when adolescents were as promiscuous as street dogs, and every movie you went to, every play you saw, every novel you read, was sex-obsessed; when the accepted way to recover from guilt feelings, if you were unfortunate enough to have them, was to repeat the offense that caused them, until you could accept it as natural; then, *then,* right at that moment of history, she would have to be torturing herself with notions like adultery.

In Arabia, she thought, they would stone me to death. In some civilizations I would not be worrying about my husband showing an emotion; I would be dead. So here what? Smooth my hair with automatic hand and put a record on the gramophone? Anyone who went so far as to get into bed with a lover ought to be able to say the words without panicking, and yet she wavered and hung, despising but accepting the rankle of conscience. Up the double cone of her headlights she stared into a future blank with what she had almost inadvertently done.

The streets of Taft offended her eyes, used to darkness. At a truckers' stop she bought gas and toyed with the notion of coffee, but she could not imagine sitting in the bright cheap café with her hair coming down and her face showing, brooding over a thick mug like some sullen adolescent. She took gas card and receipt from the station attendant without ever having really seen him, and cruised the bright deserted street and saw the lights of oil fields on the hills; and then there was again the dark rush up the road, only an infrequent car or truck now, and long stretches where she might have been a rocket in space, swaying a little in interstellar winds, with the intricate nest of stabilizers, transistors, klystron tubes, photoelectric cells, and automatic cameras in her skull turning and recording and remembering, without volition and without rest.

The hills were a dark flow along the sky on her left. The valley black was scratched with moving, tiny lights, stars of the fifth or sixth magnitude, remote in some other galaxy. Two or three times she raised oil camps, close constellations colored like diamonds and rubies, that burned with so pure an intensity they made her own passage seem a flicker of undestinationed light. Out of the torpor of driving she roused to momentary pleasure at sight of them, and wondered groggily if all pleasure were of the senses, and thought secretly of touch, the insatiable appetite of the skin. She said, tasting the word, finding it a word from the same lexicon as adultery, the word ecstasy. What did the conscience know of ecstasy? For that matter, what did Dr. Burke Castro know of it?

Then the tired reminder. That isn't fair. You've been his wife for a dozen years. Now you sneer at him because you've injured him.

The motor's steady roar had taken up the whole interior of her head, the white center line of the highway stood on end into the darkness beyond the headlights, the telephone poles fled backward with a *whit! whit! whit!* Signs glared and were gone. The parted valley subsided back into its dark. Now she met almost no cars, but only occasional semis bringing down lettuce from Salinas, late strawberries from Castroville, baled hay from the dry valley. Her companions were the wondering faces of cows caught staring across fences, and her own fleeting image, at once transparent and inescapable and tinged with green like great Hamlet's phosphorescent ghost. Those and the creatures of her mind that crept out and retreated again, and her passions that remembered, and her conscience that rebuked and denied.

Gray light lay on the smooth hills above Pacheco Pass; back of her the valley was dim. As she crossed the hills, light grew and spread back the horizons, opened up the canyon and then the westward valley and the Coast Range beyond, grayed the trunks of sycamores along the creek and brightened the shine of leaves. Once, fifteen years or so ago —more than that, seventeen—she had climbed Pacheco Peak with a crowd, and it came back on her now like a memory of lost innocence: there had been slopes of April grass, wildflowers, all the springs running and the creeks full, and laughter all that day long. They had carried sandwiches and bottles of wine to the top and eaten in the sunny shelter of the fire tower. Remembering them there, sunburned and carefree under a light as tender as Corot's, she worked her dry, tobacco-saturated mouth, feeling a hundred years old.

Full dawn caught her between Gilroy and San Jose. Against the sky west of the highway the hills were dull gold. Around the outskirts of San Jose, past Moffett Field and its enormous blimp hangars, she drove tensely, tiredly, and too fast. Her mind had given up its circling and was sullenly still.

At Middlefield Road she swung into the left-turn alley and shot across on a changing light. Then fields and shacks, a flat new school, picture-window-and-shed-roof tracts with new lawns, sapling trees, ugly fences; and so into the tree-heavy streets of Palo Alto, looking as if they cried for an old-fashioned milk wagon and a clopping horse and a man in striped overalls darting from porch to porch with a wire cage of bottles. Nothing like that, actually: only a car backing from a driveway, that she paralyzed with a blast of horn, and University Avenue with only two cars on its whole length and many of its shops empty, done in by the drive-in shopping centers, and finally the underpass and the already hurrying channel of El Camino.

She wished she had stayed on Bayshore; only old habit had made her turn up here. She had forgotten what an anguish El Camino had become. Every driver was in a rush, racing the clock to work, driving by bluff and horn. Her scratchy eyes peered; she had to force herself to alertness through Menlo Park, Redwood City, Belmont, San Mateo. It was three times worse than she remembered from last time. Why couldn't they stay home in Arkansas or New York or wherever they all came from?

At last the topped eucalyptus trees, the limited stretch of El Camino where conservatism had prohibited commercial development, the street names that from childhood had been the home names—Ralston, Floribunda—and the unchanged patrician quiet. Or not unchanged, for, though the neon and stucco cheapness was behind her, the developers had thrust in even here. The street she drove was lined with gum trees, enormous and probably dangerous. Through their close-set trunks where the fairways of the country club used to gleam, circled by kicking jets of water, she saw the houses of the newer and lesser wealth, modern or ranch style, with their unhealed grounds.

But now the discreet lane, the stone wall, the modest country mailbox: *Hutchens*. She turned between the gate pillars and the open wings of the wrought-iron gates. Her tires gritted in fine white gravel. The drive curved to expose the lawns, the banks of azalea, the big old incongruous frame house whose gables reached up among the highest trees. As she pulled to a stop the sun was coming like some thick spilled liquid through the oaks.

She got out with her shoes in her hand, picked across the walk, and was reaching a hand to try the door when it opened and there was Lizardo in his white coat. He had not heard her, and his surprise was so violent it was comical. His intricately wrinkled face underwent a convulsion of smiles; he understood at once that she did not want noise. Ever since she was six he had conspired with her against her mother. Now he grabbed for her hand. His fingers were dry and warm, and his face was brown: with a pang she saw in it the brown Indian faces of Oaxaca, and to hide her own face she bent and hugged him.

"Lizardo!" she said. "Mabuhay!" and slipped past him into the Ispahan-cushioned stillness and brown dusk of the hall. Lizardo shut the door.

"You drive all night?"

"All night. Oof, I'm dead. Look, be an angel and have Virgil put my car away right now? I don't want Mother to see it and know I'm here. I'll surprise her this afternoon. How is she, all right?"

"Miz Hutchens pine. You all right?"

"Tired."

She smiled and started for the stairs, but he said, "You want breakpast? Coppee? Orange juice?"

"Not now. Just sleep."

Her stockinged feet were soundless in the carpet. After the windy roar of driving, the hall seemed unhealthily still, as deficient in oxygen as in light. Costly chilly gleams of rubbed walnut and gilt filtered down at her, and raising her eyes she saw them all watching her, four generations of women imprisoned in gilt frames.

From the left Great-Grandmother Wolcott, bony as a dray horse, rigid in a sheath of gray silk, wearing a communion-service hat and carrying a tiny parasol: a creation of John Singleton Copley. From the right Sabrina's mother, Deborah Barber Hutchens, etherealized by the art of John Singer Sargent to a meringue lightness, floated in white organdy, the boniness of her family face softened by what Sabrina had always felt was a cowardly catering to the wealth of the sitter. Mr. Sargent had painted young Deborah at the height of his fashionable reputation, and in two sittings. Next to his idealized portrait was Frank Duveneck's extraordinary likeness of Grandmother Emily Wolcott Barber—a thing like a Hals fishwife, a pale, long, lumpy face emerging

17

from bituminous darkness. And directly above, on the landing, meeting her eyes as she turned, Sarbina saw herself at the age of six. As a child she had been enormous-eyed, rather sullen, staring some question. Even then she had parted her hair in the middle, but in the portrait it hung down her back in a sheaf. She wore a pinafore with a belt of yellow ribbon, as if she had been dressed for a portrait by Sir Joshua Reynolds.

She hung a moment at the foot of the stairs, meeting the eyes of the sulky child. In girlhood she had spent hours when the house was clear, studying herself, and she had always thought Speicher one of the best American painters because of what he had seen in a dressed-up little girl brought to his studio for a standard society portrait. It would have been easy to whip up some frothy and flattering likeness, something like the Sargent, done in two sittings with a flourish. Instead, Speicher had painted a picture that Sabrina had always felt an obscure compulsion to live up to. Who was she? What did she want? What had she wanted at six, to put that unhappy question in her eyes?

The women, herself included, leaned on her with a weight hardly to be borne. What had seemed sanctuary as she slipped into it was again what it had always partly been—a place where life was conceived and possibly valued as a sort of house arrest.

Sabrina put a shoeless foot on the bottom stair. At that moment there were steps in the cross hall leading to the library and tea room, and Helen Kretchmer came into the hall.

"Why, Mrs. Castro!"

She was immaculate, as always—the Shirtmaker type, at any time of the day looking as if the blouse were just crisp off the ironing board. Her blond hair was softly brushed. At what hour must she get up, to look like this at seven? Also, she looked confident: that meant that the change from Mrs. Brill had been successfully made.

"Hello, Helen."

"Did you just arrive? We had no word."

"I just drove up on the spur of the moment."

"How nice," Helen said. "How was Mexico?"

"Divine," Sabrina said. She felt dirty and disheveled beside this fastidious girl, and thought half spitefully that if *she* had to make her living as companion to a rich old woman she would probably look and act the perfect lady, too. Helen's head was tipped as if she waited for some explanation, and Sabrina said, "I asked Lizardo not to let Mother know I'm here. I drove all night, and I just want to fall in bed."

"Of course. Lizardo, did you get Mrs. Castro's bags?"

"I didn't bring anything." She looked the surprised blue eyes down. But she could force nothing out on the soft Gretchen face of Helen Kretchmer except concern. "Is something wrong, Mrs. Castro?"

"Why should anything be wrong?" Sabrina said, and carrying her shoes she went up the stairs and along the hall to her old apartment. The air inside was cool and stagnant, faintly perfumed, familiar as her own face. For perhaps half an hour she lay on one of the beds without removing her clothes, staring up at the ceiling and hearing the roar of the motor in her head and feeling the motion of the car in her muscles. Her eyes were dry and scratchy, she was terribly tired, but she knew from the peevish twitching of her nerves and the racing inconsecutive images in her mind that she had not a chance of falling asleep.

Eventually she rose and hunted through the bathroom cabinet until she found a bottle of nembutal. With two capsules in her hand she looked at herself in the mirror—smooth dark hair, blue eyes that even in her fagged condition blazed with astonishing lightness from her tanned face. Imperious brows—was that the correct literary word?— and the slightly Roman Wolcott nose that took charge no matter what strange company the Wolcott genes found themselves in. It was a proud face, and she was glad of it. But then she smiled at herself suddenly, and saw and felt the many-times-repeated reassurance, how the haughty lines softened and the pride gave way, how the face became feminine and full of promises.

Madonna! She let the smile fade. Still watching her eyes in the mirror, she swallowed the two nembutals. After a second she opened the bottle and took out another and swallowed that. She poured the remaining capsules into her palm and counted them. Seven. That would do it, probably. But with a tightening of the lips, with hardly more than the passing thought, she poured the capsules back and went into the bedroom and shed her clothes on the floor. Naked, she crawled between the sheets. For a while she held her mind away by a tired effort, and a good while later she began to feel how the numbness came on and flowed up her legs and buzzed in her head. She put her hand on her own soft stomach, and the touch comforted her. The motor's noise was blending with the noise of rising sleep, the car's motion was only a slight swift swaying.

CHAPTER 2

DEBORAH HUTCHENS' first look at the day was like the view she had of most things—quiet, punctual, and a little out of focus. The light touched her eyelids and her eyelids opened; she looked up into a cloudy grayness marbled with pink and gold. Awareness came upon her a sensation at a time: the solidity of her body in the bed, the coolness of the satin puff under her hand, the tinted obscurity above her that gradually became her ceiling with its border of loops and bows in ornamental plaster. There was no moment of recognizing where she was, only a gentle pleasure at the passive center from which she watched, and then later a drifting thought or memory: Good she had not permitted that decorator to become as Italian as he had proposed. She would not have liked to wake up and see fat *putti* and bunches of grapes hanging over her.

She heard soft steps in the room, and the ceiling brightened, an effect like dawn, as the other drape went back with a slurred sound. Mrs. Hutchens, now fully awake, lay quietly without turning her head. She did not like doing things suddenly. The unexpected and unpredictable rattled her. She liked to know what was coming and how she was going to respond to it, and so her first conscious act every morning was to examine the day ahead and plan its details. Constructive daydreaming, she called it. Her mother, who had had the same habit, had called it "doing her matutinals," a phrase that Deborah had once found elegant and amusing but had long ago given up using. For one thing, it was not in keeping with the psychological flavor everything had to have nowadays. For another—the admission burst with a tiny acid explosion —her mother had too much had the habit of arranging *everyone's* day. Wednesday today? No, Thursday. Household accounts with Helen, then. Good. That was one thing Mother always used to praise me for, the way I kept account of my funds. I might have done well in business or investments if I had been a man and there had been any need. Tidy desk, tidy mind, Mother used to say. So, first, accounts. Second, what? Eye exercises, must try swinging for a longer time even if it is disagreeable and dizzying; yesterday there was that one moment of perfectly clear vision. Third, golf. Not an inviting notion, but should keep up the regimen, undoubtedly. The virtue of any regimen lies in regularity, you weaken your fiber by skipping. And then Helen loves it. Perhaps only five holes, we could have Virgil waiting there by the green. Would it be cheating not to do the seven Dr. Sanders suggested? Must ask him.

Anyone for luncheon? No. Nap, of course. And then, oh, lovely, the diaries with Sue Whiteside. How splendid. We might make a habit of it every Thursday, go through them all, even that boyhood one of Mercer's. Sue has no family in that sense. Hugh's another thing, naturally, Pages and Claibornes and Whitesides from Virginia and Pennsylvania. How meekly Sue bore the cross of poor Hugh! Though it was true she had bettered herself very much, marrying him. Still, Thursday would give her a regular escape, quite apart from the fascination of the diaries themselves.

Good, then. First, accounts. Second, eye exercises. Third, golf. Fourth, luncheon. Fifth, nap. Sixth, diaries. Seventh, tea. Sue would stay, of course. And Barbara MacDonald was coming to borrow some of the old gowns for a masque or pageant her children were in. Have Helen call and ask her to come at tea time. Afterward perhaps give her and Sue a tour of the dress-collection lockers and the things from the trunks. Haven't looked through those for months. Should keep better track of things—getting as absent-minded as Auntie Grace.

That made her smile upward at the furbelows of tinted plaster, for she was not in the least like Auntie Grace, who at Deborah's age had become so procrastinating that she never managed to be up and dressed before tea time.

But concentrate, now. Seventh, tea, and eighth, visit the lockers and collections. Ninth, dinner. Oliver and Minna coming, and the children later. Perhaps Oliver would bring some movies and slides. A good outlet for him, he should be encouraged in it. I will ask him myself. No, send Helen; he might be less inclined to balk.

There. There was the day, all tidy like a drawer freshly arranged. Only when she was sure of it, and had run again through its nine items, did Deborah turn her head and look toward where Helen was sitting, hands in lap, in the bow window, with the light coming around her fair hair.

"Good morning, my dear."

"Good morning, Mrs. Hutchens. Sleep well?"

"I should think it bad management . . . not to." She folded back the puff and put her feet down and stood for the robe that Helen held for her. The weight on her feet hurt—a thing that Helen noticed.

"Shouldn't you take a tub this morning instead of a shower? I'm so afraid, with your poor feet, you'll fall and hurt yourself in there."

"My feet are splendid," Deborah said. She looked at Helen to say something else, forgot it momentarily, and stood with a smile that had meant to be speech trembling on her mouth. Then it came back. "Doctor Sanders says the . . . body . . . should accustom itself to sudden changes of . . . temperature. I feel ever so much better since I . . . started taking showers. And how," she said, fixing Helen with a humorous eye—a sweet girl, and wonderfully capable and thoughtful, but sometimes almost too serious—"how could I take a . . . cold shower after a *tub?* Can you imagine standing there up to your knees in . . . hot water . . . with the cold pouring down on you? It would be ghastly."

Smiling and murmuring, hobbling because her feet always hurt her most just after she got up, she went through closet and dressing room to the bath, and pulled on a shower cap that made her feel queer and delightfully out of character, and stepped with a sense of independence and a thrill of anticipation into the shower stall. The glass door shut behind her. She tried its catch and turned, after a deep-breathing moment, the chrome handle. She knew just where to point it now to get water of the right temperature, and after the first chilly splashes the spray came splendidly warm down on her back. She felt that it suppled her arms and shoulders noticeably. At seventy-five one could not expect to be entirely free of arthritic troubles, but by proper diet and exercise one could minimize them. She turned the tap to a hotter flow, stood soaping and adjusting, turned it again. Under the steaming fall her body cringed. She turned the tap again, almost secretly, and was emancipated into lovely unendurable heat. Then she began to brace herself; she counted slowly, one, two, three, and flipped the handle clear back to "Cold."

The icy douche paralyzed her. She crouched under it emitting birdlike cries, turning swiftly her front and then her back again, and standing it for another second, and one more, until finally she reached for the handle and the water was blessedly off and the door open and the big warm towel around her. Oh, she *was* grateful to Dr. Sanders for prescribing the showers! It shamed her to remember that at first she had been skeptical. She recalled saying that she thought showers somehow unladylike; and besides, how did one wash one's *feet*?

Five minutes later she went back through the sweet cedar-smelling closet with her shoes neatly aligned on the waist-high racks and her dresses and coats each under its plastic cover. She found her bed made up, the room tidied, Bernadette just leaving, Helen looking at the *Chronicle,* and Lizardo setting the breakfast table in the bow window. There was a vase of Chilean lilies on the table and the breakfast dishes were the green and white Meissen that had been . . . whose? Grandmother's. Nice to see those out again. Lizardo had orders to keep rotating things for a change of scene. She said to him jocularly, "Good morning, Lizardo. Do we . . . owe the lilies to you?"

She had not much varied the joke for twenty years. He had orders about flowers, too—freshly cut every morning. She wondered he could see out through his smile, his face was such a nest of wrinkles. He looked a little like a man peering out the cobwebby window of an old stable. She bent her nose to the lilies, drenched in sun from the window, and sniffed them, not for her own pleasure but because any expression of her pleasure would please him. In the same way, without any particular anticipation, with no flooding of the taste buds, she inspected the silver covers, the crisp Meissen, the food: under its cover the stone-ground unbuttered whole-wheat toast; in a tall glass the orange juice, complete with pulp—the pulp was important; in a bowl the specially prepared skim-milk yoghurt sprinkled with dark brown melting sugar. It pleased her, even though it did not rouse her appetite.

She remained bent a moment, sniffing the lilies, while Lizardo held her chair. "Lovely," she murmured, and felt the firm edge come against the back of her knees, and kinked herself cautiously, and sat down to breakfast with a little thud.

For a half hour after Helen had rung for Lizardo to clear away, they sat on in the window over the accounts. Helen laid one bill after another, with the unsigned check clipped to it, before Mrs. Hutchens. Mrs. Hutchens gave each her careful, unseeing attention before she drew her signature onto the check with a stiff hand. Between signatures she sat flexing her fingers and thrusting out her arms and pulling them back.

"That exercise looks as if you were picking cotton," Helen said once. Mrs. Hutchens spread her fingers humorously in Helen's face like a goblin going boo. She said it was important to keep the muscles and joints flexible, and this exercise was particularly good because it could be done anywhere, during a conversation or even at the theater or a lecture. While her hands clenched and thrust, she also began to roll her ankles from side to side and to curl and uncurl her toes within her orthopedic slippers.

After the checks there were letters. The first requested funds to send an orphan to a summer trade school, and enclosed a penciled description of him on a mimeographed form. Flexing, Deborah decreed that he be sent. The next asked a contribution to one of those committees for the relief of displaced Europeans, committees which Deborah could never tell apart but for which she always felt sympathy. Perhaps it was foolish of her; it set Oliver wild to have her contribute, and she knew that Pro-America and other groups thought some of the committees communistic. Still, she did feel sorry for people driven from their homes, and it was the Communists—wasn't it?—who had driven the Hungarians out. So how could this committee be communistic? Send them a hundred dollars, she told Helen. A third communication wanted letters written to her Congressman and to the chairmen of certain continuing committees of Congress. This should be done in advance of the convening of the next session, and had to do with Indian reservations. Look into it, and if you think so, send a letter, Deborah told Helen. I do think it terrible how we have treated the Indians.

She resumed the flex and thrust of her hands. "Nothing more?"

"No more letters. There's only that problem of Mr. Cantelli."

"Mr. Cantelli?"

"Who took care of the fine bindings. Who died."

"Oh," Deborah said. "Oh dear, yes." She looked at Helen's tanned, softly smiling face and groped for the response that would be right. The problem had come up too suddenly. "Oh . . ." she said. "Have we . . . sent flowers?"

Helen laughed. "Oh, yes, Mrs. Hutchens. He died a month ago, you remember. But according to your checkbooks it's time to have the bindings treated again, and he isn't available."

"And we haven't . . . anyone else."

"No."

It seemed a difficult thing. Obviously one did not go out and find a man to care for fine books the way one located a gardener or driver. She supposed the agencies had few such persons. Cautiously she said, "Where, do you suppose? Who might . . . know?"

"If you don't have anyone in mind, I can call the Stanford library, or maybe the Grabhorn Press in the City, and see if they know anyone."

"Yes," Deborah said. "Please do." She hung a moment, struck by the most sudden and glorious idea. "Do you suppose . . . do you suppose we might find someone who could do the books and also the . . . family papers?"

"You mean catalogue the diaries and all those?"

"Yes, and perhaps the collections, too."

"I shouldn't think it would be too hard to find someone."

26

"I wish us to!" Deborah cried. "I have been wishing for ever so long that . . . those things were in order."

"Good. I'll see what I can do." She gathered her papers and stood smiling. "You're very decisive and efficient this morning."

"Don't you . . . think so?" Deborah said. "It's the showers, I believe." Her fingers, weary, quit working and lay in her lap. "I have another idea. What if I . . . dressed up for reading the diaries? Would that be too giddy for an old party like me? You remember that brocade of . . . Aunt Sarah's, the one with the peplum? Once I had it made over to fit me, for a party. What if I . . . got into that and surprised Sue Whiteside? Wouldn't she be astonished if she came in and was . . . greeted by Sarah Wolcott, straight out of the year 1871? Why don't I?"

"I think that's a wonderful idea."

"I will!" Deborah said. "And the . . . diamonds, the rose ones. They were Grandmother's, not Aunt Sarah's, but . . . even so. Shall we look at them?"

She hobbled to the bureau and got the key and unlocked the metal door in the wall. Inside were tray drawers lined with white velvet, two tiers of ten drawers each, and in the drawers were all the jewels that had come to her, everything owned by anyone in the family: brooches and lavalieres, pins, necklaces, earrings, the tiara that Grandmother Wolcott had worn at a ball in the London Guildhall when Queen Victoria was present. She stirred them with her finger, opening drawer after drawer: cameos and emeralds and diamonds, a cat's-eye ring her father had given her mother in Nice, the black pearls that Uncle Mercer had brought back from the Persian gulf for her mother's wedding, a whole drawer of old fashioned round gold beads, earrings in the shape of love knots, loops, coins, drops, most of them for pierced ears. In another drawer gold pins, in another diamond bracelets, in still another a dozen engraved and enameled breast watches, in yet another cairngorms from Scotland and amber from the Baltic coast. What a lot of the family was in those drawers! It was as if the generations had been boiled down into a crystalline essence and deposited there.

At her elbow Helen said, "Every time I see those I doubt my eyesight." Deborah smiled over her shoulder; she loved to look, herself.

Emeralds glinted green from a tray that was opened and closed again, and then from the bottom drawer, a flicker of tinted light, Deborah drew the rose diamonds—earrings, necklace, and brooch of matched and graduated stones. Their size always astonished her; Grandfather Wolcott had been the lavish one of the family, though he had also been the original money maker. The heavy necklace hung across her palm, faintly and purely tinged with rose when no facet caught the light, but exploding in flashes of red and yellow and blue when she moved.

"Please wear them," Helen said. "I'll feel as if I were in the Tower of London."

"Aren't they beautiful?" Deborah said. "It's curious, I never cared especially for money, it never gave me any . . . pleasure. I like *things*, like these." With a sidelong glance she added, "You think I like things too much."

"You have such lovely things to like."

"I'm the dormouse of the family," Deborah said happily. "Isn't it . . . dormice that hoard things? Or do they only sleep?" She waved a hand. "Perhaps it's packrats. All of us have been a little that way, but I am . . . the worst."

She dropped the diamonds back in their velvet pocket and shut the drawers and locked the metal door. "Now my eye exercises. But do have Bernadette . . . get Aunt Sarah's brocade ready."

She sat relaxed, a cushion in her lap and her elbows on the cushion and her hands cupped over her eyes. After a time of soft darkness she began to imagine things for contrast: a pure white diamond lying on black velvet under a pencil-beam of light, a white heron on a black Japanese screen. Finally she took her palms away and let her relaxed and rested eyes adjust to the morning again. From Helen's rooms down the hall came the remarkably swift clatter of her typewriter.

Deborah rose and stood in the middle of the room. With her hands hanging loosely she began to swing, rotating her body from the hips so that her head and shoulders moved through a half circle and her eyes, open but unfocused, brushed across an arc of window, wall, door, a picture, and back again. The object was to catch things off guard, to see them without really looking. She swung until she felt dizzy, but the flash of crystalline vision that she wanted would not come. By the time Helen returned she had given it up and sat down to rest.

"Did it work?" said the cheerful young voice.

"No," Deborah said. "Pshaw! Perhaps we can . . . get it with the cards."

Helen raised the cards one at a time into view, held them a moment, and turned them under, while Deborah tried to read them from a flitting glimpse. She tried to sit relaxed; she tried not to strain. Between cards she lifted her palms to her eyes and returned herself to the dark, and then she took her hands away suddenly to surprise a card into visibility. Then all at once it began to come. She cried out one, then another, then a sequence. "Barn! Delinquent! Notebook! Zebra! Pimpernel!" When they stopped to rest she was totally delighted. "Oh, it did come! I saw them so . . . clearly. You ought to try the . . . exercises, Helen. They do so much . . . good."

"Unfortunately I have twenty-twenty vision without."

"Oh," Deborah said without thinking. "It's a shame." They laughed, bursting out at the same time. Deborah felt it, for a moment, a kind of treason to poor Mrs. Brill that she should be able to laugh so readily with this young person who had been with her now less than six months. Yet it was so; Mrs. Brill, especially in the last year or so before Oliver insisted she be pensioned, was not a good one to laugh with. Helen so happily was. "I'm a ridiculous old person," she said. "I think everyone is as decrepit as . . . I am." The clock on her bedtable demanded her attention. "Goodness, nearly time for golf. Tony will be kept waiting again. Helen, would you be a dear and . . . tape my feet for me? You do so much better with them than Bernadette."

While Helen worked on her feet she sat and looked down on the bent fair head. It was all she could do to keep her hand back from touching it. And such a stroke of pure luck—she had come to them straight out of the blue, just when Mrs. Brill's retirement and her own illness made it important that . . . And Oliver had managed it, and one did not, generally, expect the things he managed to be so pleasant. It made one wonder.

With moist eyes she said, "I don't know . . . really . . . what I should do without you."

Helen's eyes flashed up and then down; her lips half smiled; she murmured something.

"You're like a . . . daughter," Deborah said. "Like what one wishes a daughter might be." Though she felt that her talk was skidding dangerously close to some brink, she could not keep from finishing the thought. "Sometimes almost more like a daughter than my . . . real one."

They both watched the spiral of tape go smoothly across Deborah's instep. "That's wrong of you," Helen said. "You're very lucky in your children."

Now that they were over the brink, it did not seem so dangerous. Deborah said, considering, "Wrong of me? Yes, perhaps it is. Sabrina in particular was once a . . . great worry to me, but that was all . . . long ago. She has been married and head of her own house for more years than I . . . like to acknowledge. I suppose she must by now have conquered that . . . restlessness and dissatisfaction that used to upset me so. She responded to disappointment or discipline . . . very badly. We were never as close as I could have wished."

"She's lovely. I don't think I ever saw such a magical smile. It just illuminates her."

Deborah chuckled. "You make her sound like . . . some sort of beacon." But something vaguely disquieting had come into the conversation; even when she considered how to carry it on, she half wished it would end. She held her foot stiff against the pressure of the tape and the efficient hands. Into her mind like a splash of water came the cool thought, You too much like being taken care of, and she said, "As she grew up people . . . said she had great charm. I was always . . . myself . . . a little afraid of her charm. I was . . . afraid she would use it on people. Charm can be a very bad substitute for character."

Helen's upward look was skeptical and indulgent. "I gather she couldn't use her charm on you."

"On me? No. I tried to be a . . . good mother, not a soft one. She was terribly moody and willful, you have no idea. She seemed absolutely . . . determined not to grow up a lady. I don't know what she did want to be. Sometimes I was afraid she would . . . run off and join a circus or a . . . carnival. Can you believe it, when she was almost sixteen I had to . . . send her to stand in the closet for something, some impertinence. She had just had to be . . . brought back from school in Switzerland, Lausanne, because of . . . the war, and I was arranging to send her to . . . Miss Burke's. I forget now what it was. Some disobedience or impertinence or some . . . ill-advised thing she wanted to do. So I had to . . . send her to the closet. At nearly sixteen."

"And she *went?*"

"Of course. I . . . ordered her to. It was the only thing to be done. It was the way my mother used to . . . punish *me*."

Squatting with one hand on the smoothly taped instep, Helen shook her head. "How does that feel?"

"Splendid."

Helen stood up. "I'd about as soon tell a lion to roll over and beg as send Mrs. Castro to stand in the closet."

"She wasn't a lion. She was only a . . . headstrong girl. And she didn't stay. She appeared to think I should . . . come and apologize. When I didn't she . . . left the closet and went out into a terrible storm and deliberately tried to . . . catch pneumonia."

"Did she?"

"No," Deborah said. "She was always very healthy. But always wanting something dubious. Once just after she finished at Miss Burke's she was going to learn painting, and took a little . . . flat with bad drains up on Telegraph Hill. I had to . . . have her brought back from that, too. She didn't take it well. I should have liked to take her abroad but . . . the war was on. I persuaded her to start at Mills instead. While she was there she . . . became quite a literary person. I am surprised she has never written novels and things."

Helen had begun on the other foot. "Is she happy now?"

"Happy? Oh, I . . . think so. Of course."

"Doctor Castro doesn't have to make her go stand in the closet."

"I doubt if . . . anyone but her dragon mother could have managed that."

"You know, I think you're right." She carried the tape around the ankle and across under the arch. "You never had any such trouble with Mr. Hutchens."

"Oliver? A boy is somewhat different. One can hardly . . . expect him to behave like a lady. Sometimes I think I find him . . . *calculating*. He reminds me of his Great Uncle Bushrod. But he never seemed to have the moods that Sabrina had, and he was . . . always occupied with sports."

She brooded, wondering what it was that had flicked through her head, some feeling almost like distaste, as if she half wished he had been more like Sabrina. Maybe it was that he really didn't have a sense of humor. He hadn't the slightest comprehension of why people might laugh, though he always affected a jocular manner. Or gaiety, perhaps— Sabrina could be very gay, recklessly so. In a way it was too bad to have all those times gone, though she had never been able to persuade Sabrina to bring her friends around as Oliver did. She acted often as if she were ashamed of her home. Only a few, like Barbara; but Oliver's friends were always in and out. It had been pleasant to have the tea-room full of young people sometimes, and hear them on the tennis court or in the pool, and find books lying around that she could carry off and read.

Glancing off her own flickering thought, she said, "It's striking that they both . . . have looks. None of the Wolcotts was ever the least handsome. And yet they're different, too. Oliver has the . . . Wolcott coloring, but Sabrina in almost every way is . . ."

She stopped, staring appalled at Helen. She had been about to say, "the image of her father." As if from a distance she heard Helen say, "I've never seen a picture of their father."

"No."

As the silence of embarrassment lengthened, Deborah felt she had to say something, if only to remove Helen's discomfort. "He was not a good man," she said (and how the phrase echoed, her mother's phrase, the condemnatory voice of all the Wolcotts and Barbers, the controlled disapproval of the respectable for the cheap.) Countering what she had just said aloud, she said to herself, He wasn't that bad—he just didn't fit. They never gave him a chance.

And yet accusations trembled on her lips; with the slightest encouragement she would have told this girl things she had never told anyone. To save the moment she took her feet out of Helen's hands and tested them on the floor. Her eye encountered Helen's look of sympathy, apology, whatever it was, and for no reason she could have identified she began to smile—perhaps only because a smile might cover up better than anything else the disarray she had revealed in her life and her feelings.

"Isn't it . . . dreadful," she said lightly, "how the respectable are so seldom charming, and the charming are . . . so seldom respectable."

They had a little laugh together.

"How long ago?" Helen said.

"Mmmm?"

"I'm sorry. I thought you meant—there was a divorce."

"Oh no. A separation. Ever so long ago, so long that . . . I never think of it. Oliver was five, Sabrina only three. The marriage . . . lasted only seven years."

She closed her mouth tightly. The trembling of her lips was only a symptom of aging, an effect of her stroke. She did not want Helen to mistake it for regret or grief or something else totally ridiculous. But the bitterness was right in her throat; the injustice and loss still, after more than thirty years, scalded her. To be, as she had been, a not-pretty ardent girl, too plain to be much courted except by those of whom the family could have legitimate suspicions, too rich to be free in her affections, too shy to learn the tricks that would bring young men around, relying on her mother for her cues—and then, after she had entirely given it up, to have it alight like a bluebird on her bough, and be at first so wonderful and so encouraged by them all, and then to have it turn so bleak and awful and end in a way that could not be mentioned . . . oh!

She bent her lips stiffly. "Sabrina has his smile," she said. "Perhaps that is why I . . . put her in the closet more than I ever did Oliver."

As they went out to the car to be driven to the club, she was still reflecting on what an extraordinary thing that had been for her to say. Perhaps she had meant it as a joke.

CHAPTER 3

O NE O'CLOCK, and the midday hush over everything. Under the oaks in the protected gardens it was possible to believe that the mutter of the Peninsula traffic was only a far sound of wind in trees. But there was no wind here: the noises that were local to each morning—the birds, the scratch of lawn brooms on drives and paths, the stutter of a rototiller, the discreet sounds of gardeners grooming the place, were still. The ground smelled damp, fecund, acid. Under the oaks with their gray limbs and their surgical welts and scars the lawns were shadowed. Not a breath stirred the red-hot poker, ginger, and bird of paradise plants along the curve of the drive. In the orchard and along the walk where nectarines, pears, apricots, and apples were crucified on metal posts and tight wires, the air was so fruity with ripe apricots that Helen felt half suffocated, walking through. On the high fences of the tennis court hung green clusters of grapes.

She walked slowly, dragging her finger from post to post along the burdened wires of the espaliered apricots. A fruit met her hand and she pulled it; she held its sweetness under her nose. Across a delivery road, past an intersecting path, through a hedge, under more sculptured oaks she went slowly, not over-eager. She avoided the house, set back in its azalea gardens, and went around it across more lawn and through a rose garden and up to the hedge which had grown into and all but obscured the woven wire of the swimming-pool fence. She listened. Oliver Hutchens had been away so much during her time here that she was not yet sure of his habits. Lizardo had said that he did not go to the City on Thursdays at all, and would probably be around the pool.

Warningly she clashed the gate against its guards. "Hello?" she called. Through the wires she caught a glimpse of a blue sunning pad, a nakedness alarmingly total, and then as she stepped back in confusion the voice rumbled out at her. "Who is it?"

"Helen Kretchmer. I have a message from your mother. But it isn't pressing. If you're napping or sunning I can come back, or call."

"Stay there."

She heard him muttering and grumbling, then his feet came padding on the cement. He appeared on the other side of the gate in a Bikini so skimpy she had to brace herself to take it casually. He was as brown as an islander—after all, he should be; he had been in the islands half the spring.

She had never seen him, even fully dressed, without feeling his masculinity like a violence. He affected her now like a knock on the head. From his cropped hair to his brown feet curling against the heat of the pavement, he swelled with muscle. His neck was a corded column, his arms were herculean, the pectoral muscles lay across his chest in molded slabs, his belly was a washboard. Though she did not dare look fully at him, she had the impression of how from just inside each hip bone, and descending toward the flimsy clout heavy with his sex, there were lines of taut muscle, or the division between sets of muscles, such as she had seen only on heroic statues of the Michelangelo kind. His thighs and calves bulged and tightened as he teetered on the hot cement. Appallingly conscious of his body, she smiled blindly across the gate into his face. His face scowled and squinted.

"What is it?"

"It's Thursday," she said foolishly. "You're coming to dinner tonight, I believe. . . ."

His sandy eyebrows rose, and his speckled hazel eyes pried at hers. He began to smile. "You walked over personally to tell me that?"

35

She felt the red come washing into her face and saw his smile twitch wider. To herself she said, "Remember who he is!" She said aloud, coolly enough, "Mrs. Hutchens has an exaggerated notion of my efficiency. I couldn't leave it to chance."

"No." Oliver moved one foot onto the other instep, the movement of a powerful animal; she had the feeling she should be ready to jump away if he should rear or kick. And she could smell him, not unpleasantly.

"She wondered if you'd mind bringing over some slides or movies to show after dinner, something from the islands, and some family things. She thought there might be something the children haven't seen."

"You can report they have seen very little. I keep the kiddies in their kennel."

She could believe it. He had the look of one whose enormous virility could beget and forget children with the same casualness. Just for an instant Helen admitted the small chilling thought of what it might mean to be mated to that aggressive potency, and she thought of his wife with pity and awe. Five children already, fifteen more to come if her organs held out.

"But you do have something?" she said. "It would please Mrs. Hutchens very much. She thought there might be some old films that would give the children a notion of the family as a consecutive thing. I imagine Mrs. Castro will be there too."

"Sabrina will?"

"Yes. She drove in early this morning."

"I thought she . . ." He moved again, impatiently, and shoved the gate wide. "Come in, my feet are burning off."

"I should be getting back."

"Come in!"

He clanged the gate shut behind her. "Go sit down over there." As she started toward the chairs, she heard his running feet and the splash as he hit the pool. He swam its length in four or five great strokes and came up over the edge with one flowing motion to stand dripping beside her the moment she sat down.

"What's she doing up here?"

"I don't know. I just saw her for a minute. She went right to bed."

Impatient with herself for having blurted out to him what she had scrupulously not told his mother, she stood up again. "Really, I must be back in a minute. Mrs. Hutchens and Mrs. Whiteside are going to read diaries this afternoon, and I have to—"

"Diaries?" Oliver said. "Again? Good God. Every year or so she catches somebody and inflicts those things on her. Who the hell would want to hear about Grandmother's sixteen-year-old crushes, or the summer sermons on Nahant, or just when during the year 1868 Aunt Sarah read *Scottish Chiefs*? Did you ever look into those diaries?"

"Your mother loves anything that has to do with the family back in Boston."

"Does she not!" Half in the sun, he sat on a lounge and fingered the heavy muscles of his arm. She had the feeling of being inspected and estimated. Abruptly he said, "How is she, anyway? You see more of her than anybody."

"How is she?"

"In the head. The aging business."

"Why, there's nothing wrong with her head! She thinks as clearly as anyone."

"Na, na. I've noticed it especially since I came back. Don't tell me she's thinking clearly when she stands looking at you and moving her lips and trying to remember what she started to say."

"That's just her tongue," Helen said. "She can't always make it say what she wants it to, and her lips tremble that way. But her head is perfectly clear. Her memory is incredible, and she has a marvelous sense of humor, she sees the joke in everything."

The speckled eyes watched her steadily, the firmly cut lips were turned up a little. She was glad he had not been around much to have his eye on her while she was learning the ropes and wooing Mrs. Hutchens away from her grumpiness over the departure of Mrs. Brill. He said finally, "You're very loyal."

"I hope so."

"You're well paid to be."

Just for an instant she gave him her uncareful eyes to look at. "Yes," she said, "but that's not the reason."

He made a wet footprint on the cement and studied it. His eyebrows

37

were fair and bushy and New Englandy like his mother's. Then abruptly he was looking upward at her again from under them. "How about all these food fads?"

"That's Doctor Sanders. Since she had that little stroke he's had her on a low-fat, low-cholesterol diet."

"If she hadn't been able to talk him into prescribing it she'd have found it in some magazine," Oliver said. "Yoghurt, and stone-ground flour, and soy bean oil, and blackstrap molasses, and wheat germ. She eats what my kids feed their rabbits and bantam hens. And those God-damned eye exercises. Every swami and buttermilk drinker in California must bless the day she was born."

Helen hesitated, uncertain how to meet what seemed so outright an attack on his own mother. She laughed a little, and said, "Really, her diet isn't just a fad. Maybe it's keeping her alive and healthy. And the exercises give her something to do. She doesn't have much, except what she calls her regimen. She's almost shut in."

"How many swamis have called on her this week?"

"Not a single swami," she said, and tried to divert his aggressiveness with a smile.

He would not be diverted. "Quacks, I don't care what kind. Quakers, Communists, members of committees, jigaboos working up to a pitch. They're like yellowjackets around a fig tree. Her name is on every God-damned sucker list there is."

"No, honestly, you exaggerate. I see them all. If they're obviously crazy or out to exploit her I don't let them in."

"I sure hope you don't."

"I don't. But a lot of them are perfectly honest, only a little hipped on something. She's interested in them; it's almost the only personal life she has. The Symphony and the Palace of the Legion of Honor and things like that don't ever seem to have been her particular interest, even when she was active. Now she's nearly shut in, she needs something. The only one who comes that you could call a swami is Krishna Lal, and he's just a pleasant spiritual sort of man preaching non-violence. *He* can't hurt her."

"He can bleed money out of her."

"I can't remember that he's asked for anything since I've been here."

"Listen, I pay you the compliment of thinking you're not stupid. You know why people like that hang around an old lady with a lot of money and no judgment."

"I wish you wouldn't keep saying that. She's perfectly all right, only frail and with arthritis in her hands and feet."

He was slapping a light pattery rhythm on his thighs with his flat hands. As if he had just decided something about which he had been uncertain, he clapped his hands to his legs and held them there. "Look —in this job you're going to be pretty deep in the family. I want to know whenever Mother has some big charitable notion that she isn't willing to route through Collier at the bank. Okay?"

"She does go through him," Helen said. "She gives these little nominal gifts—" The word made her laugh. "At least they're nominal for her. But anything bigger is always referred to Mr. Collier. Like when she wanted to give something to Stanford for their library building fund."

"I remember that very clearly," Oliver said. "She was going to give fifty thousand dollars." He grinned at her wolfishly, an exaggeratedly greedy leer. "By diligent and timely effort Collier and I cut it in half."

"Yes," she said. She had the strong feeling that this was getting altogether too confidential; she did not want to be involved in arguments between Oliver and his mother. But when she stood up to go, he squinted up at the high sun and made a staying motion with one hand.

"Who's been putting the finger on her this week? Who would like an appointment to discuss an important matter confidentially?"

Now she could let her mouth bend in a smile. "You're much too suspicious. There's not a single appointment on her calendar."

"Great." He stretched all his muscles like a cat or a dog, first his upper body, then his legs, feet, toes. The water had dried on his brown skin, his wet footprints were almost gone from the pavement. "I'm telling you this for a reason," he said, and suddenly his squinting stare was as hard for her to meet as his near nakedness. "You're in a confidential position. I want you to keep track of what goes on. Mother has to be protected from her own foolishness. Plainly, she's a sucker. She's quite capable of writing a will that leaves everything she owns to Mister Krishna Lal to stamp out violence from the world. Or if she's on a cultural kick we might find when she dies that what was once a tidy little estate is now part of somebody's endowment, and we're selling off the lower forty to meet taxes. I don't care if it's the best cause in the world, I don't aim to let her make a fool of herself."

At least he was frank. Helen said only, "I don't think you need to worry. Her mind isn't failing. She's as bright as you are, and a lot brighter than me."

"I'm glad to hear it. Because you seem pretty bright." Abruptly he rose, and the muscular surge of his body and the way his speckled eyes now looked down at her instead of up from under his eyebrows gave her a wincing feeling of weakness. It occurred to her to wonder if he fancied himself that way—if he went around full of arrogant notions like a hawk over a chickenyard. "Okay," he said. "Tonight I'll come over with projectors and slides and movies and we'll have a happy hour of family records. I've got the whole works from forty years back."

"It will please your mother very much." She started to move away, but his hand took her solidly by the arm.

"I want you to do me a favor. If anybody dangerous gets her ear, let me know. I don't mean old Krishna Lal. I've had my eye on him for a long time. I love him, in fact. He writes letters to the papers protesting income taxes because they go for implements of war. Except for his half-assed reasons I couldn't be more in agreement with him. But you know the kind I mean. Steer them to me or Collier and they'll evaporate. Will you do that?"

"Certainly, if I think she's in danger of being taken in."

"Fine," he said ironically. "I trust your judgment. How long have you been here now?"

"Nearly six months."

"Like it?"

"Very much."

"I forget. You trained as a nurse?"

"No. Only secretary."

"College girl?"

"Wisconsin. You *don't* remember many details, do you?"

"I was a little pressed, about the time I interviewed you. As I remem-

40

ber, I took you sight unseen, on a week's trial. I should have paid more attention."

The smile was still curling his lips; he still had hold of her arm.

"I must say," he said, "you're an improvement over what poor old Mother had before."

"Thank you." She said to herself again, "Remember who he is!"

"Don't thank me. It's no trouble for me to be quite nice when I'm so inclined."

The smile curved higher; she noted his very even teeth, like the capped teeth of a movie hero. He pulled her wrist, pulled her against him, folded his other arm around her. She neither resisted nor yielded. For a moment he bent, looking into her eyes with his speckled hazel gaze, and then he kissed her. His kiss was instantly and hotly sexual; he was as direct as a billy goat.

After a swamped and breathless interval Helen drew herself away. Her eyes did not let themselves be put down. She said steadily, "Now I *must* go."

She knew that his eyes followed her out the gate. She knew he was smiling broadly. But all the way across the lawn and up the avenue of espaliered fruit trees she went with her jaw locked, sure that if she relaxed it her teeth would chatter like a porcupine's. The only thing she could think of was an old dirty joke that used to be told around school, about a hen that had been run over by a Volkswagen. The hen, the story said, had pulled herself groggily together and remarked that he was a rough son of a bitch, but he hadn't gotten anything.

CHAPTER 4

Groping along the shoe shelf for something to wear, Sabrina came upon the squaw boots. For a moment she stood frowning, caught in the past as a woman is caught who steps into a grating with a spike heel.

The boots were the gift of a god—a god of eighteen, a Dartmouth freshman from a Boston family, sent out to work through the summer as a copy boy at the *Chronicle,* and told, for old acquaintance's sake, to call Sabrina's mother. He had called, being both dutiful and good-natured. He had come to dinner, he had made good use of the swimming pool, he had gone sailing with Oliver in the bay. That was the only thing she knew against him, that he appeared to like Oliver. For the rest, she had worshiped him around the jambs of doors and across rooms, had refused to go swimming when he was around because in a bathing suit it was clear she was not quite yet a woman. And also, if she gave evasive reasons for not swimming, he might deduce interestingly female explanations.

Once, in the City, she had escaped the driver who had her in charge, and hurried down onto Mission Street, and there, shuddering back from frequent Skid Row bums, she had waited across the street from the *Chronicle* for more than an hour, hoping to see him come out so that she could feed on his unconscious loveliness. Her mother had been terribly upset, and been going to fire the driver, who was pretty upset himself. How had that all worked out? Some explanation suspiciously half-believed; a bribe to the driver to salve his injured feelings.

Oh, but Larry Keams! Though he had never come out of the *Chronicle* entrance into her sight, he did now and then notice her. She felt that she puzzled him, and once she remembered telling him, when he had been kidding her as if she were some infant sister of his friend Oliver's, that he had better learn how to treat women. That astonished him, and before he could laugh she went dignifiedly up to her room and lay on the bed and brooded, and kicked pillows around.

Why wouldn't he have laughed? And yet he saw something in her. She knew he did. Probably most of the time she was a skinny thirteen-year-old who was always hanging around, staring soberly across rooms or hanging indifferently on the wire of the tennis court while he and Oliver played, but once or twice there was more. He had not disappointed her. Going back at the end of the summer, he must have looked around him in the drive and said, "Where's Sabrina?" For she had fled, unable to watch them callously loading him into the car with his bags and his golf clubs and his tennis racket. So rather than go away without saying good-by he had come hunting her, and found her in the tearoom peeking at a tree through the telescope. "Hey," he said, "are you ducking out on me?"

"Oh," she said, "I thought you'd gone," and screwed her eye deeper into the brass eyepiece. He dug her out of there and held her by the shoulders and laughed at her. He had a gift for laughter; in him it was neither light-witted nor hysterical as it was in so many. Then he put out his hand and with his knuckles touched the damp spot on her left cheek. "You're a funny one," he said. "And you're going to be a heart-breaker. Will you wait for me?"

The very idea made them both laugh. He gave her a quick hug and was gone, and furiously, furiously, she scoured upstairs to watch from a window as they drove him away. Four days later, postmarked from Albuquerque and packed in a box labeled Fred Harvey, had come the squaw boots, pure white deerskin hung with tiny silver bells, and with the boots a card she could imagine him scrawling on the cleared edge of a counter: "For a girl nobody knows."

Dead center. He could not have said more plainly what she had always thought herself. And when she put on the boots and drifted softly tinkling past the mirror door of her dressing room, she felt how they transformed her, or revealed her. She became in fact the sulky-eyed child that till then only Speicher had seen. With her hand on an imagined shoulder she waltzed shut-eyed, and the sound she made filled her with such delight—the thought that they were from *him* was so thrilling—that she spun twice and flew downstairs to the door of the tearoom. They must have heard her coming like Santa Claus outside a Christmas Eve church, and then she materialized in the doorway with her smile coming and going on her face. The four women in the room turned toward the door; she saw how they sat as if all had caught a quick breath. Her mother, with the teapot raised to pour, stared with a stricken face, set the pot down on a cup's edge and spilled it, and still stared. Her underlip was bitten harshly up under her teeth.

Sabrina shook the limp, half-soled, discolored moccasins, trying the tinkle of the past. More than twenty years ago, and yet a thing she remembered intensely. Here, against all probability, were the squaw boots that had given her a notion of who she was. Against all probability, for her mother had disliked them from the first as something unbecoming a young lady, and Sabrina had had to sneak them out in her handbag and change at the club or wherever she had got away to. And she had never left them lying around: so many things of which her mother disapproved had a habit of quietly disappearing. During the time when her mother was most at her about them, Sabrina had even slept in them. Appropriate, inappropriate, those words had nothing to do with her mother's displeasure, she knew. Somehow, appearing in that doorway with her jingle and her smile, she had frightened her mother badly. The girl that only Speicher and Larry Keams knew was not a girl Deborah Hutchens *wanted* to know.

Groggy from the nembutal hangover, Sabrina stood in the closet with the moccasins in her hands, and then with a crooked smile she bent and slipped them on. She stamped her foot, and it jingled. Ah, ah! Girl-hood restored, charm reasserted, confidence reassured. Well, Mother, here we go again, she said and, faintly tinkling, went on out and down the stairs. But she heard the music of her feet as thin and brittle as vanity itself light-wittedly dancing, and she would have gone back to put on something less troubling if Lizardo had not appeared in the hall.

"Ha-ha!" he said. "You hab good slip?"

"Oh, grand."

Moving past him, she found in the drawing room the box of ciga-rettes that her mother, disapproving, kept there for callers. Lizardo's lighter snapped before her face. "You like some fud now?"

"I don't believe so, Lizardo."

"You sick?"

"No."

"You like orange juice, maybe? Coppee? Chicken sandwich?"

"Stop taking care of me. Where's Mother?"

"Got company."

"Where, library or tearoom?"

"Library. Miz Whiteside."

She had started through the double doors when Lizardo said softly, "Doct' Castro telepone."

Sabrina had a sensation like secret nausea, as if a sickness that for social reasons she had tried to ignore had now arrived. She felt over-taken, and at the same time corroborated in an expectation; it was as if she said, Of course. Aloud she said, "He did? What did he want?"

"He want to know you here okay. I tell him you slip, everyt'ing pine." From his eyes, which communicated something understanding, apologetic, and protective, she let her glance stray across the room—carved walnut and mahogany, lacquer inlaid with mother-of-pearl, an intricate rich footing of Bokhara carpets that should have been in a museum, all flooded with gray light from the battery of draped windows. Other rooms in the house had got most of the good pieces. Because this one was so big, and duplicated so exactly the drawing room of the Nahant house, all the ponderous Victorian junk had got piled in here. It was a room to make you feel three feet high and start you to talking in whispers, like a public library. Without looking back, Sabrina said, "Is he going to call again?"

"He don't say. I s'pose."

"Does Mother know I'm here?"

"I don't tell her."

"All right."

The nausea lay under her breastbone, ready to rise in one irresistible rejection. She asked herself why Burke's calling should double her guilt and depression, and then she asked angrily why he couldn't let her alone at least for a day while she thought things out. And yet if he had not called she would have been even more upset; at least she had forced him to express concern.

For a few seconds a possibility, clear and definite, completely persuaded her. It said that Bernard, blinding and ecstatic as those ten days had been, had only been a catalyst whose function was to cure Burke of taking her for granted, and bring them together again. There was a flow of daydream in which she saw them, emancipated from the clinic, alone in some place exciting and remote—São Paolo, the Greek islands, Andorra—and they came out on a balcony flooded with morning sun and looked down on people driving donkeys loaded with fruit, wine casks, flowers.

But the face in the daydream became treacherously, even while she dreamed it, the darker one with the large warm liquid eyes and the lips that she wanted to put out a hand and touch. The ridiculous travel-poster notion had twisted itself incorrigibly into a reconstruction of Oaxaca, and she looked sharply at Lizardo to see if she could find among his wrinkles any sign that he was reading her mind. He looked only anxious. "I'll be in the library if he calls again," she said.

That was when she saw Bernadette coming down the hall with some old dresses on her arm, and after her the barrel-shaped figure that walked carefully on flat heels.

"Bobbie!"

"Sabrina! Hey!"

They flew together. There was a moment when Barbara's pregnancy was like an unwanted third person between them, but only a moment.

They had each other by the arms, looking and laughing. Barbara wore no make-up, her face looked shining and broad, she had got heavier, but she still had a vocabulary like a bird for expressing pleasure, and her greatest pleasure and highest devotion were still—the fact shone out of her face—Sabrina.

"Your mother didn't say a word," Barbara said. "What a sly character."

"She doesn't know I'm here."

Lizardo was disappearing through the door under the stairs that Barbara had just come up through, Bernadette was on her way out to the car. Sabrina hung onto Barbara's arms, matronly arms, no longer the thin wings of a girl, and the thought was a pang: thirty-five, both of us. Barbara's whole expression was sweetness, receptivity. She looked always as if she were perched on some wall delightedly watching something on the other side. She liked everyone ("How *can* you?" Sabrina used to screech at her, "how *can* you not think some people are slobs?") and she liked Sabrina most. Delight came to her from outside, from her friends: she was a vessel. Now her face first showed expectancy— Your mother doesn't know you're home, and so there must be something—and then slowly faded and shadowed, following what Sabrina knew to be her own tight and uneasy expression.

Sabrina said, "I've got to talk to you, I think I must have driven up here just for that. I've got a million ugly things to tell you. Come on up to my room."

"Oh, Hutch," Barbara said, "I can't! I'm way late getting back."

"You can come up for ten minutes, surely."

Conflict and hesitation wavered in the placid face, the brown eyes hunted in Sabrina's, the mouth drew down. "Really, I can't. I'm already a half hour late. I just ran over to borrow some of your mother's dress collection for a do the girls are in, and I didn't dare bring them and let them see the whole thing, so I left them with the neighbor's twelve-year-old." Her soft eyes clung, her mouth crept back toward its native smile. "It isn't anything bad. You're kidding me."

Sabrina said something vicious and put her arm around Barbara's thick waist and walked her to the door. Her irritation was instant and real and could not possibly be allowed to show. She had a cool glimpse

47

of how they looked together, her own slim good figure beside the thickened and back-tilted one, her own hair dark and shining and smooth—she had never cut it in her life—beside Barbara's ragged dry bob, her linen dress and belled dancer's boots beside the not-new maternity dress and the flat-heeled oxfords. For the duration of the image she was close to formulating why they had always been closest friends: she had always led Barbara and always excelled her; Barbara demanded and threatened nothing.

"Damn your children and your school-teaching husband," Sabrina said. "How are they? I don't care, don't tell me. I wish I could talk to you now."

"Can't you tell me just quick? Is something wrong? Is it awful?"

"Awful. Wonderful. Oh, I don't know!" When she laughed, a sudden contraction of her jaws flooded the space under her tongue with saliva. She held Barbara with a look that her ironic sense told her was melodramatic. "I'm having an affair."

She felt that the words came out of her mouth in an absurd bleat. And what made her search Barbara's face so hungrily? Alert to her own sensations, focused upon herself, she perceived how she fed on Barbara's surprise, shock, pity, envy, whatever was there.

Envy? Did she expect envy?

"Oh, dear!" Barbara said, the feeblest of responses, and hung awkwardly in the doorway. Beyond her, across the drive and lawn, two gardeners were loading into a truck the wood from an oak that had gone down. "Who?"

"I mustn't keep you."

"Don't be mean. What about Burke?"

"I don't know. We had an awful scene last night. Oh, not awful, just . . . I guess it *was* awful. For me, anyway. He called a while ago, while I was asleep. He'll call again pretty soon, and what am I going to tell him?"

"Which one do you love?" Barbara said.

For her, perhaps, it would have been that simple. Sabrina watched the gardeners lifting a trimmed oak limb. The sound of it falling into the truck was heavy and solid under the trees. Barbara said, "If it was Leonard and me, I could tell. I'd just say please take me back."

"If it was Leonard and you you wouldn't be in this kind of mess. But maybe I can go back."

"Then it's already over."

"I hope so," Sabrina said. "I'm afraid so. Oh, it was over before it began!"

Her head felt stuffed, the way a trophy head might feel after it had been cut off and its bones removed and its shape filled out with hot sand. Through the sand she heard Barbara saying, "You *have* to come over tonight. I'll send Leonard off to bowl or something."

"All right, I'll come if I don't get hung up with Mother."

Barbara went awkwardly, turning to look back. From the window of the unwashed Chevrolet in the drive she threw an urgent smile, and as she rolled past she leaned to say, "Please! I'll hate myself if you don't."

From the doorway Sabrina looked into the summer afternoon, the familiar, protected, nostalgic green and gold of sunlight sifting through big oaks. It had always been far grander than she liked; she used to be furiously embarrassed that they kept nine gardeners busy doing nothing but grooming a walled home for self-indulgent privacy. Yet she looked into it right now with a tight throat, as if it were something dear she would have to put behind her forever, or as if, conversely, the sheltered grounds suggested everything passionate and alive that she was now putting behind her. Closing the door, she felt that she imprisoned herself beyond hope in gloomy rooms, an Emily Dickinson without a gift. That would be something—return to the ancestral halls and flit around in wispy draperies, peeking from behind curtains, hiding in closets, and being, like her mother, tended and pampered by a personal maid, a butler, a cook, a companion, a driver, and nine gardeners.

From the landing looked down her own six-year-old face, that child jailed here forever, a family relic before she ever became a person. In the brown air the painted eyes were sulky for something. Escape? Was that what Oaxaca had meant, too? Then why was she back here now? The two of them confronted one another, fearing freedom and hating sanctuary.

For she feared freedom, that kind, even with Bernard. She knew

49

plenty of women who had chosen it, some of them Burke's patients and her own companions. Their spirits responded always more tiredly to play and what they called fun, as their faces responded more tiredly to packs and massage and their physiological processes quickened and sagged always more sluggishly to alcohol, Seconal, Miltown, the desperate doses of Premarine. And the more money they had the worse it was for them.

Sanctuary, then? She could have mummification in two styles, Pasadena or Hillsborough, the Hillsborough style more fool-proof. No grief or pain, not even restlessness, could stay active long in a house like her mother's. Within days it would begin to seem historical, something that had happened to one of the family.

Burke? Bernard? Marriage, divorce, remarriage? How could a person know? She felt that her life had been flicked like a ball into a roulette wheel, and she could only watch herself until she quit spinning. She couldn't tell Burke anything; and if she called Bernard, what could she possibly ask him?

It occurred to her to suspect herself of milking an emotional situation for all it was worth, and impatiently she broke away from the stare of her own painted eyes. Softly she went down the hall. Her mother's halting voice was telling or reading something. Then a guffaw, a choked comment in Sue Whiteside's hoarse whisper—the true San Francisco croak, product of fog and Miss Burke's, the regional voice heard at Friday-afternoon symphony or between the acts in the foyers of theaters, super-imposing wry and humorous hyperbole upon vowels broader than Boston's. It was a voice that managed to be at once informal and select, Western and cultivated.

Anyone else? A murmur—Helen Kretchmer. She listened for others but heard only her mother taking up the interrupted discourse, reading something. Sabrina flattened the knots out of her forehead, adjusted her mouth, loosened her fingers. She said to herself that Burke's call might settle something. They could work it out. Depend on that.

With her smile already radiant and her feet softly jingling she materialized in the doorway.

CHAPTER 5

S HE WAS prepared to surprise them, but not to be surprised herself. From a deep chair rose up a figure out of a period drama, wasp-waisted, puff-bosomed, bustle-hipped, in white and gold brocade. Her hair and throat and ears blazed with diamonds. In her hand she held a small leather commonplace book. Her lips worked, her tongue stumbled. "Why   Sabrina!"

"Good heavens, Mother, what have you got on?" Sabrina looked a question at Helen Kretchmer—Is this something that has to be humored?—as she moved toward the daughterly embrace. "You do look gorgeous," she said, and performed the ritual kiss, touching the soft old cheek above the stiff brocade. It was like kissing the total Past, lavender, must, mothballs, and all. Over her mother's shoulder she said, "Hello, Mrs. Whiteside, hello, Helen. What is this?"

Her mother put trembling fingers up to stop the trembling of her lips. "It's . . . Why, it's . . . Oh, Sabrina, you have such a way of . . . doing these wild, abrupt things! I'm delighted to see you, my dear but you . . . shake everything . . . right out of my head. Why didn't you . . . write you were coming?" Her eyes fluttered down and up again. "And those *preposterous* old slippers!"

Helen Kretchmer's eyes met Sabrina's, and Sabrina pinched her brows together in a quick frown of incomprehension. What? Do what? "Shhh!" she said, bending laughing against her mother's ear. "You know how I am. I just found the car headed this way. What are you doing in all the masquerade? Did I interrupt a rehearsal?" A perception of something altered pulled her eyes to the wall. In the space ordinarily occupied by Monet's lilies, the only picture in the house that she liked except her own portrait, hung now the lumpy face of Duveneck's Grandmother Barber. "What on earth!" Sabrina said.

When Sue Whiteside laughed she wheezed smoke between her widely set teeth; she looked like an amiable and badly piped dragon, and it was a testimony to friendship that Sabrina's mother continued to like someone so set on killing herself with lung cancer. "We invited her in," she said. "We're reading her diaries. You've been missing the most *divine* tale. *Fabu*lous. Just like a novel. *Will* she be reconciled with her friend Harriet, *should* she accept the invitation of the handsome young Pole. *Simp*ly divine!"

"I expect it doesn't have . . . quite that sort of suspense," Deborah Hutchens said drily. She had collected herself. The look she gave Sabrina as she kinked cautiously back into her chair with a creaking of brocade was bright and searching. Careful, Sabrina told herself. She is already wondering, and she is still hard to fool.

Ignoring her mother's automatic frown, she flopped in a chair with one moccasined foot under her and lit a cigarette. Through the smoke, she brightened her face to take part in their elaborate charade, and said chattily, "As I remember, poor Grandmother had four thrills in her lifetime, each one about twenty-five watts."

"*Poor* Grandmother doesn't seem . . . quite the expression," her mother said. "She lived a blameless life, and I never saw her forget she was a lady."

"That's what I mean."

The impatient frown tightened in her mother's face. "You've always liked to make that sort of joke. I never found them amusing." The resemblance between her and the portrait of Emily Barber was more marked than Sabrina remembered, perhaps because of the antique gown; but Sabrina, passing off the rebuke with a down-turned mouth, acknowledged that her mother had a better face than Grandmother Barber. Grandmother looked as if she had never laughed. It was impossible to imagine that lumpy, long-faced, severe woman as the romantic girl who wrote diaries.

Sue Whiteside was also busy clearing the air and passing off the rebuke. She wheezed, and her eyes, wet with wildly disproportionate amusement, sought out Sabrina's with a kind of desperation. Oh, do let's make it pleasant, let's not quarrel. It's *terribly* amusing, it really is. Sabrina gave her a brief private smile and saw how at once her pleasure increased. How lovely of your Grandmother to keep diaries all those years. How *queer,* actually, how *touching,* to read her intimate thoughts when she was still a girl, before you or any of us was ever born!

Well, how queer to be Sue Whiteside, big, clumsy, nice, wry, terribly sad, saddled with a mentally sick husband too wealthy to be institutionalized and too disturbed to be soothed by anything but music —and not music from any high-fidelity set either, but only music made by performers present and in tails. Every Tuesday afternoon a contingent from the San Francisco Symphony came to the big music room in Woodside, correct in afternoon clothes, and played to an audience of that poor captive schizoid and his poor captive wife, with perhaps a nurse or servant and one or two friends. Now that Sabrina was home, there would surely be a half-swallowed invitation to come up for music some Tuesday, and a ghastly understanding of the refusing lie. In front of Sue Whiteside it would be worse than unkind to make too much of Grandmother Barber's dehydrated life.

"Please go on, Mother. Don't let me interrupt."

"Are you planning to stay a while?"

"I think so."

"You think so." The faded eyes sharpened, guessing. "Then we'll have time for a . . . good talk later."

"Maybe Mrs. Castro needs to be brought up to date," Helen said.

"I?" Sabrina said. "I know the plot."

In the hall she heard steps, and twisted sharply, thinking it might be Lizardo announcing Burke's call. No one—and anyway the phone would have rung on the library desk. She must be losing her mind. Twisting back, she ran into Helen Kretchmer's pleasant questioning look. What was *she* watching?

Her hand holding the cigarette shook so that the smoke rose wriggling. Abruptly she was furious. Of all the things to come home to! To sit while her mother, in costume no less, recreated the maidenly secrets of Grandmother Barber eighty years ago—a perfect lady, one of the best preserved and least lovable of the family relics. There was nothing alive in the whole house; it wasn't a house, it was a museum. Nobody lived in it, or ever had, but spooks and survivors. She could feel her own passionate life at the heart of it like a powder charge with a short fuse.

Helen was still smiling at her. Automatically Sabrina fixed her own smile, a disguise through which no one could see to the shadows on her face or on her mind. She swung a foot, tinkling.

"Well, *I* forget," Helen said. "Was Bushrod your mother's father, or uncle, or what?"

Sabrina gave her credit for acuteness. Nothing soothed in that house like a genealogical question. And it let Sabrina herself sink back away from them. It was five minutes past five, the office would be clearing of patients, any minute now he might be calling.

". . . brother," her mother was saying. "The oldest, born 1836. Then came Auntie Grace and then . . . Aunt Sarah and then mother, Emily . . . and then Mercer, the baby. Bushrod was always terribly good at business. He was . . . trustee. You see, my grandfather's will left everything in trust. Each child got only fifty thousand dollars in cash plus . . . one-tenth of the trust income. Grandmother got five-tenths. But Bushrod handled everything. He did . . . very well. In his own right he left seven million."

So they sat, Sabrina reminded herself, in a strategic position. Since only Emily, of those five children, had ever married, and since she had only little Deborah—and pretty late, too, it must have scared them —and since nobody in the family ever left a big bequest outside except for the hundred thousand that Bushrod left the Harvard Club, it had all come funneling into narrower and narrower circles of inheritance. There they sat like a barrel under a spout.

54

Her mother had found her place and was looking around, chuckling. "*Duckins*," she said. "They had such . . . queer words. *Duckins*, isn't that odd? Something like scrumptious, I believe. And *jol*, a great many things were jol."

Jol, yes, the duckins tribe of the Wolcotts, formidably rich, nearly sterile, physically unattractive, subject to pride and early senility; a tribe cranky and procrastinating, with snobbery where their affections might have been and possessions in place of emotions. She had never been able to imagine any of them young, in spite of her grandmother's diaries and their Victorian teen-age lingo. They insisted on remaining, for her, what they had always been: eccentrics, accumulators, indulgers of seldom generous whims, buyers of real estate, merchandisers on Boston's T-wharf, directors of State Street banks, compulsive travelers, makers of wills.

Wasn't it fair to ask what any of them had ever lived for? They had grown on the Hub of the Universe like green mold, implacably avaricious, implacably decorous, never thinking, never feeling, never a part of the stir of ideas, never touched by the arts except when they collected them as real property, never acquainted with great men or associated with wicked ones, but known everywhere without affection among the wealthy.

Four generations of green mold. And herself and Oliver? Not the children one would have expected to be the sole heirs of the Wolcotts and Barbers. (For a second, staring at the cold-suet face of her grandmother usurping the place of Monet's lilies, she felt the nembutal hangover blur her sight and she saw instead Bernard's face, the lips, the brown skin, the eyes that probed her like another kind of love. Ecstasy, my God!) She rubbed her hands up and down her suddenly goose-fleshed arms. Ecstasy would have no meaning to any Wolcott. Not to Oliver either, for all his stud-horse vitality, unless maybe the war did it to him, when he was a hero winning medals and capturing islands single-handed. Maybe danger, action, was something like ecstasy for him. On the other hand, a true Wolcott, he might have thought of those islands as strictly real estate.

She blew smoke before her face, screening it. Vitality, anyway, and that was no part of the Wolcott tradition. She knew where he had got it—from the place they had both got their looks, from the vulgar side, the unspoken-of side. And that was another thing, that insane Victorian refusal to let his name be spoken. She herself didn't know—his only daughter—whether he was alive or dead, why he had left, where he had gone. In her childhood she had used to dream of running away to him; she had liked to think that she was not her mother's daughter, but the child of some previous marriage of her father's.

Her mother's faded lips were moving as she read. The skin of her ears and throat was mottled, lightly tanned, under the glitter of the diamonds. At the point she had reached in the diary, Emily Wolcott was sixteen, a schoolgirl in Paris. It did not matter much where she was or how old she was. Sabrina knew her history year by year, detail by detail, and it was dreary all the way.

As if she were coming in near the end of a B movie she had seen before, she could take satisfaction in what she had missed: lists of uplifting books, abstracts of sermons, moral analyses of Emily's friends, most of whom she had envied, and of her sisters, both of whom she had disliked. Well past was that glum little section during which fourteen-year-old Emily stayed home for a week making a rigolette for the Milton town fair, and then went every day to see if anyone had bought it, and finally brought it home because nobody had. Sabrina nearly regretted, however, that she had missed the drama of the young man who stared at Emily in church in Nahant, and sent her through her little brother Mercer a letter which she opened before her mother could find and confiscate it. (It was all full of poetry, quoted.) Later the young man was taken off to the insane hospital, and Emily stayed in her room for three days, to emerge at last transparently pale, purged by sorrow, a girl over whom a man had lost his mind for love.

Coming late, Sabrina had missed the sequence that began when the Nahant crowd was getting up a quadrille, and George Hollis had extended his hand to Emily to choose her. But her dear friend (!) Harriet Blaney, pretending to be talking to someone over her shoulder, took his hand instead, and so Emily sat all evening at the piano playing while others danced. Next day they were having amateur theatricals and the piece was a playlet composed by Harriet. Emily could not help letting it out that Harriet's *mother* had written it. She did not mean to hurt

Harriet's feelings—the truth should hurt no one—but Harriet grew hysterical, and when Emily repeated what she knew to be true, Harriet went home. Grace and Sarah had the nerve to scold Emily for revealing the sordid little secret; they said it was *base*. At her mother's urging, Emily agreed to write a friendly letter, in which she said she freely forgave Harriet and hoped Harriet forgave her. She had it in her pocket, walking down the docks toward Harriet's, when she saw a party going sailing, and there was Harriet, and the hand she took to hop down into the dinghy was George Hollis's. Emily waited until she caught Harriet's eye and then she lifted the letter over her head and tore it into little bits and let them flutter into the sea. (Which must, Sabrina thought, have confused Harriet a good deal.) They did not make up till ten days afterward, when Emily was walking in the woods reading *Maude* aloud to herself, and ran plump into Harriet reading *Bleak House*.

Sabrina sat inattentive, reminding herself ironically of what else she had missed. Too late for the programs of the Haydn Society concerts. Too late for the closing of Emily's school, when the girls all vowed to save one dress and bonnet from each season, and when they all cried so inconsolably, Peggy Bigelow down with cool cloths and hartshorn, and Priscilla Tyler the envy of them all, for she wept steadily and serenely without hiccups or discolored eyes from the opening till the closing bell.

Those sentimental tears Sabrina could spare, as also she could spare Mme. Choteau's school in Paris, and the shopping and the balls when Emily's family came to release her in the spring. Too late this show for the handsome young Pole who at the Embassy ball mistakenly asked for a polka, which she was allowed to dance only with her brothers. He was crestfallen but eager, and waited, and was just coming forward (she was sure) to choose her for a lancers when her mother signaled that it was time to go. As they waited for their wraps, Emily saw the Pole lead out another partner, and in despair, laughing very hard, she danced her friend Emma Lacey around the foyer.

Poor Grandmother Emily was always taking her rigolette home unwanted from the fair. Sabrina, coming back from where indifference and irony had taken her, saw Helen Kretchmer listening with a soft, half-suppressed smile, and Sue Whiteside pretending with tense expressions that this was all like the climax of a thriller. And here came Emily, in her daughter's halting voice: a finished young lady who spoke French and some Italian, who was five feet nine inches tall and a little stooped (from growing too fast, they said, but she knew better: it was from bending to conceal the fact that she was taller than many young men, and to minimize what she thought the too-obvious fullness of her bust). Here she came, the source of that gloomy portrait on the wall—her face long and pointed at the chin, her smile impermanent and of the mouth only, her eyes with a trick of watching. It was her eyes, Emily was sure, that put young men off; she had been told roundabout that one of them found her terrifyingly intellectual.

Here she came, determined to be some worthy man's helpmeet, preferably a somewhat older man with hair graying at the temples, a Greek nose, and a future in the diplomatic service. She brought her hopes back to Beacon Street and waited, and before long something came to her, something thoroughly Emilian.

"Oh dear!" Deborah said, looking up, "I don't know if I can bear to read what comes now!"

"Go on, Mother, it's the climax of the show."

It took a little imagination, but only a little; the diary said as much between the lines as in them. Picture, then, Emily Wolcott looking from an upstairs window of her father's house on Beacon Street. It is evening, and autumn; the grass of the Common is already yellowed with fallen leaves, the lights down Boylston Street are distended in smoky dusk. There is yelling down by the Frog Pond—some of the rowdy Irish. It is getting so they come boldly right up to Beacon itself. Emily's father has said at dinner that between them the Paddies and the pigeons are taking over the Common.

A plain girl who knows that her soul is beautiful, Emily grasps the curtains, staring dreamily downward, listening to footsteps that approach and recede, thinking of footsteps that may walk into her own life. She wonders if George Hollis will have heard she is home: George is going to Harvard now, perhaps he will call one day. Her family do not approve of girls coming out, and she would be terrified at that anyway—she and Harriet have agreed it is like being put up on the slave block and hideously offered for sale. Yet there is difficulty in meeting people, and so many young men seem to have gone West, or abroad. Could her parents be induced to give a ball? But that would be practically coming out.

And still there is Grace, totally unattached at twenty-four, and Sarah, without an admirer at twenty-one. True, they make no effort; neither has the slightest charm. Emily is willing to make every effort, but how does one go about it? How, while keeping one's dignity, does one induce young men to take one to concerts or for drives along the Charles? Of course it is hardly yet the season; it will be different when she and her mother have found time to make some calls.

Out on the smoky Common, obscured by forked trees, framed by gas lamps, figures move, some in couples. A light buggy with a fast team drawing it clatters across Charles and comes uphill. As it moves through the gaslight she sees the horses straining into their collars, and on the seat a gentleman with a tightly buttoned coat, with a glowing cigar in his mouth and his gloved hands clenched in the reins. He is unapproachably strange, more foreign than if he spoke Arabic. The entire city of Boston seems peopled by men just as strange. And she loathes the odor of cigars, but that is a thing upon which women must be indulgent.

The casement lets in a draft of chilly air smelling of smoke and horse, of home, of walks along dim streets in the evening, of fall and fall's melancholy, of loneliness and longing. She leans her head against the window frame and makes a little noise in her throat. Then she hears a splash of mandolin music, an outbreak of laughter, a good tenor voice singing. Down on the corner of Charles three figures are clotted. Irish? Hardly, not with a mandolin, which now plinks out a few measures of a march, to which they come on in step.

They stop at the corner of her house. She hears them snickering. One bursts out with a shout of that clear tenor laughter. Up behind the curtains Emily Wolcott shakes. She does not recognize them, yet she must know them, and now they are about to make a quite unconventional and perhaps unacceptable call. Panic flutters the curtains clutched in her hand. She is resolving to fly downstairs and beg them to come another time when her mother is at home, when the mandolin plinks again and without a pause they are serenading her under her window.

She hangs listening with her heart thudding holes in her chest until they finish the song—a not very appropriate tavern song—and one of them, looking upward, says, "Juliet? Wherefore art thou, Juliet?" Emily notes but forgives the misreading. Her heart urges her outward onto the grilled balcony, hardly two feet wide, where she has begun to lure birds with crumbs and suet. Down below, the young men start another song; no men ever sang more sweetly. She thinks she recognizes George Hollis's voice. It is like him to do something like this. She has heard that Harvard men are very unconventional. But not the tenor—the tenor is a finer voice than George's. No one she knows—not yet.

They finish singing and call for her. Daring revives, and with her toe she pushes the casement wider until she can edge out with her hands on the iron rail. She is slightly uphill from them, and they do not at once see her. She takes her hands from the railing and begins softly to clap them.

Like daisies in the dusk their faces turn. One holds his hat against his heart. Another looks away toward the upper story of the house next door. Emily, following his glance, sees the glimmer of a dress at the window a floor above her own, and hears a soft snort of laughter.

Once or twice more, with dignity, she claps, bending her head to them, and then puts a foot backward and finds the floor inside, and backs out of sight and shuts the window. Faintly she hears them laughing and calling for her to come back. Her heart is rough as a pine cone in her breast, and she knows that if she ever meets the girl next door— new people have bought the house and they have not yet exchanged calls—she will die. She takes a long, cold, accurate look at her future, and that evening she sits down and writes in her diary not what her shriveled heart is saying, but a humorous little essay about her own blunder, and a chiding word about young men who will act in so thoughtless a way, and risk addling the heads of silly girls.

Sabrina moved. At the light clink of bells her mother looked up, the reading voice broke off. The French gilt clock on the mantel said twenty past five. Burke should surely be free now; was he deliberately *not* calling? Leaning back again, she caught Helen Kretchmer's bright blue look: what *did* she find so fascinating? Sue Whiteside was shaking her head, saying, "Oh dear, how dreadful, oh dear oh dear."

"But of course she met my father," Deborah said. "Later."

Sabrina swung her jingling foot, raising her eyes to the lumpy-faced woman who stared bleakly down from above the mantel. She felt light and fidgety. Without intending to speak, she heard herself say, "Much, much later! Eighteen mortal years. And all the time Grace and Sarah are getting queerer by the month, running off to Europe every summer to buy those trunk-loads of gifts they never could bring themselves to give away, and Great-Grandfather survives the big panic before the Civil War and coins money afterward, and dies, and Bushrod goes on digging his mole hole deeper into State Street, and Mercer grows up and goes traveling and sends back those pictures. Eighteen years of that, before the family manages to turn up a sacrificial lamb who will marry the youngest of the Wolcott old maids for her money, and she takes him."

Her mother was looking at her with her teeth showing. The eyes of Sue Whiteside, encountered by chance, wandered away. "Honestly, Sabrina," her mother said, "you're speaking of my mother and father . . . your grandparents."

Sabrina smoothed her dress, and turned upon them a smile so consciously radiant that she saw them all, the willing and the unwilling, begin to thaw. She felt that like Davy Crockett she could grin the bark off trees. Her fingers were twitching with energy. "I am," she said. "With respect and pity. She was unfortunate and he was a hero. He was very decent to her, I think . . . wasn't he? But of course her Wolcott luck held. He had to get Roman fever and die within a few years, and there she was again."

Her mother, watching her steadily, said, "Do you . . . find that amusing?"

"I find it ghastly."

"So do I," Sue Whiteside said. "I want to cry. Is there more?"

Deborah Hutchens made a small impatient stirring with her finger among the diary's pages. "Perhaps it is getting late."

"No, please finish."

Sabrina settled back. Her mother's diamonds shot at her a fat red ray that winked blue and yellow and then out. The steady eyes were at odds with the lightly trembling head. They asked questions, they speculated. "Of course, Mother," Sabrina said.

"There are only her resolutions. She had great character. Remember . . . she was only seventeen. And yet these are the precepts I grew up by and . . . tried to raise my own children by." Her eyes lifted a significant second to Sabrina's, and Helen Kretchmer, irritatingly clairvoyant to the ghosts of old conflict, rose and made a diversion by snapping on the reading light over the old lady's chair. The dry, wavering voice read:

"I promise and resolve:

1) If I begin a book I will read it through.

2) I will never . . . refuse to greet anyone I know, at least with a bow.

3) I will always dress properly.

4) I will ask few questions.

5) Whatever I will do . . . I will do on time.

6) I will ask help only when it is clear I cannot get on without it.

7) I will neither borrow nor lend if I can . . . help it, and I will never borrow from the servants.

8) I will be quiet, calm, and self-possessed, for I have found that . . . it is not good to show myself grateful for every slight attention.

9) I will always, when it is possible . . . to do a thing by a safe means or a doubtful one, choose the safe way. It is better to be . . . overcautious than imprudent.

10) I will not be too eager to oblige."

"My Lord, Mother," Sabrina could not help saying. "Are those things really there?"

"Of course."

"I don't remember them."

"They are . . . in the back of the book. What is it you find so strange?"

"The whole thing. The personality, the mind. 'I will not be too eager to oblige,' 'Choose the safe way.' Good heavens! If anyone in our whole family had ever had the capacity to go boom he would have shaken everything down like the House of Usher. Did you really take those resolutions seriously?"

"Is it so desirable to produce scapegrace sons and . . . wild girls?" her mother said (and once, Sabrina thought, I would have been afraid of her when she looked like that). "Other families had them. Ours was . . . mercifully free of them."

"So far," Sabrina said, holding the weakly blazing eyes, and then spun in her chair with a shaking of bells. Lizardo was there, his eyes answering hers: No, not yet. He said to her mother, "Tea now?"

When Deborah Hutchens had finished working all the anger out of her fingers and brought herself to obvious composure again, she said, "Oh, dear, it *has* got quite late. Yes, Lizardo, if you please."

Sabrina stood up. "Mother, will you excuse me? I don't believe I'll have any tea. I've got a headache, maybe I'll lie down till dinner. Excuse me, Mrs. Whiteside, Helen."

Their murmurs and their eyes were on her back as she left. In the hall she met Lizardo bringing the tea cart. His face filled with protest. "You not habbing somet'ing to itt? You hab not itt all day."

"I've got a headache." Lowering her voice she said, "Lizardo, have you got any whisky?"

"Yes."

"May I borrow a bottle till tomorrow?" (Never borrow from the servants.)

"You nid it?"

"I never needed a drink worse."

Anxiety was netted among his wrinkles; his eyes were like polished wet stones. "Where? Your room?"

"Yes."

"Soon as I serb tea?"

"You're a darling," she said, and gave him a fleeting irradiation of her smile. "If he calls, buzz me up there."

Lizardo brought the bottle, as he had brought bottles many times to her and Burke, her and her friends, in that house where orange juice was considered the best drink, though grape juice and ginger ale might be substituted if there were children present, or if the day was warm, and Sabrina lay on the chaise drinking whisky and tap water and trying to hold in her mind the things she might say when the telephone rang. She found it hard to keep the imaginary dialogue intact; it kept drifting into phrases of excuse, justification, or apology, or into resentment of the things *he* might say; or the chastened scene of reconciliation insisted on blurring out, to leave her with her blood awake and her imagination caught on some passionate moment of lips and hands in Oaxaca.

Several times she repeated the formulation she had made earlier, that a doctor's wife might as well be a widow. She had not meant to betray him, and yet he must see that only a vast boredom could have driven her to do what she did; she had a grievance. If she came back, he would have to divert some of his practice, so that they could do more things together. It framed itself almost as an ultimatum—and it was no sooner framed than she wondered what she would do if he yielded to it.

Nevertheless, something like a threat had lodged itself in her mind. He would have to see that not all the forgiving was on his side. She had something to forgive, too. She had the total pointlessness of her life to forgive somebody for—him or her mother or herself or all three.

She told herself that she would not call Bernard. That was miserably, desperately over with; they had kissed its corpse good-by in Oaxaca. She would wait for Burke to call, and then they would see whether he could be reasonable and she could keep from going to pieces.

Until seven she lay brooding, rewriting the conversation that would take place when the telephone rang, never finishing it but always starting over with new justifications or new ways of showing him she would not have been treacherous if he had not already blindly failed her. But the only bells she heard were the bells of her squaw boots when she rose to pour a new drink—those and eventually the shudder of the bronze gong that announced dinner.

CHAPTER 6

HE FILM stuttered, flapped whitely, went out. "Little too old," Oliver said. They sat in the dark until Lizardo touched switches and restored islands of light and groupings of furniture. The children argued and shoved one another, but among the adults the silence was general. No one commented to Oliver, holding the rewind switch and watching his mother, on what an interesting family record he had dug up; no one asked where he had found it. That face, mugging and grinning just before the film snapped, that figure in its ridiculous plus fours, had silenced them all. Even Helen, Sabrina saw, knew who had been shown, though she could have known no more than any of them why Oliver had shown him. He could not possibly have done it unthinking. Looking at the old, blotched, undone face of her mother, shocked speechless and shaking as if she had *paralysis agitans*, she was sick, sick, sick of all this family business. Since she came home there had been nothing else. First the diaries, now this. She put her hands on the arms of the chair, prepared to rise.

Passing among them with a tray of orange juice and grape-juice-and-ginger-ale, Lizardo paused before her and gave her a blank, discreet look. No call yet. She stood up so abruptly he had to swing the tray aside. "Excuse me, everybody," she said. "I've got some letters to write. Good night, Mother, Oliver, Minna. Good night, everyone."

As she had done that afternoon, she got out ahead of their questions
—assuming that anyone just then had any questions. In the cross hall
leading to the library and tearoom she stood a moment, her eyes burning with weariness and a hopeless premonition of tears. Burke would
have known she'd be waiting. He had deliberately done his bare duty
by calling once, and that was all he was going to do.

Anger flared up and went out in tiredness. She listened for voices in
the drawing room, but heard only the children. The hall's faint smell
of cedar oil recalled times when she had stood outside rooms wanting
things. Half her life she had stood in halls waiting for someone, or missing someone, or wishing something, or hoping for a voice, or maybe
only listening for sounds of life. If she did hear laughter or talk or the
clink of cups, as often as not she held back stiffly, repudiating what she
was drawn toward, and thinking how solitary and excluded and defiant
she was.

Why couldn't he have called, and helped her through this?

Under her fingers the paneling was satiny and cool. Her feet took
her into the library, lighted only by the reading lamp on the desk.
Monet's lilies were back on the wall. Standing by the desk, Sabrina
turned the clock and read it: eight-forty. She went around and opened
a drawer and pushed it shut again, trying the smoothness of the slide.
She opened another and there lay the telephone books, San Mateo
County on top, San Francisco underneath.

Her breathing had grown difficult and shallow. When she riffled the
pages of the heavy San Francisco book they stuck to her fingers with
static. Pinching the flimsy sheets, she turned them; her eye noted that
she had opened to the M's. McCaughey-McDermid, McDermond-
McGregor, McLaughlin-Meade, Meade-Mendes—her eye went down
the columns, her thumbnail moved along the names and stopped.
Marked now by the deep dent of her nail, the name stared up at her
from the anonymity of the page, and with a suspension of everything
in her except a half-nauseated haste, she began to dial.

Remotely the mechanism spun through its whirrings (and how
lonely a thing it is to telephone, how hopeful and pitiful a thing to
make incantatory motions with a piece of machinery and trust that
somehow magic will humanize it and the miracle of contact be estab-

lished! In Oaxaca, just before they parted, he had said, "This can't be forever, somehow we'll keep in touch," and she had laid two fingers on his lips, saying, "Touch—that's just what we can't keep. How lovely if it were true.") Now she heard the distant ringing and thought how dead and sad when the miracle didn't happen, when there was only this senseless repetition of sound like something left running on an empty planet.

And what if *she* should answer? Sabrina would not have known her if she had walked into the room, yet she thought of her as the Enemy. What a difference there might be if that woman were dead. Suddenly panicky, she thought, This is terribly dangerous! and started the instrument back toward its cradle. It clicked. A woman's voice, rising in question, said, "Hello?"

Sabrina clapped her palm over the mouthpiece as if her thoughts, racing toward some lie, were audible. Then her eyes slanted toward a shadow of motion in the doorway and saw Oliver there. Quietly she put the receiver down on the woman's reiterant voice. She looked at her brother with hatred.

Too big for the room, too aggressive for its repose, he came on in, probing with his glance like someone turning over rocks in search of fish-bait bugs. "Talking to someone? I hope you didn't hang up on account of me."

"I did. What do you want?"

"T-t-t-t-t," he said. "Why get sore? I want to talk to you."

"Well, here I am."

"Exuding charm."

"What do you want?"

"Come on, come on, you're all upset about something. Is this a bad time? Shall we make it another day?"

"Oh, get it over. Have they all gone, in there?"

"Minna and kiddies all gone home, Mother and La Secretary gone up to exercises and so to bed. We have the place to ourselves."

"How nice for us." She looked for a cigarette and finally accepted one from his outstretched pack. Across the lighter's blade of flame she looked into his square athlete's face. "What on earth was the idea, shocking her like that?"

"Like what?"

"Oh, don't play with me! Where did you get that old movie, anyway?"

He smiled. "A usually reliable source."

"I've never seen it before."

"No."

"I'm surprised she didn't burn it."

"Did you ever know her to burn anything?"

"Everything connected with him, I thought she did."

"She never had a chance on this. I just got hold of it recently."

"All right, but why did you have to spring it on her? You just let him come back to life without warning in front of her."

"Yes!" Oliver said, "and did you see how she reacted?"

She shook her head angrily. "If it's reactions you want, why not kick her in the stomach?"

"Well, well." Oliver's eyes were narrowed to bright little half-moons, his eyebrows peaked into inverted V's. "Standing up for Mother. You've mellowed."

"That was dirty," Sabrina said. "She isn't what she used to be, she has to get braced for things. What is it you want, anyway?"

Smiling, he looked around among bookcases and cabinets; he seemed to brood upon the brass footrail of the fireplace. "Why don't we go somewhere and get a drink? Or have you got any more of that whisky you were so perfumed with at dinner?"

She set her foot on the bell button under the desk. For nearly a minute she studied Oliver's amused face. He liked to act as if he found you ridiculous; his pose was that he read you like a book. Yet it would be a mistake to underestimate him. There was more to him than sports cars and skin-diving and the muscles that she knew reduced some women to jelly. His squinted eyes looked back at her with more knowingness than she liked.

The white coat glimmered in the doorway. "Lizardo," she said, "would you get that bottle from my room? And some glasses and ice? Please."

"The reaction is important," Oliver said. "I didn't show that movie just to shock her. I wanted to see how far gone she is."

"Gone?"

"All this idiotic family worship. It gets worse and worse. Grandmother's church attendance record in Nahant is more real to her than what goes on right here, today. I doubt if she can tell one of my kids from the other. I doubt if she can tell past from present, except that the past is realer. I showed that movie because I wanted to see if he was as real to her as the Wolcotts are. He is."

"Real?" she said. "Of course. Even with all the hush-hush, he's always been the realest thing around here. Remember when she caught me looking at his picture in her locket? Don't tell me she's any different than she always was. Wasn't he real to you, in his knickers and his smile? He was to me—twice as real and twice as dreadful as if anybody'd respected him while he was alive."

She felt unreasonably angry. It wasn't simply that he had been brought back, but that he had come back in that silly costume of the twenties, going through the pantomime of a Harold Lloyd comedy, turning his frantic and over-eager smile into the camera, making an ass of himself, flickering and jittering there like a parody, a puppet in boy's clothes.

Oliver said, with his eyebrows high, "How did you know he was dead?"

"I don't. How would anyone know? I don't know how I recognized him in the movie, unless from that peek into Mother's locket. Or maybe he looked like you, a little." The hazel eyes with sunburned squint wrinkles tightening at their corners knew something; he was feeling ironic and superior. "Why?" she said. "Do *you* know? Who told you?"

"I went to his funeral."

"You *what?*"

"On Kauai, two months ago. I was intending to go over and see him, and then I got word he was dead. It was his wife gave me this movie and some other stuff."

"His wife?"

"The woman he was living with. I don't know whether they were married or not. Probably were—technical bigamy. They'd been living together for twenty years."

She stared at him, oppressed by a disappointment so overwhelming that she could find nothing to say. You wondered all your life, you never quite gave up the childhood dream of finding him and knowing him, and then when you did it was just too late. If she had known two months ago, she might have gone to the islands instead of to Oaxaca. Forcing her voice, she said, "How did you know he was on Kauai? What was he doing there, beachcombing?"

"He had a ranch there," Oliver said. "I saw him once during the war. He got a pass to Pearl to see them hang a Navy Cross on Big Brudder."

"You never told me."

Acknowledging something, he ducked his head sideways with a half shrug. "I sort of thought he might get in touch with you. He didn't, ever?"

"What do you think?" she said bitterly. "I'm the one that's never known anything, not even why he left. What was it, this woman, or gambling debts, or something else attractive?"

He smiled. "There may have been women, and there probably were debts. But that isn't why he left. He left because Grandmother and Mercer, especially Grandmother, bought him off."

After a considerable pause she said, "How do you know that?"

"He told me; he was sort of apologizing and explaining. Also I've got copies of the papers he signed, a sort of quit-claim agreement, and a receipt for two hundred and fifty thousand."

"My God, Mother must have been really fond of him!"

"I doubt she even knew about it. She probably thinks he skipped."

"You mean they . . . ?"

"I mean they."

It burst out of her, the question with which she had tormented herself in childhood. "But wouldn't you think he'd have come back *sometime,* or written? At least to you and me?"

"I guess he thought the whole family was so down on him the only thing he could do was take their money and thumb his nose. One thing I wanted to check on this spring, I wanted to confirm his conscience. If Mother had died before he did he might have been able to foul up the estate but good. But he had a sort of honor; he kept his bond."

Testing his expression, which for him was singularly open, she wondered if he had some reason, like his reason for springing the movie on their mother, or his reason for visiting the pariah in his exile, for telling her all this now. "What was he like?" she said.

"You saw his picture."

"Yes, 1927, and all dressed up like Gene Sarazen. I mean what was he *like?*"

"Like anybody else. Getting a little thin on top, but still sporty. He was eight or ten years younger than Mother, you know. Loud jacket, broken veins in the cheeks, ruddy face, big smile."

"Did his smile ever look ghastly?"

He stared. Drily he said, "Ghastly isn't a word I'd've picked, no. We only had about an hour together, and he was sort of embarrassed. He wanted me to understand that it was only when he was sure there was no chance of a reconciliation that he took the money; he said he did it for our sakes, to get out of our hair. Hoped I wouldn't think he'd sold out his children. Sort of pathetic—he'd followed us in the newspapers. Had a society-page picture of you in his wallet. What makes you pick a word like ghastly, for God's sake?"

She moved the silver letter dagger parallel with the blotter's edge. A picture of her. It was ridiculous, but she felt like crying. She said, "I don't know. It's the way I've always seen him, like somebody damned, maybe like an old fairy rouged over his wrinkles." With a tight little laugh she tossed her hands in the air. "And he didn't try to blackmail you? He didn't think a quarter of a million was too cheap for so heroic a son and so beautiful a daughter?"

Lizardo brought in the tray, looking in a state of acute anxiety. But that was only his wrinkles; when he was younger he had had a face as serene as a Khmer Buddha's. He had put crackers and cheese and fruit on the tray with the whisky, that meant he had been watching her not-eat at dinner. To please him, she put a bit of cheese on a cracker and popped it in her mouth. "That's wonderful," she said. "Thank you, darling."

He went out softly. Oliver poured two drinks. "Darling?" he said. "That's a new one, with the servants."

"Love isn't so common you can disregard it," Sabrina said. "The old man loves me. He always has. He *is* a darling. It's his whisky you're drinking. Now what is it you were so anxious to talk to me about?"

"I thought we were talking about it."

"Father?"

"No, not Father. He was paid off thirty years ago and he kept his bargain. It's Mother I'm talking about. She's losing her buttons."

"Oh, come on!"

"You haven't been around. All the do-good outfits, for one thing. World Federalism, Moral Rearmament, Civil Liberties Union, League for Civic Unity, NAACP, God knows what. Stick around a week and see who calls. She used to have some contact with people you'd want to have contact with. Now it's birds in turbans who eat with their fingers, and old dames preaching Absolute Honesty, and committees suggesting donations for inter-racial friendship. The only times she goes out any more are to play golf, which her doctor makes her do, and once in a while to a crackpot meeting. And watch her play golf. She potters around talking to herself and dubbing the ball up the fairway and putting it back and forth across the green while six foursomes stack up behind, and every time a putt doesn't drop she stands there murmuring and shaking her head. "Strange!" she'll say. "Strange!"

Sabrina laughed. "I can hear her. She isn't used to being balked, even by a golf ball."

"Sure, but is that normal? Here's something else. Do you know how much she's given away in the last few months, just in driblets? You remember we fixed it so she has to fight Collier to give anything big . . ."

"*We* fixed it?"

"You approved it. When she was sick."

"I don't remember," she said. "I suppose it's a good idea."

"You're damned right it is. But I didn't allow for the nibbles. I just checked. Eighteen thousand in four months. They write in, or make a call, and bingo. It's automatic. They keep coming back, as why wouldn't they? And new ones keep showing up. You wouldn't know there were so God-damned many organizations, half of them on the Attorney General's list probably, and not one in ten that's deductible."

"Now it comes out," she said. "Money. What if she does give some away? She can afford it. There's always been more income from the trust than she could possibly use. It would just go in taxes, or have to be reinvested."

"*Have* to be," Oliver said. "You kill me."

"It does me good to have her give something away. Today Bobbie MacDonald came to borrow some of the old dresses for a play or something her children are in, and Mother *loaned* them to her. Not gave. Loaned."

"Naturally. Those dresses mean more to her than any amount of money. She'd give away her total income and be happy as a clam living in mildewed party gowns and rummaging the cupboards for pairs of Auntie Grace's eighty-year-old French gloves. The past. What I've been telling you."

Sabrina's mind had doubled back, and she was speculating on that almost-made contact that he had interrupted. If Oliver hadn't come in, she might have got by the woman with some lie, she might now be talking to him. With marriage and duty in ruins behind her, and Burke too stiff-necked to bend an inch, she might at least be in touch with love. Instead she had Oliver talking family and finances. Lifting the bottle, she sloshed a new drink into her glass.

"So what is it you want to do?" she cried impatiently. "You can't stop her from spending her money any way she wants to."

"Oh yes you can, if she's going off her head."

"You mean have a guardian appointed?"

"If necessary."

"It's absurd. She's no more incompetent than you are. The whole family's been nuts for four generations, but that hasn't kept money from sticking to them. Anyway, you have to have evidence, a court has to decide a thing like that, or a judge, or an umpire or somebody."

"Exactly. So I've been gathering a little evidence." He trickled a thin stream from the depleted bottle into his glass.

Sabrina spun clear around on the rotating chair. "Oliver, that's vile!"

"Vile? It's done all the time. Some of your best friends are incompetent. There're plenty of reasons. And there's no disgrace, people understand. It may not even be immediately necessary. But don't forget her will. How would you like it if she left five million—as she could—

to the NAACP or some God-damned outfit like that? How'd you like to strip yourself to pay estate taxes on that kind of a God-damned will? And couldn't you find any use for the fifty or sixty thousand she's going to give away to crackpots this year?"

"How much have you given to the Republican Party and Pro-America and the anti-income-tax crowd? How much have you lost at Bay Meadows?"

He grinned at her fixedly with his cropped head sunk down. "Those are personal expenses, not contributions to crackpots."

Sabrina said in anger, "I knew I shouldn't come home to this—"

The telephone rang.

Her whole body felt the impact of that strident noise. Her eyes jumped to Oliver's, her hand jumped to the instrument, hovered, drew back. Afraid of its trembling, she thrust it down in her lap. The telephone rang again.

"Shall I answer it?" Oliver said, watching her.

She shrugged. "Lizardo can get it."

"I thought you were expecting a call from Burke."

"I was." (But he missed his chance! He can't expect me to wait forever.)

The telephone began a third ring that was cut off. She did not like the bright, alert look that Oliver wore. He seemed to sniff secrets. If this was Burke, she would have to excuse herself and take the call in her room. And then what would she say? The speeches she had spent an hour before dinner in framing had all come undone.

Under the desk the buzzer made its discreet noise. Sabrina drew on a cigarette and blew out smoke, and behind that cover, with lowered lids, picked up the phone. "Yes?"

Click as Lizardo hung up, then the voice: Bobbie. Sabrina's breath flowed out slowly and easily. She sat picking a flake of tobacco off her tongue, looking away from Oliver and listening to Bobbie's light, excited patter of words that asked if she was coming over.

"I don't know," she said. "Maybe. I've been talking business with Oliver"—she flicked him a glance—"and I might be held up till late."

"No matter what time," Barbara said. "I'm terribly sorry about this afternoon, I just couldn't. Please come on."

"I'll try. If this runs too late I'll call you." She hung up. To Oliver she said, "Bobbie. I was trying to get her when you came in."

"Mmmm." He stripped a bunch of grapes, eating them swiftly, slouched far down. Abruptly he stood up. "Well, that's what I wanted you to know. You aren't around, you don't see it. But if we don't get prepared in advance we could have a hell of a time breaking some crazy will."

She sat still while he came around the desk; she felt him loom at her shoulder. He said, "There's one other thing that's come up. How would you feel about selling the Woodside land?"

"Selling it? To whom? What for?"

"To a group of developers. We'd be part of it."

"Cheeseboxes? The whole Peninsula is ruined now."

"Not cheeseboxes. No tract houses." He leered. "Junior estates!"

"It sounds utterly repulsive."

"It sounds to me like a three-million-dollar equity in a six-million-dollar deal."

"It gives me nightmares. Have you proposed this to Mother?"

Irritation put deep lines in his face. For an instant he looked like pictures she had seen of pilots testing the human effects of great speeds, like a man in a power dive or a wind tunnel. His cheeks were ridged, his mouth drew in. "What would she say if I did? If it was money she'd throw it away on the first jigaboo that asked for it. But it isn't money, it's property, and so it's sacred. Even though the damned taxes double every few years, she'd hang onto it like death."

"Well, there's your answer, then. It's her land, not yours."

"Only as long as she's competent."

"You're a charming fellow," Sabrina said. "I won't have anything to do with it. What does she need another two or three million for, anyway? What do you need it for? Pretty soon that Woodside place will be almost the only open land, except Stanford, left on the Peninsula, and even Stanford seems to be breaking down. If the taxes are too high, why don't we give it to the state or county for a park?"

"That's exactly the kind of do-good notion I'm afraid she'll get."

"San Francisco was made by do-good notions like that," she said. "The Fleishackers and Sterns and de Youngs and Spreckelses and

Crockers and Phelans can have them, even Hearst had them, but not us."

"Just the same, don't go putting ideas like that into her head."

"Oh, let's drop it," she said. "But don't expect me to conspire against Mother so you can pull off a real-estate deal. Persuade her yourself."

He circled the ice in his glass, the speculative humorous look back on his face. He said, "What the matter, Sister? You're jumpy. You've got something on your mind."

Sabrina moved her shoulders. "I just discovered my father and then lost him again. Remember?"

"How's Burke?"

"Fine, I guess. Up at six, back for late dinner unless there's an emergency, out every other evening to dose somebody's cold, always paged at the end of the first act. You know."

"What does it get him, working that hard? He'll kill himself."

Again she moved her shoulders. Then his hand came down past her, poked the page of the open telephone book. With a wild certainty, an exaggerated moment of paralysis followed by a heavy thudding of her heart, she saw his thick brown finger rigid at the indentation her thumbnail had left in the margin. "Who's Bernard Mendelsohn?"

As she swung to glare upward she saw in his face that he knew everything, just as surely as if she had told him. "Oh, damn you," she said, unutterably tired. "Go away. Go on and leave me alone."

From the unmoving swivel chair she watched him drain his drink and set the glass on the tray. "Relax," he said. "I'm not going to spy on you. You'd better get some sleep. You look bushed."

Silently she watched him go out. For quite a long time she sat still in the library empty except for spooks and relics and the dry sound of Time, a neat ticking from the French gilt clock on the mantel, an uncalibrated whirring from the electric clock on the desk.

If what she wanted was reconciliation with Burke, she had better pick up the telephone. Probably he was waiting for her to do just that —salvaging his pride by forcing her to come crawling. Her mind repudiated the notion before she had half thought it. She would do anything else first, anything.

But if he had called the second time, if he had taken a plane up, if he should walk in that door right now. She had not intended treachery, she had only exploded into it after twelve years of repression and inadequacy. He could not expect her to humiliate herself more. She had come home and told him honestly. Wasn't that enough?

But if he came in that door right now, then what?

Her eyes, smarting with snagged nerves and strained muscles, lifted to the doorway and saw only a hole between the paneling and the leather-and-gilt backs of books. At her elbow the desk clock made its dry whispering. In God's name, why all this torment about an act of nature? Why the self-flagellation because out of boredom or passing lecherousness or whatever other cause she had loved two men?

She knew, of course. Because the second was not just another man, he was ecstasy and liberation, a face and body that were sweet and secret, hands and eyes and a voice that worshiped and cherished her. And the first was not just a first man, but her husband. Her conscience was not so naïve that she could get around it by beginning to dislike the person she had wronged. Above all, it was she who was involved in this, Sabrina Hutchens, who in spite of herself, in spite of everything, had had her conscience shaped by generations of conventional puritans she had always despised.

Even as a girl who worried her mother frantic with her carelessness and sullenness and rebellion, she had been in no danger of the horrors her mother evidently feared. When she ran away to take an apartment on Telegraph Hill and fantastically study painting, she had lived like a nun, not like a bohemian. Maybe fastidiousness, maybe something psychologically juicy. But also commitment: her inhibitions were not only submitted to but believed in. If human love was the best thing in life, even if it was only the greatest pleasure, then the act that consummated it was not to be made trivial or cheap. She had always grown furious with novels or plays that represented sex as a casual letting off of steam. If that was all it was, why involve another person in it? And the psychologists who had "emancipated" love into an innocent form of play filled her with contempt.

It was not play. It was a long way from being play. The treason of the body might be only a little treason, readily understood and forgiven and forgotten. But when it involved also the treason of the affections and the trust, then it was deadly guilt. And that was what it involved with her.

It sickened her to be what she was. If Burke had called right then she would have asked to be forgiven and restored. But he had not called, and she knew he would not: she knew his pride and his chilly control. He would wait for her to come back on her knees.

She did not know, when she picked up the telephone, whether she was going to call Pasadena or San Francisco; she only knew it was a desperate choice. Her finger made it for her. It found the hole marked J, the first letter of JUniper, and the number it dialed was the one marked by the dent of her thumbnail in the open book at her elbow.

At the first ring she nearly hung up again, her lip clamped between her teeth in panic because again she was unprepared with a lie. But it was not the woman who answered. When she heard the resonant voice she bent sharply, huddling over the mouthpiece, thinking in the instant, How secure he sounds! How carelessly he picked that up!

The mouthpiece was wrapped within her hands. She said into it softly and urgently, "Bernard. It's Sabrina. Are you alone? Can you talk?"

There was a silence. He cleared his throat. He said, "Yes, this is Mr. Mendelsohn."

"Listen!" she said, very low. "I came on up. I'm in Hillsborough. Can you meet me? Now?"

She heard with admiration, even while she hated the need for it, the considering, business-like voice. "Well, it's pretty late. . . . Just a minute, let me see." A remoter murmuring as he spoke with someone in another room—her—with his hand over the mouthpiece. She waited, breathing shallowly through her mouth. He was back; he said, "I'll tell you, Mr. Hanks, it's not something I'd do for everyone. But under the circumstances . . . Could we settle it in an hour, do you think?"

"Oh, yes!" she said. "Just to see you!" before she remembered that she need pay no attention to what he said. He was speaking not for her but for the room behind him. His voice had ridden right over hers: ". . . shall I meet you?"

"What?" she said stupidly. "Oh. Somewhere. You're in Stonestown? How's the Skyline, just at the top of the ridge? There's a subdivision across the road now, but an old lane cuts off on the valley side. . . . You know that place? Right above the airport, where everything opens out?"

"I know it," he said. "Yes. Twenty minutes, say?"

Into her cupped hands she said breathlessly, "It may take me a little longer. But don't go away! Leave your parking lights on. I'll be in a gray and white Chrysler convertible."

"Thank you," the resonant voice said. "Not at all."

Frantic to be going, she was on her feet. Her hands were damp. Seeing the tray, she felt that she should ring for Lizardo, but that would take time, and anyway he knew enough to clear away before her mother came down. The thought came, I ought to change, put on some perfume, and at once, with a cunning she had not known she had, she canceled the idea. No, no perfume. She would smell it on him.

By that time she was on her way, nearly running, toward the front door.

CHAPTER 7

As she rolled out from under the oaks and through the stone gates she saw the sky clear, with scattered stars. Chilly air blew in her face, so damp that she stopped and ran the top up, encysting herself in canvas and glass. By lanes known since childhood, but confused by improvements that made even the familiar look strange, she ducked out to the trunk road, spun into it, came down hard with her foot and fled upward along the curving white line. Her lights fell on oaks, redwoods, bloody-barked madrones; and the subdivisions had been before her, spreading like ringworm to the Skyline and beyond. Swinging right on the Skyline, she held her watch under the cowl light. Five minutes to ten—she had been fifteen minutes already. On her left, along the highest crest, the sky towered with a lofty wall of fog. In anger and helplessness she saw thickening streamers reaching across the road, and heard the reedy whistle of wind. Almost at once everything went white. Approaching cars began as blurry pinheads of light, grew into threatening dazzles, crept past. Frantic and frustrated, Sabrina sat far forward to see, searching for the entrance to the blind lane.

But then the fog thinned as suddenly as it had closed in, the lonesome whistle of wind died away, the jammed roofs of tract houses ended and the air was full of the foul smell of brussels-sprouts fields. At a remembered curve she slowed, peering. It looked right, a side road that eased off into weeds between thin trees. She turned in, and ahead of her a pair of headlights flashed up bright and went down again. The road was littered with papers and beer cans and the refuse of the hundreds who had parked there above the view. Below he widened the great basin of lights, the bay a long darkness down its center. She saw the car, and its door opening. Her lights threw the shadow of a man far down the slope. Then she could tell him by the way he moved.

She snapped off the lights and turned the key and yanked on the hand brake and was out of the car before it stopped. His feet were coming through weeds and trash, his sudden arms came around her. The tears she tasted through their kiss might have been those she had shed in the shattered moments of good-by in Oaxaca, so little did the intervening time count.

His embrace was like a physical attack. Her head was hollow and humming, her breath gone. Opening her eyes to conquer the dizziness, she saw past the side of his neck to the sky, and the stars in it were whirling. Even with her eyes wide, the spangled sky spun faster, streaming stars. Dimly she felt her lips coming unglued from his. The humming stopped—had one of them been making it, a humming or crooning as they kissed?—and she felt the pain of his arm against her ribs. Bernard was saying sharply, "Sabrina! Darling, what's the matter? Are you all right?"

With the tips of her fingers she touched his face. "I'm all right. Oh, now I'm all right!"

"You fainted or something."

"You should be flattered, darling."

"Joke." He held her face between his hands. She could see only his silhouette, but she knew the warmth of his eyes and his expression of smiling attentiveness from the set of his head. He was very tall—she had forgotten how tall. And she could feel his heart hammering.

"Did I scare you?" she said, still touching his cheek. "Good. I love it that I can. It was just seeing you—feeling you." Shuddering, laughing a little, she crowded closer, and said into his lapel, "I've had a perfectly vile time, darling. I've hated every minute, and I've hardly eaten or slept. How have you been?"

"Miserable, up to now."

"I envied you having a job."

"It might have helped if I could have kept my mind on it." His fist lifted her under the chin. Even in the dark he had a flattering, cherishing way of looking at her, respectful and proud as if she were a work of art he had just acquired. "Oh, I'm glad you came!" he said.

"I couldn't have stayed away, I think. Did I make trouble calling you at home? I wasn't going to. I kept telling myself I'd never call or see you again. Then I just did."

"You're wonderful."

"I called once about an hour earlier. *She* answered, and I hung up."

"I remember, it rang." He had her wrapped completely around, rocking her a little in the wind. She felt safer than she had ever been.

"Did you think it might be me?"

"I'm afraid I didn't think about it," he said over her head, as if he didn't want to talk at all.

"You sounded so secure when I did get you, like a contented householder getting up from television to answer the phone. Is that what you were?"

"I was a householder."

She weighed the answer. It satisfied her. "What did you tell her?"

"You're an importer of Japanese woollens and you have to leave on a midnight plane."

"She doesn't know about us at all, then."

"No."

"Does she guess?"

"I don't think so."

"Everything in your family is just the way it was before."

The rough tweed of his jacket rasped her cheek as he wrapped her still tighter. Over her head he said, "No."

"Ah, darling!"

"Not the same for me. As far as she knows, it's the same."

Disappointed, she half twisted out of his arms. Below them, nearly islanded in the bay's darkness, the airport was a brilliant cluster approached by dotted radii. The Bayshore Freeway moved its opposing belts of lights all the way from Hunter's Point down to the glowing haze around Redwood City and Palo Alto. Up the Contra Costa hills lights swarmed in milky ways, and off to the left, obscured by the nearer hills, a section of the Bay Bridge crawled like an old-fashioned illuminated sign.

"I hate it that she doesn't know," Sabrina said. "I hate it that she can't *tell.*" She was shivering through her whole body.

A car's headlights touched the tops of trees off to the right, and passed. Against their backs the wind pushed heavy and wet. Ambiguous in the starlight, a paper bag blew along the ground and plastered itself against a clump of weed. "Darling," Bernard said softly, "she's only had a day and a half to notice anything." He opened the car door. "Let's get inside, you're cold."

"I'm a mess," she said. "I'm a jealous, unreasonable female."

"You're in love," Bernard's voice said softly in her ear. "So am I." They were locked mouth to mouth the moment they slid into the seat, and when they finally broke apart he said, clenching his hand up and down her arm, "You're not in any doubt, are you?"

"No." She traced his eyesocket, his cheekbone, his mouth, with her fingers, wishing it were light enough to see him. "No. Only we were going to be so big and strong and break it off. What are we going to do now?"

"There doesn't seem much *to* do," he said, and for the second time in two or three minutes a twinge of disappointment made her move a little away. How could either of them accept, in that tone of submissive resignation, the total impossibility of what they both most wanted? There should be more anguish than this; even Oaxaca, and that tortured good-by at the airport, was righter than what she had just heard in his tone. She said, "Burke knows. I told him."

The slight movement of his body expressed some meaning that she was alert to without fully understanding it. He said, "How did he take it?"

"Clinically. He'd never show anything."

"No?" he said. "People are different. It would destroy Norma."

They sat separated by the fact that she had told her husband, but he had not told his wife. But she so wanted things to be right between them, and warm and secure again, that she gripped his hand, saying, "It's harder for you, with children."

He was looking out across the lights for a second. Then he made a disgusted exclamation, shook her shoulders with his circling arm, and said, "Do you know what they'd hear and believe, if it came to a break? That I'd thrown them all away in order to marry a rich woman."

"I suppose," she said drearily. Out in the starred blackness the Contra Costa lights merged into the sky without a horizon.

"Norma, too," Bernard said. "I've thought of nothing else since I left you. She's past forty, she's a nice woman, she's been a wonderful mother, she thinks we've had a successful marriage. . . . We *have,* if that makes any sense to you. I can't get over thinking how unfair, you know? After . . ."

"Taking the best years of her life?" Sabrina said. "Please, darling. We didn't fall in love on purpose. I tell you the truth, I can't cry for her sorrows. My own are enough for me."

His profile, projected against the valley's lights, seemed aloof and brooding. The warmth was squeezed out of him. She thought bitterly, Everything I touch I turn to stone! Then his hand came rubbing on her shoulder and the side of her neck, and suddenly she bent her cheek against it and held it there. He bent down over her and his breath beat warm, faintly whisky-smelling, on her face. "And yet I love you," he whispered. "You make all the rest of it only duty. The trouble is they *are* a duty. I owe them a responsibility, but I'm also fond of them. The fact that I love you more can't make me love them less."

"No."

"I'm afraid you think I should leave her anyway."

"Darling, I don't know what I think. I want you, that's all I know."

In an extending silence the wind began to whistle around the car; the unbuttoned flaps of the top creaked and snapped. A trail of vapor wavered almost unseen past the window, and a patch of the valley's lights was dimmed. Their faces were only a foot apart, but she could see no more than the set of his head, the way he had of holding it a little on one side. His thigh was warm against hers. And she was at once anguished and reassured by the sigh, like a groan, that was wrenched out of him.

"Oh, Christ, I don't know," he said. "I suppose I might even learn to dislike her, eventually, if I took the trouble to be unkind, and forced her into nagging and fighting me. Then I could do it, at least as far as she's concerned, but I wouldn't like myself much. I've always tried to be decent. Doing something like that deliberately would be almost like plotting to murder her and throw her over the Devil's Slide. And there are still the girls."

She counted his fingers, tested that each one had a nail, felt up along the knuckles and wrist. Streamers of fog went past the corner of her eye. "So it comes down to who gets killed," she said finally. "I mean, we can have the courage of our affections and somebody else gets killed, or we can be scrupulous and responsible, and it's us."

The mere saying of it made her feel as if the top of her head were coming off. She straightened away from the fingers that were fondling her jaw and ear and cried, "Darling, did you think we could have an affair without damaging our marriages? Let me tell you something. I never believed in divorce either. And let me tell you something else. I was a virgin when I married and you're the only man since. I take this as seriously as you do. I've wronged Burke at least as much as you've wronged your wife, and I can suffer as much as she can. And I haven't got three of your children to console me."

She turned her head, grimacing in the dark against the tears. His hand was fumbling at the back of her neck, and she felt the pins of her hair come loose. He touched her wet face and took his hand away, and she sat despising their wretched condition and their wretched scruples, and then she was twisting toward him, crying, "Bernard, listen, please! I'm no good at this. If you wanted a lover you chose terribly badly. I was brought up wrong, I can't convince myself that anything I do is justified by my natural urges, and neither can you, obviously. I think we're dirty and wicked, I really do. Don't shake your head. But if we've been wicked, I've loved it, too, darling, see? I'm willing to pay the price. If we're going to be wicked, let's plunge, instead of nibbling ourselves to death with little lies and regrets. That's the only way I can feel even halfway good about it. Otherwise we'd better go back to what we decided in Oaxaca, and cut it out of us like a cancer."

The fumbling hand came through the falling sheaf of her hair and touched her neck, came around to her face. "Tears," Bernard said softly. "Poor darling."

"Don't you think I'm right?"

"I don't know," he said. "I'm trying to think."

"I can't go on being an importer of Japanese woollens!" she said. The pressure built up inside her as if every stroke of her pulse was the pulse of an air hose. "Oh, *God*," she said, "isn't it ridiculous what our emotions get us into! I wished I'd stayed in Pasadena and kept my mouth shut and lived forty years as an ornament on the doctor's mantel. No I don't. I wish I'd kissed you good-by in Oaxaca and gone straight out and slept with somebody else, anybody, some mule driver or someone in a bar, just to show myself that sleeping with someone isn't this important. I'm sorry, I'm sorry, I'm *sorry* I came up and broke it open again!"

Both his hands came down to catch hers in her lap. In a choked voice he said, "You're tearing my insides out!"

"What do you think you're doing to mine?" But it was only for a moment that she avoided his mouth. Then they were fused, the kiss clung and lengthened, his hands were on her. It was a long time before they separated; the anger was gone.

Laughing shakily, she drew her fingers under her cheekbones. "I never knew I was such a one to cry."

"I'm feeling that way myself."

"And there's no hope for us."

By the hair he pulled her head back against the seat, and with his lips against hers he said, "Darling, I don't think I could stand doing what would be necessary for a divorce."

But he would not let her move her mouth away. "I can't give you up, either," he said, and they were fused again. When they came lingeringly apart he whispered, "Some way, we've got to see each other. We have to!"

She took that in. "A love-nest?" she said. "Oh, Bernard!"

With his mouth nibbling at her ear he whispered, "How do you like your hell, partial or complete?" Looking past him, down across the bay, she saw the tilted slope of lights on the Contra Costa shore being wiped away as a wall of fog moved southward. The bridge was already gone, the Bayshore below the airport was going. It was coming over the ridge, too; the wisps were thickening past the windows. "Think hard, darling," Bernard said. "Is anything more important than seeing each other every few days?"

Hopelessly she turned her lips to find his. "I don't want hell at all, I want you. Maybe even that way, I don't know. Now I suppose it's getting late and you have to go home to your wife."

His growl was unintelligible. His hand was busy at the buttons of her dress. She rocked her head, bruising her lips against his, saying, "No, no," but she did not stop him. Her flesh jumped at the cold, complete marriage with his hand. Still clinging, not wanting to break the kiss even while they moved, they groped out of the front seat and into the back.

She was panting and stammering with passion, and yet she was not one in whom passion clouded or stopped the mind. While she fumbled in the dreadful awkwardness of finding a position, she was thinking bleakly that she had wasted her youth. A lot of girls she knew would have been handier at this. While she struggled with the clothes, and helped his hands, and heard him groan with impatience and frustration, she was thinking that this was where modern love brought you: to a lover's lane where in the desperate constriction of a back seat, in a car parked among the beer cans and Kleenex and discarded condoms of clerks and students and juvenile delinquents and the emotionally and sexually dispossessed, you dispelled the fiction that you were much better, much different, or even more fastidious.

Love turned out to be a tall man, taller than she remembered, with a face that only forty-eight hours ago she had searched and memorized but that tonight she had not once seen clearly, a face with olive skin and large glowing eyes and a habit of smiling and easy laughter: a face in which the tenderest thing was the admiration she read there for herself.

His breath beat against her. He moved, and she moved to help and meet him. Instantly he swore, and she was jammed under while the hasty spasm convulsed him. It was so ghastly and unsatisfactory that she almost laughed. It was all right, she said, soothing him. Never mind, never mind.

But she was glad that he could not see her face, nor she his.

"You're my life," he said afterward. "You're all there is. The rest is jail."

"Ah, darling." She touched his cheek and meant the tenderness even while she was reminding herself of where they sat, and how outside, on a dirty wind, trash blew past.

"We could get an apartment," he said. "Where, do you think? The City might be too dangerous, we both know too many people. Berkeley too, I went to school there. What about Oakland?"

"I went to Mills," she said, and listening to her own words she heard them as a criticism, as if she had said, "Shall we protect only you?" To rescue him, she said quickly, "But I don't know anybody there. *Nobody* knows anybody in Oakland."

They laughed. He said, "Darling, darling, I wish we could be open. But I don't think, the way things are . . ."

She saw him loom for an instant into visibility as lights brushed them. He straightened up with an exclamation. "Tidy up!" Confused, she craned to look, and saw headlights bumping down, blurred in the fog, and two red lights on the car roof, one blinking, one steady. The highway patrol. Perfect.

Bernard stepped out and spoke with the policemen outside. They did not bother her except to flash a flashlight in the window—to make sure she was not a corpse, she supposed, or a fourteen-year-old—and move it from her to the registration slip on the steering column. Putting up her hair, which had all come down, she gave them her full face to look at, thinking, Oh, the hell with it, what does it matter?

The police were evidently suggesting that they move on. She could hear Bernard asking angrily if it had become an offense to park and look at the view. Dangerous, they said. Inviting trouble, and waited, one in the prowl car, one outside. Eventually Bernard put his face in the window and said, "I suppose we'd only complicate it arguing with them. Maybe we'd better just go, before they get too nosey."

"Maybe so. You're already late, anyway."

"Can I call you tomorrow? After everybody's cleared out of the store? Five-thirty, say?"

"Please," she said, and put up her face to be kissed. He kissed her like a boy kissing his mother.

"Sweet," he said, and searched her eyes a moment and turned away. The police car backed around, but did not go. Sabrina stepped out into the sudden damp chill and got into the driver's seat and started the engine. Then Bernard came out after her, and after him the prowl car like a sheepdog. Bernard blinked his lights, she blinked hers in return, they turned opposite ways on the Skyline.

Every circumstance, she was thinking, cooperated to make the passion to which she had committed herself a pitiful parody. She hated the image of the two of them scuttling like interrupted high-school lovers from a lover's lane. Still, the parody was over, his wife was expecting him home. Stooping, she held her watch under the cowl light: eleven twenty-five. A little over an hour. The importer of woollens had not much out-talked his time.

She supposed he was feeling mean and humiliated, and yet he had no reason to blame himself. For it had been she who broke the bond and picked up the telephone, she who suggested meeting and named the place, and she who, when he might have said good night and parted from her, challenged him with having to go home to his wife. She did not know herself: ever since this thing began it had been as if she were being pushed from behind in a direction she recognized but would not acknowledge.

When she turned off the Skyline down toward Millbrae the red top-lights of the police car went on and were swallowed up in fog. Now where? Home? To bed? A good cosy re-thinking of everything? Oh, no. She could drive for a while. Or she could—and this was what instantly established itself as desirable—swing down to San Mateo and, whatever the hour, talk to Barbara.

CHAPTER 8

S HE COULD throw out her thoughts as she might have thrown out trash, but then there was nothing left. She felt dead, left-over, strengthless, purposeless, and a cigarette that she put between her lips so nauseated her that she threw it away unlighted.

In fog that was thick and coiling like cigar smoke she felt her way back along shrouded lanes and across the quickly met, quickly lost blaze of El Camino crawling with yellow fog-lights. With little difficulty she located the brick gateposts that had once marked the service entrance of an estate she knew, and that now opened on the tract called Greenwood Acres. Of Barbara's house, which she had been to only twice, she remembered that it was on a street named for some shrub, that it was on a corner lot, and that it was a flat-topped redwood. In her numb mind lay images of a short driveway, a carport, a walk of round cement pads, an overturned tricycle, an entrance under a flat overhang, a vine climbing a wall.

Turning in the gates, she brought her lights onto a white sign all but lost in the mist: Pyracantha. The street curved down toward the hazed aureole of a street lamp on the next corner. In the whole block there was not one lighted house—only saplings within their triangles of bracing poles, and angles of roofs, and box shapes of darkness melting into fog. Past her, as she drove slowly, flowed a curve of glistening curb and new wet lawns. She came to the corner—Ceanothus—and turned, hesitating, and crept on and peered hopefully at an entrance light but saw nothing surely familiar about that house, and nothing alive in it. The light was probably on to guide home some nocturnal teen-ager, while the parents got their careful sleep against the morning race for the 7:32. It seemed the wrong life for California, an inferior and imported life imposed on the place by immigrants ignorant of how life had been and might still be lived there. Bernard's life, essentially, even to the teen-ager. His oldest was sixteen. She pinched her frown down around her headache and crept on.

Dim shapes repeated one another, delusive lights appeared and were gone again, until little by little she realized that she hadn't the vaguest idea where she was. Ulysses buffeted around the whole Mediterranean could not have been more lost than she was now in what during her childhood had been a forty-acre horse pasture.

A street named for a shrub? They were all named for shrubs. From blurred street light to blurred street light the maze led her in circles and figure eights at whose re-entrant curves she found delusive names: Acacia, Laurel, Laburnum, Palo Verde. They were all fictitious—they were all the same street. The dark roofs were the roofs of the same six or eight houses, dismantled behind her and set up again ahead by some smooth stage machinery hidden in the fog. Very few were awake in this watery world. At a corner house, once, she saw the brightness of windows, and headed for them, but just as she rolled to a stop they went out. She crept on.

The windshield wipers squeaked back and forth in their hurrying semaphore. The fog lay over the whole Peninsula, over the whole of California, over the whole of America, over the whole twentieth century, like the sea over lost Atlantis, not blowing, not moving, but still, dense, settling. Her lights made momentary pearls of the fat drops hanging under leaves; a yellow sign that said "Children Playing" was streaked with forked channels of wet. The broken images upon which she had relied for recognition were worthless, for the driveway of each of these identical houses led to an invariable carport, and on every drive or sidewalk there seemed to be an overturned and forgotten tricycle. Each moment she felt "colder," like a child straying from its object in a blindfold game. There was not a gas station, not a drugstore, from which to call—zoned out, she supposed, to keep holy the bedroom suburb.

Another intersection, another hazed light, another sign. Like a person with a stiff neck who turns his whole body to look, she cramped the car to bring her lights on it. She was back on Pyracantha.

Angrily she backed and headed again into the labyrinth, ignoring street signs and hunting only for lighted houses. Barbara, she was sure, would wait up long past any reasonable time, and leave a light on even if she eventually gave up and went to bed. Finally, after three false leads, there was a corner house with a smoking cone of light under its overhang, and a long narrow lighted window screened with some sort of semi-transparent blind. When she probed her lights toward the carport they shone on the rear end of the old blue Chevrolet.

At last! She stepped out of the car, and almost before her feet were on the ground the house door opened, and Barbara's thickened figure, with the heavy shoulders of her husband behind her, bulked in the yellow rectangle, a silhouette of welcome. Sabrina heard her own heels softened and hasty on the wet walkstones, and her own voice, brittle, the kind of voice she despised and often mimicked, crying in the tone of gaiety and chatter, too loud in the respectable darkness, "My God, kiddies, where you *live!* I feel like Pavlov's dog."

Briefly, she felt warmed and welcomed and at home. They swept dolls and children's sweaters off the sofa and planted her there. They asked her what she would drink. Their voices and laughter were a reassurance. They pooh-poohed her hypocritical question whether it wasn't too late to stop. She had the sense that they made an occasion of her.

The house was jerry-built and messy, it smelled of dinner and children, everything was mingled with everything else—living room, dining room, kitchen—so that Leonard rattling ice trays at the sink half drowned out what Barbara was saying, and his bent head beyond the pass-through was still part of their threesome. The books that lay on the coffee table were *The Child from One to Six* and *Waiting for Godot*—how absolutely typical! Beside her on the sofa Barbara sat with her palms upturned in her lap like a female Buddha, and talked unhurriedly and looked upon the room without concern for its messiness, and upon Sabrina without anxiety but with sympathy and love. She was afloat like a ripe seed on the tranquil pool of her own serenity. Her manner said that there was no trouble of Sabrina's so heavy that it couldn't be floated there too.

Sabrina leaned back, cast up her eyes, stuck out her feet, and heaved a comic sigh. She almost convinced herself that she had been running a gantlet and was now safe. She reached for a cigarette, and as she did so she saw her movement reflected in the obsidian-black picture window across the room.

Instantly her mind went cautious, for her figure looked trapped and at bay in the reflected corner. The face staring back at her was haggard. The cigarette wobbled between the lips. The voice went on— too shrilly?

Then Leonard came around the partition with a tray, walking carefully in very shiny cleat-soled Bavarian shoes, his stout bowed legs filling the laundered Levis. The brilliant smile that Sabrina threw him visibly checked him, as if in his careful walking he had bumped a chair. He had a face like a Neapolitan black-marketer, and his hands, his eyes, his voice, were quick and knowing. When Barbara had met him ten years before he had been a GI student at the University of California, running around the campus on a motorcycle and dressed in Levis, a black leather jacket, and sometimes a metal-studded kidney belt. Now he hung over Sabrina humorous and attentive, weaned of the jacket and kidney belt, but still in the Levis—the least likely high-school English teacher in the entire world, probably.

Their eyes met, he seemed somehow to encourage her. Probably he had been coached to bring them all a drink, make a few remarks, and disappear. The knowledge that Barbara must have told him what she knew (I'm having an affair! How idiotically self-dramatizing could one get?) made her drop her eyes. What could her kind of trouble seem to a man like this one, this bouncer with chipmunk eyes and perceptions as quick as a gypsy fortune teller's? He would have had a blunt workman's past; the kinds of things that most troubled her would seem to him frivolous or insane.

Well, she hadn't come to talk to him, anyway. And what did it matter that Barbara would surely tell him everything as soon as they were alone? But somehow it did matter. When Barbara said, settling herself with a cushion behind the small of her back, "Now tell us about Mexico, and everything," and Leonard perched, about to take flight, on the corner of a chair, Sabrina found herself resisting them. They invited her to do something she did not want to do.

So she said only, "It was all right. Rain every afternoon by the clock, rum collinses in the zocalo, girls selling banana stalks full of flowers, people in pajamas, donkeys—lovely donkeys—American tourists who made you ashamed and who were probably ashamed of you." She looked at Leonard where he perched, and before he could make his planned move she made one of her own. "Tell me something."

His alert face waited. Still looking at Sabrina, he passed a glass to Bobbie across the coffee table.

"And don't get mad."

"Mad?" he said. "At a lady?"

"Do you wear that outfit even when you're teaching?"

The question obviously jolted them—not, Sabrina perceived, because it was impertinent, which it was, but because they had been braced for something else. Barbara giggled. Leonard peered at Sabrina, his lips moving as if he were choosing among a dozen quick answers. He said, sparring for time, "I take a Fifth."

Barbara said, "Just because *you've* never seen him in anything else. I'll have you know he's got a pair of slacks and a corduroy jacket, and sometimes he even wears a tie."

"Not willingly," Leonard said. His eyes were like a boxer's hands; he sat waiting for her to lead again.

"But unless the superintendent or the principal makes you dress up, it's Levis," she said. "What's that to prove?"

"Does it have to prove something?"

"You must think so."

"Say," Barbara said, "you leave my husband alone!"

"Not till he answers me. I've been wondering this for ten years. He even came to tea at Mother's in Levis once. He's living up to some role."

"A shrinker," Leonard said. "You got a theory?"

"You bet I have. And you'd better corroborate it."

Across his bulging shoulder she checked her face in the obsidian window: alive, interested, all right. When she looked back from that glance she saw that Leonard had taken the opportunity to shoot a look of his own at Barbara. "Fire, Doctor," he said.

"Your family were working people."

"Not willingly," he said again. "Only under pressure. My old man and my uncles were in the pokey half the time and drunk the other half. I got a brother in the pokey now—just heard yesterday. He busted a guy with a ketchup bottle in a drive-in."

"Don't brag. Maybe not working people, but proletarians, eh? The common man? The man in the street?"

Leonard fixed his mouth demurely. "Just at the edge of the street, where it humps up there. While the men-folks were sleeping it off in the gutter the women were joining curbstone religions. I got a couple of aunts—say!"

"But you liked your father. I've heard you talk about him."

"He wasn't a bad guy, just worthless. If he wanted to be good for nothing, I figure it was his God-given right."

"So he's the one the Levis are for, to show you're not giving up chewing tobacco and spitting on the floor just because you went to college. You want to demonstrate to Daddy that you haven't become a sissy."

Leonard considered. He shook his head. "It would never convince him," he said. "He'd see through it. He'd catch me reading Katherine Anne Porter and he'd *know*."

"Sure he would. Also he'd look at the Levis and say, 'What's the matter with this hood that greasy jeans aren't good enough for him? Why is he always so laundered? Is he a compulsive washer or something?' And he'd look at the shoes and say, 'No son of mine would put that much spit and polish on a pair of shoes in a lifetime, but this one shines his every day. This one is wearing Levis to kid me along, and washing and polishing like mad to please his own sissy nature and the religious aunts. This one has dangerous impulses toward respectability.'"

"It's marvelous how clear you make it," Leonard said, and rubbed his bristly poll.

"I'm glad you concur. Now tell me something else." She felt the drink, or else she was light-headed from sleeplessness and nerves. A little wildly, wanting to laugh, she thought, How does it go? My left is crumbling, my center is giving way, my right is in retreat, I shall attack? So she said, "Pardon the impertinence, but I already know all about you, so it won't matter. You'd never take any money from Bobbie's family, right?"

Leonard's eyebrows crawled upward; she was sure he would tell her to mind her own business. But he only made a hacking motion across the wrist of the hand that held his glass. "Cut off m'hand first," he mumbled, and slid his eyes sideward at Barbara with an incredulous smile.

"That also gratified the Independent Working Man in you. Besides, you had some money of your own, didn't you? Ten thousand dollars you won playing poker in the Navy?"

"I'm not talking without my lawyers." He scowled at Barbara. "There's a stool pigeon somewhere in the organization. Besides, your information's wrong. They were crap games, and the dice were honest."

"So with this suitably hard-boiled nest-egg you get married," Sabrina said. "And whom do you marry? The nicest, best-brought-up, most upper-middle-brow girl on the Peninsula. And how? Before a J.P. in Vallejo, outraging the whole family. You've been a real tough independent all the way—probably you stood up to the J.P. in Levis. After a while you buy a house, GI Bill, no down payment, and what do you buy? A house right smack in the middle of the mass-produced tracts where you have to find your own door by radar and can only tell your wife from your neighbor's by checking her driver's license."

For one cold instant she remembered the probing flashlight, the beam on the celluloid envelope on the steering column. She blinked. Leonard was watching her through slightly slitted lids, and she wondered if she had challenged him too harshly. But he really was like a boxer; he came up after a flurry from a shell of gloves and elbows.

"So which are you?" she said, and smiled to dissolve any roughness that might have crept in. "How do you justify being a nonconformist in Levis while you make dutiful monthly payments on a tract house and attend PTA meetings and belong to the Neighborhood Improvement Association?" She flipped the books on the coffee table. "Who are you waiting for, The Child from One to Six, or Godot?"

They had left Barbara behind. This was between the two of them, and somehow it had become important. Leonard took her glass and his own, looked toward Barbara's and saw it was half full, and went into the kitchen. From behind the counter he said, "That's an interesting question. Or is it a theory? Ambivalence probably explains it all." He came back and set her glass before her. "There was something else, wasn't there?"

"Yes," she said. "I was thinking while I ran this maze finding you. Interchangeable houses, interchangeable cities, compulsive traffic, we never know where we're going. We need an Ariadne and a good long piece of string. How can you and Bobbie, who aren't stereotypes at all, stand to live in a place where nobody is distinguishable from anybody else?"

"Sabrina!" Barbara said, and looked around dismayed. "My beautiful home! My adorable children! My devoted husband!"

"Reverse the laws of camouflage," Leonard said. "You know how I tell Bobbie from these other women? She don't play bridge. Know how she tells me? I wear Levis. The slightest deviation down here makes you a Character. A tract is the best of all possible places for individualism to flourish."

"When he's really a character is when he deviates from the Levis," Barbara said. "You ought to see him."

Sabrina squinted, groping. He had taken the initiative away from her, and she felt the brief energy and interest draining away. "Tell me," she said. "I'm serious, I really am. Is there enough of a life in just having children and paying off the mortgage and creating a secure little American Home? I don't want to sound sneery. I just wonder." She laid her head back on the sofa and rolled it from side to side, laughing, looking at the ceiling. She knew they were watching her closely. "I feel . . . I don't know . . . like some character out of the twenties going from party to party crying, 'What's it all for?' It's all like a big banquet during a plague. Is working for security enough?

97

Do you think security is that valuable? If you do, you're deluded I was born with barrels of it, and I know."

"Security we haven't found confining," Leonard said. "My salary is forty-eight hundred a year."

Their eyes met and held. "So little as that?" she said. "Why do you teach, then?"

"Dangerous impulses toward respectability," he said with a faun-like smile. "Your theory. A man has his little vanities. Nobody in my family ever read anything but comic books and the Bible. Naturally I can't help showing off."

She thought she had never seen anyone more intensely alive. If she had been feeling better she would have enjoyed arguing with him indefinitely. Barbara obviously adored this nimble eccentric, and she was right. With the perception of how solid Barbara's contentment was, something sad and old washed through Sabrina and she said, "I probably don't know a single pair except you whose income is that small, and I don't think I know anybody but you two who is satisfied with his life. The more freeways we build and the thicker the foam-rubber cushions get, the less we're satisfied."

At once he adjusted to her tone, hung his elbows on his knees and squinted at the toe of one Bavarian shoe, his forehead furrowed like a caricature of an ape trying to think. His bright eye cocked upward. "Satisfied?" he said. "That's a word. But when your whole world never used its mind except to outsmart the other guy and cheat on the old lady, you can tell conditions have improved when you run into some people and some books that really do mean good will to men. None of my family ever had the dimmest notion what they were heir to. History, books, pictures, music, hell, all dat was nuttin to dem. So even if I'm not satisfied, I'm not kicking. By the grace of God I've got everything to learn; there's no place to go but up."

"And it all comes out as love in the suburbs," Sabrina said.

"I'm telling you, a house is just a box. You can put anything you want into it—Christmas-tree angels, old beer bottles, busted plumbing fixtures, fertilizer, anything."

"You really think you can be yourself in Greenwood Acres."

"Just about as easy here as anywhere. Easier than some places."

"Your whole, real self."

"Never met him," Leonard said. When he drained the ice from his glass and screwed the rim to his eye she saw his eye hugely distended glaring at her through the lenslike bottom. "Look," he said, and took it down. "One trouble with my old man, he never had a job he could respect, so he never respected himself. He thought he was being wasted. He was, too. Most of us are. So all I want to do for my two-bit salary is maybe help some kid who's proving he's a real individual by the haircut he wears and the amount of rubber he can leave on the pavement when he peels off. Maybe, because I been there, I can keep some of these punks like my brother Doug from turning into corner boys, pushing tea or pimping. I pry open the lid of this kind of boy and I plant an idea, maybe, like putting a clamshell pill behind the pancreas of an oyster. Maybe nineteen times out of twenty nothing happens. But once in a while one of these kids will go to his doctor and say, 'Doctor, I got a hell of a pain, I think I got gallstones,' and it's a pearl."

"Leonard," Barbara said, afloat on her serenity, "you seem to me to talk *incessantly*. Why don't you vanish now so us girls can whisper and giggle?"

"No," Sabrina said, "don't send him away. He's my guru. I want to hear more about how not to go to waste."

"We haven't had a chance to get a thing out of you about *you*."

"No," Sabrina said, and felt her cheeks tighten. She saw Barbara begin the spinning of a theory, not too far from the facts, probably, to replace the mystery she had been left with that afternoon. But that was all dismal. She was dirtied by it, and by her contradictory self.

"I envy you, you know," she said. "I envy you both. You were lucky enough to be born poor, and Bobbie was lucky enough to be born fertile. You can be producers. The rest of us can only be consumers."

"Is that bad?" Leonard asked, as if he wanted to know.

"It's what everybody wants till he gets it."

"Is it so dreadful to have money?" he said. "Sometimes I think about it and a gleam comes into my eye."

"Bobbie, haven't you told him?"

"I was never rich," Barbara said. "I was only a nice girl who was considered suitable for rich girls to play with."

Leonard reached for Sabrina's empty glass, but she held on, talking up into his face. "Talk about your family! Put your mind to the contemplation of mine. They didn't get drunk and disorderly, but listen to the life history of one of them and you want to weep. I listened to my grandmother's this afternoon. They all went to waste, every one of them. I can't conceive any worse fate than to be born a rich woman in nineteenth-century Boston, unless it's to be born a rich woman in twentieth-century Hillsborough."

"Oh hey," they said. "Hey now."

"The difference between the rich and poor is that the poor still believe in heaven," she said, and let his hand take the glass from hers. "If you were born in heaven, and know it's a fraud, there's no place to go but hell. I'd give anything to have been born poor, so I could have tried to become something."

"Are you sure you haven't?" Leonard said.

"You know you have," said Barbara.

Now they were purveying the comfort they had been prepared to have on tap.

"I lack that clandestine impulse to respectability," Sabrina said. Wound up, hectic, an outsider hammering at their doors, she looked from one to the other, and they smiled fixedly back, shifting their feet cautiously as if not to disturb her. "Tell me the truth," she said. "Are children enough? Do they take you out of your bloody useless self?"

"Look who's been upholding the self against the subdivisions," Leonard said.

He went softly into the kitchen to renew her glass, and for an instant she was dressing a faceless but beautiful child for a party, and ragged nerves, crumbling certainties, hysterical discussions, ridiculous posturings were all washed over in a sentimental glow, and she was no longer a distracted Katherine Mansfield heroine crying, "Oh, what's it all about? What's it all *for?*" Accepting the glass, she thought, Maybe your self is only there for the making of other selves; maybe you're not meant to find meaning in your life, but only to divide its burden, pass it on.

Which was no help to her. Harshly she said to these two, "What are you going to do when your children start rebelling against Greenwood Acres and you? Will they still be enough when they've repudiated you and gone some way you don't approve of?"

"They won't rebel against love," Barbara said.

"I know some who have."

"Against too much love, or the wrong kind."

"Ah?"

"We won't give them that kind."

"Or too much," Leonard said. "All sins are sins of excess."

They smiled at her fixedly, only half joking. "My God," she said, "you're sublime."

His mobile face wheedled and beguiled her. He smiled like a kid who has just pinned a "Kick me" sign on his friend. "Can I say a word for good old Greenwood Acres, teacher? Sure some of the neighbors wish I'd wash our car; I leave it dirty for that reason. Sure we don't waste as much time in people's patios as we might—we ain't *friendly*. Sure I wear these jeans, I'm an oddball. But I remember somebody else, not from Greenwood Acres, that was giving me the needle about those a few minutes ago. What you have to remember is that Greenwood Acres lets us live. Nobody burns crosses on our lawn. People speak. Some of them even like Bobbie better because of what she married. 'Oh, his poor wife!' Eh?"

"Eh? What do you want me to say, amen?"

"Save it for the benediction. We got a PTA, sure, why not? There are a hundred kids to the block. When a school-bond issue comes up, who rings doorbells to make sure the stupids don't vote it down? Greenwood Acres. Sure we had a flurry about a colored family moving in. What happened? It turned out there were more of us for him than against him, and he's still here. That isn't usual, maybe, but it's possible. Is it possible in Hillsborough?"

"You're making me want to move right in."

"Yah," he said, a little surlily. "Tell you another fight we're in. Almost anywhere else in the world a lot of open country got preserved by nabobs and bigwigs—you know, some place for the peacocks to get their exercise in. Hell, you live in one, you know. But in tracts they don't specialize in parks or peacocks. Progress is all on the side of the bulldozers, so somebody has to snatch a few of the amenities of living out of the way before they all get flattened out. Who does? Greenwood Acres, as much as anybody, maybe because we're already living in the overcrowded future and we know how it feels. I know a dozen families that work their heads off for parks and greenbelts—small-c citizens, the poor old overworked conformists of Greenwood Acres. Even my gentle wife writes letters to the press and hectors planning commissions."

Sipping her drink with her eyes on his sharp face, she said, "You're making a case for middle-class civilization."

"You're damned right," Leonard said, "so long as it tries to be civilization."

Derisively she said, "Will you let the poor rich folks in, too, so they can have these satisfactions? Have you asked my mother to donate some land for a park?"

Barbara plumped the pillow behind her. "Heavens, no. From the estate?"

"No, the Woodside land."

"Gee, I never thought of it. Do you suppose she would? My word, it's perfect for a county park. *Would* she give a few acres?"

"Why don't you ask her?" Sabrina said, holding Leonard's eye. "Let us get that satisfied glow, too."

His lips bent, flattened, discarded two or three answers. Something stubborn and contentious showed in his face. She almost thought he flushed. "I'm not kidding," he said. "When's a good time for the Greenbelt Committee to call?"

"Why don't I find out?"

"Will you?"

"Of course. I'd love to, if only for the sight of Oliver's face." In the mirroring window she saw her image pressing its fingertips against its temples; as soon as it saw her watching it dropped its hands. "Well, so I'm enlisted in a Cause. Hooray. Do you need money?"

"Did you ever know a committee that didn't?"

"I'll send you a check. Make it out to you?"

"Sure you want to get involved in this spirit-killing little old suburb?"

"I'd be glad enough to get wound up in anything." The torpor that lay just back of her forced animation blurred her mind like a streak of fog. She had to grope for what she had intended to say. "Give me the formula," she said finally. "What else can you suggest for the girl who has everything—too much of everything, a bellyful of everything?" Her eyes, sneaking toward the window, came back to find both Leonard and Barbara looking rueful and uneasy. "Everything," she said, and straightened her slumped back with a chop of a laugh, "except love, children, usefulness, and what else?"

Stretching the laugh, she made herself busy with a cigarette. They were really watching her now—did they expect her to fly apart? A look of warning passed between them. Abruptly rising into her own smoke, she said, "I've got to go. I've kept you up all night as it is."

They protested, but she ignored their protests. She saw that they were dismayed by her sudden move; they felt that they had somehow failed her. Oddly, she was content that they should feel so. She laughed a good deal, pulling her sweater over her shoulders. "Good night, good night, good night. I love you both, even if you *are* so self-satisfied."

Her face felt the cool wet fog. Leonard grabbed her elbow as her ankle turned on the edge of one of the walkstones. "Good night," she cried again. "Bobbie, bring the girls over to swim tomorrow. How's three o'clock? Don't bother calling, just come." She waved. From their safe doorway, standing together, they watched her go.

Now again dark roads, late cars, lanes overtaken and violated in their after-midnight quiet, and the MacDonalds abruptly blotted out by the returned memory of Bernard and the Skyline. Was this how the situation began that she had seen other women get into? If Bernard took an apartment, would she live in it, or meet him there? She miserably did not know.

How many times, unwilling, dead for sleep, had she driven, this late or later, these lanes and this gateway, to find her mother waiting up, the hall lights on bright to detect whatever stigmata of dissipation clung to her. And right now she had no house key; she would have to ring and waken Lizardo.

The entrance light was on. She parked before the garage doors, found the doors locked, and left the car where it stood. Coming back to the house she walked on the wet lawn rather than on the gravel, and she tried the door stealthily in the hope that Lizardo might have left it open for her. Locked. But instantly, almost with the same depression of the latch which her thumb made, the door clicked open and Lizardo stood there. He must have been waiting on the hall bench.

She gave him not even the parody of a smile, saying only, "Couldn't you have left it unlocked?"

She stopped. Out of the web of wrinkles his black eyes looked at her soberly. He backed up, swinging the door wide, and scowled some meaning or warning. His lips pursed in a whisper she did not catch. "What is it?" she said sharply, and started past him.

From the foot of the stairs she heard the steps and saw the shadow that came to the library door down the left-hand hall. Mother? Not that, not as if she were fourteen years old! She squinted angrily, trying to see. The shadow spoke. "Sabrina?"

"Burke," she said.

The leap that her heart had given when he spoke began to shudder down into a hard slugging pound. She laid a hand, suddenly gentle, on Lizardo's white arm. "Go to bed," she said, and went on down the hall.

CHAPTER 9

B URKE did not offer to kiss her, and the impulse or habit of affection in herself was no more than a moment's hesitation, a flick of the eyes and a readiness in the muscles. Then she had gone past him without any greeting beyond her first startled naming of his name, and seated herself in the padded desk chair. She drew a deep, cautious breath to quiet her pulse, and wished instantly she had not, it sounded so much like a sigh. In her ear the electric clock made its dry whirring. Its hands pointed to twenty past one.

Her mind, leaping twenty guilty miles, imagined Bernard lying beside his wife, and she wondered if mistrust had yet begun to divide them, if suspicion had popped on its little red light in the woman's mind. Looking at Burke, she thought, My husband—my ex-husband, but torpor and fatigue prevented her from feeling anything more acute than a sort of apprehensive breathlessness. She said, "When did you get in? If I'd known you were coming I'd have been home."

"I came up on the ten-o'clock flight."

His voice was as dry as the whirring of the clock. His face, not tanned enough, gone sallow in offices and examination rooms, wore a look of almost prissy reserve; his eyes were very watchful. Beyond the clock's noise it was unhealthily quiet. She had a perception of how in all the dark house everything slept—her mother, Helen Kretchmer, the servants, the ghosts, the family hoards—while in this deep room, Rembrandt-lighted, went on something lurid, by every inherited prejudice disreputable and unclean. She said, "You've had a long wait. I'm sorry."

His watchful eyes seemed to estimate the depth and reach of her apology. He had always walked with an exaggerated stiffness of the spine, almost leaning backward, even on a golf course, and he stood now as if relaxation would have been immoral. As much a puritan as herself—a Spanish-Californian puritan with a little Inquisition relentlessness left over in him. She knew his contempt for weakness; she feared him as she feared her conscience. But all he said, and that in the voice of commonplace, was, "Not long. It was after midnight before the cab got me here."

As the silence between them lengthened, spun out by the whirring clock, what had been shame and embarrassment began to swell in Sabrina into angry bitterness. Was he simply going to stand and stare at her all night? Take up exactly where they had left off the night before, when someone's stomach ache called him away? Why didn't he ask where she had been? He was obviously wondering. Or force the talk to where it had to go, to the question of their future? Or curse her, beat her to death with the fireplace poker. Anything.

Harshly she burst out, "Why didn't you call again? I waited all evening."

He was not so composed as he pretended; she saw something happen around his eyes, some expression subtly change there. But as so often when he was outraged or angry, his feelings showed principally as an excessive, impenetrable politeness. She saw him put it on, and she heard in his words the iron of an unyielding self-justification. "Why," he said, "I was waiting for you to call *me*."

Anger, a sheet of it like white lightning, dazzled her view of him where he stood stiffly above her, judging her. "Ah!" she said. "It must be wonderful to feel so blameless!"

He stared at her hard-mouthed, and she saw in his eyes the flare of cold anger like the reflection of her own. But he only said quietly, "Do you always have to lash out at somebody else when you're in the wrong? Why wouldn't I feel blameless?"

Turning her head away, playing with the silver desk set, her cheeks stiff with the will to hurt him, she said, "Don't you generally?"

"I do in this."

"Well, I don't," she said. "Is that what you wanted to make me say?"

He moved then—she heard him cross the room and take a book from the bookcase with a slur of sound, and a second later slide it back again. Then he returned and stood across the desk from her until she shoved the pen stand furiously aside and flung up her head and cried, "Oh, take your eyes off me! I won't stand being looked at that way!"

But he would not let himself be pushed toward anger again. He had the advantage of her, he had been able to prepare an attitude for this interview. She had only her emotional disarray to cover her. Every word of their talk would emphasize his control and her lack of it, his probity and her disreputable collapse. Blameless? Of course he was, by any standard anyone would understand. Of course he had every right to look at her in fury and disgust: she granted it even while she resented it.

And listen to his voice, dispassionate as if he were interpreting an X-ray. Could he have any idea how much he had become a doctor even outside the office? "We won't get anywhere if we start out like this," she heard him say. "And we have to talk. Don't we?"

She bent her head to let her spread hand cup and support her forehead. "I suppose."

"Are we splitting up? Is that what this comes to? What do you intend to do?"

One flitting look—there he stood, judicial, courteous. "Is it up to me?" she said.

"Isn't it?"

"If it is," she made herself say, "you're being magnanimous, as usual." And cold! she wanted to cry. Icy, as usual! How can we talk about this as if we were deciding whether or not to hire a gardener? We ought to be in tears—I am in tears, I'm drowning in tears inside. And there you stand. If you were the man I married, if you were my husband, if you were anything but a graven image, you'd slap me. "Haven't you anything to say about it?" she asked. "As the . . . wronged party?"

He was like tennis players she had known, the kind who returned everything until they forced you into errors. Stonily he said, "I might have something to say, yes. I might have to wash my hands of you. Or I might even ask you to come back."

"Why?" she said, in a voice that sounded as hoarse in her own ears as a crow's cawing. "*Why?* So you could always hold it over me? So you could enjoy the penance you'd put me through?"

But he dominated her with his eyes and his stiff, polite face—the face of a man being courteous under provocation—and he said, "If you've got anything to say I m bound to listen. You said last night you wanted this affair to be over. Is it?"

Her moment's spiteful resistance already spent, she put her hands fingertip to fingertip on the desk blotter and studied the light shaking in them. She was all to pieces, all to pieces. "I don't know," she said.

"Where were you tonight?"

She saw the opportunity and its impossibility at the same time. The first disaster, the one which had shaken her down, she had brought herself to tell truthfully; tonight's gave her no alternative but a lie. Without looking up she said, "Over at Bobbie's. Before that I was driving around."

"Alone?"

"Alone. Does it matter?"

"It matters a great deal."

"You don't have to cross-examine me," she said stiffly. "I told you, without your ever asking, about Oaxaca. It all happened."

"You didn't come up here to see him?"

"No."

The pulse beat like a little life between the taut cords of her wrist. It beat five times before he said, "Are you in love with him?"

The life in her wrist went three ticks toward its death. "I don't know," she said, very low. She was aware of his height above her, straight and severe; she knew the way his teeth would show under the tight lips. He would not run from unpleasantness, and he would not lie, as Bernard would and as she herself just had. And yet his gray eyes were chilly where Bernard's were brown and alive, and his voice had long ago forgotten warmth. There was a sadistic streak in him. She had an almost irresistible impulse to glance up sharply, sure she would catch some expression like enjoyment in his face.

"If you're not in love with him," Burke said steadily, "then what is all this about?"

She shivered her shoulders.

"Is it that you're just sick of me?"

"No!" she said. "Oh no! Not . . . anything like that."

"Have I done something?"

She shook her head. No, nothing you have done. Only something you have been, or become, or not done. Something *I've* become.

"Then what?" She could not answer. She heard the breath whistle between his teeth. "There must be some reason why you disgrace yourself and shame me. You can't pretend it's like you. Or I hope it isn't. Maybe I've been deceiving myself."

Without strength left to combat him or even resent him she sat inspecting a chipped nail and let the lash fall on her, accepting its justice. She had admired and respected and slightly feared him for a long time. Huddled and submissive, she was thinking irrelevantly to herself, To-night was the night I lost my father, too. With a hopeless movement of the shoulders, she said, "I don't know, I've just come all apart."

"People don't come apart without some cause."

"Oh, you're so . . ." Her eyes were up. He had not moved, his expression had not changed. "Cause!" she said. "The same old cause, I suppose. There hasn't been any room for me in your life for years. What if I was tired of going to waste?"

For once she had stung him, she had stung him like a wasp. He bent from his stiffness, his knuckles came down on the desk, he glared at her with his face full of outrage. "No room in my life? Going to waste? You're out of your mind. What do you mean, no room in my life? That I'm busy?"

"That's part of it."

"Then it's hopeless," Burke said, and planted his knuckles with a hard wooden sound, once, on the desk. "I'm a doctor, I'm bound to be a doctor, I've got an obligation to my patients, and the profession, and myself. Would you respect me if I shirked it? I wouldn't respect myself. We've been over this fifty times."

"Yes," she said. "Many times. And you're absolutely right."

"But you still hold it against me."

"Not that," she said. "Just . . . Oh, I don't know! You've quit being yourself, you're *only* a doctor! You're thinking about the clinic or some patient all the time. You keep yourself wearing that bedside manner, you've always got on your crisis mouth. Even when I drag you out to something, you don't enjoy it. I don't think you enjoy anything any more but work. You don't enjoy *me,* I'm sure. You never let yourself have a strong emotion or even an affectionate impulse. . . . If I hadn't had to go all bottled up for ten years I might not have come apart. You *freeze* everything. . . ."

Their eyes were hard now, locked like wrestlers. She had said more to him than she had ever managed to say; and it struck her as a hopeless corroboration of her own tirade that his face showed no sign of comprehension, but only stubbornness and resentment.

"I've paid you the compliment of thinking you didn't need to be patted like a lapdog," he said. "I thought we had a relationship that let us function as individuals. You're not a woman without resources, Sabrina. You haven't had to sit around pitching cards in a hat. Even if I've been as occupied as you seem to think, you've still had a beautiful house, money, position, looks, youth, health, interests, friends, everything you needed to make a—"

"Life of my own?" she said. "Oh, *God,* Burke! The same old life I was brought up to, only without Saint Matthew's Church. Bridge luncheons and cocktail parties and charity balls and lying around pools."

"A lot of your friends seem to find things to absorb them."

"Sure. Pottery kilns in the back yard. Studios for the writing they hope to get around to. Anti-Income Tax agitations. Planned Parenthood. Neighborhood racial councils. Junior League theatricals."

"You've been marvelous in every one of those you've acted in. As you know."

"Yes," she said. "I could probably make quite nice pots, too, and write poems that the *Los Angeles Examiner* would print."

"Well?" he said, impenetrable.

She made a weary gesture. "The Intelligent Woman's Guide to Time-Killing," she said. "I could write it without notes."

"A lot of people would call it a satisfying life."

"With a lot of people I have never agreed," Sabrina said. "A lot of people probably envy Mother's combination of ancestor worship and charity and self-indulgence, too. But if you recall, I never wanted it."

"You're saying I've only substituted one kind of jail for another."

Propping her forehead with her hand, she stared at the desk's inlaid intricate edge.

"If you've been going to waste," Burke said—a voice as unmodulated, as disengaged from personality and feeling, as the crackling of a paper bag—"if you've been going to waste, you chose an odd way to become useful."

Eyes up, eyes down: his were coldly burning at her. She was too tired to quarrel or defend, she was too sick and sad. But however he or her conscience might shame her, neither could shame away the thing that lay coiled as real as a worm at the heart of her discontent. She did not even brush Burke's words away, she ignored them. "You remember Bobbie," she said. "She married this Leonard MacDonald, strictly from nowhere, and typed theses to help him through graduate school. Now he's teaching, and they're still as poor as mice. She's got a crackerbox house and one good dress and two children and another coming, and how fast I'd trade her!"

The clock whirred out another raveled length of Time. At last Burke said—and she heard the impatience as a sharper, challenging note in his voice—"It won't do you any good to manufacture artificial responsibilities. You wouldn't seriously want to teach, would you?"

The thought made her laugh. "It sounds grubby, doesn't it? Maybe the last resort of the blind is to lead, though."

"Or adopt a child?"

She sat still. Careful, careful. She had always backed away from that decision; maybe she would always back away from what she most wanted or needed. Or maybe she still had hope. "You get such lemons sometimes," she said. "It wouldn't be like your own. I still don't think I'd ever feel right about having one without the pain."

They had run down; anger and recrimination had petered out together, expedients had proved too heavy to lift. She watched Burke examine the palm of one hand as if for blisters. He glanced up, squinting; his lips tightened and loosened again; he looked like a man weighing a bargain in his head, balancing advantage against disadvantage. His shoulders moved. "Well," he said, "I seem to have failed you somehow, or you seem to think so. I don't understand how. It doesn't seem to me I could have done much differently. I can't be someone I'm not."

He sounded not self-righteous but hopeless, he spoke obviously less in accusation than in bewilderment. The stiff watchfulness and politeness of his face had dissolved into something twisted and pained. Wildly her eyes clung to his gray glance, and she saw the spasm contract at the outer corners of his eyes. For a moment he glared out like a man from behind bars, and instantly she was flooded with a contrition so terrible that she wanted to claw her face and scream.

"Burke, I . . ."

"Sabrina . . ."

"I'm the one!" she burst out. "Oh, I *hate* myself for what I've done to you!"

He watched her with eyes that glittered; his severe outline melted and ran with the massing of her own tears. "Please!" she said. "Can you believe that I wouldn't deliberately . . ."

Abruptly he moved, he came around the desk behind her and laid a hand on her shoulder. With a feeling close to horror, intensely recalling having done the same thing with another hand only a few hours before, she bent her head sideward until her cheek touched his knuckles. He said thickly, "They gave you a difficult temperament, Sabrina."

To that she agreed with a choked laugh. The horror remained, but like a wind that blew past a corner and did not touch her. Sometime she would have to come out into it, but not yet, not now. Her face turned further until her lips touched his hand. What was the matter with her that she could not make a life out of what was the envy of every outsider? One prison for another? Most women would not think so. Both what she was born to and what she had married into were scale models of paradise, where the fortunate could enjoy lives of luxury and gratified desire. And all she found was chatter, hollowness, horror. She felt like crying at him, If just once a day you'd remembered to lay your hand on me the way you're doing now!

He stood stiff and still, only his fingers moved lightly on her collarbone. The silver base of the desk pen swam and spun in her tired eyes; blurring in her unfallen tears her face looked back at her, distant in the rounded metal, with his face even more distant beyond and above.

In a moment her whole head was full of another picture: he did have his arms around her, she hung breathless and laughing where he had caught her in the upstairs hall, directly in front of the pier glass. In the glass she watched his face come close beside hers, over her shoulder, and his arms come around her from behind. Their eyes hunted mirrored eyes, it was a moment all the more intimate for its doubling, for their being able to watch themselves watch it: their bodies and legs overlapped like figures in a Greek frieze. "Answer me," he said, and she said, "Yes." "Why are all other girls thick-ankled?" But she only laughed, and he said, "What kind of magic do you use in your smile? Do you have any idea what your face with that smile chasing across it can do to me?" "I hope so," she said, watching his mirror eyes, holding his arms tighter around her breast. "I hope so. I practice it in front of mirrors." Locked together, watching themselves in the pier glass in the gray light of a winter afternoon, they laughed, and liked the look of their own laughter. "Not what I mean, you don't," Burke said. "What I mean, you were born with. You're one of those who were made to enhance life."

Twelve years. Twelve years of enhancement since then. "Sabrina," her husband said, and she could see him, small and distant, in the rounded silver.

"Yes."

"How bad is it? If I could forget all this, could you?"

"Ah, Burke!" She stood up, twisting, ready to cry, ready to have his arms come around her, but he had dropped his hand and moved back—still in part an antagonist. Her lips pulled up against the resistance of all the muscles of grief that wanted to pull them down. "Give me a little time?" she said. "He isn't the real trouble. I am. I don't understand myself. I go around beating my breast searching for a function, but I never really want any of the functions that are possible. I foundered and went down halfway between duty and desire. Can I try to straighten myself out? Would you give me some time?"

And at once she met the iron in him; he had not modified by a single detail his original insistence on fair, hard justice. "Is it over?" he said.

"I want it to be."

"You want it to be."

"Yes."

Almost as if she embarrassed him, he studied her face. "All right, time. How much?"

"I can't tell. What it takes."

"You baffle me," he said, and turned away and stood looking into the pooled light of Monet's lilies. The desk lamp threw his shadow folding up the corner of the room and onto the ceiling. When he turned around again he had given up trying to keep the polite impenetrability he had worn most of the evening. He looked middle-aged and tired, with bags under his eyes, and his right hand jingled small change in his jacket pocket. "I was thinking coming up," he said. "If you . . . This makes me want to commit murder, Sabrina. It may be just as well you take some time; I may need some, too. But I want us to get past it, if we can. And if we do, I was thinking . . . why don't you start in with the Pasadena Playhouse, go into acting seriously. You're such an absolute natural. Or organize a group yourself, you could."

Something in her face must have told him not to go on. She could not help saying, "Have a life of my own? Run out and play?"

He flushed dark red, so that at once she tried to turn the edge of her remark, crying lightly and hopelessly, "Maybe I could become a middle-aged character actress and win supporting Oscars. Mother would be so proud." Her eyes smarted; she took his hand and pressed it between both of hers, saying, "Burke, darling, maybe we *can* get past it. But don't be kind, or I'll weep."

The red still hung in his cheeks; his expression had again hardened and become formidable, and in spite of her words, she wanted him kind. Stubbornly gnawing at something already gone past, he said, "What do you mean you don't know whether this other business is over or not? It's not exactly the sort of thing you'd be vague about, is it?"

A retort flew to her lips and was blocked there. She faced him across the consequences of her lie: driving, and alone. The thought of how recently she had been locked in unlovely fornication up on the foggy ridge made her physically ill; she would never be able to pass the place again without a shiver. It seemed to her that Bernard, whatever he had been—ecstasy, anger, a dare, a substitute—was already past, and what he had been was so tainted in her mind that she wondered she could meet Burke's eyes at all. And she was dismally tired.

"It's late," she said, "and I've hardly slept for days. Can't we talk tomorrow? How long can you stay?"

"I shouldn't stay at all. I've got two patients going into surgery tomorrow morning—*this* morning."

"But you *could* stay."

"Yes, I could."

"Please. I'd like you to."

"All right." He stood with both hands in his jacket pockets; his shoulders lifted with a conclusive deep breath. There was an uneasy hangdog smile around his mouth. "Is there some guest room made up where I can sleep?"

Steadily she took his arm and turned him toward the door. "Could you bear to sleep in my room?"

"Bear to? Yes."

"It might look funny if you didn't."

They went upstairs under the somber lowering of Emily Wolcott, past the egg-white organdy of Deborah Barber, straight into and past the sullen stare of Sabrina Hutchens. Her door clicked behind them and shut out the sleeping house.

"The far bed is yours," Sabrina said. "I'm going to have a shower to relax me." Just for an instant, as their eyes met, Burke smiled—his old smile, questioning, even diffident, the mask of imperturbability and purpose wiped away: a smile of real sweetness, with both a question and a promise in it.

She had a tumid, oppressive feeling in her lungs, a difficulty of breathing, a sense of something dramatic and dangerous about to happen. Carrying fresh pajamas and robe, she went into the bathroom. Under the shower she hardly moved; she felt like a primitive woman in a purification ritual, as if the scent or stain of uncleanness were to be washed away and she restored to touchability. And it was as if a pair of eyes inside her mind looked steadfastly straight forward so as not to see what was in their periphery.

Tiredly refreshed, she dried herself and got into the plain blue pajamas—she had always despised nightgowns—and pulled the cord of the robe around her. Leaving the dressing room she hesitated, almost knocked, before she pushed through.

The bedroom lights were off except for a small lamp on the bedtable. Burke sat on the edge of the bed in his shorts. As she came in he stood up, and then once more there was a dueling and searching of eyes in semi-darkness. She heard him say something short and strange.

They met on a white goatskin rug between the beds. Saying nothing, looking into her eyes with a strained, harsh glare, Burke raised his hands and loosened her robe and pushed it off her shoulders to the floor. He unbuttoned her pajama tops and pushed them after the robe. Then abruptly he was on his knees with his face buried in her belly. With her arms around his head she hugged him, and heard the grinding of his teeth. She tipped her head and stared up at the ceiling, crying silently, Oh my God, what am I, what am I!

"No!" she said aloud. "No, oh no, no!" Violently she twisted away from him, tangled her feet in the goatskin, half fell against the bed. He was still on his knees, clinging to her legs. "No!" she said again, hoarse and gasping. "Burke, I wasn't just driving around. I'm not fit to . . . Oh, God, Burke, please, I was with him. *I was with him!*"

He let her go; on his cheekbone the bedlamp lit the shine of tears. She scrambled up to sit on the bed, and watched him assemble himself bit by bit, breath and emotion, body and mind and pride, and stand up. Their glances crossed once, grating like the ends of a broken bone, and after that she could not look at him again. She heard him dressing, heard his feet moving around the room, but she continued to sit huddled together on the bed with her hands pressed between her knees, and long shudders every few seconds ran the length of her body.

Still without a word, he had started for the door; and still she could not look at him. Through chattering teeth she said, "Take my car, the keys are on the dresser," and he said, "Shall I leave it at the airport parking lot?" and she said, "Yes, Virgil can get it tomorrow."

The long shiver came up her legs and through her body and contracted her shoulders. She waited for what else he would say.

But he said nothing at all. Just for a moment she summoned the courage to look up. With his hand on the doorknob he was devouring her with a look pale and terrible. Then without a word he went out.

CHAPTER 10

STRANDED by receding sleep, the mind flopped on the margins of consciousness. Unwilling, it turned and turned, tried to dive, floundered against the immovable, threshed in panic, and woke.

She lay staring upward, just as she had been doing when she last remembered. Her mouth was dry, her eyeballs ached, she felt how she had awakened frowning, pinching her brows down upon light or trouble or both. For a second the rasping of the breath in her throat sounded fantastically loud, until she recognized the sound as not her breathing at all, but the regular *scratch-scratch* of a rake on the gravel paths outside. Through the blinds, a golden gloom; under them, a leakage of gray.

Her hands at her temples felt dried salt. Between the beds the robe, the pajamas, the twisted goatskin, lay where they had been kicked. As the memory came back she had to clamp eyes and teeth shut upon the picture of him rising from his knees as if his whole body were tied together with bandages. That repudiation would burn on his pride like napalm; and though he might find relief by plunging into work as a bomb victim burning alive might plunge into water, he would be afire again as soon as he came out. And herself, who had done it, done all of it? Not much better. It seemed a pitiful thing that a person should cry in her sleep and awake with a knitted frown.

Her eyes opened again and she stared dully at the light below the windows. Words revolved in her head, a sentence stupidly intact from some book, repeating itself as if it meant something. *When I awoke, it was broad day.* Now where? It seemed important to place it. But she had not the pleasure of an extended search, for almost at once she recognized it. *Robinson Crusoe,* the morning after shipwreck.

Years ago, she used to spend hours in this room reading, sprawled across the bed with her chin over the edge, the book on the floor, her heels in the air, assuming postures that her mother said were neither ladylike nor good for the eyes. The gray light now was the same, the words brought back something that once her imagination had leaped to take in: hope, activity, self-reliance, the magical island to be explored, the ship to be plundered of everything needed for the re-establishment of a life.

She worked her dry lips. Her eyes, slanting again over the bed's edge, caught upon the tangled rug and the clothes that love had cast there. How *could* she re-establish a life, after what had passed? On what basis of trust or confidence, and with whom? Burke, stabbed and stabbed again where he was most vulnerable? Bernard, netted in a web of conventional responsibilities? She had even less hold upon the illicit warm one than upon the one who held himself stiff and austere.

The scratching rake went on, diligent and absorbed. How beautiful to get up every morning and make neat comb-marks in a path, or milk goats in a corral, or coddle the shoots from a rescued handful of grain. Or walk into office or clinic with the mind fixed on lovely simple problems: an overdue shipment, a child's broken bone, the lump in a frightened woman's breast. It was unfair that they should both have the solace of work, and she should not. She coveted the peace of women who stitched the seams of shirts. How cunning of people to enslave themselves, as the phrase went, to a job. Then the days would go down sweetly, one by one, each with its teaspoonful of responsibility, accomplishment, and reward.

As for Mrs. Burke Castro, she could cry in her sleep, awake frowning, borrow whisky from the servants. Unless—and she looked the possibility in the eye for a moment, recognizing it as the broad day to which she had awakened—she could do what shame and conscience told her she should do, give up what she could probably not have anyway, and learn the cool consolations of obedience as the society doctor's society wife.

She rang for the maid, and to the discreetly opening door threw an order for coffee, orange juice, and cigarettes. In the shower she stood chattering under the cold water as long as she could bear it. Later, toweling herself, she looked out the dressing room window into the gray lichened limbs of oaks. Below those lay the familiar horseshoe of tree roses and the striated walks. The man who had combed them had gone. It was very quiet. The swarming streets and ringworm subdivisions of the Peninsula might have been a hundred miles away. Intelligent people held back the intrusions by owning their horizon. Then, liberated from obligations, protected from interruptions, they could sit in the midst of order, beauty, and harmony and contemplate the disorder of their own lives.

A quail came out of the leaves and walked along a horizontal limb. His vest was slate blue, his belly patterned like rusty chain mail, his throat and eyebrows outlined in white, his back gray. His plume bobbed jauntily over one eye. Altogether a spruce, plump, self-satisfied bird. Behind him, nervously hurrying, came a female, a demure gray devotion. When the male stopped to peck at a knot on the limb, she waited, and after he had passed on she stopped and pecked the same knob. He walked to a bend in the limb and hopped down to a lower level. She hopped after him. He paused to rub his beak, both sides, against a patch of green lichen. She came behind and sharpened her bill on the same patch. One after the other they disappeared into the leaves, a paradigm of conjugality.

Fidelity. Sabrina framed the word at her naked image in the dressing-room mirror. Fidelity, another of those words from the dictionary of archaisms. An unthinking and excessive devotion, a quality of the female quail. And yet why must she poison with irony something she had already lost the right or title to? Why *must* she lash out at something or somebody when she found herself in the wrong?

With her hair falling forward on her shoulders she looked like a North Beach weirdy. When she gathered and held it at the nape of her neck she became the Speicher portrait, great-eyed and somber, asking something. Her dark-tipped breasts moved with her arms as she brushed; when she set the brush down they drooped—too far? As if putting hand to a pain she cupped, lifted, and let go, watching the effect. Catching her eye in the mirror, she grimaced. Is that it? she asked herself. Is it only the old *démon du midi?* As commonplace as that? A woman of thirty-five frightened of middle age? It angered her to have felt that pang of dismay, for she knew its source—an anxiety as old as adolescence, or older, the apprehension that in love she might be—had been—inadequate.

Nakedly mirrored, a shamed and reluctant maenad, she watched herself, remembering. With Burke, yes. She admitted passivity, habit. Whose fault, she would not have dared to guess. Sometimes, when he did become heated with desire, she had been embarrassed, nearly, by his compulsion to name what they did, verbalizing organs and act as if only words made them real. Last night, if she had been able to go on with it, would probably have been like that. But with Bernard? No. Even that horrible business in the car had shaken her and left her tender. So I am not cold, she said to her questioning image. I'm not, I never have been, it's only that Burke hasn't known how to let himself go, and I haven't known how to. . . . If I'd had more practice in expressing emotion I might not have been blown up by it in the end.

But that was practically to admit her own inadequacy. Testing the idea, she said to herself, "I have been loved by only two," and she felt how meager, after all, was the experience that had blown her life apart. Nearly all women had been loved by several, some by many. She knew an arty Hollywood couple who were always talking about group sex; you kept hearing of these orgies where men and women crawled together in a stew of naked bodies, tangled like angleworms, exciting themselves with pornographic movies and a slither of promiscuous touch until, she supposed, a maddened female simply impaled herself on the handiest erection. Once she had read the memoirs of a prostitute who boasted of having forty men in one day.

Ah, but that was the ideal, that was not for ordinary mortals. She turned her lips inside out in disgust. Her breasts were watching her like dark eyes. Sickened of herself, she turned away.

In the bedroom she heard Bernadette put down the tray. With a name like that, she should have been the sort of maid that male guests cornered in the pantry. Instead, she was a thick Alsatian woman addicted to television and pentecostal tent shows. The last time Billy Graham had been at the Cow Palace she had gone to hear him seven times. How did someone like Bernadette wake up? Singing, chirping God's grace? Heavily and gloomily, in rebellion against a mean fate? Or placidly, finding the job adequate to fill the whole mind, the spirit content to attend on the dumbwaiter, bring trays, make beds, polish up bathrooms, replace damp towels, take a little ironing down to her room where it could be done while she watched with one eye the nervous flicker of love and trouble on the television screen?

"Mrs. Castro?" said the German voice through the door.

"Yes?"

"Your mother would like to see you."

"All right. Has she had breakfast?"

"Two hours ago."

"Is she still in her apartment?"

"She don't feel so good, she's in bed."

"Why don't you take my tray in there, then? I'll be right along."

She took a last look at herself and put away the uneasy questions to which she had awakened. She supposed she owed her mother a visit—they had hardly done more than greet each other so far. It was even a sort of pleasure to have the obligation. She reminded herself to call the beauty parlor and see if she could be squeezed in. And she had asked Barbara to bring the children to swim. Already, she saw, it was nearly ten—broad day. Even without wrecks to plunder or goatskins to sew into clothes, there had to be ways of passing the hours.

Her mother lay propped against several pillows, a froth of lace at the throat and wrists of her dressing gown, her hands limp on the Florentine leather of a writing portfolio. She looked as if she might smell of some ingenuous apple-blossom scent. Since she had given up her glasses and adopted the eye exercises, her face seemed less severe than Sabrina remembered it. She had a soft, peering look, an expression that was eager and almost wistful. In the bow window the long white nylon curtains rippled, chasing sun and shadow across the round intarsia table with its tray and its vase of copper-red roses.

"Mother," Sabrina said, "you look like someone's painting of a Dear Old Lady."

"Grandma Moses?" Her smile was shaky and her skin palely blotched; she seemed frail and very feminine. In fact it was an astonishment to Sabrina to comprehend what must have been apparent all her life, how utterly feminine was everything in this room. The fact had its probable explanations, simultaneous with the observation. It was shrewd of her, Sabrina thought as she moved toward the bed. It was shrewd, finding herself abandoned, to leave behind her the place and people associated with her humiliation, but bring along everything that constituted her defenses. Reproduce the Nahant house and build a wall around it and fill it with the family accumulations. She had made a nest as snug as the inside of a satin cushion and as elegant as the boudoir of a French king's mistress.

The cheek she touched hers to was withered and soft. A stiff hand came around Sabrina's shoulder as they kissed.

"You're not feeling well," Sabrina said. Helen Kretchmer, passing the door, smiled in.

Wincing at some obscure quirk of real or imagined pain, Deborah Hutchens said, "I regret it . . . only because of my regimen. If Doctor Sanders knew I was not out playing golf he would be . . . very upset."

"And it wouldn't do to upset Doctor Sanders."

"He's very strict with me."

Which, of course, she loved. This bossy woman loved to be bossed, and that was a surprise. Or was it only that a rich woman needed a doctor the way a Catholic needed a priest—a fact that Burke had built a career on.

Sabrina sipped her lukewarm coffee. Her mother, after watching her for a while, said, "My dear, you're looking . . . tired. Have you been overdoing?"

"How can you overdo, doing what I do?"

"You have great circles under your eyes. Maybe you should see Doctor Sanders while you're here."

"And get put on a regimen? Golf and cold showers?"

"Cold showers are perfectly wonderful for you."

"I hope so," Sabrina said. "I just got out of one." She drank her orange juice and lighted a cigarette. Helen Kretchmer, solid-legged, tanned, honey-haired, immaculate, a girl beside whom Sabrina felt obscurely corrupt, leaned smiling in the door again.

"Excuse me, Mrs. Hutchens. I just had a call from the library. They don't have anyone to suggest except the man who does their own rare books, and he's tied up for months. They think the best places to call would be bookbinders in the City." To Sabrina, smiling in her exaggeratedly friendly way, she said, "We're hunting someone to treat the fine bindings and catalogue the family papers."

"Whatever for?"

Instant displeasure showed in her mother's face. "Please don't let us . . . begin on your cynicism. The papers are the intimate record of an important family. A historian would . . . find them invaluable."

"Are you going to turn them over to a historian? Will we have Carl Sandburg and everybody digging through the archives to find out what Uncle Bushrod wrote to the *Boston Transcript* about Mr. Lincoln?"

Her mother's hands moved with a touch of the old peremptory impatience on the tooled leather. "In spite of your jeers, it is not impossible. Eventually, perhaps, scholars will work here as they do in great houses . . . abroad."

Through the steam of the refilled coffee cup the collapsing face with its mulish chin seemed braced back in the nest of satin and lace, a face still stubborn, and with its old glare, but without its old force. The shaking hurt it; it made her look weak. More than ever, as she grew older and frailer, she was a Wolcott, one of a predictable tribe. What Oliver thought senility was no more than the tribal habit of accumulation; but where others contented themselves with material things, she also collected Time. In one way Oliver was right—the past was every bit as real to her as the present. Save it all. Some day Grandmother Emily's diaries might be revealed as greater than Pepys or Evelyn.

Helen was still in the door. On impulse, Sabrina said, "It doesn't sound like a very technical job. Have you thought of someone like Leonard MacDonald?"

"Barbara's husband? That queer fellow? Could he do it?"

"Why not? He could find out how to treat the bindings. And he likes books. He might get a chuckle out of the Wolcotts."

"Then he is . . . not the right person."

"Oh, Mother, he's literate, he's intelligent, he's a friend, he works for less than five thousand a year, he's got a third child coming, he's in his summer vacation and would have the time. Who's a better person?"

Deborah fingered her lips. A look like daring glinted in her eyes, a bubbly little snort escaped her. "I imagine Uncle Bushrod would be . . . astonished . . . to find himself being catalogued by a fellow in those workmen's trousers. Bushrod was always so . . . correct, he'd expect a librarian in morning clothes."

"Jol," Sabrina said. "Shall I ask him? How much do you pay?"

"Mr. Cantelli charged thirty dollars a day for doing the bindings," said Helen Kretchmer from the door.

"I don't know," Deborah said. "This requires a person of . . . special capacity. We might have him list the collections too, if he has time. Would that be enough, do you think?"

"If you offered him more he'd probably think it was a handout, and refuse."

Mrs. Hutchens frowned, not irritably. The light of anticipation grew in her widened eyes. She began to stretch and clench her hands, working them in the air. "Splendid!" she crowed. "Oh, I do hope he will consent. I'll . . . help him, if he'll allow me."

"Why wouldn't he? You're paying him." Thinking of the night before, and the odd, truth-party sort of talk they had had, she said, "Maybe he and Bobbie will convert you to their current cause."

"Cause?"

"Conservation, sort of. Planning. Last year I suppose it was interracial housing, or protecting the national parks against power dams."

"Oh yes, I think I recall that. I believe we . . . contributed something. Helen . . . no, it was before you came. But now it's something else, you say."

"These American domestic types fool you," Sabrina said. "Who'd ever picture Bobbie challenging boards of supervisors and throwing herself in front of bulldozers . . ."

"*What?*"

"Oh, not literally. But organizing, and propagandizing, and ringing doorbells. Maybe they have to prove an education wasn't wasted on them."

"But what is this new cause?"

Sabrina had to laugh. "Mother, I've discovered the perfect red herring for you. Drag a cause across the trail and you quit sniffing even after the family collections. Parks and greenbelts—you know. Make developers put a park in every subdivision, make planning commissions reserve open land when they approve site plans, make the state landscape freeways and the towns prohibit billboards, get landowners to donate land for future parks."

"Why it sounds like . . . a perfectly splendid thing," her mother said. From the nest of pillows, her eyes (she had pouches of her own) forgot to frown at Sabrina and peered into a future California ponded with open fields, dark with copses (she would have called them copses, following Mr. James), lined with poplars or whatever they planted along roads. Her mouth, opened a little, trembled, and she raised a furtive hand and pressed it firm.

"It *is* a splendid thing. Want to donate the Woodside place?"

"Oh my goodness!"

"That's what I thought."

"Please do not . . . bait me, Sabrina. I am not well."

"I'm not baiting you. They asked me to ask you if you'd like to give some land."

"I consider that your air of knowing in advance what my answer will be is . . . baiting."

"All right, I'm sorry." She tried the coffee pot and found it empty. "Why not give some, then? They'd put your name on a bronze plaque, and mount a portrait bust of you on a concrete pillar, and call the oldest tree the Deborah Oak."

"You make it sound splendid," her mother said. Her bulging glance was retracted, her voice was dry. "I shall have to brood upon it."

And if she brooded upon it, it was sure to take fifty years at a minimum. Her heirs could settle that one. Sabrina said, "As long as you own it, it won't make much difference, it'll still stay open country.

Maybe it's better if you do keep it. I must say it gives me the crawling itch to think of the Great American Public swarming through there scattering beer cans and stoning the squirrels to death."

Over her shoulder she saw with annoyance that Helen Kretchmer still leaned in the doorway, listening and smiling. "Helen, call Boris, will you, and see if he can work me in this morning?"

An abrupt order, as if to a servant. And a slow, hot, comprehending flush. Good.

"Of course, Mrs. Castro." She went away, and Sabrina said to her mother, "If I look as bad as you say, I'd better get worked over."

"You seem very nervous," Deborah said. "Were you serious about the portrait bust?"

"Sure. Why? Would you like that?"

"It would be interesting to see oneself . . . turned to stone. In our family we were always painted." Her hands worked in air. She changed the subject, as usual, without transition. "Should you like to have a . . . dinner party or luncheon for some of your friends?"

"There's nobody I want to see, especially. If I feel like looking anyone up I can take them to the club."

The weak blue eyes lost interest and rolled away in an exercise that showed their whites horribly. "For heaven's sake, Mother, must you?"

"It's important to keep at them," Deborah said. "Eventually the exercises will . . . change the shape of the eyeball. I see ever so much better since I . . . gave up glasses."

"If you keep on looking like that, it won't be a portrait bust. They'll mount your head on a totem pole."

Deborah giggled. "Perhaps I could haunt houses." Her hands quit working and dropped on the portfolio. Out of a clear sky she said, "Is Burke coming up?"

Her eyes now, for all their watery weakness and the light shaking of her head, were hard to evade.

"Not that I know of," Sabrina said.

"Lizardo says he was here last night."

Sabrina snapped to her feet. "Lizardo does? What kind of Meddlesome Matty has he got to be?"

"I heard someone. I asked him who it was. He didn't want to tell me but I . . . made him."

Steps approached the door, and Sabrina twisted around. Tattletales and snoops, there was one at every entrance. But the soft face of Helen Kretchmer smiled in at her—carefully, correctly. Being put in her place had taken some of the dewy stare out of her. "Boris says he could take you at eleven-fifteen, Mrs. Castro."

"Yes, all right." The girl went away, but not until the typewriter started up down the hall did Sabrina let her eyes meet her mother's, watching from the bed. "Yes," she said, "he came up. But he couldn't stay. He had to be back at the hospital this morning."

"Sabrina, I hope you haven't quarreled."

"We haven't quarreled."

"But there is . . . some trouble?"

"Yes, there's some trouble."

"Oh my dear!"

"It's all right, it'll work out."

"Is there . . . another woman?"

"What? Oh no."

The slow, growing alarm in her mother's face mounted to a pitch too well remembered, repeated at every adolescent crisis. It amounted to a certainty that something dreadful had happened, and an equal certainty that the fault lay with Sabrina. "Is there . . . it's not you, Sabrina? You haven't been foolish?"

"Did you raise me to be foolish?"

Her mother sighed. "You're a grown woman. But grown women have been foolish . . . before this." Clumsily opening the portfolio, she scattered papers around. Blindly she fumbled them together again. Her mouth trembled into violent helplessness and then was pinched firm. She said, "My dear, if you're even *thinking* of . . . separating, let me tell you . . . there can be many years ahead and they can be . . . lonely as the grave." With frail violence she sat up, straining forward; she alarmed Sabrina with her paleness and weakness; she seemed to be issuing a warning from her deathbed. "I was reading Mr. Longfellow's translation of the . . . *Divine Comedy*," she said.

"The innermost band of the . . . ninth circle of hell . . . did you know . . . is lonely and cold."

"Let's not get upset," Sabrina said after a moment. "If I have to live alone, I'll have to live alone, even if it is lonely and cold."

"You won't like it."

"I don't like it now. I never have liked it."

They were closer to intimacy than they had been in thirty years. Deborah Hutchens' head moved as if in pity, and Sabrina, stung, said, "Were you surprised at that movie last night?"

A forbidding glaze came over her mother's eyes. "You recognized him."

"Yes."

"And what did you think of him?"

"Naturally I was interested."

"He is not worth your interest."

"My *father?*"

"He was not a good man. Oliver should have had . . . better judgment than to resurrect that old film."

"Where is he? Or is he dead?"

"I don't know. I never heard."

"You despised him so much that you just wiped him out."

Her mother's face was as stiff as carved wood. "Yes."

"So then," Sabrina said, "you *prefer* your hell lonely and cold."

She was unprepared for the shaking anger in the old blotched face. "Sabrina," her mother said, kneading her trembling hands, "I was . . . concerned about you. I tried to . . . offer you some advice. I did not look for insolence."

Sabrina stood up, her eyes locked with the faded blue ones in the deathlike head. The smile on her face felt stiff and inadequate and sad. She thought, My God, she's as confused as I am, the minute you flush her out of the cushions she's lost. "I'm sorry, Mother," she said. "Would you rather I took my troubles away?"

"You know better than that. You know you are always welcome here."

"All right." She stooped to the cool kiss of armistice. "But please, if

I'm going to make a mistake, it's got to be mine. You can't believe—can you?—that a person's family has any business interfering in her marriage."

On that note, which was perhaps not fully understood, and which she would not have sounded if she had thought it would be understood, she left. At the garage door Virgil touched his cap to her. "Have you got a car I can take?" she said. "Mine's at the airport, I'd like you to take somebody and go get it sometime today, if you will. The keys will be in the parking-lot office."

Was it the uniform cap that made chauffeurs seem the most servile of servants? All her life servants had embarrassed her, all except Lizardo. In her childhood, when she had to be delivered or called for, she had made drivers leave their caps off, and maids wear a coat over their uniforms, to avoid the look of pampered wealth that she hated. Now, irritably, when Virgil brought out the station wagon, she climbed in and slammed the door, and smiling into the teeth of his deference, flung off the hand brake and tramped down on the throttle and peeled away like a hot-rodder, shooting gravel in the doors of his immaculate garage.

CHAPTER 11

F OR A HALF HOUR Boris's equivocally erotic hands massaged the knots out of her mind. Then for a while she was trapped in a row with four others under the roaring helmets of the dryers, and could fall back on a copy of *Vogue,* turning coated pages in which bony women demonstrated the astonishing ingenuities of elegance: women uplifted, corrected, disguised; women gorgeously jeweled and intricately coifed; women with hair that looked as if it had been cut by satyrs pursuing them with hedge shears; angular pen-and-ink women with autumn mist mink in natural color superimposed on them; women in sacks with bows on their behinds; surprised-looking women in baths and barrels; women in towels on bathroom scales; proudly fastidious women with notably exposed armpits; women aphrodisiacal beside phallic perfume bottles.

It was certainly nothing new; it was, for that matter, paleolithically old. But her own involvement, once she noted it, tempted her to scorn, for this was a game, apparently, that she played as helplessly as any. Let a woman be vain, proud, ambitious, insane, cruel, goody-goody, restless, bored, anything, still her body was the seat and instrument of her preoccupation. Mostly it came out as glamour, and glamour could be defined as intention, and fashion was intention's dramatization. The business of a woman's life was contained in the ritualized progress

131

from the invitation to the embrace, and even when leaving one embrace she could apparently go nowhere except into another.

And after the embrace, after the sticky flower trapped its pollinating quarry? And especially if no pollination took place? Then what? They forgot to say in *Vogue*. Repeat until tired, maybe. Take it for a free cadenza. But sooner or later, after the body's rapture, the mind's unease, if you had a mind, and if you tried to be honest. After the embrace, the questions. Even she had helplessly gone that road; her discontent was a discontent of the mind, but she had found no expression for it except the body. Hating going to waste, she had found, Burke said, an odd way of becoming useful.

Vogue made it clear to her all over again what she must do if she wanted to live with herself. A wife without ecstasy was better than a mistress with a hurting conscience. Yet as she thought this she found herself sitting tense and rebellious, and her hands were aching from their clutch on the magazine.

Boris shook her hair, released her, led her back to a booth. The woman opposite, a little withered woman, was having drawn upon her eyelids a line of turquoise, and around her lashes a line of black. Her claw rested upon the arm of the chair. The nails were long ovals of polished black horn; on one finger was a ring with a set the size of a half walnut. Not Hillsborough or San Francisco: more outlandish than the local taste. New York, possibly; Texas or Los Angeles, possibly. But female. As the operator stepped back, the tipped head came down and the rimmed and green-shaded eyes examined themselves with unsmiling seriousness. Then the woman's glance met Sabrina's in the glass, and became at once a beam of the coldest malevolence.

Boris began brushing back the heavy sheaf of her hair, and she was recalled to the scrutinizing of herself.

Later she escaped into the early-afternoon heat, tainted with smog. She had not gone a block before she felt faint and queasy. Ahead was a dingy stucco front, a neon cherry on a neon toothpick in a neon glass. She stuck her head inside and saw three empty tables, a bar with two men sitting at it and one behind it. The bartender tilted his head back and stared at her. She felt like someone in a foreign country, unsure of the local tongue.

132

"Lunch?" she said.

He flipped his towel. "On'y sandwiches."

It was not inviting, but she was there. The two men at the bar watched her in the mirror. Over the radio, tuned intimately low, the Giants were getting their brains beaten out in Cincinnati. The bartender brought her the stinger she ordered and shook his head over them. On the road they stank. Pitching. They needed a left-handed reliefer bad, especially against an outfit like this Cincinnati outfit, with all that left-handed bench. He stood relaxedly. "You a baseball fan?" he said. "Some women are, some ain't."

The sweet, cold, minty drink calmed the fluttering in her stomach. She had another, and then a tuna sandwich and a glass of beer, while a thin trickle of trade came and went and the game with its distant-waterfall sound of the crowd murmured on. The bartender came and slid pretzels across the table to her and said that Mays wasn't hitting, either. His average stayed up but he wasn't getting them where they mattered, and he wasn't hitting the long ball. How many runs had he driven in on this road trip? How long since he homered? "But I forget," he said, smiling with black teeth. "You never did say whether you was a baseball nut or not."

The Giants scored twice while Sabrina finished her beer, and the bartender felt better. So did Sabrina, restored by drinks and food and the sleazy gloom and the masculine rumble and putter. The bartender's confidences flattered her. Men were more restful than women. She left him a dollar tip, and when she went out she threw back from the doorway a smile that she saw him store away.

Shopping occupied her for another half hour: things for Bobbie's children. Then, thinking ahead, she turned into a liquor store and ordered two mixed cases delivered to Lizardo. She didn't want to go out every time she wanted a drink, and she had her grandmother's word for it that one should not borrow from the servants.

Back home, Lizardo opened softly to her ring, and she dumped her parcels in his arms and told him to have somebody take them to the pool. She told him also about the liquor he could expect: he could put it in his closet. But she did not escape without pacifying his anxieties. "You itt something?" he said. She knew he smelled her breath.

"I et something and I drunk something. Is Mother napping?"

"Yes."

"Anybody call?"

In his eyes she saw the reflection of the startled, insistent expression of her own. The shake of his head twisted in her feelings, and it was all she could do to avoid bursting out in an exclamation. Neither of them! Bernard she had not really expected until five-thirty, and yet she found that what had not even been an anticipation had turned to a sour disappointment. And Burke, whom she had put aside in her mind as too painful to face, but whom she had already half returned to in her thoughts, why couldn't *he* have picked up a telephone while he was out at lunch? He might have wondered how she was.

At the pool, Oliver lay as limp on the diving board as if he had fallen there from ten thousand feet; his heavy arms hung down, his face was turned into the matting. Minna and a maid were shooing shrieking children into the dressing rooms. Nobody paid any attention to Sabrina as she came in and closed the gate. Oliver did not move. A boy pursued by another ducked around her, and pursuer and pursued feinted and jockeyed with her in the middle like a tree. The pursued one skidded sideward, slipped, caught the other's shove, and went sprawling into the water.

"Here!" Minna said. "You two! Come on now, get dressed." From the dressing rooms came roars and squeals. A naked boy skittered past a door, shrieked, clapped his hands to his loins, vanished. The one in the pool dragged himself ashore and staggered in, shaking water off his fingers.

"I'm taking the whole bunch to the Redwood City rodeo," Minna said. "Aren't I the lucky one?"

Her figure had sagged and widened with child-bearing, she had unattractive white strap marks across her freckled shoulders, her hair was mussed from the white rubber cap that she held now in one hand, and her smile was a little crooked, one cheek lifting more than the other as if she had had a mild stroke.

"Yes," Sabrina said.

The crooked smile widened, the eyes opened until wrinkles rose clear into Minna's hairline. "Don't be sarcastic, I can't bear it." Distracted, she shouted into the bedlam, knocked on the wall until she got a lessening of the noise. "I'm going in and get ready. We're leaving in exactly ten minutes. Anyone who isn't in the station wagon when I come out will get left."

"Daddy will see they get there," Sabrina said, and dropped into a lounge.

"Daddy!" Minna said. "That hound!" She limped off on wooden clogs, an effective exit. Lying back against her cushion, Sabrina let the sun cover her. Children pattered past; she opened her eyes to smile and speak when someone she never did see said, "Hello, Aunt Sabrina." Whispers, giggles, noise diminishing to two or three voices, then to none at all. Smell of chlorine and wet cement and lawn. A little wind moved the wistaria pods hanging from the arbor along the front of the dressing rooms.

Oliver groaned. The back of his neck wrinkled like a movie Prussian's as he raised his head. The side of his face was waffled from the matting, and his mouth made wet sounds. "Is it safe?" He sat up, straddling the board, rolling his shoulders and stretching his arms, powerful and loose. "Ah, Sister." He looked like something on a billboard— It's Lucky when you live in California. Sabrina recalled a novelist friend who after a Hollywood contract went away cursing everything except the bodies of the natives. "They're creating a beautiful race," he said in envoi. "The brain may wither away to the size of a lentil and the moral sense may atrophy entirely, but they're going to look like Tahitians."

"Sun god," she said to Oliver, and went in to dress. The dressing room was soaking. She kicked sodden towels around the floor to take up the worst of it and then kicked the towels under a bench. When she came out in her suit, Oliver had not moved from his straddle of the board. His shrewd squint was on her as she turned over a red-hot mattress and lay down on the cool side.

"Feeling better?"

"What is this?" she said. "Everybody asking me if I'm feeling better."

"Who's been asking?"

"You, Barbara, Mother, Lizardo, everybody I've seen, practically."

"You looked spooked yesterday."

"And today I don't look so spooked?"

"Not quite."

"Then you shouldn't go by what you see. I'm worse off today than I was yesterday. So's Mother, thanks to your film premiere. Did you know you put her to bed?"

"She'll get over it."

"I suppose. Maybe you did some good, at that. At least she talked about him a little. She said she didn't know if he was alive or dead. Didn't you tell her?"

"Why should I have told her? I wasn't supposed to know myself." Varnished with sun and sweat, he bounced gently on the stiff board. "What do you mean, you're worse off than yesterday?"

She turned her face downward on her crossed wrists and did not answer.

"You're mixed up with Barney Mendelsohn, is that it?"

Stricken, she reared up on her elbows. *"Barney* Mendelsohn?"

"Isn't that the one? Tall guy, used to sing—big rich voice?"

"You know him, then. Last night you knew him."

"I see him around here and there. Isn't he at the Emporium?"

Sabrina lay down again. She was too tired to be much upset. The very fact that Oliver knew Bernard made everything seem less frantic and impossible, somehow. "Well, so now you know," she said into the mattress, and turned her head a little to see him. He had gripped the sides of the diving board and was raising and lowering his body with his arms. Grunting with strain, he said, "He married?"

"Oh sure. I wouldn't have it any way but the hardest."

"Yeah. Well don't let it get you down. It happens all the time."

"Does it?"

"Doesn't it?"

"If it does, that's one of the things that get me down."

The great triceps ridged as he raised himself. He crossed a leg, did a momentary one-hand stand, brought the leg under, and came down crosswise, facing her. "No kidding, why all the tragedienne postures? You'll dramatize yourself into a breakdown."

"Will I? That's one way to make myself seem important."

The expression he wore, somewhere between bewilderment and amusement, nettled her, and she rose up on her elbows again. "God, Oliver, don't you ever question the life you live? Sometimes I think I got involved in this business just to prove that something was worth getting excited about. And if I'm worse off today than I was yesterday, it's because I've begun to doubt even *it*."

Scratching his shin, he regarded her. "That's quite an attitude. Barney would be flattered."

"Oh!"

He said, "You always did want to live every minute as if you were the first monkey being sent to the moon in a rocket."

Again she lowered her cheek to the hot, plastic-smelling pad. "No, I'd just like things to mean something. I'd like to mean something myself."

"You're wound up like a little tin automobile. Practice some of Mother's yoga. You need to learn to relax."

"Relax?" she said, glaring at him. "You too can be happy and contented? Try our improved pre-frontal lobotomies, certified by hundreds of satisfied users?"

"Or try a psychiatrist. I'm not kidding you, Sister, you sound as if you could use some help."

"You bet I could use some help, but not that kind. Original sin according to the gospels of Vienna. The hell with it, simply. I don't believe in those people, not as healers. If I've got guilt feelings, I'm good and sure I ought to have them. I don't care to find out whether I'm animal, vegetable, mineral, anal, oral, or genital. I'm not going to spend three years on a couch while some medicine man tries to get me to admit I remember a time when Mother repudiated me or when I wished my brother was dead. She's always repudiated me, and I've wished you dead plenty of times, but that's not what's bothering me."

He bounced the board lightly. "What is?"

When she sat up suddenly, the blue pool, the lawn, the lounges, the arbor, the white refrigerator in its alcove between the dressing rooms, darkened to a tintype indistinctness, almost disappeared. Then the diz-

ziness passed, color and sun and sharp shadows came back. "I wish
I knew," she said. "The world, maybe. Being female, maybe. Burke,
maybe. Too many existentialist novels, maybe. A lack of opportunity
—something. Is there anything to drink in that icebox?"

"Beer. There might be gin and tonic."

"Want one?"

"Not now."

When she came back with her drink and sat down in the half-shade
of a hooded lounge, Oliver was under the board. The water sloshed
around his thighs as he chinned himself six or eight times. Then he
hung, half floating.

"You really manage it, don't you?" she said.

"Manage what?"

"You've got everything the way you want it."

"Aside from taxes, government red tape, five kids, the necessity of
keeping Mother from playing the fool, et cetera, et cetera."

"You never get wondering if just managing the estate is enough?
You never wonder if you have a right to be alive? You don't have to
be reassured you're doing something useful?"

"Oh, come on, Sister, for the love of God!" He surged upward and
his frowning face appeared over the end of the board, glared, went
down again. *"Useful?"* he said from below. "Useful who to? I'm useful
to you and Mother, I trust. And I'm useful to myself when I'm well
fed, well exercised, comfortable, and entertained."

"What kind of entertainment? Danger? Spear-fishing, things like
that?"

"That's all right. Gambling. Women. Ball games. Bottles. Movies.
TV. Comic books. I'm not fussy."

She drank half the bitter contents of her glass. "There you are," she
said. "Rich, healthy, handsome, the father of sound children, a lifetime resident of Paradise, with just enough responsibilities to make
playtime pleasant. You're almost the American ideal, do you know
that? You're what this civilization has been working up to. When
everybody gets like you, we're in."

"The hell with you." The arms flexed, the face rose, subsided, rose
again. She thought in contempt and admiration, He *is,* he's a pure

Whatd'yecallit, a somatotonic. He's worse than Mother. Even when he's talking he can't help flexing his muscles.

His head rose and hung there with the amber, light-lashed eyes glinting at her. "You need a breeze through you. You're morbid. Why don't you go up to Carson City with me tomorrow?"

"What for?"

"The ride. Some fun. We'll take the Mercedes. Chase the cobwebs out of you. The sports-car races are on over at Minden."

"Are you driving in them?"

"Not this year."

"Who's going?"

"Just me."

"I might at that," she said. "Are they likely to pile up and roll through the bales of hay and catch fire and kill forty spectators?"

"Why, do you want them to?"

"I think so. If you'd guarantee it I'd go. I'd like to see a good bloody disaster."

Casually and mindlessly active, Oliver chinned himself. It seemed to her a deficiency of consciousness in him that he could so enjoy sun and water, air, light, the senses, the activity of the muscles, without being in any way aware of how much he was enjoying them. He closed his eyes and let go with his hands and sank soundlessly under. Many seconds later he came up a long way down the pool, to lie brown and buoyant, sustaining himself with the gentlest of breast strokes. His arms thrust once, hard, and he surged forward, pushing a wall of water. "Okay," he said with his chin down, his mouth at the very surface. "We'll make it an expedition."

"Don't count on it," Sabrina said. "Only maybe."

In the drive a car door slammed. Excited children's voices, running feet on the path, the clash of the gate, and here came Barbara's two hurling themselves toward her, crying, "Sabrina! Hey, Sabrina!" Hastily she put the glass under the lounge where it wouldn't get kicked over, turned loose her smile, and braced herself for the theatrical hugs, the wet kisses.

"Hello, darlings!" she said. "Hello, Louise, hello, Dolly, hi, lovers, how've you both been?"

CHAPTER 12

FOR A WHILE, Lady Bountiful, she could distribute gladness out of packages—a curly dog with a red tongue, a tiger with a plush tail, two rubber swans, a set of play dishes. Extravagantly loved, she was made to become one of them, and swim and splash and chase and be chased until she fell into a lounge, exhausted, and repudiated them, referring them to the pool and the sandbox. Barbara, her center of gravity so wrong that she could neither sit up nor lean back comfortably, eventually shooed them off. "Sabrina's tired," she said. "Go entertain yourselves for a while or I'll have Daddy drown you both."

Sabrina waved them an exaggeratedly limp good-by. Through the shadow of the headache that darkened her sight she saw the smile and the pucker of a question in Barbara's face. All the time, probably, she had been sitting there waiting for the confidences that had been promised yesterday afternoon. And yet not even to Barbara would it be possible to tell what she had been through since then. Coldly reported, it would sound like the doing of a woman completely out of control. As, perhaps, it was. She heard Barbara say, "Is it . . . are things any better?"

"No," Sabrina said, and groped under the lounge for the melted-down remnant of her second or third—good heavens, what difference did it make?—gin and tonic. "No, no better. But maybe closer to a solution."

Barbara waited; her eyes were brown and full of light, like the eyes of animals, like Bernard's eyes. It seemed easier for brown eyes to look love, somehow. "What?" Barbara said. "Go back to Burke?"

Sabrina looked down her brown legs to her brown feet. Without turning her eyes back toward Barbara she brushed away a patch of sand from her knee. "I guess," she said.

More sympathetic silence—and she found that she could grow as impatient with sympathetic silence as with many other things. Abruptly she stood up. "Let me fix your drink," she said, and took the glass over Barbara's protests that there was still a lot in it. Starting away, she stopped, looked back, and said into Barbara's manifest bewilderment, "I forgot to tell you, I've got Leonard a job. Is he doing anything?"

"A job? No, just repairing television sets."

"Starting Monday, how'd he like to be Mother's rare-book man and archivist?"

"What?"

"Don't spoil it with whats. It's all arranged. Mother really has a job she wants done. He'd be doing her a mighty favor. The pay is thirty dollars a day. If he wants to work more than five days a week we can probably arrange time and a half for overtime."

"But Sabrina, wait. Could he do it? I mean . . ."

"He's fully witted, isn't he?" Sabrina said. "None of the Wolcotts and Barbers was. Anything they could write he ought to be able to catalogue."

She went off to the refrigerator and fixed two more drinks, and then with the sweating glasses in her hands she slipped into the dressing room and looked at her wrist watch on the shelf below the mirror. Ten minutes to five. To her own face, vivid and ice-eyed in the cool mirror, she whispered, practicing, trying the meaning on her mind, "I've been thinking and thinking, darling. We were right in Oaxaca. We have to stop right here. We mustn't see each other again, we mustn't call each other. Ever! But oh, darling . . . !"

She closed her eyes, opened them, turned away out into the shade of the wistaria arbor. The shadow lay so dense it was almost black, and beyond it, blazing under the afternoon heat, the pool and its borders were bone white, chemical blue. She saw the underwater light shake along the pool's blue side, and the steps in the corner crawl like something seen through flawed glass. The children's heads were bent together in the sandbox, Barbara from her lounge was craning toward the refrigerator alcove where Sabrina had disappeared. Of a sudden she was furious to have them gone. If he should call early, she would not be there; if he called once and missed her, he might not call again.

"My word," she said, coming from the shade into the blaze of sun. "Where's the afternoon gone? It's already five."

She made it so plain that even her protests did not keep them there another ten minutes. Before she heard the Chevrolet start on the other side of the fence she was in the dressing room and racing into her clothes. At five-fifteen she was in the front hall of her mother's house, breathlessly asking Lizardo if there had been any calls. None.

The drinks she had had pounded in her breathing and pulse as she hurried upstairs. Dialing, her finger slipped so that she had to start over. She got the switchboard and gave Bernard's name. There was an immediate honking of the busy signal. "I'm sorry," the operator said. "That line is busy. Will you wait?"

She waited. What fool could be calling him now, after closing time? Or had her own call cut across his? Had she, by her impatience, only— "I can ring now," the operator said. A click. The voice.

"Darling!" she said.

She realized at once that the word must have sprung at him out of the telephone like an armed robber out of an alley. He said, fumbling, "Just a minute, please." Noises—the closing of a door? Offended, she waited on the signs of his discretion.

"Now!" he said. "Ah, sweet, I was just going to call you—"

"I was afraid you wouldn't. I couldn't wait."

"I was just waiting till the switchboard operator goes off. This isn't too good, any minute somebody could plug into the line, so take it a little easy. Maybe I ought to call you back."

"No!" she said. "Now that I've got you!"

He laughed softly. A pause. "I've been thinking about you all day."

"I too," she said. "And trying not to."

"I feel lousy about last night."

"Don't."

"It was messy and stupid, and humiliating for you."

She said, "I saw you, at least. We were in touch."

His laugh again, low and secret, his voice resonant and tuned for confidences. And this was the thing she had been wanting more and more as the afternoon wore on—this whispering contact, this conspiratorial closeness. The room spun, not unpleasantly. It seemed a long way to the ends of her fingers, and when she spoke it seemed that her voice was like the magnified whisper of a movie screen where lovers mutter for their own ears alone but must be heard in the back rows. She said, "It's like a disease. Do you have any idea?"

"None whatever. Tell me."

"Ah, you. I wish I could touch you now."

"So do I."

"It *is* a disease. You'd think going to bed would cure it, at least for a while, but it only makes it worse." Hearing him say something, she listened. "What?"

"Remember the switchboard."

"Sh, sh!" she said, mocking him. "There are ears everywhere. I've just lost my upbringing. I was never like this before."

"You're wonderful."

"Am I? I feel like one of these snake women. Pure evil below the belt. That's one view of women, isn't it? And yet I think I love you, and a snake woman isn't supposed to be able to do that."

"Darling," he said, "don't you think maybe I'd better call you back in five minutes? The operator will be trying to clear the lines."

She sat up straighter. "We can hear her if she cuts in. I wanted to tell you, Burke was here when I got back last night."

His answer came only after a pause, and veiled with caution, "He was? What happened?"

"Nothing. He went on back." (But something did happen, something sickening that makes me ashamed.)

"For good? What's he going to do?"

"I didn't ask him." Rocking her head, the edge of the mouthpiece hard against her cheek, she cried, "Oh, Bernard, does it matter what he does? I tried to care and I can't. I wish we could just worry about *us*. I wish I could have lunch with you in the City, I wish you could come down here for week ends, I wish we could just be open and not afraid of being seen. . . ."

"Garden of Eden," he said neutrally and regretfully. "We had Oaxaca."

She was tempted to take desperate and ill-tempered hold of that "had," it made everything so past. Instead she said as if playfully, "But we weren't Adam and Eve, darling. We were trespassers. We sneaked in from the Land of Nod."

From his uncertain laugh she judged that she had been in some way troubling. He said, "I guess that one went by me. What's this Land of Nod business? Are you high?"

"No darling. I'm low."

"I'm sorry," he said, so softly she hardly caught the words. "I wish—"

"Darling," she said, "listen! This isn't what I was going to say when you called, but listen. We can't just sit around being sorry. Let's go away somewhere. I don't care where. Let's go down to Big Sur and sit on the lighthouse steps and watch the whales go by, or let's go to Norway salmon fishing. I don't care. But let's not hesitate and quibble, let's plunge. This is the only life we've got."

"It'd be lovely," he said in his low, regretful voice. "It'd be heaven," and again she found herself picking at his tenses and from them deriving disappointment. The conditional. Would be. He was going to make excuses, he would evade her. The excitement died, anticipation collapsed, she slumped on the bed and everything bright in her went dull.

"But you won't," she said. "I don't mean enough."

"Sweet, I wish you'd try to understand. You mean everything. But I'm not free, I'm tied."

"Untie yourself!"

She heard for answer only the humming line.

"*I* did," she said.

More humming. "You make it awful hard," he said finally. "Darling, who gains if you get talked about and I become something treacherous to my children? Listen, I heard today of a place in the Carmel Valley we could get. It's off by itself, walled patio, pool, everything. We could have it from now to the middle of August. I could cook up some excuse to get away nearly every week end, or I could maybe send the family off to Huntington Lake or somewhere. . . ."

"Bernard," she said, "it's an ugly dishonest dream."

He was talking fast and earnestly, and she sat cupping her right elbow in her left hand, her right leaning the receiver against her ear. Didn't she think this was the wisest way, at least for now? It would let them see each other, they could keep in touch. Maybe later, sometime when he had to make another buying trip, they could . . .

She listened with her lower lip bitten thoughtfully under and her eyes on the dense leaves and lichened limbs of the oak outside her window. Sun infiltrated the whole mass; for every leaf of green there was a leaf of hot light; dappled afternoon fell through her windows and lay across the floor nearly to her feet. A little wind stirred, and the air, the whole room, shivered. She heard Bernard's voice pause on a question, and in the humming moment, over it or through it, from another world, a quail's anxious three-note call, twice repeated.

"Darling?" he said. "Don't you see that? Don't you agree?"

The wind moved again, the air shivered. There was goose flesh sudden on Sabrina's bare arms. Bernard was still talking. Quietly she lowered the telephone from her ear and laid it in its cradle. Already remote, he died in the middle of a word.

Principally what she felt was shame.

Almost absently, she walked to the window and stood looking out into the green and gold. From the hall beyond the closed door at her back she heard the squeak and rattle of a tea cart being wheeled from her mother's room to the dumbwaiter, then the sound of the sliding door, then a remote, internal murmur of pulleys as the old rope operated elevators went down. She saw how the disturbed sunlight moved on her arm and on her dress.

Still quietly, not questioning the impulse, she opened her door upon the padded hall, and went down the stairs past the glower of the generations. No one was in the lower hall or—she looked in—the drawing room. Lizardo had Friday night and Saturday off. She turned around the newel post and opened the backstairs door, and without snapping on the light went down the narrow coil of steps. The air was cooler, the light from the half-windows in the foundation wells was greenish and subdued. She had a strong sense of descending through deeper and deeper crypts toward some catacomb.

In her childhood this had been one of the refuges. The great dim room to the left, with its white wooden lockers along two sides, had been one of the stages for their theatricals at the infrequent times when she could coax the keys to the dress collections from her mother. A maid had always come along to see that they did no damage, and the maid generally brought washing or ironing. That whole area of the past smelled of camphor and laundry soap and steam and hot cloth, and of the fuel oil from the furnace room. The ghost of its old smells lay on the air now, a thin odor of preservation and disuse.

For a while she stood looking at the lockers, filled with the dozens and dozens of dresses and hats that, if she had been permitted to use them freely, would have made her into anything she desired. She could have plucked personalities out of those closets as freely as people now plucked them out of pill bottles, if hers had been a house where things were for use instead of for keeping. Instead of that opulence of opportunity, only an occasional skimpy masquerade with the three or four inner-circle friends before whom one need not feel too embarrassed at the restrictions and the inhibitions. Those few, and a maid to watch them, and a meager dribbling-out of one costume apiece from the closets of plenty.

Sabrina took hold of the handle of a locker and pulled. Locked. Why not? The lesson of her childhood had been that nothing you really wanted could be had.

Whatever it was she had come looking for, the past or some impossible comfort, it was not there. This was only one more room in the family museum; it told her neither who she had been nor who she should try to be. She turned and went down the hall of whitewashed concrete, one side light-welled and the other close-hung with framed pages of illuminated antiphonals—something that Aunt Sarah, in a religious or historical phase, had collected. Their gold leaf gleamed, their square black notes climbed and descended on the staff lines as overgrown with gold and lapis lazuli as old rail fences might be overgrown with blackberry vines. She tried again, as in the past, to puzzle meaning from the crabbed and abbreviated Latin: frozen music, petrified worship, unintelligible, quaintly attractive.

Raising her hand to knock on Lizardo's door, she had a dreamlike vision of her own face, serene, looking out from a starched white coif, her pale lips forming the murmur of hymns or prayers, and she thought, That's one way. Wouldn't it be a joke if I wound up a Poor Clare or something.

The door opened and Lizardo looked out, but a Lizardo so changed from what she anticipated that she dropped back a step. This one wore light blue gabardine slacks and a cream-and-tan sport shirt with a yoke. The flashy clothes changed him utterly; he looked like a worn-out roué, fastidious and corrupt, like one of the gamblers and pimps she had seen outside bars and Chinese gambling houses on Stockton's Alvarado Street, waiting for the pickers on a Saturday night.

"Are you going out?" she managed to say. "You're all dressed up."

"Not yet," he said. "Plizz!" He rushed forward one of the heavy, dark, over-carved walnut chairs that had once occupied stiff space in the Beacon Street or Dartmouth Street or Nahant house. Sabrina, sitting down like an embarrassed caller, found herself smoothing her face with her flat hands, feeling safe and shaky. "I hardly recognized you," she said. "You're so *elegant*, Lizardo."

But she recognized the room. It was a little blurry from all she had drunk, but hardly changed. The neat bed wore its serape cover, the guitar hung from the wall with its tasseled cord drooping, the desk held its row of magazines and paperbacks neatly on edge between the plaster bulldog and the terra-cotta bust of Jiggs from whose head, in the past, had grown green grass hair. Above the desk, six square feet of wall were solidly filled with newspaper and magazine pictures of General Douglas MacArthur in black dime-store frames. That gallery had doubled in size, but otherwise things were the same.

Lizardo's uncritical adoration beamed on her and warmed her, and that was surely a part of what had drawn her down here. It had been Lizardo much more than her mother that she went to when anything was wrong—perhaps because it was usually her mother who made things go wrong. She supposed Lizardo had fulfilled some of the functions of a father, a father without authority or punishments. Smiling into his smile, she said, "You're so elegant you must have a date with a girl."

An indescribable expression moved in his wrinkles, something gratified, wistful, lecherous, and sly. "Yes."

"Really? No kidding?"

"Oh, yes. But she waits."

"She must like you."

"Oh berry much!"

"Well I'm astonished at you, you old Romeo. You never used to go out with girls. You used to sit home and compose songs." Privately, she had always wondered what he did for women. There were practically no Filipino women in the United States; a Filipino was caught between the immigration quotas and the miscegenation laws. She supposed that like other lonely bachelors he must sometimes have gone to some miserable whorehouse that ignored the color line. That could be where he was bound tonight. But at his age! His wrinkles were deceptive, but he must be sixty at least. She looked again around the neat, sailor-like cell, and pity made her shrug her shoulders together and exclaim, "I've always thought yours was the nicest room in the whole house."

"Yes," Lizardo said. He could not keep his lips over his teeth; his smile kept breaking out white and toothy. He went over and laid a finger on one of the pictures in the MacArthur gallery. "This my girl."

Sabrina went to look. Hemmed in by two dozen reproductions of the general's godlike profile was a newspaper photograph of a very pretty Filipina, perhaps eighteen, wearing an evening dress with an orchid at her shoulder. She was clinging to the arm of a dressed-up Filipino boy, and she had smiled shyly into the camera at some dance.

"That pretty girl? Who's the rival?"

"Oh, him," Lizardo said. "This was bepore I met her. You like to hear?"

"I certainly would."

"On my bacation," he said, "I go to San Prancisco, I hab nice rooms, suite, in Pilipino hotel. I like t'ings nice por my priends. So somebody comes, and manager asks me gib up one room, all rooms are pull. I say all right, sure. He say we hab to share batt, but doors lock inside, no trouble. I am not knowing who comes into my place. But when I come back at night I go into battroom and I smell perpume. I say, 'Aha, it is a lady in here!'"

Sabrina moved a little. He was leaning, literally panting to tell his story, and when she moved, his eyes followed her quickly as if looking for signs of disbelief. The skin of his face was dry, beardless, shrunken on his delicate skull. "It's romantic," she said. "Like a movie."

"Better than moobie." But her little movement had thrown him off, he evaded the consequences of his own tale. "So . . . I met Estrella."

"In the bathroom?"

"Ah-ha! No. She stays a while, we got acquainted."

It was on the end of Sabrina's tongue to ask what a girl of eighteen was doing staying alone in a hotel, but that did not seem discreet. Something tired, disillusioned, and sympathetic in her said that if poor old Lizardo had got taken in by a whore, at least he was getting some excitement and some love. So she said only, "It really *is* romantic, Lizardo. When did all this happen?"

"Fibe, six mont's ago. Christmas."

She leaned to look again at the picture. The iron beak and imperial stare of General MacArthur were focused in upon the girl and her escort from every side. Most of the MacArthur pictures were from the years of the war and the surrender, and the newsprint was yellowed under the protecting glass. The picture of the girl was at least as yellow as the yellowest of the general.

Pity moved the heart in her breast like a disturbed toad. Not daring to look at him, she said, "She's terribly pretty, Lizardo. You're lucky." When she could stare at the photograph no longer she turned on him, gay again, and said, "It seems like old times to be down here. Remember when you used to sing me your songs? Sing me one now. Is my contraband booze here? Let's have a drink and you sing me your song about General MacArthur. Have you got time? Will your girl wait?"

"Oh, yes." He stood before her in his libertine's clothing and looked at her with concern. "All these drinks not good por you."

"What *is* good for you? Come on."

"You pilling okay now?"

"I'm feeling divine."

"I t'ink you got some trouble."

"I think so too. Lizardo, darling, come on and sing me a song to cure my woe. But give me a drink first, please."

He brought a bottle from his closet, went to the basement refrigerator for ice, and brought her a drink. He did not take one himself; she had never seen him take one. "What you do?" he said as he handed it to her.

"Do?"

"You stay here, go back to Pasadena, what?"

"Ah, if I knew the answer to that one!" But feeling what a bleak look she gave him, she sipped her drink and said brightly, "Actually there are a million things to do. Tomorrow maybe I'll go to the road races with Oliver. Then maybe I'll go abroad or get a job. Or enter a nunnery. Or devote myself to social work and take sewing and deodorant soap to delinquent girls at the county jail. Or maybe I'll build a house at Carmel and cover my hollow heart with a green copper roof and warm it with radiant heat and furnish it with Finn Juhl chairs and hang Weston photographs of Point Lobos on its grasscloth walls and peek out at the world from under a twelve-foot overhang. That would be in the family tradition, at least. And I could always ask friends down. What would *you* think I ought to do?"

His worry was all over his face as he took the guitar from the wall. He shook his head, and while he tuned he watched her askance across the varnished curve of the guitar. Sabrina, prickling with irritable energy, her teeth on edge, wandered to the desk and picked up a magazine and put it down again, throwing a brilliant, encouraging smile back at Lizardo. "I've tried to remember that MacArthur song a dozen times. It's a great song. This time I'm going to write it down and get it right."

She pulled open the desk drawer to look for pencil and paper. Staring up at her was a flat black automatic. With one knee up, his foot on a chair, the guitar across his body, Lizardo leaned looking as if he might cry.

"Well my goodness!" she said. "Are you scared of burglars?"

His eyes would look everywhere but at her. They wound up fixed on the ceiling, as if they found there the pure tone his fingers were trying to pick out of a string. He bleated, "I hab enemies!"

Quietly Sabrina shoved the drawer shut. Without paper or pencil she went back and sat in the carved walnut chair.

"It is por protection," Lizardo said.

"Of course. I didn't mean to rummage your things. Forgive me."

For a few seconds longer he plinked and tuned. Then he took his foot off the chair and straightened to attention and cleared his throat. Sabrina filled her mouth with cold, hardly diluted bourbon. Smiling a pleading smile, Lizardo strummed an entry that was martial and severe, and at her nod, began to sing.

"Oh, General MacArt'ur, he say, 'I come back to Pilipines,
I come back to Pilipines,
I come back to Pilipines.'
General MacArt'ur, he say, 'I come back to Pilipines,
I go now, but I return.' "

Lower and sadder than she had been at any time that day, Sabrina sat listening, applauding with her eyes and her smile and thinking of the dream girl cut out of a newspaper fifteen years or more ago, and the enemies, imagined for no conceivable reason except to ring the too-safe refuge with dangers and light the drab life with melodrama. She listened to the guitar style, flamboyant but not very precise, and looked at the pictures of the Hero, the General, Captain Jinks of the Horse Marines, and she thought, You poor old devil, you too! Her heart moved again in her breast, sluggish and heavy, and when Lizardo finished she saluted him with a smile that felt as stretched and unreal as the painted smile on a balloon.

She left word with her mother that she would not be at home for dinner. Some time—not long—she spent in a bar on El Camino. When the incoming dinner crowds drove her out, she turned as if in obedience to an accepted penance up toward the Skyline. Steadily, with her eyes and mind wide open, she cruised between alternating stretches of subdivisions and heath until she saw approaching the mouth of the blind road. Her foot did not ease on the throttle, the anticipated shudder did not come. The lane opened briefly and passed, no more than a littered dirt road ordained shortly, with its history of furtive loves, shabby quarrels, and desperate men hooking hoses to the exhaust pipes of cars, to be graded down and built over by the oncoming tracts. She could not persuade herself that anything vital to her own life had gone on there. And yet how much like turning homeward from a cemetery after a funeral.

Closer in toward the City was a place she had loved since childhood, a gray farm anchored like a lighthouse on the sea cliffs, with a pond behind it to mirror the sky and the buildings and the windbreak of cypresses. This too, she supposed, was doomed—would be gone by now if whoever owned it had not loved it and hung on. She pulled off the highway at the turn and shut off the engine and sat looking, as nearly blank in mind as if she had been on the edge of sleep.

The sun was setting in the offshore fogbank. She sat unmoving, not taking her eyes off darkening sea and darkening sky until land and sea and sky had dissolved together in dusk, and lights that she had not seen born winked all along the curve of shore. Eventually she started the engine again and drove on. She had a sensation as if the car were the little boat of a Ouija board, pushed by fingers or forces, it didn't matter, but pushed; and she herself helpless but unattached, until through traffic lights and unfamiliar new suburbs she reached what she was headed for, and her right tire rubbed the curb of a dead-end street in Stonestown.

Now torpor and indifference were taken away like a bandage that had bound in and deadened pain. She watched like a wolf from the dark, greedy for every sign, every detail, of the way he lived. For she had taken it in completely that this security was what he feared to lose. His two-story stucco shouldered its neighbors for room on the narrow lot, everything in it incorrigibly, predictably, upper-middle. House, lot, neighborhood, flowerbeds, patch of lawn, even the aralias in tubs on each side of the blue door, could have been duplicated two thousand times in the western subdivisions. House built ten years ago to sell at $27,500. Neighborhood carefully restricted until discriminatory clauses in deeds were invalidated by the Supreme Court; since then, zoned by quiet neighborhood consensus and realtors' precautions.

She lighted a cigarette, and at once, because the glow showed her ambiguous image brooding in the windshield, jerked her hand down into the dark seat. Except for her own car and two others, the street was clear. All up the hills, toward the darkness of the Sutro Forest, lights bloomed in lines and circles and crescents. The wind sliced into the car with a night-time edge.

What were they doing in that house, he and his possessive wife and his three probably silly and unattractive daughters? In God's name, why should *she* sit out in the dark as furtive as a thief while they inside owned him completely? What were they doing—playing cards, records, radio? Reading? Doing crossword puzzles? Or glued to television like forty million other idiots?

If she chose to, she could walk up to that door and push the button, and, whoever answered, demand to see him. Before them all she could force a show-down. In three minutes she could crack that secure middle-class home like a walnut. Whatever else she was, she was a power for destruction. Remembering Bernard's voice shushing her on the telephone, proposing secrecy, hypocrisy, evasion, she thought, He's afraid of me, and he's right.

Then she froze. His door let a slash of light down the front steps. She saw him plain in the opening, tall and bare-headed in a short-sleeved sport shirt. He seemed to sniff the air, he looked at the sky and then casually at Sabrina's car. Did he recognize it? Could he see her? Had he come out to signal her? She eased toward the far side of the seat, gradually turning her face, and saw him put a letter under the flap of the mailbox to be collected by tomorrow's postman. To her? But then he wouldn't leave it around for everyone to see.

Once more—keenly?—he looked across at her car. She half lifted her hand to beckon, but he had already turned. The slab of light narrowed and vanished across the steps, leaving only the diffused entrance light on the aralias.

With her heart thundering in her ears she opened the door and stepped out. Somewhere two radios or television sets were antiphonally discordant. Sauntering, she went around the eye of the dead-end street and back down his side. Her eyes pried at the edges of the windows where the drapes did not quite close.

Ring his bell? Present him an outright challenge to the choice he had made? For he had made it, not she. The acknowledgment left her eyes so hot she felt they must glow in the dark. She swung a blind look at the lights scattered all above her on the hills. She had thrown herself at his head and he had ducked. It was unthinkable that she would be that shameless again, but even if she were, he wouldn't come on her terms. He would have his cake and eat it too, or he would go without his cake. Behind his passion and his warmth, behind the deference and admiration he showed her, behind the hard kisses and the soft words, was the immovable fact of his previous commitment, which he would not break.

She could burn his house down, shake or break his marriage, but she would get out of it nothing but revenge—surely nothing of what she had hoped to fill her life with. She went on past his walk.

A few houses down, a door opened. Sabrina controlled an impulse to get away. Girls' voices, the stomp of a rock-and-roll record, people shouting. Then a girl in toreador pants and pony tail ran down the walk. Passing Sabrina, she glanced up, and Sabrina saw a young face still lighted by what she had left—dark, inquiring eyes, heavy brows, a face slightly chubby, teeth that showed in an even, curious half smile. The eyes that looked at Sabrina would have looked at anyone else with the same interest, and forgotten with equal promptness anyone they encountered. Just passing, she slowed toward dignity, and then her sneakers were pattering again. Sabrina watched. Of course. Up Bernard's walk, slamming through Bernard's door. One of his daughters, secure, contented, full of thirteen-year-old excitements, fond of Daddy, snuggly and affectionate and thoughtless. She thought of herself at thirteen, and heard down some corridor of her mind the receding jingle of bells on the squaw boots that had first taught her she was female, mysterious, and to be loved.

Instead of that, she lurked outside the door of her reluctant lover, a vampire driven by an ancient incurable ferocity. How might she look to anyone inside there, to that chubby innocent with the eyes like a painting of Ruth or Naomi?

"My God," she whispered, "is this *me?*"

In a direct abrupt angle she crossed the street, slid into the car, started the motor, circled the turnaround, crept on past his house as slowly as the car would move. She did not pretend to herself that she would ever come back, or that he would come to her. Whatever possibility had been there she was relinquishing. But that could not blind her to the amount of hope she was leaving behind her. She watched his house until even by craning she could no longer see it, and the breaking of contact was as reluctant as the last touch of fingers in good-by.

CHAPTER 13

THEIR WAITER was a man with a soft, corrupt face and a voice like a shy girl's. The two boys at the corner table back of Sabrina's kept arguing about him. One was positive he was a castrato, the other thought he was a flit. They bellowed joyfully into the Wagon Wheel's din, a yard behind Sabrina's back.

"I don't *give* a damn, you understand," said the advocate of the castrato theory. "It's nothing to *me*. But I can tell the difference between the *wrong* hormones and no hormones at all. Look at his face—no beard, skin like a woman. And a choir-boy voice."

"The voice doesn't prove anything," Flit said.

"The hell it doesn't."

"What?"

"The hell it doesn't."

"The hell it does."

"The hell it doesn't. How do you account for it, then?"

"You can be born with funny vocal chords. Maybe he's a male alto, or a counter tenor, or something."

"What?"

"Maybe he's a counter tenor!"

Castrato groaned. Into their low-ceiling corner the incomparable clatter of two hundred diners crashed and pounded. "Oh, man," Castrato said as if in pain. "Counter tenor, he says. Under-the-counter soprano, you mean. Man, you don't know anything. This guy's *deprived*."

The babble broke and drowned them out. "Isn't it nice," Sabrina said, forming each syllable for lip-reading.

"Mmmm?" Oliver had been looking down at the lighter in his fingers. His forehead wrinkled as his eyes came up in question. His cigarette hung steady in the very middle of his lips.

"Other people's conversation."

He looked uncomprehending, and she gave him one of the dying-fish faces she was accustomed to draw in the margins of letters. But her depression was only too real. Too hard a day: an early start, a hard, fast drive over, too many martinis before lunch, a hot and blistering afternoon, too much talk, too many people, too much dust. The only good hour of the whole day had been lunch at Addie McAllister's ranch. She had wandered outside with her barbecued-beef sandwich in her hand and found a calf that had sucked her fingers. But that was only an interlude. Most of it had been as stupid as this overheard conversation in a corner thick with cigarette smoke and the reek from the charcoal broilers. She felt drained, dried out, coated with an ugly film, and she was hot enough to die.

"I wonder how many places like this there are in the United States?" she said. "Places that smell and taste and sound exactly alike, where they anaesthetize your taste with alcohol and then throw steak and french fries at you? And where you're not at home unless you're loud."

From two feet away he looked into her eyes. "I'm sorry," he said. "There wasn't much choice if we wanted to eat on this side. This is the best place in Carson."

He looked almost offended, as if she were blaming him unjustly for the institution of the charcoal-broiled top sirloin. "Oh, don't mind me," she said. "It's just that I've had about all the heat and noise I can take."

His eyes were quick and judging, and at once his hand was in the air, his fingers snapping for the waiter. It occurred to her that he was being considerate; he could be a brother if he tried. He said, "Are you all right? Would you feel better waiting outside? This is going to take a minute."

"Maybe I will go out." He rose when she did, watching her, perhaps to see if she would fall down. She was not so sure herself that she would make it, the room spun so, layered with smoke and detonating with sound. The boys in the corner stopped talking to watch her leave, and she dropped on their brown, flat-topped, insolently healthy heads a look that should have scalded the hair off them. She felt like crying at them, You brash cubs, sometime you'll find out every poor maimed unfortunate in the world isn't there just to joke about. Why not a little pity, why not a little decent silence?

The tables were packed so close she had to wedge through. From the bar, where people were lined up two deep waiting, someone called, but she waved blindly and went on. The headwaiter by the door creased his underworld face at her, and then the hot air of the street flooded around her and she stood breathing quickly against a pole. Second by second the smoke and hysteria and the nauseated feeling of pollution evaporated away. She filled her lungs many times; she looked around.

Carson City's main street was surprisingly quiet after the clamor inside. The sun had been behind the Sierra for some time, and the light, though not the air, was cool. Eastward and southward across the tops of buildings she saw lion-colored mountains still in sunlight. The wind that came rattling the leaves from cottonwood to cottonwood down the short side street was warm, dry, faintly scented with sage and even more faintly with something rarer—the pines on the mountains.

Oliver came out and stood at her side. "Feeling better?"

"Much better, thanks."

"I thought you were going to conk out."

"I'm all right now."

"Not a very successful day."

"You won two hundred dollars."

"I mean for you."

Though she had learned long ago to be alert for the tone of irony in his voice, she did not hear it now. He seemed honestly concerned; he had actually proposed the races as therapy. She said, "It wasn't your fault I wasn't up to it."

"No disasters."

"No," she said. "Not enough blood."

158

They walked through a blast of barbecue smoke to the parking lot. Three quarters of the cars in it were Porsches, Mercedes', Austin Healeys, Jaguars, MG's, Triumphs, Lancias. Oliver pointed to a squat gray racer as if he expected her to say something. When she turned a blank face he was astonished. "Reventlow's Scarab," he said. "The winnah. You weren't paying much attention."

"I was never a very good spectator."

When he opened the door of the white Mercedes he had to brush and blow at the drift of cottonwood fluff that had gathered in the seats. The corners of the lot were white with windrowed cotton. Sabrina got in and closed her eyes. She heard the door shut solidly, heard Oliver walk around, felt the car lean with his weight. The key clinked in the ignition. She rolled her head sideward and looked and saw Oliver, in his plaid cap, pulling out of the boot the hooded jacket she had worn coming over.

"No thanks," she said. "I'd rather blow."

She lay back, looking up into the big cottonwood that spread from the lot beyond. The breeze was rattling up there, and she looked into thousands of heart-shaped, trembling leaves that glinted like light dry metal and pattered like a shower of rain. From all through the tree, from the split clusters of bolls, seed-fluff streamed off across a sky as blue as a Dutch tile. When Oliver reached to turn the key she laid a hand on his wrist. "Wait. Let's sit a minute."

"We'll get home about two as it is."

"Just for a minute. I like the sound of the leaves."

He turned his back half against the door so that he could watch her. After perhaps two minutes while she sat with closed eyes he said, "Mother told me Burke came up the other night."

She concentrated on the lonely and musical sounds of the tree. From a distance she said, "The news does get around."

"You didn't make it up, I gather."

She opened her eyes and came back. "Oh   you know. He thinks he's furious at me but I wonder if he really cares. I'm only a postscript on his life. He's married to a medical practice."

"I wonder."

"Don't wonder. He is."

"Even if he is."

"Even if he is, what?"

"Even if he is, make it up."

"Just like that."

"Just like that."

"Suppose he wouldn't?"

"He would."

She captured a filament of cotton, lighter almost than the air that carried it, and tried to lay it on her palm, and when it wouldn't stay she blew it over the side of the car. "I don't know," she said. "Maybe he would. What about Bernard?"

He was doodling the gearshift stick around through four positions, and while she waited for him to answer he began to whistle "Siboney" through his teeth. The stick moved jerkily in the parody of a rumba step. His hazel eyes glinted sideways.

She took his meaning, but the momentary angry defensiveness that came bursting up toward speech stopped short of words. For his contempt was not too different from the feelings she herself had had the previous evening, while she prowled Bernard's middle-class street hunting the ghost of ecstasy behind his blue door. Blue doors in New Mexico, she remembered, were supposed to keep witches away. Well.

Oliver said, "Your disease isn't so uncommon there's no known cure. It'll cure itself if you'll let it."

Her lips thrust out at him. "Relax and enjoy it?"

Her brother's exclamation was almost a grunt. "Wear it out," he said, "then go back. If I know Burke, he'll take you. He'd think he had to keep you on a short lead, and he'd get pretty prissy, I would guess, but he'd take you, partly because he thinks you're Bewitching Womanhood on a patty shell and partly because he knows damned well how much you've meant to that fancy practice of his. The other business is no good. If you will pardon my crude terms, Barney's a weak sister. He couldn't hold you three weeks. He's nothing—I don't know how in hell you came to pick him in the first place. Wear it out and get over it. These things happen. There's no reason they have to last."

"Unless you can't shake them, or unless they're only symptoms of something else."

"Oh, for Christ's sake."

While she sat sullenly, sunk in the bucket seat, he turned thickly behind the wheel and said, "You *like* this God-damned Madame Bovary act. Come off it. And let me tell you something else. You're a little too noticeable to go around making a spectacle of your blasted life."

"Isn't that quaint, that was a point Bernard made."

"Then he's got more judgment than I gave him credit for."

"It's the worst thing I know about him. He's afraid."

Just for a moment he squinted, guessing. "Balls," he said. He turned the key and the motor chuckled. But before he could drop his hand to the shift stick she was out of the car. He regarded her grimly.

"Now you're sore. Good God, Sabrina, you act fifteen years old. Get in and let's go home."

"I'm not going back yet."

She turned her face upward to the myriad tremble and glitter of leaves, the silent snow of fluff. With a gesture as positive as unleashing a dog she let her mind escape his insistence and run loose. Without taking her eyes off the stir and shimmer of the tree she said, "Oliver, did you ever think of buying a ranch? Raising cattle?"

He barked out a one-syllable laugh. The moment she looked down he began ludicrously and savagely to bounce up and down, tossing imaginary flowers to both sides, a two-hundred-and-ten-pound Ophelia. Here's pansies, that's for thoughts.

"Seriously," she said.

"Oh, *seriously*. Well, seriously, no. Taxwise it has advantages—guaranteed and fully chargeable losses. Likewise Nevada has a pleasant absence of state income tax. As a way of life, however, I mean as a way of finding something *positive* to do in the world, no. If you remember, I am tied to certain properties in Hillsborough and Woodside." He barked again. "Why? That the latest project?"

"I was just thinking how lucky pioneer women were. I wish Burke had been driving a covered wagon when I met him, and I'd had to clear away the rattlesnakes to build a cabin, and wash clothes every

Monday in a boiler set on a greasewood fire, and make soap out of ashes and bacon fat, and stand off Paiutes with a Sharps rifle."

She said it principally to get a rise out of him, and yet there was a streak of truth in the fantasy. Preposterous as it was, she had seen herself in calico at that cabin door. Oliver was shaking his head slowly back and forth.

"Can you imagine me in Addie McAllister's shoes?" she said. "Boots, rather? Out in the corral with the men at roundup time stabbing steers with hypodermics and notching ears and clipping horns and branding—even castrating? I've seen her."

His morose eyes never left her face. "No," he said.

She paid no attention. "Burke could come up on week ends and for his vacations. In the fall the cottonwoods would be all yellow and in spring there'd be pussywillows and in winter we could run up to the Snow Bowl or Squaw Valley. And in summer you could bring all your fifty children to ride the horses and catch pollywogs in the irrigation ditches. And I could have a million dogs. You know the first thing I did when Burke and I were married? I got a dog, just because Mother would never let me have one. Do you know my dog Fat Boy? I wish he was here now."

"So do I," Oliver said. "I'd have him bite you. Where does it get you to wallow around in all these daydreams?"

"Somebody's got to raise the steaks for the nine million charcoal-broil steak houses in the United States."

"Have you forgotten all the people you know who set out to live the healthy outdoor life here or down in the Santa Ynez or somewhere? The few who make it go grew up on ranches in the first place. The rest go to shrinkers twice a week or have already taken their overdose of sleeping pills. Cattle ranches are a symptom, not a cure." He caught her smiling at his violence, and made a disgusted *pft!* with his mouth. "You pernicious hag, get in, so we can get started."

"I told you, I'm not going back."

His eyes cocked up at her from under bushy brows; his face went through several expressions and settled on one of polite interest. "So what'll you do?"

"Maybe stay here for a while."

"Here? In Carson?"

"Somewhere around here. I like the way the trees sound."

"That's fine. What do I tell Mother?"

"Do you have to tell her anything?"

"Cut it out. Of course I'll have to tell her something. She'll ask. She's so convinced that the dissolute Hutchens strain is breaking out in you that she'll ask in fear and trembling."

"All right. Tell her I stayed over with Addie to learn cattle ranching. Or tell I went into the desert to purify my soul. Can't you see the headlines in 1970? Tonopah Mystery Woman Believed Lost Socialite. A woman who lived for ten years in a Tonopah hotel room may be socially prominent Mrs. Burke Castro, wife of a Pasadena physician, Tonopah police said today. Mrs. Castro disappeared from a parking lot in Carson City on June 21, 1960, after an argument with her brother, wealthy playboy Oliver Hutchens of Hillsborough. Contacted at his mother's Hillsborough estate, Mr. Hutchens said . . . what *did* you say?"

"Choose any four-letter word."

A party came out and crowded into two cars and pulled away. The cottonwoods pattered overhead, the breeze was almost cool. She thought that if she could find some place to walk, the half-stupefied headache she had carried out of the restaurant would go away. She had no heart for fencing with Oliver, and less for listening to his advice. She wanted contact with clean things, wind and trees, sagebrush, desert, stars. And no people.

Eventually Oliver accepted the fact that she was not going. "Got money?"

"Enough. And credit cards."

He swung his sunglasses by the earpiece. His head bristled with virile short hair. At seventy he would have it as thick as ever; he would be a white-haired, pink-faced old man dangerous to waitresses and his younger friends' wives. These things happen; there's no reason they have to last. He said, "Let me ask you straight, are you responsible? Sober? In your right mind?"

"Of course."

"How long do you expect to stay?"

"I don't know. Until I think things out."

"Want me to stay over and drive you back tomorrow?"

"Oh, Oliver, let up! I'm not staying over to meet Bernard, so you can't embarrass me that way. Stay if you want to, but I'd rather be alone."

"So," he said, and, straightening, laid his palm on the gear shift knob. "Well, *coraggio*. I'll tell Mother you're at Addie's. You might check in there if you decide to stay more than ten years. There might be messages." She stepped aside as he cramped the car around, and from his angled position he said, "Don't get lost."

"Ah, wouldn't I like to!"

He did not shoot forward as she expected. His face was scowly. "Sister mine, I wonder if I ought to leave you?"

"Go on, your chivalry is showing. I'll be all right."

"Where'll you stay?"

"I'll find somewhere."

"How'll you get home? Plane?"

"Or rent a Hertz car."

"So," he said again. "Well, whatever it is, find it." He laughed. "Or lose it." He burst away, bounced at the driveway entrance, shifted with a *whurt! whurroo!* and was gone.

At once Sabrina walked around the Wagon Wheel and across the highway and down a side street that shortly dwindled away into desert. Out ahead to the left she saw U.S. 50 cutting eastward toward the broken country where the Carson River made a belt of trees. Ahead to the right was the high desert range she had seen over the roofs; she thought she could see the Indian School at its foot, miles away over a sloping patchwork of alfalfa fields and pastures. But she bore away from the cultivated land, heading into the scabby flats straight eastward, parallel with U.S. 50. As a gauge of how much was left of afternoon she watched the shadow of the Sierra that crept up the face of the eastern range.

In the flat heels she had worn for the races she found the walking easy enough, but she was offended by the scattered refuse. Every clump of sage or rabbitbrush wore flags of Kleenex, around every stalk was folded newspaper or waxed bread wrappers. Glass was everywhere, and bullet-plugged cans, broken toys, cartons, dried and curling shoes, crockery. Instead of being gradually engulfed in its own rising rubbish, as ancient cities had been, Carson City tossed its litter out and let it blow, so that archeologists of the far future would find the town's life spread in a thin geological horizon across miles of valley.

The breeze puffed at her back, flowing down from the cooling mountains. She tested the air for unpleasant odors and smelled only dust and sage. Very quickly the desert took the pollution out of the garbage people flung across it. Not even carrion retained its stench long. But it was all ugly, especially the cans, one of the ugliest shapes of human waste. Only glass, which lasted forever, might ultimately acquire beauty on that dumpheap. Over many years it acquired a delicate ultraviolet tint. Remembering Addie McAllister's mantel with its row of those relics, Sabrina found herself examining the rubbish as she picked her way through it, hoping for the sight of an unbroken flask or medicine vial with the lilac of fifty years of sun in it. She would have taken such a find as an omen.

The rising line of shadow had overflowed the broken country along the river, as well as the shoulder of the southeastern range. North of her was an irregular noise of speeding cars. Walking with her eyes on the rosy spurs of rock that were still in sun, she thought, Maybe I *should* go out in the desert somewhere. What if I just kept on walking? Maybe Manitou or somebody would send me a vision and tell me my secret name, out in the middle of some dead sea bottom with my tongue leather in my mouth and my skin burned black and the sky like tin, and all around a horizon like the backbones of dinosaurs. Maybe suffering and purging would bring an inward look so profound that ever afterward a person would be unshakable. Maybe then I'd know what I should do, and be able to do it.

She went on between clumps of sage, down curving channels of ash-like earth. The sun on the peaks had shrunk till it was on only one face of rock, and then between the time when she lifted a foot and the time when she brought it down, the peak went dun. While she counted one, the light that had been dammed there went a hundred and eighty-six thousand miles into space, on its way to make a sunrise on some other planet.

Out of breath, she paused. The pounding in her temples, the dilated look of everything, the grayness that seemed instantly to flood the world when that candle peak went out, her recollection of the uneven course she had pursued out from town, made her realize that she had been quite drunk, and was still far from steady. Never mind: the desert would purify her as it purified everything.

She was perhaps a mile and a half out on the flats, excruciatingly alone, a sparrow whose fall might or might not be noted. Above her the sky was full of light, though the earth lay now in its own shadow. On the other side of the Sierra the last sunset on the continent was in progress. How strange and sad to be a living, feeling thing!

She heard the whispering hum of cars from the highway. The wind that in the parking lot had brought to her nostrils a touch of coolness and peace touched them again with the warm, unmistakable scent of pines that it had kept intact across all that aromatic reach of sage.

Like a hope? Eager for portents, she grasped at the possibility that recommended itself to her like a patent medicine. Tired? Run-down? Out of joint with your world? Scared that the fault is really in you, not in others? Then simplify. Find a world you can quit being afraid of. Try fresh air, work, the company of animals less troubling than twentieth-century human beings. Head for the desert or the woods.

Briefly, experimentally, she saw herself walking a night road with someone, their footsteps soft in dust, the ranch house windows lighted, the barns dark, the night wind stirring and rattling the leaves, and beyond them, enclosing it all, the far, soft, hollow roar of the mountains.

Then she saw whom she was walking with, and the image cracked like cracking glass. Where on earth was her pride? She said aloud, "Bernard, damn you, I will pick you off me like a burr! I must!"

Abruptly there were tears on her face. She sat down with a moan, and leaning back on her braced palms among the runty forest of sage, she stared blindly at the sky. For a long time she sat without moving. The tears stopped, her cheeks dried. A small boatlike cloud coasting over the southeastern range went red, then pink, then mauve, then gray. The greenish sky deepened, the sage plain filled with shadows that between the dark clumps became almost as dark as the sage itself.

166

There was a soft sound of wind, like a sigh: another day endured and survived.

Purify me, she said to the shadowed desert. Tell me the name to go by. Tell me what to do, and teach me how to do it with a whole heart.

She tuned her ear to the stealthy night wind. Much of the day's heat had already radiated away; the air was cool. A few stars had revealed themselves brighter than the sky they were set in. This was the hour, she remembered, when sidewinders came out of the sand and the desert's nocturnal life began to stir. Her ears strained against silence, whispers, rustlings.

Carefully she leaned forward and rubbed her hands, pebbled with indented gravel. Beside her her handbag was a swimming paleness. She grasped it and rose, bringing into view the wider darkness and the uneven line where earth fitted sky. Only then, up to her waist in sagebrush, glaring into shadows, did she comprehend what a figure she made—a woman in a cotton print dress, clutching a white summer handbag, all alone a mile or two out in the scraggy desert, with tears dried on her face and her ears alert for the sandy slither, the small dry coilings, of danger.

Lashing her fear with irony, she assured herself that it must happen often. All the time, distracted women must wander away from gambling joints, divorce courts, bars, motels where they lived with one man while divorcing another, and jounce and stumble ridiculously, in angry or lamentable tears, out into the wilderness, to be rescued later, hysterical and panic-stricken, by bored lovers, deputies, posses of excitement-hunting loafers. Whatever the desert might offer a savage living out his ritual obligations, it didn't offer much to modern woman. The contents of her bag recommended themselves to her notice: a partial pack of cigarettes, a compact and lipstick, a broken roll of Lifesavers, a crumpled handkerchief, a purse, keys to the car she didn't have with her, a gas card, a restaurant credit card. Not exactly what the well-equipped hermit should take along.

To think of doing anything alone, anything whatever, was preposterous. She turned, and the neon halo of Carson City bloomed against the wall of the Sierra like the lights of rescuers. Through wind-moved trees, or what she imagined were trees, the town's lights flickered and shook.

She started picking her way—most carefully, for she had not entirely shed her fear—among the gnarly clumps, the glass-and-can-strewn ground. Hunt her soul in solitude? There was no one she less liked to be alone with than herself. Search her soul for answers? There was no more answer in her than there was in an echo. She gave back nothing but questions. Sneaking from the image of herself self-exposed on the dreary flat, she groped toward the lights of Carson, and when she paused, hunting a passage among the shadows or listening to a frightening sound, she heard the traveler wind, the growing and then diminishing of cars on the highway, the troubling sounds of her own difficult shamed life: the breathing, the beating of the heart.

Whatever she needed, it was not herself. She did not like herself. She needed someone with whom to keep in touch, someone to comfort her when she whimpered and reassure her when she was scared. And that had to be, could only be, Burke.

Hunting a way to come into town unnoticed, she found herself at the edge of the State Capitol grounds. People were strolling there, sitting on benches; she fitted herself among them and took her unnoticed place. There was an air upon the proprietary couples of comfortable relaxation after a day's work. They spoke in low voices, their laughter was gentle. They seemed another race from the tourists in the bars and cafés and gambling joints along the highway.

For a time, shoes in hand and the lawn soft-prickling under her stockinged feet, she watched a boy hunting nightcrawlers with a flashlight, pushing a can ahead of him, probing his light among the grass blades for the telltale reddish shine. Around her among the smells of cooling night under the rattle of cottonwood leaves the slow couples moved. She would have liked to live and belong and take part in this town—not the hoked-up tourist town, but the working town, the cattle-raising, alfalfa-growing, politics-arguing, intimate, practical, Biggest Little Capital on Earth.

Was that so insane as Oliver said it was? Was that impulse to find a healthy world and make herself a place in it only another of the emotional explosions that had begun in Oaxaca and left her in bits? Or was it the beginning of reconciliation and wisdom? She had hated her un-rewarding life; here was an alternative, possibly even a way to lead Burke out of that highly paid attentiveness he enslaved himself to. She could heal the healer. What you did conditioned what you were; if you did trivial things, you were trivial; nothing, you were nothing. The Wolcott tradition might tell her to collect sun-tinted bottles, but she wanted more. There was too much life in her to let it be frittered away. Made to enhance life, Burke had told her long ago. Here might be a way.

In the soft dark, full of a growing excitement and triumph, she said with her lips but not her voice, It all changed, it all started to go right, one night when I was up in Carson and fell in love with the sound of cottonwood trees.

There was a drugstore in the next block. Standing at the cashier's desk between a counter of cheap bright goods and a bank of slot machines, she changed a dollar into quarters and dimes. As she turned away, to test her luck she dropped a dime into one of the slot machines and pulled the handle. The wheels whirred, clicked: cherry. Spun, clicked: cherry. Spun, clicked: bar. Into the cup, with a tinny clink, the machine spit four dimes.

An omen. Sabrina scooped them out and slid into the telephone booth. One of the dimes revived the telephone into a hum, and she dialed operator. When the voice came she shoved the hinged door shut with her knee, enclosing and illuminating herself, and lifting her mouth close against the black cone she called collect. The intricate system made its heard connections, voices passed on data. Then the number answered not in Robert's or Annie's voice, but in Burke's own.

"Hello!" she said. "Hello!" The operator cut in and cut out again. Then they were alone on the line. "Hello, Burke?" she said, and had to clear her husky throat. "It's Sabrina."

"Yes," he said, "I know."

"I thought we ought to . . . talk things over."

"I'm surprised you think there's anything to talk over."

"At least I can say that I'm miserably sorry."

"Yes," he said. "That's what you said the other night."

"It's true! It was true the other night and it's true now."

"I'm glad to know it," Burke said, "but does being sorry help?"

"I hoped it might help a little."

"Maybe it does, a little. Maybe we need something that helps a lot." Stalemate, so soon. He was a stone. Once he had said to her, joking, that he couldn't get mad but he could certainly hold a grudge. Already the mood of penitential optimism that she had brought to the booth was heating up toward hostility and self-justification, and that was not what she had wanted or intended. She could imagine his head bent down as he listened politely and unforgivingly to her humbling of herself. Bitterly she cried into the mouthpiece, "This time *I'm* calling *you*. What do you want me to do, get down on my knees?"

It was a moment before he answered. She thought she heard a dry little cough of a laugh. "I doubt that that would help either," Burke said. "I tried it. Remember?"

"Ah!" Sabrina said. "Ah, that's dirty!" The booth was so airless that she kicked at the hinged door and kicked herself into darkness. Sitting in the bluish radiance from the drugstore she said urgently, "Darling, please let's not quarrel! Can't we try to be reasonable people? I take all the blame, I'm crawling. It's all over, I've given him up totally, I'm asking you to forgive me. Can you?"

She hung upon the lengthening, stubborn silence. "I don't know," he said.

"Oh, please! Because if you can I've got an idea for us."

"Do we need an idea?"

"Doesn't it seem to you we do?"

"Ideas sound about as useful as feeling sorry. You can't smash . . . smash everything and then smash it again and then expect to kiss it better."

Now for the first time she heard the quaver of anger in his voice, the way he swallowed a word to get his breath, and she gripped the receiver as if it were the receptacle of all her own anguish. She said to herself, This is how you decided, forget what it costs, and cried into the listening, unsympathetic wire, "But darling, if we both tried! You said you wanted us to get past it. So do I. I want us to get a ranch up here, like Addie McAllister's, and get back to some healthy kind of life. I could be of some use, I could *do* something! And you could come up week ends, or oftener if you'd turn over more patients to the others, and ride and relax and get over all that strain. Maybe if you liked it you'd want to give up your practice down there and move up here permanently. I should think you'd want to heal people worth healing instead of all those . . . people such as I've been . . . Darling?"

She was talking to silence; for a second she was afraid he had hung up. Then she heard his breathing. Without inflection he said, "It might be a good idea for you. Why don't you go ahead?"

"For us?"

"For you," Burke said. "Not for me."

"Oh, darling, why not?"

The connection was very good; she could distinctly hear every breath he drew. "You want to know?" he said in a quacking voice.

Sabrina moved her knee, and the light came dingily on in the booth. She saw her own face uptilted to the mouthpiece, furiously listening like someone caught at a keyhole, and though she could not see the lips move, she heard the stiff words. "Say it."

"Because when I left the other night I was through," Burke said. "After that, how could I ever trust you again? How do I know what you're doing in Carson right now? How do I know you're not snug in some motel?"

Strangling, Sabrina kicked the door: the light went out and left her in the cold radiance of diffused mercury vapor. Whispering, she said, "I'm not. I've talked to him once, on the phone, since I saw you. He wanted me to go to Carmel with him and I wouldn't. It's over. And that's the truth."

"Maybe," he said. "How would I know?"

"Darling . . ."

"You do anything you want," Burke said in a high tight voice. "I'm out of it."

"I knew you were heartless," she said, still whispering. "I knew you were as cold as a lizard. But I never knew that if I came on my knees you would care so little that you would . . ." A high shelf of blue boxes of Kleenex outside the booth burned for a moment as yellow as fog lights and then came fading back to blue. "When you were on your knees," she said, "I hurt you because I had to, because I'd lied and I couldn't go on lying. But when I'm on mine you take your revenge as cold as ice."

She reached to hang up, and from a foot away the receiver said, "Sabrina!" She kept the receiver hanging over its hook. "Sabrina!" it said. She dropped it in its holder.

The booth light somehow was on again. She pushed through the door to avoid it and the sight of her own reflection. Her hands were shaking; she braced them against a counter, hesitating in the strange, somnambulistic unreality of mercury-vapor blue.

A girl with loaflike buttocks crammed into flimsy slacks was hanging on the handle of a twenty-five-cent slot machine, watching while the bands spun and stopped. "Pfffft!" She let the handle bang up and said to the girl behind the counter, "Jeez, I should have stuck with the one at the Western. That paid *once* in a while."

"This is ripe," the clerk said. "It's hardly paid all day."

They stopped talking as Sabrina came between them with the remnants of her change in her hand. As she might have dropped a scrap of paper in a wastebasket, she dropped a quarter into the machine and pulled the handle. She heard it whirring behind her as she walked on. When she was halfway to the door it clicked, after two steps it clicked again, after another it clicked a third time. The fat girl bleated and the jackpot crashed.

Sabrina looked back from the doorway. Coins were still rolling; the fat girl was on her knees, the clerk with a look of glad envy was leaning over the counter. "Jeez!" she said. "Irish dividends!" Their heads turned as Sabrina moved, and when they saw her starting out the door the fat girl screamed, "Hey, you leaving your *jackpot?*"

"Keep it," Sabrina said. "Maybe it'll bring you some of my luck."

The street was Christmas-colored with neon. She went down it blindly, thinking, Oh damn him, damn his coldness, damn his hurt grudge-holding vanity! If he'd only been the slightest understanding, we might have . . . He didn't have any reason to . . .

Might have what? said the cynic in her cerebellum. And didn't he have reason? Didn't he? And won't he? Oh God, won't he?

CHAPTER 14

"ALL RIGHT," Barbara said. "Tell me all about your first Monday among the rich folks."

The children were in bed, there was an undemanding tootle of Haydn coming in from KPFA, the house had been aired of dinner smells.

"They are different from you and me," Leonard said.

She bit off a thread and laid aside the dress she had been mending and picked up a pair of faded jeans. Her ankles were giving her trouble with this baby; she had to stay off her feet as much as possible. "I know all about that, all that about they have more money. I want to know what you did."

"It won't instruct you much. That's a funny household." Sprawling on the sofa, he laid aside his book and put his foot carefully in her lap among the sewing. She lifted it off and dropped it on the floor.

"Funny how? What happened?"

"Funny any way you look at it. Nothing happened. I dusted off some books, and treated some with my secret formula, and talked some with Mrs. Hutchens, and had tea with some people you wouldn't believe them if you read them in Dickens, and then on the way home I spent four eighty-five for paperback editions of books I had coveted up at the castle."

"Oh, come on, Leonard. You don't have to make up melodramas or anything, but I've been an understanding parent all day, and now I just want to sit and listen to you talk, and sew tiny garments, and be cozy."

"So," he said. "Well, I reported for duty at eight a.m.—"

"Which was too early. I kept telling you."

"It was not too early. That is a spartan house. I was greeted without enthusiasm by the Filipino butler, who obviously wished I would use the servants' entrance."

"Lizardo is an old sweet."

"With me he is an old sour. He lets me into this gloomy ancestral hall. There is not a sound except a vast ticking from the grandfather clock, like a time bomb. Then as I stand there it strikes one—just one. A couple of portraits on the walls, real old ravens, fix their eyes and beaks in me as soon as I turn my back. My shoes squeak. Eventually I sneak into the library and shut the door."

"You liar," Barbara said. "You walked in there bold and bow-legged as a lion."

"So now," Leonard said, "I am safe except for Brutus or Cassius or somebody on a bronze manhole cover above the door. He is trying to stare me down, and succeeding. They have swathed the whole room in sheets and drop-cloths and have put up a big trestle table for me to work on. It's so much like the funeral parlor I worked in in Schenectady that I begin to feel at home. So I start at the upper left-hand shelf and remove all the books. Then I wash down the shelves. Then I dust the books I have removed, a book at a time and sometimes a page at a time, with a clean flannel cloth, and I lay them in order on the table and I start painting their bindings with a mixture of lanolin, beeswax, cedarwood oil, and some additive whose name I forget. This is called the British Museum Mixture, a formula courteously provided me by the curator of special collections at the Stanford University library. Tomorrow I will rub all these treated bindings down and put the books back. Is this the kind of details you want?"

"Tell me what books."

"Kee-rist," Leonard said. "Did you ever look into those shelves?"

"Not really, I guess."

174

"Everything you ever wished you'd read. I am Don Juan in a nunnery—three thousand well-preserved virgins yearning to have their covers cracked."

"Do you have to be dirty?"

"You wanted details. Today I handled about two hundred, and while I was about it I admit I cracked a few. Given my health I will crack a lot more. Studs MacDonald."

"Ah," she said, "can I help it if I'm pregnant and useless?"

Their eyes met; they smiled deeply. "How is he today?" Leonard said. "Kicking you around yet?"

"Not really. Just sort of push-ups." He put his foot on her thighs again and she left it there, pulling her sewing free on top of it. Haydn paused, murmured a moment, and became Wolfgang Amadeus Mozart in a musical-comedy mood. "You haven't told me what books," she said.

He lay back with his hands under his head and shut one eye, then the other, squinting at the ceiling. "Jowsus, the books. Folios, quartos, crown octavos, duodecimos, cordovan and tree calf. She has two of these unique jobs—plates destroyed after one copy, laid paper, original water-color illustrations by Matisse, Dufy, and Pissarro, bindings in pastel leather by some fabulous bird in Paris. I became a hand-washer, believe me. But those aren't what I got hung up on. They're only for admiring, not reading. What slowed me down was the ones I'd have liked to curl up with. Ever look into a veritable Audubon? Or *A Pictorial History of the Civil War?* Or *Sylva of North America,* with those illustrations of trees and leaves and twigs that make you wish you were a bird so you could perch on them and sing?"

"You had fun. I told you you would."

"Fun, sure. Also twinges of proletarian unrest, thinking of all the time book dealers have spent finding those mint sets of Parkman and Motley and Prescott and Henry Adams and Gibbon and Macaulay and Carlyle, just so they could sit unread in Mrs. Hutchens' library. It would almost be better if they weren't real. My God, there's a set of Thwaites' *Western Travels* six feet long that nobody had ever opened, I think, till I spent fifteen minutes on the company time this afternoon sneaking a few pages of Maximilian of Wied. Fun? I guess yes."

"Did you see Mrs. Hutchens? I'll bet she'd let you borrow things."

"I did indeed see Mrs. Hutchens. She was in every thirty minutes. I babbled my enthusiasm for her library, too. But when she murmured and hesitated and boxed her ankles and finally came out with the word that I might want to take certain things home to read, I got cold feet. She'd relish a gap in those shelves the way she'd relish a gap in her teeth."

"Oh, well, if you can get them in paperbacks. Anyway Dolly or Louise would probably have cut the illustrations out of them. What else did you do? Did you see Sabrina?"

"Sabrina went up to Nevada on Saturday."

"Reno? Do you suppose she . . . ?"

"I don't know. I couldn't exactly ask."

"Gee, I hope she hasn't decided to divorce Burke."

"If you ask me, she's one jump ahead of the shrinker man."

"I don't know. Maybe she *should* divorce him. He's so much older, and so busy all the time, and so sort of stiff. She needs something to do."

"Is a job so hard to get?"

"How could you convince yourself a job was necessary if you could buy out the company? She's had jobs; she just couldn't take them seriously. She's got the notion she and her whole class are parasites— she's got this New England notion of usefulness in the world but she can't think how to be useful."

"She hates being a flea but she won't hop off the dog."

"She's too proud to do a lot of things, and too restless to just enjoy herself. And she thinks she's scornful of luxury, but she isn't."

"Well," he said, "she's a charming girl. She's so charming she can make you nearly forget how selfish she is."

"Oh, Leonard!"

"Isn't she? Hasn't she always used you like a human hot-water bottle?"

"You don't have to be insulting. Anyway what about that five-hundred-dollar check to the Greenbelt Committee?"

"Yes," he said. "That shakes me. But man, I find it hard to establish sympathy with somebody who can't find anything to do with ten million dollars, or a hundred million, or whatever it is. There must be *something* money's good for."

"She doesn't want any place in the world that she has to buy."

"So it isn't good she wants to do. It's herself she's worried about."

"But I thought you liked her!"

"I like her fine. I just think she's dangerous."

"Only to herself."

"Mainly to herself. But she wants other people to watch while she goes to hell no-hands. She hates being a woman."

"*Sabrina?* She's got more charm in her little finger than most women have in their whole body."

"Sure," he said. "She can focus on you in a way to melt glass. But take it from an old cover-cracker, hers is one cover I wouldn't ever be tempted to crack."

That left her astonished. She spread the material of the jeans across his shoe and studied it. "That's funny. I would have thought . . ."

"So maybe I'm wrong," he said. "After all, she's got this red-hot affair going. Anyway I'm only tempted by ancient virgins in half leather."

"Ahhh," Barbara said comfortably. "Poor Sabrina. Well, tell me about tea. Who was there?"

He removed his foot from her lap. Mozart caracoled on. Leonard happened to smell his fingers, held them for her to sniff too. "The odor of learning," he said. "Ineradicable. Lanolin to soften the leather, cedarwood oil to keep out bookworms and silverfish, beeswax for a hard sheen. Tea? That was something. This Helen Whatsername summoned me about four-thirty and I had to go. They were all too well bred to comment but not too well bred to stare. My shoes do squeak, too. They don't squeak anywhere else, but in that house I sound like a Japanese student in buttoned cottontops.

"So here I come, *creak, creak,* and cringe down on a satin sofa smiling and smiling and sniffing my fingers at them. There is a gal with gap-teeth: Mrs. Whitebread? Whiteside. Also a Moral Rearmament lady just back from a convention on Mackinac Island. She has blue hair and gentle gentle eyes that she fixes on me with a hungry imperative. Also a gentleman who was once religious editor for the Des Moines *Register*. Every time I look at him his paw is in the cookie plate. He nibbles like a rabbit, *mnmn, mnmn, mnmn,* with his lips sticking out and his eyeglasses flashing at me. *Mnmn, mnmn, mnmn,* and away goes his paddy into the cookies again. He parts his hair like T. S. Eliot, and when he speaks he bends his head down sort of demurely, and you can see clear to the bone.

"This editor tells me he has been commissioned by *Reader's Digest* to do four articles on The Religion of Everyday. The price of these will be twenty-five hundred dollars each, *mnmn, mnmn, mnmn,* and off goes his hand into the cookies. *Mnmn, mnmn, mnmn,* restores your faith in humanity that a great magazine read by forty million people in seventeen languages should be willing to pay so well for articles on faith and good works as exhibited by the simple everyday American."

"There isn't any such man. You're making him up."

He raised his hand for an oath, sniffed his fingers, smiled. "Nothing but the truth. I think they did commission those articles, too, and I think the price was twenty-five-hundred apiece. But about that time the Filipino renews the cookie plate, and passes the orange juice. The Moral Rearmament lady asks him if he's ever been to Baguio, where her outfit has another conference headquarters and where she was recently thrilled to hear delegates from Japan publicly apologize to the Filipino people for starting the war. The editor is on fire at once. Snatches a cookie. Restores your faith in humanity, *mnmn, mnmn, mnmn.* The Filipino says he been to Baguio many time, he come from Ilocos Sur, berry close by. The Moral Rearmament lady tries to make him admit the Peninsula hills are very like the hills around Baguio, but I don't think he buys any of that. The woman with the teeth, Mrs. Whitebone-Whiteside, lights up a cigarette that Mrs. Hutchens and the Moral Rearmament lady courageously overlook, and the editor gets another cookie as they go by. Mrs. Whiteside gets the word from Helen Whatsername that I am going to catalogue the family papers, and she tells me what a delightful time I am in for, simply divine. Then Mrs. Hutchens tells us a story about Uncle Bushrod, how he could never bear the undignified postures of crawling in and out of early automobiles, so about 1912 he had a special Silver Streak Rolls built for him, so high he could walk straight into it with a tophat on."

"I know," Barbara said. "We used to play in it sometimes. Oliver still drives it to these antique-auto shindigs."

"Well, I have always had to stoop. But just when Mrs. Hutchens has finished her tale, and the Moral Rearmament lady is looking yearningly at me, bent on conversion, I see my chance, so I stand up, *cre-e-e-a-a-k!* and announce that it's time I got home."

"You make yourself out such a goof. I'll bet you were the life of the party."

"I was mute. But I was getting away with a strategic withdrawal when in comes Oliver Hutchens, and Oliver is less than overjoyed to find us there. He gives us this little steely glint, you know, like a house detective. He does not shake hands, neither does he bow. He looks, he ticks us off. Mrs. Whiteside, how do you do. Mrs. Bent— I believe I have met Mrs. Bent, yes. Moral Rearmament, is it? Buchmanites? Yes. Mr. Spencer? Good afternoon. You're . . .

"A writer, the editor tells him, and is about to fill him in on the *Reader's Digest* articles when he notices that the opportunity is gone by, the Young Laird is on me now. MacDonald? Oh, Barbara's husband. No smile. The bastard has met me at least five times, each time all afresh. So then the horrid truth comes out, that I'm the new archivist, and that catches his attention all right. Really? he says. *Really?* I thought you were a schoolteacher, he says—you know, like saying to the chimneysweep, What are you doing up the chimney, I thought you were the guy we called to pump the septic tank.

"Old Mrs. Hutchens is murmuring, and old Mrs. Whiteacre is looking pained, and old Mrs. Bent is fumbling at her reticule and shooting her stole, and the editor is screwing his chin out of his collar and flashing his eyeglasses around, and Helen Whatsername—who incidentally is something of a dish, did you ever notice?—sits there with her knees and ankles together. This Oliver has quite a knack. I wait till my defrosters are working and then I creak away, and the editor grabs a last cookie and follows."

"You're exaggerating."

"Naturally. What I really did, I stepped up to the insolent bully and said, Who do you think you are, shouldering your way into an innocent tea party and insulting your mother's guests? You cad, I said, I'll teach you the manners you seem to have missed learning, and with that I—"

"Was he really nasty?"

"Yeah, sort of. Definitely, I should say."

"I wonder why?"

"Deponent sayeth not. As I was creaking out the door with the editor behind me I heard Mrs. Hutchens ask about Sabrina, and he said she'd stayed up at somebody's ranch. Then I found myself in a column of two's with the editor. First thing I know he skips to get in step. I stumble and break it up. Right away he skips back in. He will not be denied. He is full of togetherness and vital adjustment. I try little mincy steps and he's right with me. I step out, and here he comes, hup two three four. I almost expect him to call for a cadence.

"He is telling me it restores his faith in humanity to know someone like Mrs. Hutchens. Great heart, wonderful woman shedding good on every side. Clearly I am one of the sides. He will put me in an article, a workman brought into the library and given an opportunity to know Great Books. The Filipino pursues us and opens the door and we bump each other around bowing ourselves out. He won't go first because then he couldn't keep in step, and it's obvious he doesn't trust *me* to keep the faith. So we go out together, and sure enough I catch my cleats in the mat and spoil his exit."

Barbara sighed and rolled the Levis and stuck the needle under the threads of a spool. She said, "I wish I was a man and got to meet interesting people. Now would you like to hear about *my* day? At nine-fifteen Louise and Dolly had a fight over the things Sabrina gave them yesterday and I had to separate them for an hour. At ten the dishwasher overflowed and spewed suds all over the kitchen. At eleven I discovered we were out of butter and lettuce and you had the car. At eleven-thirty—"

"Peace," he said. "Peace, perturbed spirit. How about a stroll through the quiet streets of Greenwood Acres?"

"All right. I guess I should give him some other kind of exercise than practicing pushups against my kiddlies."

"Kiddlies?"

"I said kiddlies, didl't I?" she said. She stood and smoothed the maternity dress across her front. Her eyes met Leonard's, and she laughed.

CHAPTER 15

O LIVER let the silence extend itself, looking back at his mother with a controlled absence of impatience or rancor. The mulish, pebbled tightening of the chin meant that she was feeling balked or rebuked. A dim pink showed in her cheeks. The secretary, apparently not sure whether to go or stay, had poured his tea and then gone over by the windows. The afternoon behind her hazed her head and shoulders with gold; the back of her neck looked as fuzzy and soft as a pussywillow. When she saw him looking, the easy flush rose in her throat and cheeks. But not confusion, he assured himself. Complexion, not confusion. She struck him as a girl who knew what she was about. No matter what horse she was riding, you would not see daylight between it and her.

Presumably she had felt his remarks as partly a criticism of herself, and that was all right too. It wouldn't hurt her to be a little off balance for a change. In his controlled, pleasant voice, he said, "Mother, don't be absurd. I'm not accusing you of extravagance, or trying to put you on an allowance. I'm only saying that the expenses of this place are getting so high we ought to talk them over."

"Are there any more expenses than there have . . . always been?"

"No more people, no. Just everything costs more. Taxes double every few years, wages are three times what they were in 1940. You know what the monthly payroll comes to, your house and my house and the grounds?"

His mother put her fingers against her trembling mouth; he half expected her to stamp her foot. "I should think it petty to inquire."

He nodded. "Above arithmetic."

"I should think we are not in danger of becoming insolvent."

"No, just in danger of sleeping past our station."

Helen Kretchmer murmured something and moved toward the door. Oliver acknowledged with his eyes the discretion that prompted her, as well as the smoothness of the way she moved. She had a molded, muscled look like a well-shaped mare. He looked back at his mother.

"I've just been going over the accounts. Nine gardeners, a driver, a secretary, a butler, a cook, and a maid, and at my place a cook and a maid. Altogether, just about five thousand a month. Ten of those people we also house, and seven of them we feed. We maintain six cars and two trucks. It's about time we asked ourselves how long we can support all that goes along with thirty acres and a castle."

"They increase in value all the time."

"What good is that? Unless you sell, all it means is more taxes."

"But we still qualify as a . . . ranch, and many expenses can be deducted."

"Two acres of pears," Oliver said. "Believe me, I stretch those as far as they'll stretch. But you don't justify a five-thousand-a-month payroll on two acres of pears."

His mother's hands rubbed and rustled in her lap, then hung and flexed beside the chair. He saw her thoughts working outward, stiffening her neck and her long, shaking head. Her lips came together in a parody of firmness that exasperated him. "I'm sure I don't understand why you accost me this way," she said. "There are no unnecessary persons on the place. Do you want me to . . . , *economize?*"

"Look, Mother, you don't know what's been happening. What was a dollar is a quarter now. The only things you can do in this market are to speculate on the future earnings of common stocks or play real estate. You can't do the first right as long as there's only a dribble of income above expenses, and you can't do the second unless sometime you're willing to sell."

Her hands hung down, unflexed; her clouded eyes watched him with suspicion. "You have some proposal."

"I might have a half dozen proposals. But we can't just sit." Timing, he had told himself before he started in on this, was most important. You aimed yourself like a torpedo boat and at precisely the right minute you let fly. And sometimes you bluffed in one direction and came in at the last second in another. He said casually, "I suppose we could sell some of the excess acreage of this place. That's what a lot of people have done."

Her eyes looked absolutely white. *"Subdivide?"*

Crossing his legs, Oliver set his cup on the teacart. Pleasantly he said, "No more than twenty acres, maybe. You could get forty thousand an acre. And you'd still have ten. That's a duchy, these days."

"Oh, no," she said as if her wind had been knocked out. "No."

"You'd rather dwindle."

"Don't we simply remain?"

"We remain till costs and taxes whittle us away."

As if looking for support, she glanced to both sides. "I couldn't think . . . Sell off part of the estate? Surround ourselves with little . . . neighbors . . . people we don't even *know?"*

Her snobbery was so unconscious it was innocent, and it gratified him because he had been counting on it. He said, "I wouldn't like it any better than you would, but I'm telling you, it's time to do something. We have to make more or spend less. If you want to live at your present level I've got to have either land or some free capital to work with. Between you and that white elephant of a trust, Collier and I are handcuffed."

"I handcuff you?"

"You won't agree to what's necessary."

"I will never agree to . . . sell off part of the estate, no."

"Or anything else."

"Have you proposed anything else?"

One for you, Mother, Oliver thought. He said, "Give me your power of attorney and I won't have to bother you. I can make a little deal here and a little deal there and that's all I'd need."

"You want my power of attorney so you can subdivide?"

"No. Give me that and I wouldn't need to touch this place."

"What would you do?"

"Whatever's necessary." He hunched down, squinting quickly at her face: still mulish and suspicious. At once he changed direction. "There's something else, something I've mentioned before. These charities of yours. I've been adding them up. If I had what you've given to your committees and councils and suffering souls in the last three years I could have built it into a million dollars."

That brought her head up. Snort fire, he thought, paw the ground. She said, "I have never given to a cause I did not think worthy. I'm surprised you should suggest I might become . . . small."

"I'm not suggesting anything. I'm only saying that if I had that much free capital I wouldn't be bothering you now."

"I think you were suggesting that I . . . turn them away."

"I'm dead sure some of them should be turned away, but I never suggested it. I only suggested you look closer before you shell out. Or set yourself a flat sum, twenty or twenty-five thousand a year if you want to feel that noble, and stay within it. Even if you just made sure you only donated to things that are legitimate and deductible it would help some. But somehow get a lid on. And also give me your power of attorney and turn me loose to make a little money. If you did that you could double your charities without hurting anything."

Quiet and reasonable, he slid down in the loveseat. The midsummer-afternoon sun outside flickered and sifted through the oaks and scattered halfway down the long room. Everything around Oliver reminded him of the inertia he had to overcome. The furniture was the same old ornate wicker that had furnished the tearoom in the Nahant house. Because the Nahant house had fronted on the sea, and had had a vast window to view it through, this tearoom had the same window, though it looked out only into lawn and oaks. Because in the Nahant tearoom there had been a brass telescope through which the family and guests had watched seabirds on the buoys, the same brass telescope stood on its mount here, ridiculously aimed out into the live-oaks fifty feet beyond the glass.

His mother watched him with an expression of furtive dismay, and in irritation he stood up, walked to the telescope, and put his eye to the eyepiece. The crotch of an oak leaped into view, modeled by light and shadow. In the crotch was a small fold or pocket, and from the fold, as he watched, popped out a small sharp bill, a lively gray shape. A wren. He made a mental note to have Jameson do some surgery on that tree. Oaks that got over-watered as these did grew too fast and were likely to fall of their own weight, simply collapse some morning and with a slow soft concussion lay their tons of limbs on the lawn. And a hole like the one the wren was nesting in would catch water, rot, and weaken the tree.

When he took his eye from the cool brass, his mother's face was still turned toward him. "I am trying to understand what it is you want."

He reminded himself to be pleasant and controlled. In most things, his mother liked to be bossed and liked to unload responsibility, but if she thought her personal security was threatened she could pinch down like an abalone to a rock. He felt like taking her by the shoulders and shaking out of her the simple document that would free his hands.

Ominously she said, "Oliver, my dear, I . . . think you have some scheme in your head."

"Would you like me to bond myself?" he said bitterly. "Then could I be trusted to handle your affairs? If not, you'd better get a new manager."

"My dear, you know—"

"All I know is I can't do it if I have to come to you *de novo* on every little transaction. Suppose you had another stroke, or died. Can you even imagine what a mess you'd leave things in?"

"My will is . . . in order," she said. Her mouth was slightly open, and trembling; her eyes begged him. She did not like to discuss death. But though he might upset her, he had not persuaded her. She wanted not the slightest change, she willed to remain immovable in transplanted New England, and she would shrewdly keep in her own hands the power that would let her do so.

"Of course your will is in order," he said. "The trust is in order, too, tied up so tight Houdini couldn't untangle it until you die, and after that not even Houdini could keep the bureaucrats from gobbling most of it. Do you have the remotest idea what the . . . blasted confiscatory estate taxes would do to us? That's why I want your power of attorney

—to take advantage of the boom so that when they cut us in half we'll still be as big as we are now. To keep even you have to move, Mother! You can't just hang onto property. They'll tax you out of it."

"So it is some sale you want."

Oliver tossed up his hands, shoved them down into his pockets, strode up the room six steps and back again. He spun the telescope and looked through it backward. Far, far down the receding reach of the room her tiny figure sat motionless as an idol—the goddess who insisted that everything come to a dead stop.

She said, "Oliver, you know I don't . . . wish to hamper you. I appreciate what you do. But you and I want different things. You're aggressive, you don't like . . . simply to enjoy things. You want to buy and sell. You're like Uncle Bushrod, he was always deep in some scheme or other, Mexican silver mines and things. You will have . . . full control soon enough. Do let me have . . . my last years free of worry that you might . . . subdivide!"

"I give up," Oliver said. He came behind her and laid a hand on her shoulder; he could have crushed the bones under the white blouse like dry weeds. Strangely they moved him; she was getting old, and you forgot, seeing her putter around playing golf every day, how frail she was. And she had never opened her mouth to him about that movie. Was that behind her stubbornness now? And yet he could not afford to let her have her way. He said, "Look, forget the power of attorney if it bothers you that much. But give me just one thing. I'd like to develop the Woodside land."

He felt in her fragile bones how she took that in, first as a hope, an escape from his first proposal, and then as a possible trap. "You don't need *that* for your personal comfort!" he said. "That's only raw land. You bought it for forty-five thousand and I could sell it for nearly three million tomorrow. I can organize a development corporation and make twice that."

"Houses?" she said faintly. "Little . . . ranch houses on that lovely hill?"

"How long has it been since you've been down there? Minna may ride there ten times in a year. The kids hardly use it at all any more, they're always around the Circus Club. What else? A family picnic once a summer. You could keep some acreage if you wanted. Keep twenty acres along Canada Road. But open up the rest, the freeway's coming right past it."

His mother rose, saying shakily, "I . . . had other plans for it."

"What? Build a country place? I'll give you your choice of lots."

"No, I . . ."

He planted himself before her, prying to know what she was faltering about. But she escaped him. Shaky-lipped, she said, "Please, you have . . . upset me. I want to . . . go to my rooms."

"Mother, this can't wait, honestly. Will you give me or my corporation an option on that land—at least three hundred and eighty acres?"

But she groped and fumbled away so that he took her arm, afraid she would fall. "Please," she said. "I shall . . . have to think."

"And meantime the opportunity goes down the drain."

He was walking beside her, attentive and angry. Her palsied head turned and the opaque watery blue eyes looked into his with withering shrewdness. "Does it?" she said.

Grimly smiling, a Disney wolf that had missed its spring, he escorted her to her room, rang for Bernadette, stooped to kiss the withered cheek. Sitting on the edge of the bed, his mother looked at him accusingly.

"Think hard, will you?" he said. "This is important."

Down the hall Helen Kretchmer's door stood open. She sat brightly smiling behind her typewriter, and as he paused she said, "Is Mrs. Hutchens all right? Does she need me?"

He stepped into the room, once his own bedroom, now joined to another bedroom and bath and used as an office. Anger and frustration still tightened the tendons of his fingers. He said, "She's all right except she's out of her mind."

As she stood up he saw again the sheen of light across the back of her neck. The hair was short, and for all he could tell, naturally curly, the kind of mop that could be shaken but never got much out of place. With her athletic figure, her pale blondness, she looked like Miss Minneapolis Milling Industry. "What?" she said uncertainly.

He stepped past the typewriter table and with his spread hand took her by the back of the neck. Steering her, he walked her to the win-

188

dows. She did not resist, but only looked at him astonished out of the corners of her eyes. He said, "Look. You like your job, do you?"

"Very much."

Her neck felt firm and strong and soft-skinned under his fingers. He squeezed, and then suddenly fury was in his hands; he tightened his grip and saw fear come into her eyes. She bent away. He relaxed his clutch but kept his hand on her neck. For a blind second there he could have squeezed her head off. "You want to keep it?" he said.

Perhaps it had not been fear at all he had seen in her eyes; certainly there was none now. She turned against the pressure of his hand. Almost scornfully she said, "Are you firing me?"

"I don't think so. You're a poor girl, are you? Need all the money you can make?"

Now she gave him a curl of red lips. "Heaven will protect me."

Oliver began to smile too. "I think it will. You might hold your job. You might even get a raise. Listen. If Mother says anything to you about me selling some Woodside land, you think it's a good idea. People have to have homes. The land sits there eating up taxes. It's time it was developed. Got that?"

Her hunching blue look might have meant anything, and yet he would have bet on her. Like a serving maid making a prissy mouth before the young master she said, "I hope you're not asking me to do anything she wouldn't like."

"You know the score," he said. "If she wants to keep up a palace—and that includes you—she has to agree to some sensible management. Collier is in favor, I'm in favor, now I want you to be in favor. Okay?"

Hunched against the gripe on her neck, she looked at him sideways. A slow, warm, unhurried stir began in him. He said to himself, Why in hell haven't I been doing more about this? The whites of her sideward eyes were very clear, the iris a pure Dutch blue. For a moment they stood with their noses no more than ten inches apart.

Then Helen spun away. Her transparent skin warmed with the easy flush. Her cool voice said, "Thank you, yes, I'll remember." Stooping forward, looking in as she passed, Bernadette went heavily past the door.

"You're all right," Oliver said. "You're all . . . right!" Her eyes did not go down. They followed him to the door, and were on him as he went out. "Remember!" he said around the jamb, but got no answer.

At the foot of the stairs he was stopped by Lizardo—and that was another thing. Sabrina ought to have her head examined, getting that familiar with a servant. He'd get too much into the family and he'd have to go, or else he'd be found foxing or finessing somebody on his own hook. Smuggling in Sabrina's whisky was only a beginning. Darling. Good Christ.

"What?" he said.

"Telepone," Lizardo said. "Doct' Castro."

Oliver took it in the library, picking up the telephone after one look of angry distaste at the signs of MacDonald's labors and one sniff at the taint of cedar oil and beeswax on the air. "Burke. Hi."

"Hello," said Burke's reduced, clipped voice. "I'm calling to see if you know where Sabrina is." Oliver looked up at the ceiling. The minute a man got caught in what Burke was caught in he even began to *sound* like a cuckold.

"God, no," he said. "That's a hard question, these days. She told me to *say* she was going to stay with Addie McAllister."

"I'm at Addie's now. She hasn't been here since lunch Saturday."

"How about the hotel or one of the motels?"

"I've checked them all."

"She said something about renting a Hertz car. Try there?"

"Both in Carson and in Reno. She hasn't rented one."

"Oh, fine," Oliver said. A concentration of irritations and frustrations shook him for a second like a tree in a blast. Of all the things he didn't need, the least necessary was a cops-and-robbers search of Nevada for his berserk sister. "Goddamn, she's got a genius. When I left her she was full of the love of cottonwood leaves and talking about disappearing into the desert for ten years. She might have, I suppose —she's crazy enough to be camped out in some wash in the Bullfrog Hills."

"I've been trying the real-estate offices, but no luck there either," Burke said. "She called me about ten Saturday night and was talking about buying a ranch."

"She was singing that song to me too. Health, the outdoor life, animals, no more cocktail parties or bridge luncheons."

"Yes," Burke said, "but where is she?"

Oliver said what he thought was true. "I expect she's out in some sagebrush joint playing Emma Bovary before an audience of barflies, if you really want to know. I gather you didn't go for the ranch idea?"

"There are certain limits," Burke said.

"Then she's probably in some desert garden eating worms."

"That isn't a lot of comfort. Was she drunk?"

"Maybe a little. Maybe later a lot, if I know her. She's been pretty upset about something. Maybe you know."

He listened carefully. After a moment the wistful cuckold: "Was she alone?"

"She was passionately alone," Oliver said. "I offered to stay with her but her soul craved solitude." The gust shook him again; he damned all women to hell. "Look, boy, Mendelsohn wasn't around. I doubt if he's with her now."

With his eyes on MacDonald's sheet-draped table and careful piles of books, he listened. The voice was dry. "Oh. You know about that."

"She talked to me about it. But I think it's all kaput."

"That's what she told me." A pause. "That doesn't tell us where she is," Burke said. "If I thought he was with her I wouldn't be hunting her. But I've combed every motel and beer joint in the valley. Now I don't know whether to raise a search party, or go to the police, or what."

Oliver drew his chest full of cedary, waxy air and let it out slowly. "I shouldn't think you'd want to go bleating around Nevada, 'Has anybody seen my wife?' Would you?"

"I guess my embarrassments aren't the important thing right now," Burke said. "Something's happened to her. This is all so completely unlike her."

"Not so unlike," Oliver said, "and for God's sake let's not get noble." He made in his mind certain calculations and, irritably, some postponements. "Look," he said, "tell Addie just enough so she won't talk. I'll get Harrington or some other peekhole detective and catch the first plane to Reno. I'll telephone you from the airport just before we leave, so you can meet us. Where you staying? Hotel? All right. What?"

". . . quite like this private eye business," Burke said.

"Balls. Would you prefer going to the cops? How'd you like the headlines from that kind of search party?"

"That's not the important thing. She may be in trouble."

"It's important enough," Oliver said. "Even if you'd like those headlines fine, I wouldn't, and neither would Mother. I'll call from the airport."

"All right," Burke said reluctantly. "If I was only sure she was perfectly safe, you wouldn't find me pursuing her like a—"

"But you're not sure," said Oliver. "I am, but you're not. After about two hours, you'd better stick in your room for my call."

He hung up, and for several seconds sat drumming his hard fingerends on the desk. He cursed his sister systematically as an emotional fool. He wished he had muscled her into the car and brought her home by force. But then she probably would have waited for a chance and jumped out on her head at seventy miles an hour. When she got in one of these moods, she would do anything to demonstrate how shattered she was.

CHAPTER 16

THE FEEL of smooth dark motion broke. She was jerked forward and back and joggled half awake. She heard the engine sputter and then, faintly creaking, they had coasted to a stop, and a silence like feathers began to drift around her; she began once more to tilt over into unsupported fall. A pounding broke in, a voice grated. She came back a long way from exhaustion, apathy, sleep, space, death, wherever she had been, to see the Member from Petaluma leaning, glaring at the gasoline gauge and knocking with the heel of his hand against the cowl.

There was a greenish, pre-dawn light. Outside the car there were pines. The Member from Petaluma swore sullenly and unbelievingly. All the elaborate pantomines and the vaudeville routines had been worn off him; he was no longer Good Time Charlie, the master of the revels. He looked jowly and mad, and his stale night-time breath filled the car.

"Where are we?" she said.

"How the hell would I know?" the Member said. "Twenty half-assed miles from anywhere. Somewhere out along beautiful Tahoe, the Lake of the Sky."

He climbed out and slammed the door and stood looking uncertainly

193

up and down the road. His sport shirt was pleated into wrinkles across the small of his back. He looked at his watch. Behind him the roadside was bulldozed bare clear to the edge of the pines. The tips of the trees all wore extensions of new light-green growth. She could smell the quiet, and the duff of the forest floor.

"Do you want me to do something?" she said.

The Member looked in the window, opened his mouth, and shut it again. Slamming his palm against the fender, he stared sulkily up the highway. Sabrina rolled her head and looked the other way, down past a cottage to a leaden pane of lake, and beyond that to the misty far shore, with its rim brightening to sunrise. Her head rolled back and her eyes met the Member's, glazed and streaked as marbles. "Why don't you stay right here and immerse, for Christ sake," he said, and started off up the road.

But in a moment he came back, and, glaring at her accusingly, took the car keys. Without lifting her head from the seat back she watched him lurch away up the shoulder of the highway. Then she closed her eyes, and when she looked again there was only the curving road and the line of white posts and the pines.

The moment she pushed herself erect in the seat her head began to pound. Her mouth was woolly. The front of her dress was unbuttoned, and when she started to fasten it she found the brassiere undone too. Her whole body winced in a numb, unbelieving shudder. Had she, with that animal? Trying to clear her mind, she pressed her eyes tight shut and opened them again, groping back through the long blurred ugly dream.

How much was dream, and could be awakened from, and how much was reality of an unbearable kind? And how long had that night been? Her mind teemed and swarmed, and she sat with gritted teeth, letting the clearer images boil out toward the edge of memory like trash in a boiling spring. Bars and gambling houses, several, perhaps many, in Carson, Reno, around Tahoe. Once she had fallen in with acquaintainces from San Francisco who were worried about her, and fed her, and said they would take her home. But she had hidden in the women's room until they faded, got lost, anyway were gone. She had stood against the rails of crap tables until her hips were sore. Up-welling memory overflowed with reaches of white-lined green baize, with lights, eyes, the lick of dealers' rakes, the staring faces of dice.

In the chilly car she shivered her shoulders suddenly together, sickened by the image of herself: possessed, furiously gay, and drunk, drunk. How long? A night and a day? Another night? She did not remember eating anything except the charred steak the San Francisco party had insisted on ordering for her, and that she had barely touched, drinking double old-fashioneds and laughing all the time. She did not remember sleeping at all, though she must have, somewhere. The shudder went through her again. She stared out at the empty arc of road and the absolutely motionless pines. Somewhere, somehow, into that spiteful debauch had come the Member from Petaluma, a creature of fable or farce. She had recognized him at once as someone she was looking for. Multiplied in reflecting surfaces of metal and glass, he hung in her memory like twenty identical jack-o-lanterns.

Oh, she had fallen upon him. Before five minutes had passed they were collapsing with mirth. He had a ponderous deadpan soggy-drunk approach that struck them both as incomparably witty. Out of a blur of light and color he came looming, confidential and avuncular, hand on her knee for friendly emphasis.

—What I can't unnerstan', how we happen to get together? Splendid thing, can't unnerstan' it.

—I was out looking for men to match my mountains.

—Absolutely astonishing. That you should fin' *the* one man.

—There's a divinity doth shape our ends.

—Ha! May I pay you a serious complimen'?

—Would I have to stand up and turn around?

Laughter. They hung on each other. He was a dumpy man in a loud sport shirt. His throat and arms were hairy, and he had a bronchial coughing laugh that purpled his face and left him staring glassy-eyed, wheezing at intervals, patiently waiting for the consequences of her wit to pass.

—*Never* fin' a girl like you in place like this. Hardly believe it. You min' saying again how we happen to meet?

—My psychoanalyst told me to go out and in the destructive element immerse.

—Oh now hey. No destructive elemen's here, all gen'lemen. When I'm home I may live with fifteen thousan' white leghorns but when I'm on party I know how to ack. Uh? What is this, destructive elemen's?

He stared in upon her, wheezing. Behind or before and beside his face in the continuous filmstrip of phantasmagoria she saw her own. She had been watching herself while she laughed with him. Once her face looked back at her from the round of a glass with hopeless, open-mouthed terror, and it seemed to her, thinking about it, that just then she had had to force herself almost sober in order to go on with the antics of drunkenness. There was another time, clearly remembered, when she looked at the Member and saw him with ass's ears. He mugged at her, and she reached a fairy hand to touch his red face with love.

Sometime she must have slept, for how could anyone have kept it up without passing out? She had been out on her feet half the time. There were great absences in her memory. Just now there had been lipstick on his mouth as he stamped away. It destroyed every notion she had of herself; she could have lifted her face and screamed. To be, by despair or spite or self-loathing or anything else, so totally transformed. To lie down with pigs, to be pawed, and perhaps worse, by an animal like that. The only thing that gave her half a hope was that he had gone away furious. And yet even if the worst had happened, it was not so bad as that telephone call.

"Excuse me," she said to him at some point, "I want to call a friend."

"Good idea," the Member said. "Call one myself. Haw-haw."

Swimming below the breakers of noise, they moved effortlessly past crap tables and a chuck-a-luck cage. A change girl crowded past them leaning backward against the silver pregnancy of her tray, and Sabrina dropped dollars and took quarters and dimes in exchange. Through the open doors she caught a glimpse of a bright street, a neon wink and stare, reflections multicolored from multicolored parked cars, and thought how not so long ago all this had been deep mountains, softly roaring with silence like a seashell. Now all the beauty of Hollywood and Vine. Vulgarity, vulgarity. In desperation she reached out and took hold of the loose tails of the Member's sport shirt. He pranced, and she drove him. Immersing, she plummeted like a stone.

The four-way clock hanging from the rustic ceiling beams said 3:42. Touching the faces of slot machines to keep the floor steady, she made the corner where signs said He's and She's. The Member winked and disappeared. She went on, wearing on her face a smile that felt like a swelling, and feeling in her mind a . . . could it have been a hope? Before the telephone booths, suddenly shaking-handed, she dropped some of her change on the floor, and a man on the way to the He's stooped and rose again, handing her two quarters. She went into a booth.

That far she thought it was memory. But as she stood waiting in the booth it began to tip smoothly into a continuous turning fall. Weightless in space, she knew neither up nor down nor sideways; and feeling or dreaming how desperately she needed solidity, she opened her eyes and fixed them with hard effort until in an unexpected quarter the steadying chrome ring of the telephone swam into focus. That too could have been reality. But she did not remember calling. And was it reality when the sharp, frightened woman's voice cried out, "Hello! Hello!"?

Dreaming or waking, "Mr. Mendelsohn, please," she said.

"But he's asleep! What is it, at this hour? Who is this?"

"I'd like to speak with him, if he's there."

From her toppling suspension it seemed she listened. Whisperings. Then his voice, clogged and breathless. Through all the narcotic layers that muffled her fall—for she fell, it seemed now, through gelatin— she heard the fear in it—the fear, perhaps, of *her*. "Yes? Hello?"

"Hello, darling," she said. "I wanted to hear you, I've been going through hell—"

"*What?*" His voice was so hoarse and flat she would not have recognized it. "What is this? Is it some crumby joke?"

"You know it's no joke," she said. "Is she right there? Maybe that's better, maybe it's better she knew about us. . . ."

"Well, you had your joke, whoever you are," Bernard said loudly. "You woke us up at four in the morning. Very funny." Click, she was hanging to a dead wire.

She toppled, toppled, toppled. Once, from the rim of the Canyon de Chelly, she and others had rolled a bare dead tree into the canyon, and thrown themselves flat and hung their chins over the cliff and seen it fall slowly, spiraling, dwindling to a switch, to a match, until it jumped into fragments at the foot, and a long time afterward the unwarrantably solid *whomp!* of the tiny crash came up to them on their brink of stone. She fell like that in the booth, but interminably, without the comfort of an end, for the bottom fell away beneath her as fast as she fell into it. After light years of that, she came to herself with sweat starting all over her body and her hand clenched around the receiver. Shivering, she hung it up, found her handkerchief, patted her face and throat. When she stepped out of the booth, the Member from Petaluma started from beside the door of the He's and greeted her with warmth. He, at least, was no dream.

"Hey, you really were calling somebody. Thought you were kidding." He loomed comradely, his hand around her arm. "Tell me again," he said, "how the great flat feet of Fate led us two together. Then I can forget there's somebody else you call at four bells in the a.m."

Swallowing her nausea, she yanked his shirt tails. Dear Vulgarity, dear Caliban, dear Bottom, you will do as well as anything else to shatter on. Meantime I have to get used to the image my face throws on a mirror.

Then everything was sick and dizzy. She said, "Let's get out of here!"

Gallant, he offered his elbow. "Assolutely. Any particular elemen' you wanna immerse in?"

"Just let's get out."

"Drink firs'?"

"Let's get out!"

His face looming multiplex through the gelatinous air, he steered her toward the door.

Sitting in the dead car, Sabrina began to comb her hair, and before she thought, she had tipped the mirror to see. It gave her back her distracted gaze; her eyes stared and stared until she had to look away. The brightening sky was not a finite dome, as it so often seemed, but soft blue-green space, interminable, and the planet Venus that still had strength to glow above the eastern rim was not set in the sky but adrift in it—she saw past it. Feelings that she had not known since adolescence rose in a cold tide and swallowed her as the space between the stars might swallow a grain of dust.

What folly, what posturing, for one grain of dust to fall with so much anger and pride and self-pity, and to imagine that its self-destruction made a track like Lucifer's, and that there would be some bottom, and at the bottom a crash, and that from the crash a sound of meaning would go up. What did she want, lamentations? Did she want to be brought home on a shutter so that Burke could throw himself weeping on one end and Bernard fall on his knees at the other?

And yet with almost the same impulse of thought that lashed herself, she was asking them, Is it messy enough to prove I was *serious?* Could there be an uglier way? Would either of you have preferred it if I had jumped under a train or stolen the apothecary's arsenic?

She opened the car door and stepped out. The air was pure and keen, a patch of grass running down the slope was blue with wet. In the gray clarity she felt furtive, a slug uncovered by a kicked stone. Against the pounding in her head and the insistent hammer of guilt in her pulse, she closed her eyes, and in the clenched darkness of her mind she simply hung on. After a while she said, from a thick throat, Nobody, not anybody, would believe what's happening to me.

If Burke had valued her in the slightest. If he had ever valued her. If anyone had ever valued her! My God, must a person go crying through the world for love, and be turned away?

She moved like an old woman a few steps along the road, and the moment she looked she recognized where she was. Ahead of her a graveled drive looped down past four or five sleeping cottages to the lakeshore. There was a horned point thick with pines, then a meadow; and in the meadow was Charlie Grulich's boarding kennel. Three times she had boarded Fat Boy there; last summer Grulich had helped her prepare Fat Boy for a show.

At once, without a second's pause, she started down the drive. She still wore the flat heels she had worn—how long ago? Two days? Three?—to the road races, but even so she turned her ankles on the stones. At the sound of a car she hid behind a tree until it had passed. The edge of the sun brimmed over the lake's great bowl and dazzled in her eyes. The amethyst water disappeared in light, at her feet the pine-needled ground was suddenly gilded. Her nose took in the medicinal witch-hazel smell of mountain misery and the lake-edge smell of wet stones and roots. A Canada jay squawked off through the trees. Far off, an outboard exploded in a hot snarl and was throttled down. There was a whiff of woodsmoke on the air.

Then she heard the slam of a door, a whining and barking of many dogs, and the growl of a man's voice talking and crooning in an unimpatient monotone. She hurried past the gate in the woven wire fence and on around the house, and there in the flat gilding of sunlight was Charlie Grulich unlatching doors and letting dogs out into the run.

CHAPTER 17

Leonard MacDonald awoke and lay listening for the sounds that traditionally meant morning, and heard none of them. No roosters, no milkhorses, no buses or early-to-work trucks rumbling across the bridges of sleep, no chirp of sparrow or hammer of woodpecker, no curtains moving in light auroral breezes with a slur of fabric on wood or screen. What Greenwood Acres awoke to were the sounds of the over-crowded future, where what is good is what annoys least. Morning in Greenwood Acres was zoned out.

No rooster crowed because it was forbidden to keep chickens in Greenwood Acres—or chinchillas, or peacocks, or any other form of livestock. The paper thudded on no porch because, though the architect's basic design might be flopped, or added to, or reversed, or rotated on the lot, no one of the two hundred sixty examples of that design had a porch. The milk came only every other day, and not early in the morning, and not by horse, and not in glass bottles; most housewives bought it at the supermarket and saved a cent a quart. No sounds of building rebuked the sloth of sleepers, because in a tract developed by mass methods for maximum profit and utility there was no room for more building. Two boys who had built a tree house in a big oak that had somehow escaped the bulldozers had been made to take it down because they did not have a building permit. No kids were playing baseball in vacant lots: there were no vacant lots, and some day both big-league baseball and the American soul would suffer for that lack. No trees gave back oxygen to the air and tickled the nostrils of sleepers with freshness, and the meadowlarks that had used to sing in that horse pasture had moved elsewhere, for though there were thousands of saplings, all planted to a plan, there was nothing much that a bird could make use of.

Mosquito abatement had forestalled the thin evil whine to which dwellers in less fortunate places might awaken. The housefly, with his droning and his butting against the screens, had been zoned out with the horses and cows. No traffic disturbed the rest of last-minute sleepers because Greenwood Acres had been carefully designed without through ways. It lay sinusoidal, looped back upon itself, celled with little family units and patios behind screening fences, as peripheral and—the thought was not unheard of among its citizens—as subject to stoppage and infection as a vermiform appendix. Nevertheless, the true social shape of the future.

Exclusiveness with crowding, Leonard said to himself, and turned his head cautiously and saw that Barbara was still asleep. He reflected that awakening in this house was a little like awakening in your coffin, for the functional design was not only functional, it was all but hermetic. Plenty of glass—it had been fifteen years since a builder could sell tract houses without picture windows—but it was mainly fixed glass that looked out into the fenced patio, and not much of it was in the bedrooms. Why should it be? The first thing newcomers learned was that the California night air was more destructive to pharynx, tonsils, and sinuses than chlordane was to ants. Hence no nostalgic but unhygienic New England or Midwestern or Southern open windows; no matinal movements of curtains (no curtains); no shivery lung-filling drafts of new day. Here the householder opened his eyes to the dusk of drawn drapes, to walls and ceilings of natural plywood (no maintenance costs), and to the many-times-rebreathed air in which he had lain down.

In Scandinavia or Scotland, Leonard sometimes maintained in argument, people cursed with a gloomy climate learned long ago to touch their lives with crimson and gilt, to reflect and make use of what little light they received. But it had not yet occurred to Greenwood Acres that it could learn that trick, for Greenwood Acres had not yet comprehended that at least in its plywood sleeping cubicles it lived with gloom. It would not tolerate hearing this. Its people thought of themselves as sun-dwellers, and had tans to prove it.

Carefully he folded back the covers and stepped out on the cool asphalt tile. For a second, head tilted, he listened to the airless silence. Stepping into shorts and Levis, he watched Barbara's bulbous unmoving shape, and heard her breathing sweet and soft. She had had a restless night; let her snooze. Barefooted, bare-chested, he went into the bathroom and stealthily closed the door.

The bathroom, landlocked, with only a plastic skylight bubble for a window, was even more hermetic than the bedroom, damp and breathless and hung with drip-dry laundry. He moved quietly among light clinkings. Shaving, he confronted himself. Black hair sprouted springy from his chest and belly, with a line down the middle that divided him in halves. His wrists and forearms were thick and hairy, fuzz spread across his upper arms and shoulders, curly tufts sprang from the hollow where his collarbones joined.

Ape, he said. He lathered his face and throat. Scraping with the razor, he leered into the mirror like a trapped ball player into the television camera. You bet, he said, only way to get a decent shave. Barefooted he capered. Down his right cheek he scraped a clean swath; the mown skin looked shiny, almost opalescent. From the ape began to emerge, decorous, barbershop-smelling (a he-man aroma), the householder of Greenwood Acres.

Tiptoeing to the girls' bedroom, he peeked in. Louise was only a tousle of pale hair on the pillow, but Dolly was awake, drawing on the air with a forefinger. She started to sit up, but with his finger on his lips Leonard nodded his head at Louise and then tipped it back toward the other bedroom. Tucking the corners of his lips up under his earlobes in an idiot grin, he tiptoed on past.

It was stuffy in the entire house. He opened the front door, the half-door into the patio, the kitchen door. There was a gray morning overcast; the air was chilly, with a faint sour smell of smog in it. The lid of the garbage can was wet. From the patio came the kitten, to stand looking up at him soundlessly mewing. He stooped to run a hand along her back, along her tail, lifting her hind quarters off the floor.

The refrigerator showed him an unopened package of bacon, a canteloupe, milk. In the cupboard a package of Zing informed him that all he needed to do was stir into boiling water, set aside a moment, and serve. Whistling between his teeth, he measured coffee into the percolator and turned on the burners under it and under the tea kettle. His bare feet, moving him along the counter, stepped into something sticky, and he went to the back door to scrape his sole on the cement step. The cat rubbed back and forth against his leg.

"All right, all right," Leonard said, and poured a saucer of milk which he set down beside the refrigerator. Within a minute, getting out bread for toast, he stepped in the saucer, and he was on his knees with a sponge when Dolly came in dragging her teddy bear.

"Are *you* getting breakfast?" she said.

"Did you think I couldn't?"

"Why?"

"Why what? Why am I getting breakfast? Because pretty soon you're going to have a new brother or sister, and I'm getting in practice for extensive fatherhood. Want to help?"

"I want strawberries and Cheerios for breakfast," she said without a smile.

"Petition denied." Smoke accosted his nostrils, and he jumped to release the fuming toaster, whose pop-up didn't work. The toast, burned black, he dumped into the garbage pail. "Petition denied for these reasons," he said to Dolly. "A, we have no strawberries for your Cheerios, and B, we have no Cheerios for your strawberries. You're having Zing."

"Oh poo. I hate Zing." She leaned against him, and when he moved she put her arms around his leg and moved with him, riding his instep.

"Not the kind I make," he said. "How about bringing in the paper?"

"I want some Cheerios."

"Listen," he said, with her round silky head under his hand. "We're giving the old lady her breakfast on a tray, as a surprise, and I can't do it without you. Suppose you get your slippers on, so you don't get cold, and get the paper to put on her tray."

While he talked, her face puffed out at him, her eyes were squeezed down to glints. Then she exploded in a laugh and started running. "Shhh!" he said through the pass-through. "Let's not wake the customers." He jumped to the smoking toaster. Burned black again.

The tea kettle began to get its breath for a whistle. Leonard poured two cups of hot water in a saucepan and set it on a burner, shook salt over it, hesitated, shook again. Dolly came in with the damp paper. "Here," Leonard said. He moved aside a pitcher, glasses, an unwashed broiler pan, a can of cocoa, a roll of waxed paper, and some other items to make room on the crowded counter. He got out their biggest tray and showed Dolly where to put the paper. "You're the maid," he said. "See if you can remember all the things like napkins and spoons."

The water in the saucepan was boiling. He poured in Zing, stirred wildly to keep it from boiling over, and yanked the pan off the flame when it boiled over in spite of him. A smell of outraged cereal arose. "Look," he said to Dolly, who was laying spoons in a mathematical row on the tray, "see if you can toast some toast and keep from burning it, baby. I've flunked twice."

With one eye on the subsiding cereal he stooped to the vegetable cooler and found a net sack of oranges. The day was accelerating around him; it was a juggling act to keep all the essentials in the air at once. Coffee, yes; then down the burner some to keep it warm. It spit over its spouted chin at him when he had his back turned squeezing oranges. Zing—off the fire now, and safe. Sugar, cream— he steered Dolly to them and she got them on the tray. She wanted brown sugar on her Zing; he found it for her. The smell of smoke swung him around. His round-eyed helper confronted him with a scorched finger in her mouth. "Sister," he said, "you're going to grow up as incompetent as your old man. On the ball, baby, what do you say? Let's see your poor finner." He examined it, cured it with a smack.

Eventually there was cereal, coffee, orange juice, a cantaloupe cut in four. He had long since given up the bacon as involving insoluble problems of performance and personnel. He felt good. It tickled him to see Dolly putting the napkins in one corner of the tray and then, reconsidering, moving them to the middle, patting them smooth. His mind idled along while his hands jumped from job to job, and stumbling upon an old song, he fox-trotted around with it:

"My pet, how I love her,
My pet, thinking of her . . ."

With the toaster filled for the fourth time, and his eyes glued on it, he sang,

"I pet with nobody but"

He flipped the toaster release. Too pale. Down again.

"My pet."

Louise padded in with a knuckle in one eye and the kitten hanging limp under one arm. "What's the matter? What's burning?"

"Love like a burning city in my breast," Leonard said. "Have you washed?" He leaped. Ah, just in time. He said, "It's about ready. You two go run a washrag once around lightly, and then rouse up your angel mother and when all is ready you slip me the signal."

"Ow!" Louise said. "You darn naughty kitty!" The dropped cat slid behind the stove. Leonard stooped and kissed the clouded blue eyes. "You're cranky from too much Fourth of July. Come on, Plumbbob, get ready, hey? And a little brush on the hair."

He got another round of toast through the toaster, put butter and honey on the tray, and spooned out four bowls of cereal. Somewhere down by the bay, far-off, incongruous, peremptory, mournful, louder than usual under the overcast, a factory whistle blew seven o'clock. There was a sound of activity from the bathroom, the sandy hiss of water in the pipes. Leonard got two more slices through the toaster. Just as he was removing them, two brushed, shining, round-eyed faces leaned, one above the other, around the doorjamb, mugging silently at him: *She's awake.* He mugged back. Then he hoisted the overloaded tray onto a backtipped palm and marched, barefooted, bare-chested, and hairy, into the bedroom, singing,

"She's so refined, sweet and kind, perfect gem.
Has she got It? Lots of It. Oh baby she's got Them . . ."

The girls jumped around, yelling, "Surprise! Surprise!" Barbara, sitting up, scowled blackly. "Them! What an omen to wake up to." She smiled. "But I forgive you, you're so sweet. Give us a kiss." After a frantic sweeping aside of bottles, magazines, and clothes, he lowered the tray to the dresser. When their lips met she yanked the hair on his chest. "What makes you so sweet?"

"It's me nature. How do you feel?"

"I must be sick, if I get breakfast in bed."

He went out and returned with a small tray that he put in her lap, or rather on her thighs. She had to reach blindly for things on it like someone groping for lost objects behind a bureau. While he sorted her out juice, melon, toast, cereal, and coffee, he said, "You were up and down a good deal last night."

"I couldn't seem to get comfortable."

"I can stay home today, if you want. I don't have to go to Mrs. Lofty's."

"Oh, no. You go ahead. If I need anything I can call you."

"At least you've got two superb helpers." He got them seated on the foot of the bed and handed them orange juice and Zing. They gulped their juice, looked into their bowls, made identical faces, and laughed. "Let's eat in here every morning," Louise said.

But Leonard looked around the tiny dark cell packed with double bed, dresser, bed table, and chair, and at his daughters spooning cereal and dripping milk on the spread, and said, "I'd find it a trifle confining, wouldn't you? Of course when Mummy has this baby there'll be more room."

"Honestly," Barbara said, "what *are* we going to do? We never have worked that one out. As long as he's in a basket we can manage, but what about when he gets bigger?"

"He can sleep in my bed," Louise said.

"No, in mine!"

"Quiet, please," Leonard said. "This is what we'll do. We can either, in a dignified way, box in the carport for him when he gets too big for the house, or we can purchase a larger dwelling. How about something up on the hill, with a view of the bay and a patch of woods out behind full of horses and rabbit hutches and poison oak for the children?"

"Yes, please, Daddy! And a swimming pool."

"First things first. First Mummy has this baby, then I modestly accept a ten-thousand-a-year raise from a cheering school board, and then we go to our favorite real-estate agent, a jovial, Santa Claus-like fellow, and we say, 'We'd like a small estate, please. Something spacious, gracious, indoor-outdoor, for modern living. Because if we're anything, we're . . . gracious.' What is it?"

Dolly stared with porridge on her chin. She giggled. "You're all curly." He looked down, clutched his naked chest, and rushed from the room. In a minute he came back in a clean T-shirt, mumbling apologies.

As they ate in their mussed plywood box they heard Greenwood Acres empty itself. Voices, cars, the clicking sprockets and chains of bicycles, receded toward the gates and the SP station. By the time Leonard had rinsed the dishes and put them in the dishwasher, and had got into socks and shoes and a checked shirt, wives were beginning to return with the family cars. The house, wide open, let in their motor noises, the metal slamming of their doors. Somebody scolded somebody. The radio next door, tuned unneighborly loud, reported that the weather would be clear except for morning fog near the coast, westerly winds ten to eighteen miles an hour, high in San Francisco sixty-four, in San Mateo seventy-eight, in San Rafael eighty.

Barbara sat enthroned in the cluttered bedroom. He liked her best just this way, without make-up; her essential, even-tempered, placid sweetness was then undisguised. The skin under her eyes, slightly darkened, looked so petal-soft it tempted his fingers. For almost a minute he stood looking down at her. "You call me," he said. "I wonder if you shouldn't have your bag packed, just in case."

"I've had it packed for two weeks."

"All right. I just want you to live up to the solemnity of the occasion."

"You go ahead and worry," she said. "It's good for you. But don't expect me to be a month early. Do you think I want it said I had my third child in a Chevvy that hasn't been washed for a year and a half?"

"Criticism?" he said. He bent and kissed her. Her brown eyes were very soft, very deep, amused, untroubled. "Take it easy, now."

"I will. Don't drink too much orange juice."

He lifted and bussed his daughters. Before climbing into the old Chevvy he bent to look at the oil drip underneath it. Sooner or later he was going to have to put the old crock up on blocks and pull the rear main. He looked inside. Papers, dust, Dolly's lost sweater, a political sticker he had been going to put on the bumper and not got around to, a loose speeder wrench, a sack of tire chains that had been in there since a ski week end late last winter. He took chains and wrench and sweater out, crumpled the papers and the bumper-banner, found a stub of broom and swept out the worst dirt. Then he brushed off his clean Levis, checked his gleaming shoes, climbed in, and stepped on the starter.

Sedately, shaved and laundered, his thinning hair bristling, he drove off toward Pyracantha Avenue and the main gate, satisfactorily later than the commuting slaves, but still in time to make the Hutchens door by eight o'clock.

By suburban ways he reached the hurrying channel of El Camino, where he was stopped by a long red light. Ahead, back among the discreet patrician lanes, waited the world of Mrs. Howard King Hutchens. For all the resemblance it bore to his own, he might as well have been going to work for Harun al-Rashid. With his nose full of the exhausts of El Camino he thought of that dustless, purified, humidified air and that underwater quiet. To be involved in this solemn business amused him. Some morning he ought to arrive in a skin-diver's mask. Dr. Jekyll, I presume.

It isn't much, he said to himself, watching the interminable light. Only about four an hour, and the working conditions aren't so hot. But it's a living.

The stream of cars slashed by, unbreachable. Then the red changed to yellow, the latecomers scooted through, a channel appeared. He gunned the old Chevvy across like the hosts of Israel before the waters could roll back again. As he drove along, already half metamorphosed, under the great gum trees, he said to himself that Mrs. Howard King Hutchens was something. She entered into this archive business as if it were an elopement.

CHAPTER 18

S OMETIMES she got to help with little chores. She could hold a
scared dog while Grulich removed a foxtail from ear or eye;
or she could bathe and strip some terrier out in the yard. That
was a job she liked: at home she often took Fat Boy into the
shower with her, and roughed him up with a towel afterward until
he tore around the house shaking himself and rolling and running
his face along the rugs. But here bathings and strippings happened
only when someone wanted to take a dog away, and every one meant
the loss of a friend.

And there were great reaches of empty time. Sometimes she tried to
read. Grulich was an amateur pot-hunter, and his parlor was full of
mealing stones and Paiute baskets and the publications of the Bureau
of American Ethnology. Selecting something more for its weight than
its interest, she could go outside and let a few dogs into the exercise
yard and sit down in the white coveralls Grulich had loaned her,
and with her back against a tree consult the burial habits of the
Mi-wuk. That way she could maintain her daytime apathy, built on
the pretense that her stay here was a kind of convalescence. With
Grulich she exchanged perhaps a hundred words a day. He was as
taciturn as a stump; at meals, if he looked at her at all, he looked

outrage and accusation: What are you doing in my house? What do I get by letting you in? Embarrassment, and the neighbors talking.

The dogs would willingly have got mixed up in her troubles, however, and it was the dogs that kept her here. Thank God a dog was without embarrassments, ambitions, moral judgments, responsibilities, or fear of what people said. If he loved you he licked your hand and lay down by you and came when you called, and if you went away he waited hopefully in the driveway until you returned. If you got angry with him or hurt him, he forgave you at once, unasked. Also, no matter how badly a bitch treated a dog, he would never fight with her. Uncritical love plus chivalry to females: where were you likely to find a man as decent as almost any dog? But she did not pursue that ironic strain, or wallow in her own distress. More often than not she sat with her mind passive and nearly empty, in her lap a heavy book open to engravings of naked women gathering acorns or making soap of yucca root, and ran her hand absently over the ears and the blissful, blinking eyes of the red setter or the Irish terrier who were her favorites among Grulich's boarders. That was another thing about dogs: they loved to be touched.

Off in the blue daytime air was the pulse of the lake's summer life, rising sometimes to the roar of a motorboat towing water-skiers past, falling sometimes to the fused murmur of the highway, the boats, passing airplanes, the noises of the lakeshore resorts. She could sit with her eyes out of focus, staring at the twiggy ground, and let her mind go slack and dreaming, and in that mood could hear, back of the healthy outdoor sounds, a throb that was compounded of all the yells and groans and sighs of a vast hell. Dante, passing around the lake's basin asking questions of these shades, would have found here the usual lustful ones, the avaricious, the gluttonous, the sinners through wrath, the flatterers and those who dealt in simony and barratry, the envious and the proud. But more likely, crowding around the traveler who spoke with a human voice, these Tahoe shades would have reported their own special sin of sensation and excitement, their lust for kicks. They would have found Dante himself a sensation, and trampled one another for a sight of him: a freak of the moral intelligence. And they would have pointed out, and he observed, their special punishment, which was the same as their sin—to indulge themselves. The pleasure halls of their hell never closed, the neon burned twenty-four hours a day, dealers succeeded one another in shifts, any hour was the hour for a drink. The food of hell was charcoal-broiled New York cuts and french fries; the change girls were selected for their figures and probably for their complaisance. Panting, the Members from Petaluma drove through the neon-tinted murk screaming with laughter. Where they found quiet, they destroyed it; where they encountered beauty they left their pleasure palaces or their beer cans.

But where she sat it was quiet. For ten years she had gone through all those other circles herself, boredly or angrily or restlessly or spitefully sampling their sins and their punishments, and then in an hour, in an instant, she had smashed like a light bulb, she had betrayed Burke, her marriage, and herself. She sat now in the place reserved for traitors, and there, as her mother said, it was lonely and cold. One thing, she assumed, would reprieve her: the touch of unqualified love. But from whom? How? She had the dogs, and no one else.

At night, when the lake's hum broke down into single, far-heard voices or motor sounds, and stillness began creeping inward like nighttime animals edging closer to a sleeping camp, she hooked one of the dogs on a leash and walked him down along the shore. She told herself that whether she was involved in a cure or a punishment, there ought to be comfort in darkness, quiet, the cold wet fishy smell of the lake, the night sound of water on the beach, the companionship of a friendly little animal.

But she resisted the comfort she went hunting. When at night she shed her apathy, her jeering intelligence came out and told her that what she was undergoing was neither punishment nor convalescence, but evasion. She could not pretend to herself that she was thinking anything out, or making a contrite peace with her own motives, or finding justifications for her disintegration, or arriving at any plan for her life. That sort of reconciliation would have to be built on the assumption that for every action there was a specific

213

motivation, which once understood made everything balance out neatly: if B stood for boredom, N for neglect, D for a do-nothing tradition, I for instability, T for time, and C for conscience, then

$$\frac{(B^2 + N)T + I + D}{C} = X, \text{ for explosion.}$$

But what about the violence of her collapse, for which there was not only no adequate motivation, but very real and puritanical inhibitions? What if, a normally intelligent, highly fortunate, reasonably sophisticated woman, you suddenly blew to bits, and nothing set you off but accident, and nothing steered you from then on but furious uncharacteristic feelings like those that must drive the she-murderers of the newspapers? What if all unexpectedly you found yourself vulgar, hysterical, spiteful, and uncontrolled? What if one hour you were frantic with lust for one man, and the next anguished with pity and duty for another, and the next wild with revenge against them both, and all the time full of desperate loathing for yourself? What if your metabolism, personality, mind, changed suddenly as if you had been fed a horrible mess of personality-changing drugs, Miltown and benzedrine, bolts and jolts, Spanish fly and whatever it was they were supposed to put in the men's food in the army—saltpeter?

There was no equation that would make her understand herself. And anyway, what good would it do her to bring her own emotions under control when others, whose actions were out of her hands, continued to be motivated by coldness, suspicion, timidity, God knew what? Renounce her desires, like a good girl? She had *been* renounced, doubly renounced, and with reason.

Halting the straining terrier with a pull on the leash, she sat on a stump, with a great spruce behind her that stood for all land, all forest; and in front the glimmering, misty, light-starred lake. It was a very big lake, a Shining Big Sea Water that reached to the far edge of the world, where it was fenced by mountains. Overhead there were stars, but in the south a lick of lightning showed the loom of thunderheads. The water was stealthy-still. It made only a tiny sucking, a sigh like breath, a lip and a lap against the shingle, and then stillness again. The air was tumid with coming rain.

The terrier came against her knee and she closed her fingers in his fur. Her other hand felt around on the ground until it found a pebble to flip into the water. The lonely, forgotten *plunk* brought the dog up quivering, sniffing and straining toward the lake, and she hugged his head against her leg. They heard the thin sounds of water lapping at the edge of a great stillness, and she thought that anyone, hearing that sound, might be reminded of tide-pool Eden. Some half-man stooping alertly beside an African waterhole a half million years ago might have cocked his head at it, obscurely knowing his source. The last survivor of a humanity that had destroyed itself might take what consolation he could from that watery promise of resurrection and renewal.

Wade in? said her mind, watching her brightly. Stand up right now and walk in? The shoes would be full at once, then it would be cold around the calves, the coveralls clinging and motion difficult as the knees went under. Then water dragging at the thighs, the clothes very heavy now and the breath catching in the chill, cold gripping waist and breast until it lapped at the throat, the feet tiptoeing and the chin tilted to keep the mouth out. A last look at soft dark, soft sky, gathering storm, the lights along the shore. From behind her the anxious yip of the terrier, uncertain whether to follow. Then the settling of the heels, the relinquishing sag of the weight, the burying of the face, the slow deep inhalation.

Beautiful, a lovely sentimental satisfying ending. So young, so unhappy. She would keep it in mind. The coveralls would be a good touch, a sort of sackcloth. And there should be incidental music: from a cottage not far away, where lovers were kissing and whispering on a dark porch, a phonograph would be playing *Lu Mer*.

She threw another stone. Her fingers, lifted from the needles and litter, smelled of earthy, moldy, aromatic things, penicillin, earth's mysterious curatives.

It was fantastic that after a week here she should still be swinging in so wide an arc. Having exhausted herself in a vulgar tantrum, a melodramatic outburst, a Walpurgisnacht (give it a fancy name and it wouldn't sound so dirty, vengeful, and stupid as it really was) she did not feel in the least steadied or healed. She only felt sickened, and she had no idea what medicine to take, for she diagnosed her sickness as herself. When she was quiet in her mind, the quiet was only apathy; and when she emerged and began to think and feel, as often as not she found growing in her an unreasonable and implacable conviction of wrong and hurt. And when she became aware of how she was twisting to throw the blame back on Burke's chilliness or Bernard's cowardice, then she retreated into the self-loathing and disgust which was her apathy's truest center.

Lord God, how to *be?* A woman, a sack of organs, a creature whose center of gravity was in the pelvis, how did she justify herself when the pelvis proved unproductive? Not with pleasure, for pleasure with Burke seemed increasingly less possible, and pleasure outside she had sampled to her sorrow: it lay like a colony of streptococcus in the throat of her conscience. Quit being a woman then, forget she was a walking womb? Become some busy Neuter, lady executive or chairman of committees, put to what was called productive use the education that had been wasted on her?

The phrases for it came into her head, bitter as acid: a life of her own; find an interest.

Well, she had found a doghouse. Charlie Grulich escaped from people and hid himself among dogs and ancient cultures. Why not she? Become a goddess of fertility, learned in blood lines, steering by however little the history of living things? Imagine! they would say. She was wealthy, well-born, the world at her wish, and yet she chose to retire into the country and breed schnauzers. Ask her why schnauzers and she will reply with a smile that they are the most faithful of all dogs. But look at her hands, how brown. Look at her face, how serene.

Yes? her scornful mind answered her. Haven't you seen them around dog shows all your life? How vicarious do you want to be? They're worse than the blue-ribbon horsey kind, worse than the promiscuous kind, worse even than the busy Neuters. Or more pathetic.

The southward clouds had piled up, sneaking toward the zenith between flares of sheet lightning. Leaning from under the spruce tree's blackness she saw them engulfing foot by foot the Milky Way. A bright flash, like the cracking of a dish with light behind it, and this time a low roll of thunder.

Assuming that her trouble involved more than a choice between two men—or the loss of both of them—and accepting such other whimsies of luck as a tipped uterus, then the problem clearly was to find something worth her commitment. Start at the top, the greater glory of God? Hardly. One could abstractly comprehend the problem as a religious problem without being persuaded to denominational answers. If she wanted to do the work of a Poor Clare she would have to do it without the habit.

Or pleasure, the glutting of the excitable organism with sensation? That was the special sin of her class and her country, what occupied the Tahoe or California circle of Hell. But she herself had never had a gift for enjoyment; pleasure had always left her uneasy; her conscience always got involved in it. When she jumped into the flesh-pots, as last week, she jumped as if throwing herself into Kilauea.

So make a virtue and an existence out of pure discretion, take all things in moderation, exist by willed temperance—and for it, too? All sins, said smug Bobbie and Leonard MacDonald, were sins of excess.

They were so right. Even the examination of one's personal difficulties ran at once toward excess, until the soiled conscience swam into mere spots before the eyes. She wondered bleakly what Burke was doing, and imagined him eating moodily and alone in the house they had shared. She could not believe that his self-righteousness would permit him to regret the choice he had made; and yet she could not believe he was happy there, either. The house was hers as much as his—which was to say that it belonged to neither of them. Three times in eleven years she had redecorated it, trying to bend it into something personal, and every detail in it was of her choosing, and yet it had escaped her. Like everything else in her life it took what she had to give, and gave back nothing. She could see Burke, for comfort's sake, eating at the coffee table in the living room, or relaxing with a late highball in the patio; and yet the living room reached out behind him in shadowed spaces unfriendly to him as to her; and upon the patio fell an invisible, dampening bloom of dew.

The bowl cracked again, the thunder rumbled closer. It occurred to her, not for the first time, that she might try to get something out of talking to Grulich. At least he had made a sort of life that could be lived singly. But Grulich went around encased in his own silence like a deaf man, chewing on his dead pipe. He had sagging angry-looking German cheeks and he took no interest in human problems. He did not like humans, he liked dogs and dead cultures. The only reason he had ever let so ambiguous and dangerous a creature as herself take refuge in his place was the reverence he had for Ch. Bernsdorff von Bernsdorff, that product of carefully controlled incest that she called Fat Boy. There was a picture of Fat Boy on Grulich's wall.

Under the loose skin of the terrier's neck she could feel the solid column of muscle. The image of Burke alone in their house was pitiful to her, and yet she knew what would happen if by any impulse of affection or magnanimity he should ask her to come back, and she should go. They would both try, they would will themselves toward consideration, she would try to be humble and he would try to forgive. But the tensions of their life would go on, the first time he had to choose between her and some patient he would choose the patient, both his self-righteousness and her conscience would lie in wait for some moment, and when the moment came he would reveal that he thought of her in exactly the same terms she used for herself. And she would not take it. Being in the wrong, always in the wrong, she would strike out, and there they would be, glaring at each other across some pitiful, intolerable, unhealable gulf. Other women might slip and learn to forgive themselves; she could not. Other husbands might forgive fully, and forget; Burke could not. He would forgive in the mind only, never as an act of love. And he would always go where his duty led him, and she would always mistrust his duty because he had chosen to naturalize it in the country of the well-to-do.

Start all over, then? Go back into circulation like an eighteen-year-old, with an eye to the availability and possibility of every unattached man? She had seen the look on the faces of many divorced women; she had seen them set themselves like traps. The very thought repelled her. She had been for twelve years a trusted and faithful wife, she had known for ten days Bernard's corrupt sweetness. She could imagine no relation with a man that would not be spoiled by the memory of one or the other.

The terrier quivered under her hand and whined in his throat. Then lightning cracked the bowl, forked and bright, and she saw in the white instant his rigid, prick-eared head, the lit side of the spruce trunk and the droop of a branch, and the lake blackly shining like wet asphalt, and up above, in the periphery of her vision where the place of the flash ached in the firmament, a turmoil of boiling cloud. Then blackness with a vivid after-image like a faded negative, then real blackness, then the thunder.

The dog lunged against the leash. She pulled him back and he whined, licked her hand, leaned out against the chain testing some smell that fascinated him. He lifted his feet nervously, his body shook. How queer, to live so alertly by a sense that in her hardly existed. Her own nose could barely smell the needly ground and the lake's wet margins and the indefinable promise of rain on the air. He could sift out and sort every stray wisp of night wind, and know by pure mystery whether a taint at his nostrils was a woodrat that had poked its head out of its nest, or a deer that had come down stick-legged to drink a half mile away.

"Ah, Muggsy," she said, "smell me an answer! I've got to have something to live for. I can't just *be,* like you and Fat Boy. I've got to matter to somebody, or to myself, or why am I human?"

The moment she whispered it, she felt the twinge, the angry hurt. Her pride was as stiff and sore as a hand that the cat had clawed.

The forest breathed at her back. Off somewhere, suspended apparently in upper air, was a residual noise of humanity—a horn, a boat getting in fast ahead of the storm. She lifted her face from the wiry fur and rose and went to the water's edge and dragged a hand through the water. It felt milky warm, and she thought how everything is only seeming, how everything has definition only with relation to something else. A flashlight moving on a dock could be bigger than a star. An indiscretion that many women would shrug off, an unrest that some would cure with a sleeping pill, could tear her apart. A lie that some would tell as naturally as breathing she could not persist in at all. Bernard, who had added lying to disloyalty, kept his Stonestown security and the trust of his wife and daughters, while she, who had taken both her marriage and her emotions seriously, kept nothing.

The dog pulled her sideways and entangled himself in bushes, so that she had to grope in the dark to free him. Immediately he burst off up the shore and upset her. Angrily she yanked him back, but at once squatted among the stones and hugged him. Trembling, he strained away.

"I suppose I could give up my life to other people," she said into his hairy ear. "Mmmm? Like Schweitzer? Go off and become a nurse in a Navajo hospital, or use my money to establish schools for spastic children? But it would be such a phony thing—I'd know all along I was buying off my conscience. People who do things like that want to be called saints, and being called a saint would gag me."

The breath of air from behind her came again, and with it a brilliant zigzag of lightning that hung and quivered, visibly rushing down its crooked length. Under it the lake's livid surface stirred as if its hair were on end. Sabrina shortened her hold on the lead and pulled the dog around, feeling for the path back to the house. "So many things gag me," she said.

The terrier did not want to come. Dragging him, she emerged into the little meadow and looked up and saw the whole sky without stars. All around the edges of the bowl world, lightning flickered and winked. The sense of coming storm awakened and excited her, and she hurried. Still reaching and clawing back toward the woods, the terrier yapped, agonized, and at once the kennels broke out into ragged barkings. Against the lighted window of Grulich's parlor a shadow passed: Grulich, rising to investigate what was upsetting the dogs. "See what you've done?" she said.

He scrambled and clawed away, striving after impossible happinesses in the dark woods, so that she had to wrap the leash around her hand and haul him across the meadow, feeling with her feet for the path smooth and sunken in the turf. A gust of wind stormed around her, the horizon all around flickered with light, and she saw the path, the gate in the wire exercise yard, the line of cages down both sides with dogs standing up against the screen. Then out.

She stumbled. A splash of rain hit her in the eye. It was all she could do to drag the terrier against his desire. "Come on," she said, out of breath and laughing, more alive than she had been for days. "Come on, you little beggar, before I make a symbol of you."

The rain caught her in the exercise yard. On both sides, stretching against the screen of their pens, the dogs whined and roared and yapped. Pulling sideward and backward, the terrier walked hind-legged, pawing at air, choking on his collar. By the flashes of lightning Sabrina saw the first big drops pelting down, and twigs and dust jumping. Wet blotches spread on her shoulders, her face was wet. The air, the open ground, the pines, were alive with a gravelly rush. The terrier stood on end, crosswise, backward, between her legs, wild with excitement, so that she had to land him in his pen by the leash, like a heavy struggling fish. When she closed the door on him in a great sheeted flash he was leaping high against the screen and adding his frantic yapping to the uproar of dogs and the rushing of rain.

She closed the gate and fumbled with wet hands in the dark to snap the padlock shut. The rain came slanting thickly across the hooded night light. At a brilliant flash she jerked her hands away and then put them back, cringing against the splitting sky, and got the padlock closed. Her hair was beaten across her face; the shoulders, arms, and thighs of the coveralls were soaked; her face and hands streamed. Running, she made the door of Grulich's cottage, burst it open, and shut it behind her.

Wind and rain were shut out, noise dropped away. She stood there with her heart and her eyes as still as the still air of the kitchen. "Oh," she said. Burke and Oliver were sitting with Grulich at the kitchen table.

Immediately Grulich got up and went into the front room. His look said to her, accusingly, that he didn't want anything to do with it. In a minute they heard him going up the stairs. The floor above them creaked. They heard the hiss of rain. "Well, Sabrina," Oliver said.

He was looking his customary ironic self, but Burke, with whose eyes hers had been locked from the moment she slammed the door and turned, looked ill, white and pinched around the mouth, pouchy under the eyes. The thinness and narrowness of his face and the length of his teeth were accentuated. She thought a little wildly that he looked like Woodrow Wilson about to scold someone. But mostly what she felt was a kind of panic like a schoolgirl coming to an examination for which she has not studied—the panic that recurs in anxiety dreams, decades after one leaves school: the course one signed up for and forgot all about, the examination overlooked until there is nothing to do but take it and fail. This was the end of her lull, and she was still unprepared.

Though she had imagined their meeting, she was no surer than she had ever been about how to face him, and she was caught unbraced for the emotion she felt: not shame, as she had anticipated, but something awkward as a fishbone in the throat—pity that he looked so bad, almost gratification that she had done it to him.

To evade his eyes she went into the little room off the kitchen that Grulich had turned over to her, and got a towel off the door and came out again wiping her face and hands and patting her wet hair. Around the towel, lightly—but it came out flippant and wrong—she said, "Well, how did you find me? Hire Peekaboo Pennington?"

Oliver bent his head in ironic acknowledgment. Burke said nothing. Busily Sabrina dried herself, an extended and closely followed pantomime. Her hair was so wet that she took the pins out and shook it down and rubbed it with the towel. Then she had to go and get a comb and stoop to the mirror above the sink and re-part the hair into its smooth wings. She gathered the sheaf at the back of her neck and held it until she could grab up a piece of brown cord to tie it. In the mirror she saw what the backward weight of her hair did to her eyes, and then she shook the long pony tail loose and turned.

"You'd better get out of those wet clothes," Burke said.

For answer she reached Grulich's canvas jacket off its nail beside the sink and draped it over her shoulders, hooking back a hand to pull her hair free. The night outside winked brilliantly twice; she saw the nervous response twitch in Burke's eyelid. They couldn't talk for thunder. Burke's nostrils flared out and then in, and she thought, He's putting that on, he thinks that communicates both his strong disgust and his self-control. The yellow blind, drawn over the open window, sucked strongly outward, kinking like tin.

They waited. She saw that the spasmodic contraction around Burke's eyes, which sometimes had touched her because it seemed to mean a warmer man trying to break through the repression, had become a tic. His left eye winked at her three times while the thunder rolled and rumbled down. So he couldn't be putting it on. He looked tired and ashamed.

Oliver rose. "Excuse me," he said. "Now that the family is reunited I guess I'll wait in the car."

"You don't have to," Burke said.

"I know I don't. But I'd rather. Excuse me?" He jerked a thumb significantly at the ceiling and went out. They heard him running past the window; at his heels came a blink and a shattering crash as if someone had been waiting for him with an anti-tank gun.

Sabrina, trying to smile, felt that she only grimaced. She had difficulty in facing Burke squarely. The composed, pale face with the uncontrollably twitching eyelid was both too steady and too shattered. "Now what?" she made herself say.

"I suppose that's up to you."

For a moment a hope; she felt how her eyes jumped to his. But his glance was gray as granite, unwarmed. "Why did you hunt me down?" she said.

"You might have been in trouble."

"Yes," she said, disappointed. "Of course you'd do your duty." She stood up to the painful flickering wink. Smiling, or trying to, she produced again the crooked grimace. "Well, I was. I still am."

"What are you going to do? You can't stay here."

"I don't know," she said, and felt how little kept this dialogue from breaking into a melodrama of accusations, tears, blame, reconciliations that reconciled nothing except the moment's hysteria.

He reached out a pack of cigarettes. His hand, she saw, was as usual very clean and perfectly steady. Even more than his emotionless face, it contradicted the twitching lid. When they had settled her little problem he would go on back home and at seven tomorrow morning he would be on his rounds of the hospital.

Seeing that he was still holding out the cigarettes, she shook her head. "I've quit."

Quietly he put them away without taking one himself. He said, "I gather you didn't buy that ranch."

"No."

"It might be a good idea for you."

"Well!" she said. "Change of tune." For a moment she let her eyes blaze at him the blame that she was never quite able to suppress, and she said, "When I thought of that I was on my knees, I was thinking of ways we might work it out."

The twitch became a series of quick flutters. He bent his head a little down, and frowned as if pain had gone through his eye, but he said nothing. He looked withdrawn and waiting. Remembering his face buried in her belly, his tears on her skin, she could hardly see him for a moment, the room cracked and shattered so. Right then, with a little lie that did not even need to be spoken, she could have healed it, probably. By not acceding to the lie she had perhaps made it incurable. And yet he had come hunting her.

"You're not on your knees now," he said finally.

"Would you be, after your husband told you he didn't care what you did?"

"I was mad."

"Yes," she said, "so I gathered."

With an upward, squinting look, an incredulous shake of the head, he said, "I can't believe this is you. Overnight, practically. It's like being bitten by a shark you never even see till he hits you."

"I suppose," she said wearily. "But it didn't come on overnight."

"You never gave me the slightest sign."

"Were you ever looking?" Angrily she pushed away from the sink and went to the window and grabbed the cord of the blind. When she swung around to face him she saw that impatience or anger had put whitening lines around his mouth. So here they were back at it—recrimination, hostility. It was hopeless. Raising the shade halfway, she looked out into the streaming dark. The air smelled of wet pines and wet grass. The dogs had evidently been chased into their tepees by the rain. She heard only the pelting downpour.

"Both at your mother's and over the phone you said this affair was over," Burke said.

Without turning, she made a bitter face into the washed darkness, renouncing what had never been hers and what she had mistaken for something better than it was, but renouncing it in pain. "Over? Of course it's over." She turned. "I'm ashamed," she said. "Apparently that isn't enough, but it's all I can do. I'm sick of myself, I'll never understand it. *It's* over, but I'm not."

The tic in his eye was very bad; he stared at her with his lips grinning back from his teeth. "No," he said. "Apparently not. There's for instance the report of this detective."

"Oh, you did hire a detective!"

"What other way was there? I couldn't just let you disappear, not knowing whether you were dead or alive. Would you rather I'd gone to the police, so everything you've been doing would be plastered all over the newspapers?"

Sabrina looked warningly up at the ceiling. She could imagine Grulich up there with his hands over his ears or his head under the pillow. She found that she had braided the shade cord into a chain stitch; now with a jerk she unraveled it, watching Burke's strained, twitching face.

"Not that it made much difference," he said. "You were in and out of every club on the lake, blind drunk, cashing checks, showing your credit cards. It didn't take any detective to trail you through those two days and nights. You left your name and address everywhere."

He was showing no excessive self-control now. His head was drawn back in a curious stiff way and his eyes were half closed. He kept stretching his lips over his teeth as if they had shrunk and would not quite cover. His voice, though he kept it low, was full of hissing s's and plosive t's and c's. Silent, she watched him, thinking, It's like sex with him, the more he names it the realer it is, and the more it maddens him.

He looked down irritably as if he might give it up and stop talking, then his eyes came jolting back. He said, "If you're so ashamed, what about your friend Henderson?"

"Henderson? I don't know anybody named Henderson."

"Lying again?" he said with a terrible look. "Your friend Henderson from Petaluma."

Her heart and her breath had stopped. "Oh," she said. "Him." She ran the chain stitch up the cord again.

"How else do you suppose we found you? He told us where he'd left you and I thought of Grulich." The short leg of the table clacked down as he leaned forward. Intensely fixed behind the irrelevant winking and narrowing of the tic, his eyes looked insane. "I never thought my wife would let herself be picked up in a bar by somebody like that."

Unexpectedly her breath started again, a short, jerky inhalation. "I picked *him* up," she said. Her fingers unraveled the cord. It slipped from her hand, the shade flew to the top with a horrible racket. For a moment there was the rainy dark, then a flash lit up the whole sodden yard, the threshing pines, the path shining wet across the meadow. Afterward she felt her own cut-out silhouette in the window. Without the cord she needed something to do with her hands.

"Why?" Burke said at last in a cracking whisper. "Why? *Why?*"

Under the canvas jacket she was shivering, but when she put her hands inside, on her shoulders, they felt warm and steamy. "Why?" she said, and bit her chattering teeth together. "To make everything as bad as possible, I guess. To be real somehow. To die somehow. I don't know."

"Because I was mad, because I told you I was through, you go and do something twice as—"

"Oh, sure," she said drearily. "Of course."

His face looked as if he might shout something wild. After a hard, unbelieving stare he passed his hand along his jaw and looked down at the floor. His eye jerked so rapidly that she wondered why he didn't clap his hand over it. She could no longer believe he was only acting the appropriate but controlled emotions of a wronged husband. He shook like a dog, and stared at her in silence with his wild twitching eye, and she could have gone to him in pity and put her arms around him and held his face to her breast, but something aloof, quick, and cool that had watched her through the whole scene said, "No, it would only be pity. When he got over the bad spell and you got over your pity he would still not have forgiven you, and you would still not have forgiven yourself. Of course he's shaken, of course he's hurt, but unless he makes a move that means love, it won't do. Dirty as you are, he's got to want to touch you, he's got to hold you, and shut his eyes and hang on. If you matter enough to him so that he'll . . ."

"Sabrina," he said, "do you think you're sick?"

A long breath, a sigh really. "In the head, you mean?"

"Nervously."

"It would be nice to have such a nice simple comprehensible explanation, wouldn't it?" she said with a wan smile. "No, I'm not sick. Sick in the soul, maybe, whatever that means."

There he sat, his neat long head, his narrow jaw, his familiar bony shoulders, his hands, his wrists—her husband, intimately known. "Oh, Burke!" she said, and now he blurred through tears. "I tried too hard for too long. I married you for the wrong reasons, and tried to pretend they were good ones, and it didn't work. I've never belonged to anything, really belonged, in my life. I never even belonged to my marriage. No, that isn't quite true. I loved you, I did. But you never gave me any chance to be a woman, darling. If you had, maybe I could have become one."

He was at his old trick of examining his hands. Squinting painfully upward, he said, "I'm afraid I don't know what you mean."

"I suppose not," she said. "Maybe all it means is that I'm a wretched neurotic female. But I've told you I hate myself for what I did to you, and that's the truth. You told me on the telephone you didn't care what I did, and maybe I wanted to do something so vile you'd *have* to care. But I tell you this, I pushed myself into that filthy business the way you'd sweep a crippled cockroach into the fire. I was giving myself what I knew I deserved."

She waited. He did not say, "Let's go somewhere and heal this together." He did not say, "Poor darling, you've had a bad time." He did not say, "Even after all this, you're the one important thing in my life." He sat at the table and said with a twisted smile, "You're sure you weren't giving me what *I* deserved?"

Miserably, with chattering teeth, she turned away from him. "I suppose it's possible," she said.

She heard his dry voice, intolerably steady again—how could he?—say, "Well, if you meant to punish me, you did the job."

Sabrina shrugged. She might have said, "I'm sorry." She might have said, "I'm glad." She said neither. And at that moment, too late and in the tone of stiff correctness that made her want to screech and fly up the chimney, he said what she had been wanting him to say. "In spite of all this, I'm asking you to come back," he said. "Will you?"

She snapped around and was met by the wink and flicker of the tic. But his face was composed, his mouth steady; his hands, crossed on the table, looked relaxed. He seemed almost amused, as if he had posed her a riddle and was waiting for her to give up, and she understood that one of her deepest, longest-standing, and most ineradicable grudges against him was that he felt no guilt himself. No matter what he might say or how miserable she might make him, he took no blame for what had happened. Of that crushing rejection on the telephone he said only, "I was mad." He saw nothing demanding change in their marriage, but asked her now, as he had asked her in Hillsborough, simply to come back to what had been. Other grievances she might have manufactured in self-pity or self-defense, but that one she had not made up.

And yet she wanted to go back, she wanted to be safe, she wanted to quit being what she had become, she wanted—and would have melted if it had happened—his hand on her. A touch, a human touch, in place of this judicial withholding while she made up her mind.

Then she made up her mind. "I'm not fit to," she said, and wondered why she had fallen back on that hypocrisy.

"I'm ready to forget it."

Their eyes met in a crooked, glancing look. He squinted his eye nearly shut to stop its twitching; but except for that galvanism he had completely regained control of face, hands, voice. Not she. She choked on the word, and tried it again and choked a second time, but got it out, as thick as the word of a moron. "No," she whispered.

He sat stiffly with his hands on the table, he did not look pained and he did not plead. "Do you want a divorce?" he said.

"I . . . No."

"Would you fight it if I started proceedings?"

"No. You've got every reason."

"But maybe I don't want one either."

She shivered inside the canvas jacket, and felt the wet coveralls clinging to her legs. "All right," she said.

Now his mouth did twist; she thought for a second he was going to rage and quarrel at her. But his teeth came together; he smiled. "Right where it was before, then."

Sabrina moved her shoulders. "If you want."

"Where will you go?"

"I guess if Oliver will give me a lift I'll go back to Mother's."

The rain was slackening. A flash lit the window and she counted four before the thunder broke, receding. By the hanging kitchen light they stared at one another. He had not lifted a hand to touch her. She could see in his face nothing of what she realized she had hoped to find.

CHAPTER 19

T HE TRESTLE table had been removed from the library. What confronted him on these mornings was not a workroom but a solitude fit for a worldly pope. The air smelled with thin richness of his late preservative oils; the light was cool; the day ahead promised its agreeable inconsequential labors punctuated by anecdotal visits from Mrs. Hutchens. And first there was the pleasant business of readying the tools.

From a cabinet he took the card file in which he had indexed every item thus far examined in the Hutchens archive. Beside it on the blotter —somebody changed the desk blotter for him every two or three days— he laid two ballpoint pens, one blue and one red, and several folders of un-indexed papers. On the shelf he placed, open side out, the labeled pamphlet cases, for which Mrs. Hutchens would substitute permanent boxes in full calf with gilt lettering as soon as the bookbinder had them ready.

This was how people, of a kind, were transformed into history, of a kind. Energy, if it could be called that, into matter, if that was what these papers were. Substance into essence, if you preferred it backward and in another terminology. Like a bleat from a dusty throat the labeled cases insisted, "I was. Never mind what, I was. Here is proof." And in the end there was a sort of lesson in them; the acquisitiveness and eccentricity and conspicuous waste of a whole family became representative of something, and worth preserving. Now Mizraim cures wounds, and Pharaoh is sold for balsams.

Meantime he was a monk in an opulent cell. He pulled up the padded leather chair, looked at it with respect, sat down, opened a folder of papers, and began listing.

A child's penciled letter: *My dear Emily, we are glad you had a nice journy, we hope Mary Stillman will come and stay with you, when are you comeing home? I went to the Public Garden and saw the beautiful two lips (tulips) arnt they pretty? It is very windy today, I hope all are well. I went in the beach wagon with Magwire to Aunt Sarah's. Please tell me what part of what day you receive this letter. I would just as leave lief you would have somebody read this letter. I send my love to you all. I hope you will not care because I dident write the letter very nicely. Affectionately from Mercer G. Wolcott your Brother.*

A note from Harvard University, School of Veterinary Medicine, Hospital Department, dated June 17, 1884, addressed to Bushrod Wolcott and dealing with the discolored teeth of his setter.

A folded paper containing a reddish, five-pointed pressed leaf and the date July 6, 1865.

An envelope addressed "Cornelius M. Wolcott, Present," and inside it a note marked "Confidential": *My dear Sir: In the discussion about uniting the parties on one candidate for Gov'r against Mr. Andrew, we have had a good deal to say about yourself. The Comce's may not be able to agree upon anyone, tho Yr. name meets with the least opposition. If they agree at all it must be upon an "old Whig," and a man of buss'ss is preferable to a lawyer. It will be you or nobody. Yrs. truly, Somebody Illegible.*

So Mrs. Hutchens' grandfather, an energetic man of buss'ss, had almost made it into another sort of distinction, or at least into candidacy therefor. Inscribe on his tombstone, "He nearly met with the least opposition." Evidently that was the extent of it, for if the Comce's, whoever they were, had been able to agree, there would have been a vast body of documentary evidence preserved by the family. Even their apparent method of wildly random sampling would have preserved something more than this one note. A close miss, then. Leonard made a card for Cornelius's file, marked it "CORN." in red ink, and put the letter in its chronological place in Cornelius's pamphlet case. Diuturnity unto his ashes.

Now a green *Eintrittskart* to an Innsbruck circus, clipped to a menu from the Albergo Danieli, Venice. A clipping from the Boston *Transcript* for August 14, 1900, entitled "An Interesting Letter from Bangkok, Siam," addressed to "Dear H.H." and signed with the initials M.G.W. This began, *Where in the Far East do you imagine I am on this quiet, beautiful Sunday morning when the sea here in the Gulf of Siam is like the waters of Vineyard Sound on a perfect July morning?* and it ended, *The thermometer is only 87 degrees, but it seems much hotter, and I am constantly obliged to use my handkerchief.* Running his eye down the two columns, Leonard encountered such comments as *What a dirty, unattractive people the Chinese are, to be sure,* and *Singapore, the capital of the Straits Settlements, is a lively and most cosmopolitan town, on an island 275 square miles in extent,* and *We have seen the king four times now: twice he has bowed to us. He is a genial, and rather short man, 47 years old.*

There went old Mercer, gathering data on exotic ports and being bowed to by kings. I would just as lief you would have somebody read this letter.

There was a carpety shuffle in the doorway and Mrs. Hutchens' face, long, liver-spotted, and smiling, appeared around the jamb. She was followed by Helen Kretchmer, and they were dressed as usual for golf; Mrs. Hutchens even wore her spike shoes. "Good morning!" she cried. "Hard at work . . . as usual. What interesting things have you found today?"

Leonard had risen. With his hip he pushed the card file more safely onto the desk. He said soberly, "I wonder if I should bring this to your attention. . . ."

"What . . . do you mean?"

"These papers." He tapped them with the backs of his fingers. "Your Uncle Bushrod seems to have been a little indiscreet. This business of smuggling opium into San Francisco from Hong Kong, for instance."

"What?"

"Also the charges that were brought against him as a Czarist spy during the Russo-Japanese War. He just barely got out of that by taking refuge in the Tokyo Embassy."

Mrs. Hutchens' face had gone slack and flabbergasted; her jowls drooped and shook, her eyes were idiotic with shock. Leonard was already regretting what he had started; he didn't need Helen Kretchmer's quick frown to tell him to lay off. But he was started. The glib foolery spun itself out, getting lamer with every word. "Then there's this item about the colored woman he lived with in Barbados, the one who claimed his estate when he died . . . Jeez, I don't know."

"Uncle . . . Uncle *Bushrod?*"

Leonard smiled, and he aimed his smile to be of maximum voltage. "Maybe I put it too strong. They didn't ever pin it on him. There was a chance the dope was smuggled in by a Chinaman of the Gee tong, and the Czarist spy turned out to be an adventurer named Bushmill's Potstill. And the woman from Barbados, she wasn't quite on the up. She admitted later it was a frame. She was sore at all the Wolcotts because Mercer had killed her brother in a duel one time."

With relief he saw in Mrs. Hutchens' face signs of recovery. He told himself, Never try *that* again. You don't kid her about the ancestors. She said breathlessly, "My goodness, it seems it was . . . time we had someone go through those papers. I hope you have . . . destroyed anything incriminating."

"Oh yes ma'am. You want me to go on burning such things?"

"Things like that I . . . certainly do." Peering, she regarded him. Helen Kretchmer had begun to smile; he had the feeling that she smiled at whatever Mrs. Hutchens smiled at. The old lady pulled a golf glove over her enlarged knuckles. "Shall you have time to . . . finish them all?"

"I ought to get through the papers without any trouble."

"But not the dress collection and other things?"

"There may be an interruption. Pretty soon I'm scheduled to become the father of triplets."

"Triplets!"

"At least."

The old blue eyes peered, the sharpness of the expression a compensation for the dimness of the sight. "You will have to put labels on your jokes . . . for me," she said. "I'm afraid I was not . . . trained to your kind of humor." Then she was shaking with silent laughter. "But I find it amusing," she said. "How is dear Barbara?"

"Right in the pink. I think she enjoys being pregnant."

"How . . . nice," said Mrs. Hutchens. "How very nice. And in the autumn you go back to being a schoolmaster."

"Happy golden rule days."

"Don't you have some . . . holidays? At Christmas, perhaps? To finish?"

"I might have a week or so. But why don't you get someone else? Helen, maybe."

"No, no. Helen will be . . . sufficiently occupied. I should be . . . ever so much obliged if you would do it. I think you would do it with sympathy and understanding."

Obviously she meant it; he was touched. Her eyebrows were as gray and fuzzy as strips of rabbit fur. She laughed to herself, and her eyes peeked up in a glance that he could only think of as coquettish. "And who besides you could find the . . . daggers and dueling pistols hidden in the . . . hems of the dresses?"

"Maybe you're right at that. Not everybody is qualified."

"Then you will?"

"If you want me to."

"Splendid!" she crowed, with the sudden bugle-like sound she made when pleased. "How perfectly . . . splendid! I'm so grateful to you for all you have already done. And please carry my love to Barbara. I remember her ever since she . . . was such a little round-eyed girl."

"Mrs. Hutchens," Helen said, "if we don't get along we won't even finish five holes before lunch time."

Two smiles, one abstractly pleasant, the smile of a good receptionist, the other old and yearning and fond. They went on out, the old lady picking up her feet from the priceless rugs like a cat walking in the wet.

Sometime later, another sound of interruption at the door. He looked up, expecting to see Lizardo, or Mrs. Hutchens returned from golf, and looked instead into the face of Sabrina Castro. She had the air of having been waiting there until he noticed her; he detected the symptoms of held breath that one of his daughters would have displayed under the same circumstances. His first thought was that she had deliberately posed a picture for him. His second was a question: Is she cured? Is she over the lover man? His third was jarred out of him by the almost trembling eagerness of her smile and by the fact—it took a second to see what it was—that she wore no make-up, had scrubbed herself plain as a nun: Lord, she *is* good looking when she forgets to be Eustacia Vye.

"Well, hi," she said, and came on in. "I never saw such concentration. You must like being a librarian."

"It's nice clean work," Leonard said. "Saves on laundry."

She was paler and thinner than when he had seen her last, and it was hard to say whether the hysterical tension that had been evident in every move and word was gone, or only under control. Even without make-up she made such a package of elegance that it was hard to see her plainly. It was that air of fastidious elegance, more than anything else, that always made him wary around her.

Her eyes, a ruinous and shattering blue if you were inclined that way, were on him curiously. "How's Bobbie?"

"Great with child." The image of *her* face, also without make-up, but how different smudged with violet under the eyes, puckered with smiling as she kissed him good-by in the plywood cell—made such a vision of reality and worth as against the groomed spuriousness of Sabrina Castro that he moved a little way down the desk.

"She's not close?" Sabrina said.

"About a month."

"I meant to write, but I didn't. I just got home last night."

"From Reno?"

"Reno?"

"I thought you were up there on a ranch somewhere."

"Oh. No, I've been staying at Tahoe."

"Rugged duty," Leonard said.

Her eyes touched his slantwise, out their corners, and he wondered if it was that trick, not so much coquettish as curious and alive, that gave her her charm. Because he granted the charm. It seemed to him all the greater with her lips pale and her eyes unaccented and her cheeks an even, fading tan. He could see how it would be a real discomfort to a lot of men, the way the skin tightened across her cheekbones when she smiled, the way she seemed at once to ask and promise something. Her voice was husky and confidential, and she had an interested and alert air, the sort of manner that could attract you to a bright pupil in a class. Maybe her charm was no more or less than intelligence. And yet admitting all that, he retained the impression of something acted, of self-consciousness being persuasively natural, and as usual their talk went like light sparring.

"Very rugged," she said drily. "How're my girls?"

"Your girls are too much with us, late and soon. They're like a recurrent virus, or undulant fever."

"I want to see them."

"There's nobody they'd rather see."

"They're darlings," Sabrina said. She studied him with disconcerting interest. Her eyes were steady, but with a kind of flickering in them as if by a thousand all-but-invisible movements of the eyeball she focused many details in a single glance. He had the naked feeling that she was observing every fleck and marbling in his eyeballs and every winker in his eyelashes, and for some reason, while he held her eyes with what he hoped was an expression of friendly irony, he thought of Henry David Thoreau and his habit of putting visitors clear across the cabin on Walden Pond, so as to leave room between them for conversation.

Sabrina looked down with a half smile, a half shrug. "How are you getting on with the Wolcotts?"

"So far they haven't kicked me out of the family tree."

"Wasn't it a tribe? Especially Grandmother's generation. Not one of them ever did one solitary useful thing."

"Oh now," Leonard said. "Look what an interesting pattern of challenges and responses. Bushrod I don't dig—he was just a sort of checkbook—but Emily, and Grace, and Sarah, and Mercer, those were all people. Especially Mercer."

"Why?"

"Why? He's interesting."

"I remember him," Sabrina said. "He was a little crabby vain man. Everything he had had to be better than anyone else's, and nobody ever did anything to suit him. Once when he was out here—it must have been right after we came, I couldn't have been more than five or six— he got the idea the gardeners weren't taking proper care of the roses. Nobody in California knew anything, naturally. So he made them mix up about five tons of manure and leaf mold and peat moss and sand and whatnot, to some recipe passed on from gardener to gardener, in Nahant, or maybe learned from one of those Boston historians who were such rose fanciers, and he had them dump it right by the rose gardens and he was going to show them how it was done right."

"Yes?" he said. She had a glint in her eye, a pursed curl of self-deprecation on her mouth—the bright pupil reciting.

"It turned out he didn't have his gaiters with him. He was furious with his valet, because ever since Mercer had gone grouse shooting with the Prince of Wales—that would have been Edward the Seventh, wouldn't it?—he never did anything outdoorsy without his gaiters on. Of course San Francisco couldn't provide any; the barbarians didn't know what he was talking about. Mercer sent back to Boston for some, or was going to, but they never came. After he went home, the gardeners did something with the fertilizer, I don't know what. Stored it, maybe."

"That sounds pretty standard for Mercer."

"Strictly standard. He went forth to battle but he always fell."

"Poor old Mercer."

"He was the most incompetent of the whole lot," Sabrina said. "Some people probably thought he was a great swell, though. I'm sure he put the fear of God into what he would have called tradespeople. But sad. Did you know that in his will he left one whole house—he had about six—with a valet to look after it, and a fund to look after them both, so that his whole wardrobe could be preserved intact, not a stud or a necktie missing? I suppose Grandmother's dress collection gave him the idea. The collection was to be open to the public once a year. Probably it still is."

"If the valet can find his gaiters."

"Any valet who had learned anything from Mercer wouldn't be able to. My Lord, think of all those empty suits with Mercer inside them."

They laughed, and for the space of the laugh he felt easy with her. The air was not charged with her usual challenging, competitive, essentially hostile irony. Then she turned her eyes on him sideways again, and his wariness returned—why, he could not have said. She just looked, for that second, scornful and discontented. "Challenges and responses my eye," she said. "What on earth, in all their lives, ever challenged any of that bunch?"

He spoke before he thought. "Money, maidenhood, sterility, plenty of things."

Now she was looking at him hard and directly, and the scorn that had been only a curve of the lip was unmistakable. "The last time we talked you didn't think those were much of a challenge."

"I've been converted," he said pleasantly, and kicked himself for giving her the opening to air her grudge against the world.

But she shrugged, looked around the library, gave a light laugh. "Well, hooray. Are we going to carry the challenges and responses down to the present?"

"Not much data after Mercer. You got any personal diaries?"

She pulled down her mouth. "Not to be opened till the year 2000."

"A pity," Leonard said. "It might be the gem of the collection."

She was leaning on the desk on one hand, the fingers bent back so far they looked painful, while she looked over the papers spread there. "I'll tell you what I will do, though," she said, and gave him a glance dark and frowning. "I've been thinking about my family lately. I keep thinking what if I descended into this family and snooped around among the frustrated and lost and asked them who they were in life and why they were punished by being made empty and ridiculous. Do you think that would teach me anything?"

From three feet away she compelled his eyes. He saw a tiny brown mole, beauty spot till now unnoticed, at the corner of her right upper lid. Carefully and with a smile he said, "Trying on the different styles of damnation?"

She did not want to joke; she seemed to insist on sober attention. "Would it disturb you if I came in and read through the record? Can I be the first visiting scholar?"

"Why not?" he said. "Your mother is in all the time, and Helen

238

Kretchmer is typing all the diaries so we'll have copies for public use. Come join the seminar."

The doorway gleamed with the white jacket. "Lunch, Miz Castro."

"All right, Lizardo, thanks." To Leonard she said, "You're staying, aren't you? Don't you, usually?"

"Your mother felt it demeaned the family for the librarian to eat out of a brown bag. Excuse me a minute, I ought to call Bobbie." He picked up the telephone and dialed, holding it on his arm. Sabrina said, "Let me talk to her when you're through." From the receiver the crackling homunculus voice said, "Hello?"

"Hi. How's it going?"

"Nothing stirring."

"Feel all right?"

"Like an elephant in a hammock."

"On you it's looking good. Guess who's here."

"Sabrina?"

"Check."

"Let me talk to her!"

He kissed the mouthpiece and handed the instrument to Sabrina. "Two minutes only, the patient is very weak."

Exclamations and questions and answers and assurances burst out behind him as he went into the lavatory. Myna birds, strictly. This Sabrina was a different person with Bobbie: chirps of extrovert affection, endless reminiscences, a closed culture shared only by the two of them.

He washed his hands, ran his fingers along his blue-bearded jaw—still reasonably smooth. In deference to his surroundings he smoothed his shirttails and buttoned his collar, thinking of the snottiest advertisement he ever saw—three disturbed and sneering golfers glaring across the green at an ugly duckling, sartorially unkempt. You tell him, Joe, he's your friend.

"Mind your own business, Joe," Leonard said, and opened the door. Sabrina was saying, "We're just about to have lunch. I'd love to, if you feel all right. I'll come over early and help. Don't tell the girls I'm coming, I'll surprise them. Really? I sure do. I'll see you then."

She hung up. "Brace yourself," she said. "You're having a guest to dinner and after dinner we're all watching meteor showers."

"Not a flicker of emotion showed in MacDonald's gaunt face," Leonard said. He offered her his crooked elbow. "May I guide you to the Heppelwhite room?"

"You ass." She took his arm elaborately; she almost skipped. In the hall they encountered Helen Kretchmer, waiting for Mrs. Hutchens, who had stopped to talk to Oliver up where side hall and main hall joined. Good God, Leonard thought, are we going to have *him?* I'll eat windfall prunes in the orchard first.

"Hello, Mrs. Castro," Helen said. In anyone else, the chemistry that reddened the face would have flustered the mind and tangled the tongue, but in her, blushing operated on a separate thermostat. Leonard could see straight through her rosy cheeks and demurely lowered eyes to the steady, interested, calculating regard that she fixed on Sabrina; and when he diverted his own attention to Sabrina he found her intently watching, with a mouth that forgot itself, the conversational pair up the hall. He did not feel that he should wait for the watchful triangle to break itself up; he broke it by offering his other elbow to Helen.

Now here came Mrs. Hutchens hobbling toward them, alone. They waited for her outside the tearoom door. She too, Leonard saw, had acquired the blushing habit: a blur of faint red lay on each temple. Her mouth was pursed and trembling. Well, Oliver was an adrenalin competent to stir the metabolism of the most torpid.

Sabrina detached herself and went to meet her mother. Her eyes were very bright. When they had leaned into a brief embrace, Mrs. Hutchens, the tired red fading from her temples, held her off and looked at her the way a woman might squint at the eye of a needle in dim light. "Good . . . morning, my dear. Lizardo told me you were back. Did you . . . enjoy Nevada?"

"It was a change."

"And how is Burke? Or have you seen him since you were last here?"

Ah, the bright glance, the blinking and the smile. And ah the bright eyes at the keyholes, secretary and archivist. They became aware of each other's interest at the same time, and were, Leonard supposed, mutually embarrassed. Sabrina said in a tone as dry as her mother's,

"He's well. I saw him last night at Tahoe. Didn't Oliver tell you?"

"Oliver these days has little to say to me except to . . . urge his schemes. At Tahoe, you say? He came up?"

"He was too busy to stay more than the day."

The squinting regard persisted, trying to thread the needle of the bright smile. Then either she thought she had it threaded, or gave it up till another time and a better light. She tottered a step into the tearoom and Leonard, disengaged now, gave her his elaborate arm: MacDonald, Elbow in Waiting. Sabrina said, "What scheme has he got on now?"

After golf Mrs. Hutchens walked as if, once she made it to a chair, she would never move again. Hobbling, she said, "He is absolutely intent upon . . . developing the Woodside land."

"And you don't want him to?"

"I intensely dislike being . . . pressed."

Ahead of them waited the table by the windows, with Lizardo standing behind one chair. Sabrina turned toward limping Leonard and said, "I should think that by now, with all your opportunities, you'd have your park."

He found the watery old eyes upturned at his shoulder. It made him uncomfortable to be caught in the middle of a family disagreement, and he would have said nothing whatever about a park rather than get involved any deeper. There were thirty things that occupied as much of his mind as parks and greenbelts, anyway, and though he believed in them he would have been embarrassed to be taken for an apostle. He said in a high whine, "Well, Jeez, if I'm sitting at the family table, can I go around with my patch-eye and my tincup?"

Clinging and tottering, Mrs. Hutchens laughed and said chidingly, "You must not let our . . . friendship keep you from working for what you believe."

"If that's an invitation . . ."

"It is. We must talk at length before . . . too long. I have been guilty too. The excitement of the papers has driven everything else . . . quite out of my head." Her glance trembled on him fondly, and she leaned on his arm. A dappling of sun came and went in the big bright room. The canted telescope winked at him one slow brassy wink. "But I have not forgotten your suggestion," she said. "I have been . . . seriously thinking about it."

"So now," Sabrina said with a dark eyebrow cocked at Leonard, "it's up to you to see that Oliver doesn't get there fustest with the mostest."

Mrs. Hutchens frowned: not before the servants.

Lizardo was holding Mrs. Hutchens' chair so that Leonard, frozen out, had to hustle around and hold Sabrina's. Helen Kretchmer made it to a seat by herself.

"But tell me," Mrs. Hutchens said while her arthritic fingers worked at unfolding her stiff napkin. "If one . . . decided to give some land, or put a clause to that effect in one's . . . will, is it certain that . . . it would be accepted?"

Leonard said, "You've been pondering the quality of vision that motivates boards of supervisors."

"It occurred to me to . . . wonder. They seem so mad to get new industries and new . . . people, but they seem not to . . . do much about keeping the Peninsula a fit place for the new people, or the old either . . . to live."

"You should write our circular letters," he said. He unfolded his napkin and noticed how brown and hairy his hands looked. The faces of the three women were turned on him: Tell us a story, Daddy. He said, "I can't answer that one, you know. If it was just a few acres, suitable for a town park, I suppose incorporated Woodside could accept it, and undoubtedly would. Most of the people out there are breaking their necks to stay country. But whether the county could accept a bigger tract within the incorporated area of Woodside, I don't know. There's even some question whether it *would*."

"Oh dear, really?"

"Maybe not a real doubt. But an argument. You know? There's always some six-volt intelligence on these boards that's scared of things that could mean maintenance costs. There's always another that doesn't like to see land removed from the tax rolls. There's still another, always in the real-estate business, who is full of stern questions about the waste of living space for our exploding population et cetera. Economy and caution are such good substitutes for brains that these little politicians work them to death."

"Oh," Mrs. Hutchens said, "I had hoped it . . . would be different."

"Oh now, don't worry about difficulties! If you're serious, let us cope with those. I'll inquire around down in Redwood City, and plant a few seeds among the Planning Commission people, who do know the score and do have some non-political, non-real-estate sense. If the county shows signs of not wanting to accept a gift, we'll have a delegation at every board and commission meeting, and a propagandist on every newspaper, and a thumb on every doorbell, and *then* if they don't accept it, our whole park and greenbelt committee will line up at your front gate and commit hara-kiri."

"I wonder if that would help the situation . . . materially," Mrs. Hutchens said. She shook silently, and then her blotched, soft-skinned face firmed itself for further serious discussion. "How many . . . acres, do you think, such a park . . . should contain?"

Leonard felt like a hitter sneaking a look at the third-base coach. Sabrina's bright, amused eye said, Hit away.

"How big?" he said. "That's a hard one. Or rather, it isn't. How big should Hyde Park have been when Henry the Eighth stole it for a deer park? How big should Golden Gate Park be—or can you imagine San Francisco with only the Panhandle, say? When you go to New York do you wish Central Park was bigger or smaller? The Peninsula is building up so solid that pretty soon even an acre of green will be priceless, because there'll be no more where it came from. Two acres better. Ten acres much better. Fifty acres wonderful. A hundred acres magnificent."

"What's the matter with four hundred?" Sabrina said.

"Is that what there is in this tract?"

"Yes."

Leonard spread his hairy hands in a gesture meant to be eloquent, and with a movement as precise as a movement in ballet the Filipino set a cup of jellied consommé between them. It struck Leonard that something momentous might be happening, and he wished it had not come up so casually and caught him unprepared. This was the sort of discussion, and decision, that helped establish for years, perhaps for decades or centuries, the character of a community. And does one, he asked himself seriously, really care about the character of the community? and had to answer yes. Yes, one did. It was one of the things worth caring about. The incidence of goons and do-nothings and grabbers could be depended on in any country and any time, but you worked like hell for every decent and responsible human being: they took a lot of making. And not many of them, statistically, ever came out of the warrens of over-crowded cities. Those were places where boys from the country could go and make a reputation, but they were bad places for the poor to be born. So you did care about the character of your community, and you worked as you could for a little open sky, a little public grass, some playgrounds, some public pools, some walks or bridle paths, a little shade for the parked perambulators of the tract and apartment dwellers. And you kept steadily before your eyes that if it was crowded now, it would be twice as bad by the time Dolly and Louise grew up.

Mrs. Hutchens was musing, her consommé untouched. Her amethyst pin caught pale light; she seemed herself to be made of something pale and thin-colored. She said mildly, "The decision is made . . . difficult by Oliver's scheme. He and Sabrina, being my heirs, would have to consent."

"Why?" Sabrina said. "It's your land. Do what you want with it. You'd never get Oliver to agree. Why ask him?"

"Part of the difficulty . . . He assures me the land is worth nearly . . . three million dollars."

Leonard made a motion of throwing in his hand. He said to himself, "Who the hell am *I* to go around soliciting three-million-dollar gifts for a county that might not take them?" But Sabrina said to her mother, "Tell him it's worth ten times that as a park. Tell him there are some things you don't measure in dollars."

"Then do I understand you, my dear . . . you would not oppose my giving it all?"

"No. I mean yes, you understand me."

"Why, my dear, that is . . . very generous of you."

"Of me? It's your land, therefore your generosity."

"Oliver would be . . . furious."

"Oliver's got enough to keep him in comfort."

"Yes," Mrs. Hutchens murmured. "If one could be assured that

244

it would be . . . accepted and that . . . nothing could be *broken* . . ."
A glance—wait, wait—flickered from Sabrina to Leonard. Then something stretched too far, a possibility went by like a side road not seen in time. Mrs. Hutchens wavered a benevolent smile around the table and said, "Helen, how does this idea . . . strike you?"

Helen blushed, not the coming-and-going tinge of pink that was so often in her face, but a hot suffusion of red. She said, "It takes my breath away."

Which, Leonard thought, was neat, if not precise. You would not find that one putting her foot down on any side of any fence until she had verified in the dust the prints of Mrs. Hutchens' ground-grippers. He waited, his consommé neglected. The Filipino stood by the serving cart with his hands clasped in front of him. Then Mrs. Hutchens picked up her spoon.

"Yes," she said, "we shall have to . . . talk seriously about it. I should much like it if your committee could call. But I would not, of course . . . say anything definite. And if you had some . . . figures, statistics of growth and so forward. It is well to have . . . everything well in mind before . . . acting."

Sabrina first turned her eyes upward, and then fixed them, wide, dark blue, hot with impatience, on her mother. "It's better to be over-cautious than imprudent?" she said. "What earthly difference can it make whether there'll be four million or six million people on the Peninsula in 1980? They'll still need a park."

Her mother ignored her, saying to Leonard, "Perhaps you and Barbara and . . . your committee would come to tea sometime." She brought a spoonful of quivering jelly to her mouth, captured it, melted and ingested it.

Anticipation, two minutes before red-hot, had already grayed over with ash. Leonard did not look at Sabrina, partly because she had just been silently rebuked and partly because he was afraid she would bring out in his face his own disappointment. Heartily he said, "Just name a day, we'll be there."

"If anybody can find his gaiters," Sabrina said.

"Mmmm?" Mrs. Hutchens' face lifted, her eyes glinted sharp and hard. Nobody said anything.

Sabrina's expression was one of cynical amusement. In silence they addressed themselves to the consommé. After an interval of rather awkward non-conversation, Mrs. Hutchens pottered off into an Auntie Grace story, and before long they were on the amusing procrastination of the Wolcotts. They all had it; it was part of the family character. All except Bushrod, who was very able and energetic in matters of investment banking, and Mrs. Hutchens' mother, who had great powers of will, and who more and more, as they all grew older, took her place as the real head of the family.

CHAPTER 20

THEY WERE still sitting at table when Louise rushed up to the patio door. "They're beginning! We saw one!"

"Go on," Leonard said to Barbara and Sabrina. "Go entertain the young. I'll clean up here."

Protesting, they went. He filled the dishwasher and did some pots and pans and left to soak the most gruesome ones. When he came outside it was full, soft dark, then back yard's fragment of sky was hazy blue, with pale, almost effaced stars. Somebody's radio or television was going. As his eyes adjusted, Leonard saw two shapes sprawled on a blanket on their patch of lawn, and two in patio chairs. "Seen any?" he said.

"I saw four!" Louise said from the chair beside Sabrina's. "Big streaky ones."

"I saw six," said Dolly from beside her mother.

"You didn't."

"I did so."

Barbara said, "Pretty soon there'll be so many you won't be able to count them, and then it'll be silly to quarrel, won't it?" They lay quietly, their faces palely upturned, and he heard their little rustlings. Sabrina turned her head, but did not speak. The bulky shape that was Barbara drew up its knees. "Lie down here, there's room."

247

"Yes, Daddy!" Dolly rolled over. Louise left her chair by Sabrina and flopped down.

"Okay," he said, "but no climbing on the chest. No fair doing anything but watching for shooting stars."

"I wished on every one I saw so far," Louise said. "All four. Didn't I, Sabrina?"

"I wished on all six," Dolly said.

"Hush," Leonard said. "Operation Starwatcher calls for reverent silence."

He groaned down, exaggeratedly weary, and they made room. They lay four in a row on the blanket, and the smell of lawn and sprinkled bricks, of the day's heat, of flowerbeds and the sunbaked redwood fence that locked in their little family space, rose around them and filled the night air.

"Isn't it warm," Barbara said.

"It's like a Midwestern night."

"No fireflies, though."

"We've got meteor showers instead."

"Ah, California!" said Sabrina from her chair. "Always bigger and better." They laughed; from their solidarity they acknowledged her.

A scratch of light crossed the sky, and a hand shot upward, an elbow dug Leonard's ribs. "There's one! There's another!" The streaks were gone.

"They made an X," Louise said. "I didn't get to wish on the second one."

"I think only the first one counts when they come in showers," said her mother.

"Does it, Daddy?"

"You wouldn't want to be a pig, would you?"

"I've got lots and lots of wishes. I wish—"

"Shhh," he said. "You tell 'em and you louse 'em all up."

"Ooooo!" A bright streak slashed halfway across their patch of sky, trailing a fading tail. "A *big* one!"

Then came three in quick succession, then one more, then a very dim one. Leonard, comfortable with Barbara's hand on his stomach, said, "The Russians are busy tonight, sputniks all over the place."

"Those aren't sputniks," Louise said.

"Baby sputniks. Spitniks." They snickered, thinking about it. "They give Daddy a bad time," he said. "Every time the Russians shoot one of those up there, some Congressman wants to melt Daddy's grammar books down into rocket fuel."

"You're kidding," Dolly said. "You're lying," said Louise. "Isn't he, Sabrina?" (And that was well done, Plumb-bob, he said to her silently, with a squeeze. She seems sort of lonesome out there. Invite her in.)

"Isn't he usually?" Sabrina said.

"Me?" He lay comfortable. He said to Barbara, "I suppose you girls shredded up all the gossip this afternoon, but what did the doctor say? Still guessing August fifth?"

"Yes."

"Everything okay?"

"Everything dandy except I can't breathe, sit still, or get into my shoes. Poor Sabrina would just get settled to talk to me and I'd get kicked out of my chair. This is the comfortablest I've been all day."

"No gemini?"

"Jiminy who?" Loiuse said. "Jiminy Cricket?"

"Jiminy your ears hang out," Leonard said. "I bet I see a shooting star before you do." But she saw one before he stopped speaking, and he had to eat crow.

Then meteors began coming thickly at angles over their private sky—thin cool ones, steady ones, an occasional hot bright one. The girls lay with their arms up, tracing the trajectories as they passed and crossed. "Hey, you can see them even when they're out," Louise said. "Why, Daddy?"

"You see that sky up there?" he said. "That's the bottom side of the celestial carbon paper. Whenever anybody up there makes a line, it copies off onto your little old eyeballs."

"It's an after-image, Lumpschen," Barbara said. "Daddy is being anti-scientific again. Wouldn't you think a man who can repair television sets would respect Modern Science?"

Leonard reached an arm to snuggle the two girls. The warm little bodies crowded against him, piled like puppies. "Let us not leave the wonder out of the universe," he said. "Which would you rather have, poetry or kilowatt hours?"

"You talk funny," Dolly said.

"So I do." Craning to look toward Sabrina, quiet in her chair, he said, "Still persisting in that temperance pledge? Sure you don't want a drink?"

"No, I'm very happy."

Outside their pocketed night-smelling patio a car started, raced, slammed past, shifted, shifted remotely a second time, and was gone down the curving, scientifically designed, carefully zoned streets of Greenwood Acres. Above them the sky rained down its silent incandescent dust. Energy into matter, matter into energy, substance into essence and back again, groupings and scatterings, creations and destructions, affinities and repulsions. He felt how the four of them lay clustered like the balls and sticks of a model atom. "Tell us a story," Louise said.

"I thought we were watching stars."

"We can watch while you tell us."

"Well," he said, "once upon a time there were two little particles—only some people called them charges. Their names were Proton and Electron; the Chinese called them Yang and Ying. Electron was a very busy little bird, and kept running around all the time, and was negative in his attitudes, but Proton was adjusted and positive and just liked to sit. Like Mama there. So Proton and Electron got to going around together, or rather Electron went around and Proton sat, and after while they got married and then everybody called them Atom."

"Adam and Eve?"

"Just Atom. Hydrogen J. Atom. That was the beginning of everything. We all lived uneasily ever after."

"Oh, Leonard," Barbara said.

"Hmmm?" He craned again at Sabrina. "Wouldn't you like a cigarette?"

"I've quit," Sabrina said.

Louise was pounding his chest. "That isn't a story!"

"That sure is a story. That's the whole story. If it wasn't for that story where would you be?"

"Where?"

250

"You'd be sitting around in space being positive and adjusted and waiting very anxiously for the phone to ring."

In the starlight he saw the dull shine of Dolly's eyes. She was the solemn one, the dumpling. Louise was another kind—she sparkled where Dolly glowed. It spoiled his story that they were both girls, but he would not have changed either of them, even to create a world. The two of them seemed an extraordinary thing. People. Energy into matter.

Louise bit his wrist, increasing the pressure until he yelled. "Tell us a real story."

"Why don't you make us a pitcher of Kool-Aid first?"

She scrambled up and was gone. The dumpling came snuggling closer, the atom became an isotope of itself. In the kitchen a light went on, and a clump of bushes in the corner of the fence gleamed enameled leaves at them out of the dark. He saw Sabrina plainer, lying quietly back in the chair. No part of their family atom—with them but not of them. A wandering—what? Neutron? That didn't sound very good. Beside him Barbara, veritable Nucleus, stirred with heavy, comfortable discomfort.

"Sabrina says she's going to help you sort the papers."

That was news. "We're all in it together," he said.

"Are you still finding interesting things?"

He felt the little clinging shape at his side sagging away. "Hey, Dolly Dumpling, you falling asleep?"

"No," she said, barely awake.

"Maybe I should put her to bed," he said, and Sabrina, rising at once, said, "I will." But Dolly in her stupor groped and grappled closer, and Barbara said, "I don't see any harm if she stays a while, it's so warm."

Louise came to the door. "Ice in it?"

"What *would* you put in it?" Leonard said. "On the ball, baby." To his dark cluster, or cluster plus, he said, "Sabrina, I'm surprised at your ancestors in one way. Wouldn't you think a prominent Boston family would have had some literary friends and acquaintances? I was looking through the literary collection this afternoon. Pretty meager."

"Literary contacts why? None of them could read or write."

"Oh yes they could. There's evidence, and your mother values it above rubies. Three letters. One from Mr. Longfellow. Seems Emily and Sarah were coming back from the White Mountains one time and met Mr. Longfellow on the cars. They had quite a thrilling chat, and next morning the girls put one another up to sending the old boy a bouquet. This note is his thank-you note, four lines. Then there's one from Oliver Wendell Holmes, answering a question of Bushrod's about a point of grammar. The third item is from Charles Dickens *fils*. He wants an appointment with Mr. Wolcott on Tuesday next to discuss a business matter."

"Well," Barbara said, "wouldn't the autographs be valuable?"

"Maybe a dollar apiece. This is three generations of the family's contact with Culture, though. If there'd been anything else they'd have saved it; they saved everything. In three generations, these giggling girls recognize Mr. Longfellow's distinguished beard on the cars, and dare to talk to him; and old Bushrod is so sure of his grammar that he asks the Autocrat, whom he has obviously never met, to join him in disapproving Mr. James's usage; and a banker is approached on business by the traveling son of a British novelist. That's it. That winds it up. What the hell did they *do* all the time?"

Louise came tottering with a tray in both hands, and Leonard helped her lower it to the ground. Dolly did not stir. "Let her sleep," he said. The tray was afloat in sticky juice. He wiped the bottoms of the glasses on the grass and Louise passed them around; when she was through she sat down against his shoulder and he touched his glass to hers. "Thanks, Plumb-bob. You're a model daughter."

With her head against his arm and the glass at her lips, Louise watched the sky. A meteor scratched the soft, dark blue. He saw her squeeze her eyes shut to watch the after-image, and he kissed the top of her head.

"This is delicious," Sabrina said with an incredulous laugh. "What on earth is it?" To make up for what he heard in her tone, Leonard took a noisy gulp of his sweetened water. He could drink it at all only because Louise so loved to fix it; but he would have drunk two gallons before he would deny its deliciousness.

He said, "Stop me if I violate the family honor, Sabrina, but is it fair to think of your ancestors as stuffed? Bushrod, I guess he was stuffed with stocks and bonds. But here's a six-by-six cabinet full of etchings: Mercer. Here's an enormous armoire with nothing in it but Toby jugs: Mercer again. Here's a cabinet full of porcelain miniatures: Aunt Sarah. And a shelf of great missals that would run six thousand dollars in gold to the ton: Aunt Sarah once more."

"Go go go!" Sabrina murmured.

"I'm gone. Up in the attic is a whole room full of Carcel lamps. Know what a Carcel lamp is? Your mother tells me Auntie Grace always insisted that four candles made a perfect reading light, but if one simply must have lamps, she preferred the Carcel, which ran by clockwork, to the Moderateur, which had to be pumped up. I ask you. When she went to her reward she left at least four dozen of them, brand new, and when they unpacked the famous trunks there were two full of green silk that old Gracie had bought for lampshades but never got around to using. Besides all the other stuff that was in those trunks. Bobbie, you must have seen the attic—two big rooms with cabinets to the ceiling. And all that dress-and-bonnet emporium in the basement. You know what I think?"

Barbara waved her arm in circles above her. "Isn't Leonard wonderful? He's sort of like a fountain playing."

"Not by the slightest sign did MacDonald indicate he had heard," Leonard said. "I think your mother would love to be the heroine of a costume novel. I can see her yearning at me, wondering if under my crude exterior I may not turn out to be Edith Wharton. I know she thinks Henry James used some of the family in his books. That's why she had some bookseller get her every James first edition, English and American. Have you seen those? I did them all up with my little pot of British Museum Mixture a while ago. Your mother cuddles the thought of being Milly Theale or Isabel Archer or somebody, I think. And there's always Mercer, out on tour, buying up little *objets d'art* and attending little receptions and being bowed to by little kings—a perfect Little Bilham. But I don't know what even James could have done with Grace and Sarah. There was a pair of real sad dinosaurs, guaranteed pure Jurassic."

"Who, Daddy?" Louise said. "Grace and Sarah who?" She spoke

with her glass clenched in her teeth, and he took it away and set it down.

"Sabrina's great-aunts," Barbara said. "A couple of queer rich old ladies who died a long time ago."

"I thought you were getting fond of all those people," Sabrina said.

"I am. That doesn't keep them from being dinosaurs." To Louise he said, "Listen, quit screwing up your face, and if Sabrina will let me I'll tell you that story. This is a sad story, and probably ridiculous, so I want you to laugh out loud at the funny parts and cry when you see tears running down my nose."

She was looking from him to Sabrina. "Can he tell it?"

Sabrina nodded.

"You won't cry," Louise said.

"You never know." Lying flat on his back with her head in the hollow of his shoulder and her hair tickling his jaw, he wondered if old Cornelius Wolcott, the one who made the money in the first place, had ever lain on a dock or lawn with his daughters snuggled against him. No. He could see old Cornelius in morning clothes, with his beard parted in the middle. No place in that frontage for a child, no loose pocket that a daughter could have slipped into past the watch chain. He must have seemed as awesome to them all as God.

He gave Louise a hug. "Once," he began, "there were two old maids. Most old maids were little girls originally, but not these two. These were born old maids. They lived in Boston and were very rich, and when they were young old maids they went to school. In those days going to school was standard for old maids, and was called being finished. Boston was what really finished these two, but other things helped. As they grew up they realized there was nothing doing in Boston, and so though neither one liked the other very much, they started going to Europe together because there was no one else to go with. They went every summer for twenty-five years, and then the younger one died."

"Shall I cry now?" Louise said.

"If you want." They cried together for a minute.

"So after the younger one died, the older one kept going back to

Europe alone for another twenty-five years, and finally *she* died."

"Cry again?"

"Let's not overwork it right at the beginning, shall we?"

"Tell me when, then."

"I'll tell you. Well, so every summer the two old maids booked the same cabins on the same ship on the same date. They had cards printed up well ahead of time, years ahead, saying that Miss Grace Wolcott and Miss Sarah Wolcott were sailing on the S.S. *Westminster* of the Cunard Line on June tenth. Their brother Mercer did the same thing, only he always goofed and missed the boat and had to come on later. But they all had these cards, and it must have upset them like anything if the dockers struck, or the Cunard Line changed the *Westminsters*'s sailing date, because Grace and Sarah always sent out their cards weeks in advance to dozens of acquaintances, none of whom gave a whoop in a rain barrel whether the two Wolcott old maids went abroad or stayed home. Cry."

"Wah!"

"All right. In Europe Grace and Sarah always went the same places. First Paris for shopping, then London, then Switzerland so they could sit in the rain in a hotel in Montreux where every year the same hatchet-faced English women in the same Irish tweeds occupied the parlor after dinner and whispered and peeked behind the same copies of the London *Times*. Then the old maids went on to Venice, then Florence, then Rome, then back to Nice, and then they sailed for home from Marseilles. If they didn't get the same cabin on the same ship they had last year they thought it was very disagreeable. In hotels they wanted the same rooms, and in dining rooms the same tables. They were returners; they didn't like uncertainties. And because they were very rich, people strained themselves to see that uncertainties didn't happen to them."

"Do, Lawd," said Sabrina from the shadows. "Amen, amen!"

"Thank you, Sister. So these old maids wouldn't stand for anything but the best, either. They were fussy, oh my. They hated imitations. They wore only handsewn gloves and dresses, and when gloves got soiled they threw them away. I was reading one of Auntie Grace's letters this morning. She'd been to a reception where a woman was wearing gloves that had been dry-cleaned. Grace's whole day was spoiled because this woman 'smelled of economy.' "

He buried his nose in the silky hair at his shoulder. "That's what we smell of, Plumb-bob. One of the nicer things we smell of. Because we are not rich, or afflicted by uncertainties, or old maids. Or are you?"

She hammered the back of her head against his arm. "No!"

"No? Well, you have to have a calling, so to speak. Old Sarah, for instance, always wore a gold locket around her neck on a gold chain. Know what was in it? A lock of her dog's hair and a feather from her canary. And old Grace was always correcting people's diction. She thought you should say 'dahg' and 'fahg' instead of 'dawg' and 'fawg,' and she was fit to be tied when some vulgarian said 'Toosday' instead of 'Chewsday.' Also she could tell a lady from a non-lady by the way a lady said 'tiss-you' paper. Diction was one of the things that had finished old Grace, and she was bound to pass it on."

"Tiss-you," Louise said. "Tiss-you."

"Obviously you're a lady. Now. All this time brother Bushrod is back in Boston getting them all richer and richer. And since the old maids have seen everything they travel through forty times, they've got nothing much to do. So they shop. Sarah buys old-fashioned ribbons to take home for the maids to make into work bags. Grace buys bolts of green silk to be made into lampshades. Also they buy dresses and bonnets and Irish linen and Venetian glass and Florentine gloves and Roman silks and everything you can name, always by the gross. A lot of what they buy they intend to give people as presents. But these old maids suffer from an inherited disease, something that the whole family has, called procrastination."

"Wha . . . ?" Louise said.

"Procrastination? A disease of wealthy old maids, male or female. At first you just can't get up before ten in the morning. Then it gets to be eleven, twelve, one. You get an increase of phlegm, your blood pressure is low, you have cold feet—"

"Amen, amen, yes good Lawd," Sabrina said.

"Did she get well?" Louise said.

"They never get well of that disease," Sabrina said.

"Shall I cry?"

"I guess so, yes. If Sabrina's right."

"Wah!" Her face bent far back, upside down, to look at him. "Oh boo hoo hoo hoo!" She began to giggle. He reached down and closed thumb and finger around the nervous little ankle. On the other side he heard the even breathing of the dumpling. Louise's hand shot up. "There's a star!"

"Attention. Having bought things, the old maids had to buy trunks to send them home in. Every summer they bought six or eight trunks from M. Louis Vuitton of the rue Scribe, Paris, and they shipped them home and had them carried up to their rooms that were already overflowing with trunks from twenty years back. Mrs. Hutchens told me that when she was a little girl she used to go up to Auntie Grace's rooms and there was only a narrow aisle between trunks piled clear to the ceiling. By that time, Sarah had given up the ghost."

"Wah."

"You've already cried for her. But now Grace can't get up before two p.m. any more, on account of her procrastination, and by the time she's dressed it's time to take her drive along the Charles—that's a river. When she gets back it's time to get ready for dinner. After dinner she reads some uplifting literature, or corrects somebody's diction, or argues with Mercer about Phillips Brooks, who has been delivering some dreadfully low church sermons at Trinity Church, and plays a game of patience, and then it's bedtime. She's been intending all day to get at those trunks, but when she goes to bed, there they still are. There they always are, and every summer six more of them."

"For heaven's sake get those trunks open," Barbara said.

"Oh, no. Not for years yet. Correction: a few did get opened. Mercer got so exasperated about them that once he had a carpenter put up shelves in a guest room, and one day for a surprise he opened three or four trunks and displayed the contents. When Grace came in from her drive she thought it was quite nice, quite a good idea, but a little *shoppy*. There were two hundred pairs of gloves in those few trunks, among other things. Laugh."

"Why?"

"All right, don't. I'll hurry up and let Grace die so you can go to sleep like Dolly."

"No, tell some more. I'll laugh."

"Brave girl. Well, at this point Grace still lives with Mercer and Bushrod in the family house on Beacon Street. Her rooms are so barricaded with trunks that they have to move a lot of them to a warehouse, and when that overflows they take two drayloads out to Nahant—that's an island. About that time Bushrod gets a fat offer for the Beacon Street house and wants to sell it. It wouldn't have bothered him to move, because he did most of his sitting at the Harvard Club anyway. And it didn't bother Mercer, because he was always building or buying houses he never got around to moving into, and he had about four he could have used. But it bothered Auntie Grace, because there was no place for procrastination quite like Beacon Street among her trunks. You know what she told Bushrod?"

"Careful," Sabrina said.

"She told him she wouldn't agree to sell the house, she'd die first. So she did."

He paused. Louise said on a rising note, "Is that the *end?*"

"Unfortunately no," Leonard said. "There's still the trunks. They had a man come and list everything—this is Daddy's profession nowadays—and then they locked them up in a warehouse. They filled seven storage rooms. And there they sat for another fifteen years."

Louise lay quiet in his arm. He could see her staring up into a warehouse sky piled with stars as numerous as trunks. Barbara shifted, saying, "Is all this true? The family was always talking about the trunks, but I never heard the details. Is this all in the papers?"

"This is mostly from Mrs. Howard King Hutchens. She can't stay out of the library, and every time she comes in I get a new installment. She thinks it's terribly comical, but it's been like a treasure hunt to her all her life. It's what the family had instead of distinction. It had trunks. She was always after her mother and Mercer to open them up and have a fair—you know, issue invitations and make it a gay do. Mercer had a house on Dartmouth Street, brand new, that he'd built and never lived in, and Mrs. Hutchens persuaded him to let her hold the trunk fair there. It was going to be a big lark."

"Was it, Daddy?"

"Ah, pet, it was bigger than a lark, even a big lark. It was a turkey. See, Mercer wouldn't think of doing anything till the house was in perfect shape. It was getting on to the chilly season, and grate fires would be agreeable for the fair, but as a New Englander and a Wolcott he wouldn't light a fire in a fireplace that was all bare. A proper grate fire has a slope of ashes up behind it, to hold the coals. So Mercer sent a servant over to Dartmouth Street with half a dozen baskets of wood ashes, and had him shovel them into the nice clean fireplaces. Then Mercer got a fit of the procrastinations, and they never did get the trunks up or hold the fair. All they had was this empty house with its cold fireplaces and imported ashes. Cry."

"Why?"

"Don't ask why, honey," Sabrina said. "Just cry. It's indicated."

"Wah. But didn't they *ever* open the trunks?"

"That's the happy ending. Many years later Mrs. Hutchens got married and had a house of her own, and then she held her fandango, the way she'd always wanted to—opened the trunks and invited everybody. She was going to give gifts, sort of delayed, from Grace and Sarah. But it seemed a shame to break up the collection, don't you know, so she eventually had them packed up and sent back to the warehouse. Another five or six years, and finally she moved out here, and when she built her house she had her attics built specially for the stuff in the trunks. And there it sits to this day, two mighty rooms of it, all wrapped up in tiss-you paper—nice, but a little shoppy. And that *is* the end."

"That's a silly story," Louise said after a moment. "I don't know whether I'm supposed to laugh or supposed to cry."

"Neither do I," he said. "You hit the nail on the head, Plumb-bob."

A star streaked down a whole quadrant of sky and was followed by a thin weak one, like a match that does not quite take fire. Sabrina said, "I can see why Mother's got such a crush on you. You're ready for your doctor's orals in the family history."

"The hell of it is," Leonard said, "I'm like Louise. I keep wanting to laugh, but I think of those old girls with their diction and their trunks and their hand-sewn seams and I have to cry instead. Don't you?"

"Laughter seems a little more to the point."

"I think," said Barbara in a schoolteachery voice, "that it's a moral fable meant to show us we all should have something to love. Not things. That's awful about those cold fireplaces."

"Sarah had a dog and a canary," Louise said, "because she had the hair and the feather."

"All God's chillun got things," Sabrina said. Her laugh sounded to Leonard edged and unpleasant. "I've got a dog myself. If I had him here."

Here we go, Leonard thought. He said to Louise, "Time for bed—way past. Kiss Mommy and Sabrina."

He got the expected yowl and the expected clinging. But Sabrina came across the patch of grass and put down a hand and pulled dragging Louise to her feet. She stooped and lifted baglike Dolly and then gave a hand again to Louise. "Come on, lover-duck." Flying kisses, smotherings, reassemblings; off they went.

Leonard had not needed Barbara's elbow in his ribs. It made him, in fact, a little mad. Women assumed that every social situation, including their own kicks and silent roundings of the lips and frantic eye-and-eyebrow signals, was totally obscure to male perceptions. "I can see a barn door if my nose is caught in it," he told her.

They lay on in the soft night air. The kitchen light dawned again, the enameled leaves gleamed from their corner. Barbara said, "She's been telling me about it. She's sort of gone all to pieces."

"Well," he said, "I'm like the sparrow said about the badminton game—I don't want nuttin to do wit it."

"She was deliberately going to hell up and down Tahoe for a while."

"Watching herself all the time."

"You're mean. Don't you feel sorry for her?"

"Partly. Partly I want to spank her."

"Why? She's terribly unhappy."

"Then why doesn't she do something? Take hold of something? Stop watching herself in mirrors?"

"She can't. She's always watched herself in mirrors. She's an actress. And while you were noticing barn doors your nose is caught in, did you ever notice she's got the family procrastination as bad as Auntie Grace? She can't make herself take one way and stick to it."

"Procrastination?" he said. "Maybe, at that. All right, I won't slang her. She was damned near magnificent this noon—I thought we had a four-hundred-acre park in the bag. So I give her her right to have troubles."

"She said that up at Tahoe she was sort of committing suicide, trying to vanish, only she couldn't do it because she didn't *deserve* to vanish."

Leonard stretched irritably. He heard remote voices inside. A night plane winked over. He could feel the air cooler. "As to that," he said, "if a man might offer a suggestion, Tahoe is deeper than a shotglass."

"Leonard!"

"Ah, it's all so posey," he said. Steps coming; the door closed softly; cautiously he sat up. "All tucked in?"

"They're absolute angels, both of them," Sabrina said. "I could have dumped Dolly like a load of wood, she'd never have known the difference."

"I hope you did," Barbara said.

"I did not. I washed her sticky little mitts and her sticky little face and I wadded her into her Danny Dentons." She stood looking down on them; even in the dark she had a trim and elegant look. Leonard could smell her faint flowery scent. "I've got to go," she said. "No, don't get up."

"Don't want to drop off the wagon? Stick around, there's a lot more stars to fall."

"No," she said in her husky, confidential voice. "I must go. But thanks —you know? Thanks for letting me in."

She was gone, waving from the dim half door. Later they heard the sound of her engine starting. "Letting her in?" Leonard said. "Boy, this is the high-school dramatics club, for sure."

But it jarred him a little to think that all evening she had been sitting there outside the edge of their family cluster and thinking of herself in exactly the same terms he had used for her himself.

CHAPTER 21

F
OR THE first time since she had moved into it, Helen's room was
hot. She laid down the nail file, put her thumbs under her slip
and pulled it away from her sticky skin, and looked toward the
windows in oppressed hope of a breeze. Between their slack
curtains they gaped on a night too turgid to flow. She had the claustro-
phobic sense of walls too close and trees too high and dense. Her moist
skin contracted in quick gooseflesh, and reaching to snap off the light,
she felt her way to the window.

Gradually, sense by sense, another night gathered and formed itself.
First she smelled it, lawn and shrub and deep mold and the tannic odor
of oak leaves, and rising through those a rank exhalation as if from
meaty stalks and mats of sweating humus. Then she felt the night on
her skin, soft as the air of a summer night at home, or the water of a
pond entered secretly after dark during a heat wave, when water and
air were so nearly the same temperature, and the body so near the
temperature of both, that the passage from air to water was hardly
more than a change of buoyancy. Then what she had been smelling
and feeling began to grow apparent to her eyes, and she thought she
could make out the flat darkness of lawn spreading from the gray of
the driveway, and higher up, hardly distinguishable from the bluer
darkness of sky, the uneven mounds of trees.

262

The sill was hard against her body under the ribs. Leaning, she listened: only a low steady humming like the humming of telephone poles against which, as a child on the farm, she had put her ear—the voice of the world talking. Looking straight up she saw a star fall.

In six months she had permitted herself no homesickness, because if she allowed herself to grow sick for home she would grow sick for other things as well. She had gone through her whole life setting herself sensible goals. This was only one more—a year's waiting with everything she wanted at the end. What you wanted to do, you could do. And yet the soft air beguiled her now into admitting that she had missed the summer nights. In the Bay Area it was nearly always too chilly after dark for sitting outdoors, or even for walking unless you wore a sweater. In all her stay here she had not had one dark cotton-dress-y walk along a country road, or taken a night swim, or seen more than glimpses of the stars.

A year ago tonight, maybe, she and Walt might have come out of a movie and gone walking, talking, and planning, sitting on stone walls and watching fireflies scratch the dark woods. They would have walked with their arms around one another, tilting their heads together; or they might have stood still to hear radio music, or some dog woofing at spooks. Their feet were quiet in country dust and solemn in empty streets; they went through the half-lighted edges of town and into starlit country where the sky was very open. In a walk like that, with all they had to plan and talk about, Cassiopeia and the Dipper might move a full quarter circle around the north star, one rising as the other fell. On some lawn—hospital or school or park, or even mown roadside —they would have lain on their backs, the grass cool on their bare arms, and talked up at the stars. She remembered how it smelled walking along a street in late May when the snowballs and lilacs could make you drunk on the dark sweet air, and how heavy hydrangeas felt, brushed against in the July dark, and how all overhead in deep summer the locusts would fill the trees with the noise of thousands of thumbs drawn along the teeth of thousands of combs.

She listened. The murmur of the excluded world, a long way off. From the black gardens nothing.

It *is* worth it! she told herself. This is fifty times more sensible than any other way we could have done it. But she didn't want to think about that. What she had promised them both she could do, she would do. And yet the garden below her was as lonely as some empty island in the Pacific, and the mutter of the Peninsula's traffic was surf on a hollow shore. For the catch of a breath, her life was an intolerable exile.

The moment's sickness passed as a shiver, and she gave herself the prompt, sane preventive against its return. Walk it off. She fumbled a dress out of the closet, and still in darkness pulled it over her head. The hall was still as midnight, dim under the night lamp. Mrs. Hutchens had been in bed for nearly two hours. For a moment Helen came toward herself menacingly in the pier glass, and she got by that only to run the gantlet of the portraits in the lower hall. Since she had been typing Emily Barber's diaries she had conceived a real dislike for that woman—a martinet and a prude and a snob. She felt the eyes on her; the lumpy face seemed stiff with disapproval that anyone should be young and warm and wanting.

Then the front door, the momentary hesitation to make sure she had her key, and with relief she waded into the full outdoor night.

It was not as warm as most July or August nights at home, but warm enough. From the driveway, where the sky was open, she looked up into many pale stars. Another one fell, reminding her that she had seen something in the paper about meteor showers. It seemed a special piece of luck: fireworks to celebrate her escape outside.

When her feet found soft lawn, she stooped to touch it. Not wet, as on an ordinary California night. She stepped out across noiseless grass. An oak came over her black as a photographer's cloth, then sky again. Watching for meteors as she might have looked for four-leaf clovers, she saw one fall into the Dipper.

Oaks again, and for quite a distance the deepest blackness. She went impatiently, wishing for the open, steering around the trunks of trees more by the swelling of the ground than by sight. She met the drive once more, but the sound of her feet in the gravel was too loud and she turned across to the tennis court, where a light in a big oak threw druidical shadows across the grapevined fence; inside, the court lay gray and empty as a deserted quarry. The smell of peaches led her past, and on between the espaliered trees, where she could walk unhesitat-

264

ingly by holding out her hands on both sides to brush against the pipe frames, the leaves and gnarly branches, the heavy fruit. The air in that tight place was syrupy with peaches.

At the end she stopped and listened. There should be peepers, locusts, owls, whippoorwills, something. But she heard no sound at all. Then she thought of the pool—filtered, cool, available, empty, her suit hanging in the dressing room where she had left it that afternoon.

The gate squeaked only a little as she opened it. With more sky to see by, she made out the white stone steps and the white edges of the pool and the angled shapes of lounge chairs. The water was only a kind of shimmer of the darkness, a freshness of the air, a faint smell of chlorine. Looking and listening, she saw that it was deserted, as she had hoped it would be; she heard only the faint sucking of the outlet.

The wistaria arbor was so dark she bumped her shin on an iron chair. Her hand groped and found the dressing-room door open; she smelled Ivory soap and wet wood. The notion of turning on the light she considered and discarded: she didn't want some watchman or gardener coming around suspecting burglars. In blackest dark she fumbled at the suits on the hooks until she recognized her own by the braid on it. It was soggy wet.

Without it, then. Why not? It would be like the old pond, a secret slipping into the water with no more noise than a fish surfacing to bubble air.

Stripped, she peered around the dark doorway. Watch was kept in the grounds at night, and the main gate was locked when none of the family was out, but she had been abroad so little in the evenings that she had no notion of the watchman's habits. Her eyes pried at all the shapes angling around the pool. The pool and its borders were still.

She sneaked to the steps at the shallow end, felt the water with a toe, found it chillier than she had expected, pinched her knees together and hugged herself for a moment of shivers. Then she took a deep breath and went steadily, without a splash, down the steps into the three-foot water. Her jaw locked, she wanted to yell and thresh around; instead, very quietly, she squatted and ducked under to the chin. Under the water she waved her arms gently, she rubbed herself until the chill passed; and then on her back, swimming only by the fluttering of her hands, she coasted out into the middle and lay there looking up at the sky. She could see her own dim length and the bulge of her breasts above the water. Observatories. In the flaky starlight she smiled to herself and rolled over and swam two lengths breast-stroke as silently as she could. The water mounded up ahead of her shoulders, she felt how crystalline it was around her kicking legs. She was a figure in Swedish glass.

I can do it, she said to herself. I've already done it for six months and I can do it for another six. Whenever I get feeling sorry for myself I'll take a midnight swim or walk ten miles. You can do anything you want to, if you want to bad enough.

Touching the end of the pool she did a cautious, too-slow, awkward flip turn that made her want to laugh, and came up in the low swash of her wave. Rolling on her back, she floated, showing herself shamelessly to the stars. In quick succession three fell. Wow! She giggled, sustaining herself with light motions of her fins.

The gate squeaked.

Her head craned upward from the water like a swimming snake's; her fins became frantic. She glared down the pool and saw a shape come to the deep end, no more than thirty feet away. She heard sandals kicked off. The shadow came out on the board and bounced it; she could see it go up against the sky and cut off some stars there. Its weight came down on the board with an excruciating *whomp, whomp, whomp.*

Flat on the water, afraid to move her legs, she inched toward the steps by the slight paddling of her hands. The steps were no more than fifteen feet away. But when she reached them what would she do? She saw all the possibilities and they were all bad. There was hardly a chance that she could slip out and get to the dressing room without being seen or heard; neither could she stay in the pool and let herself be discovered.

Feeling with her feet for the bottom so that she could push herself along, she tried to call out, but found her throat locked tight. Then she cleared it with a noise that cracked the silence wide open, and half-screamed, "Mr. Hutchens?"

His response scared her to death—the harsh, fighting exclamation of a man totally surprised. The board stuttered, but there was no splash: he had run to the corner of the pool. "Who is it? Who's in here?"

In despair she tried an ancient joke. "Ain't only us chickens, boss."

"Helen?"

"Yes."

"Ah!"

She grounded on the steps and got her feet under her, crouching up to her neck in the water. Then she thought his shape moved toward her down the side of the pool, and in a panic she shoved out into the water again. "Don't come down here!"

"Why not?"

"Just don't, please!"

Oh, she should have taken a chance and run for the dressing room. She heard laughter rumbling up out of him. He said, "Haven't you got a suit on?"

"Oh, yes—well, no."

"Isn't that a coincidence," he said. "Neither have I."

Helen's mind, between the moment of considering an expedient and the moment of discarding it, told her quite coolly, This could be bad. In the casual tone of social ease, she said, "If you'll just stay down there a minute and look the other way, I'll go in and dress."

"Oh, don't go in. I like this."

"Well, I don't," she said. Then without warning he hit the water, and in a rush she floundered for the steps; but looking back as she came up streaming she saw the outline of his darker head against the light coping, and there was no noise of swimming. He was just hanging there at the edge. And if she couldn't see him any plainer than she could, he could not see her either, which was some comfort.

"Don't get excited," he said, and blew at the surface of the water. "You use that end and I'll use this. We'll play we're Japanese."

The wave of his dive finally reached her and washed the reflection of a star against her. "Really," she said, "I do want to go in."

"Why?"

"It's late."

"That's a pretty feeble reason."

"I'm cold."

"I doubt that."

Everything he said came out with a burble of laughter. But Helen was a long way from laughing. Her mind darted at possibilities. Stay here? He could swim faster than she could, he would corner her or have her by the foot before she could get out. Run for it? She had seen him come up over the edge in one smooth motion—he would intercept her before she could make the dressing-room door. She had a second's panicky imagining of being caught there one step short of safety, as in a nightmare. Oh, why hadn't she brought out at least a towel!

She told herself that after all he wasn't a sex maniac. Couldn't she simply turn on some dignity? But she had, and there he was, a round dark head like a seal's, blowing gently under water. But if he tried anything she could scream. And wouldn't that be dandy, scream and yell and be found struggling naked with her employer.

Damn him, he could spoil everything, he could make things just awful.

"Please, Mr. Hutchens," she said, "I *am* cold, and I want to go in."

"Worst idea I ever heard of." It seemed to her that he had been stealthily moving along the coping toward her. His head now was halfway up the pool. "Mr. Hutchens!" she said. "Don't come up here!"

"Mmmmrubbmmmlll," he said, laughing under water. Was he still creeping along there? She thought so.

"I'll yell," she said. "I promise you, I'll yell bloody murder if you come any closer."

"You wouldn't do that."

"Oh, yes I would!"

"That doesn't seem very friendly."

"Just the same."

"Oh, all right," he said, disgusted. "Go on in, then."

"You go on back to your end."

"My God you're modest. It's *dark*."

"Not dark enough."

When he moved with a heavy splash she crouched again, ready to leap out and run. But he was going the other way. She saw the glint and flicker, the disturbed shine of stars, and he disappeared under the diving board. From there he said, "I thought you and I were going to get along."

"I hope we can get along," she said, "but this is pretty embarrassing." She rose one step, cautiously lifting her shoulders from the water. He did not move or speak. Estimating the darkness, she came out to the waist. Nothing happened. Unless he could see in the dark like an owl, it was all right. Relieved, she came on out, saying, "Thank you, it's nice of you to let me off. I won't trespass again. It was such a warm night."

"Trespass all you want," he said from his cave under the board. "When a lady is truly modest I know how to behave."

Then in an instant shocking beams of light shot end to end of the pool. She saw the blue wriggling bottom, the copings, the board, and under it *him,* brown in the snaky blue water, reaching half out of the water to the switch under the fulcrum of the board. In that blasted instant she saw herself too—it was quite light enough—like a deer that had tripped a flash camera, and then she was running, slipping on the cement, squeaking and gasping. New lights glared on under the wistaria arbor: she ran right under one. The dressing room door slammed behind her, she flipped the lock and leaned panting against the wood, naked and slippery as a fish. Outside she could hear him dying of laughter.

CHAPTER 22

WHEN OLIVER reached the stable he found that of the eight horses he maintained there, not one was in. Three were at the Menlo Circus Club being groomed for a show by his daughters. One had had his feet trimmed too close by the horseshoer, and going lame had been turned into the hill pasture with the two mares and foals. The sorrel gelding and the black mare were in the small pasture just up behind. The boy had turned them out because they weren't getting any work and were going soft. He would run up and bring them in.

No, Oliver said. Was there a saddle, or had the kids hauled all those off, too? There was a saddle. He threw it into the car along with a bridle, a neck halter, a pail of oats, and a pair of brushes.

The Hutchens property ran to the first lane north—first a long hayfield with a farmhouse, then a pasture and corrals and ring and hurdles, then an orchard, and finally woods and semi-open slopes. All of it was belted in tight by a fence made of solid redwood rails mortised into railroad-tie posts. He saw the horses as soon as he turned left along the pasture's top edge. With a crunching of dry weeds he pulled off and parked. The fence he looked across was magnificent, made to last a hundred years; his mother's manager McIntyre, who had run the place while Oliver was away in the Navy, had spent twenty-two thousand pre-inflation dollars putting that thing around the property. Which was one of the reasons McIntyre was no longer around. Slanting down through the tall eucalyptus trees along the lower fence, the sun threw a net of shadows among the gold of wild oats and rye grass; below the white stems of mustard it cast forked charcoal lines. In the strong light the runty tarweed flowers looked like just-opening daisies.

Oliver rattled the pail with a dry calabash sound, grunting out a peremptory "Huh! Huh!" Rooted in their stretched shadows, the horses stood prick-eared.

"Huh! Huh!" He rattled the pail again. The black mare, Minna's horse, shook her head with an extravagant gesture and lifted her tail and rushed off quartering across the pasture. Her mane streamed, her tail floated, she trotted with a high clean action. The sorrel followed at a canter: he had to canter to keep up with that trot. Morning flamed off him in a red halo.

Darkness and light. Oliver watched them running just to feel the wind up their noses, playing their game of freedom before they came around. He did not begrudge them their game. On the contrary he felt tranquil, all his insides in place, not a kink anywhere, and that was surprising, considering everything. As he hung his chin on the top rail, leaning and shaking the pail gently, he smelled the night's damp in the angle of the grained and weathered wood. From the shaken pail came up the mealy smell of oats.

The mare stopped, the gelding beside her. For all their game of running away they had swung around closer than when they began. The black shook her head in exaggerated impatience and pride.

"Come on," Oliver said. "I know you want to impress your boy friend, but I've got the oats." He tempted her again, knowing she would come. They would always come, except once in a while in late April when they got drunk on green oats and prowled the impregnable fence indulging dreams of freedom.

They came walking toward him, and stopped thirty feet away. He looked into their dark intelligent eyes and shook the pail with a Cuban, caressing sound, and said to them softly, "Come on, kids, you're not something on a Mobiloil ad. You've made bargains with fate like the rest of us. You live inside a fence. Be realists, my friends. These oats are authentic."

The gelding came and dropped his nose to the oats Oliver poured on the ground, but with a rush the mare nipped him on the shoulder and drove him off. "Which demonstrates something I have known for a long time," Oliver said as he moved along the fence a few feet and reached through to pour another pile. "Which demonstrates that the attachment of the female to life is more ferocious than that of the male. There is no greedy-guts like a lady greedy-guts. I will cite you the example of old Mrs. Mantle, a friend of my mother's, who is eighty years old, toothless, probably hairless, half blind, hearing through the bones of her head and not quite straight inside the bones either. You would think this old girl would let go and dwindle out of existence with a faint odor of lavender and incontinence . . ."

In the sudden rich smell of horse and chewed oats he reached and laid the neck halter on the black's neck, and as she threw up her head, pretending, he snubbed her down and snapped the hook in the ring. With a brush in each hand he crawled through the fence and began to rub the dust out of her hide. "Does she do any such thing?" he said as he brushed down the molded chest. "Does she submit to our common mortality with stoicism or grace? She does not. It has been my misfortune to sit beside her at dinner. . . ."

The mare lifted her hind foot nervously as he rubbed down her leg. He picked up the hoof and held it between his knees while he opened his jackknife and dug hardened mud and gravel out of the hollow. He sniffed it for signs of thrush, dropped it, cleared out the other. "She eats like a pig in a trough," he told the chewing mare. "I was afraid to look away for fear my dessert would disappear."

On the mare's belly he found a bloated tick, picked it off, bent under and found another, monstrously swollen, between the black flaps of her teats. When she turned her head he held it for her to see. "A lady tick," he said. "Feel how hard she came loose?"

The mare lipped oats off the dry ground. He laid up the pad and then the saddle. As he hauled the cinch tight she groaned and eyed him; he hauled it a hole tighter. "I may say to you," he said, "that this . . . ugh . . . characteristic of females irritates the hell out of me. That much attachment to anything, even your life, is disgusting. How about these women in automobiles that scream and clutch handles and make intense suggestions to the driver? Who the hell are they, that their lives are so valuable? Are they worth more than other people, or are they only greedier of life? Aren't they just hooked a little closer to their bowels and glands? And how about my charming sister with her hair all wild, hanging onto the center of the stage. Didn't *she* play hell persuading herself she doesn't wear a halter."

Thinking of Sabrina made him, for some reason, think of Helen Kretchmer, squeaking and skidding around the corner of the dressing room, and he laughed out loud. That was one of the funniest of all freaks of the female universe, that his mother should find herself with a companion like that—built like a scatback, and with more on her mind than blushes. He had not seen her for a week, but that was all right. Something for the future; no need to rush it. But how she did scuttle! Nevertheless, not bashful; she had too steady an eye to be bashful.

When he slapped the mare on the haunch his hand left a spread print on her satiny hide. "Ha?" he said. "I leave it to you." But when he came with the bridle she pulled her head up and held her teeth shut. "Come on," he said. "You don't think you're a beast of burden, either, is that it? You never surrendered your sovereignty? Or are the oats all gone? Come on, open up, you old dog."

Her lower jaw dropped reluctantly to the pinch of his thumb and forefinger. The bit went in, the headstall went up around the ear. She chewed on the grass-stained iron. Reins in hand, Oliver stood for a second, whispering to her, smelling horse and dew-dampened dry grass and the sudden hot smell of manure from the gelding.

"I'll give you another example," he said softly, scratching in her dandruffy mane, "I invite you to consider my mother. She is the original groundhog that's been scared by her shadow, she's down her hole for keeps, and in the hole she wants everything she ever owned. She hangs onto things as if they were some God-damned relic from Tutankhamen's tomb. Look around you, what do you see? Houses, don't you, good houses, sixty, seventy-thousand-dollar houses on a couple three acres. Bridle trails all around here, room for horses like you, pleasant kind of country life. And what do you see up here on the Hutchens place? Weeds and woods, a howling wilderness. Why? Because my mother is a groundhog."

He held her in and swung up. She picked up her feet and threw her head up and down. That damned habit again. He'd cure her of that when he had time. She needed a martingale on her; she could bloody a man's nose for him.

As he bent to straighten a stirrup leather the mare spun, and he brought her around and down. His mind had not deviated from its train of thought, and his voice, though momentarily interrupted, went on again as a confidential whisper. "Women. Females. They're good for some things, let's admit. But there was never one born that would either accept facts or stick to a bargain. You never take the bit without making a face, and if it's pushed into your teeth you keep on making some God-damned attempt to avoid the inevitable. You step out of bounds and the first thing you do, you run to the referee to get the rules changed so your touchdown will count."

She had springs in her feet, she moved with snap. As far as the trail gate the gelding came with them, and would have come right on through if Oliver had not spooked him off. As they turned into the disked bridle trail between fence and woods, the gelding ran along inside the fence whinnying. "Oh, boo-hoo," Oliver said. "Yes, she's gone, you big ass. You remind me of my brother-in-law. Assert your independence. Learn to take 'em or let 'em alone."

He lifted the mare into a trot. She reached, flattened, put on speed. "Now!" he said. "This is the way females were meant to run, baby— with a bit in their mouths and a boss on their backs. You may run, and I will tell you where." The pound of her feet was no radio-sound-effect noise of the Lone Ranger or the Seventh Cavalry, but a steady even drumming. There was nothing to post to, only a vibration as even as the vibration of a motor. He had forgotten how good that gait was. Sitting her trot was almost like sitting in a sulky with a clean coarse tail in your face and smooth wind in your ears. His blood began to move. Morning was at the bottom of his lungs, cold at the roots of his hair.

Without slowing he leaned into a narrow trail that entered the woods. Gray oaks writhed up out of poison oak and coyote brush and the flick and flash of asters and ferns. The sun flaked down on the trail; he ducked for trailing branches. Under a bay tree he snatched upward and caught a handful of leaves, and from then on rode with his mouth slowly pickling from the oil of a chewed leaf. The world lay back of him as unvalued as the droppings the mare left in the trail.

"Ah, now," he said to her working ears. "Peg it, baby, peg it. The old vibrator. No no no no no, not that lousy string-halted canter. Come back down, come back to what you're good at. Now you've got it, now you're clipping it, here we go again. Huh huh huh huh, go it, you old dog. By God you've got the best God-damned trot in the God-damned world."

Where the trail grew rocky he pulled her in, jolting, throwing her feet, blowing. Up a crooked path among boulders and around the roots of big trees, across a dry arroyo where they slid down one side and lunged up the other, under the dapple of big oaks spaced along a narrow valley, they went at a fast, picking walk. There were thick-bodied, short-legged Angus steers grazing there, and the sight of them irritated Oliver. A few hundred dollars in grazing fees, the total income from four hundred acres of land worth, conservatively and in large lots, eight thousand an acre, and some of it, or in smaller lots, twice that much. If his mother would come out of her dream and listen for five minutes. Here would come the new Junipero Serra freeway, here would come people frantic for good country land, good views, oaks. With people outside the window jumping up and down and waving handfuls of money, her reaction was to draw the curtains. Leave the best raw land on the Peninsula to a bunch of beef.

The mare, soft, was sweating. There was a scum of suds along the edge of the pad and under the cheekstraps of the bridle. Coming to a steep pitch she lunged to take it running, and he held her down. "How long has she been thinking, now?" he rumbled at her. "How long since she said, 'Oh, don't press me, give me time to think'? Two weeks? Nearer three. And how long would she go on thinking if I'd hold still? Till the end of the God-damned world. So will I hold still? You just come along and see."

Farther up the climbing valley he met two riders, father and son, both riding muscled-up quarter horses. The three of them stood blowing companionably in the shade. The younger of the two riders was a horse breeder, and kept eying Oliver's mare. Good conformation—little soft? Seemed to lather up. Whose get? Purple Heart? That Arab? His respect increased. He rode around Oliver looking her over. He recognized her now, you could tell that stud's get anywhere. What dam? A rotgot mare? Just the same. You could get an awful nice little horse, just for general use, crossing a coldblood mare with a sire like that Purple Heart. He threw good bone.

The climbing sun reached down to him as he rode, squinting and drawling, once more around Oliver. You bet, *nice* little mare. Going to breed her! No? Why not? Know what he'd do? He'd breed her right back to Daddy. You might get something very nice. Right back to Daddy.

They parted and rode their ways. "How about it?" Oliver said to the mare's flattening ears. "Want Daddy? He throws good bone."

She scrambled over the last pitch and onto the back of the plateau, open, nearly level, scattered with fine old oaks. The sun on Oliver's back was hot. Gnats hung in busy nebulae at the outward edge of the oaks' shadows. Ahead of him, where the fire trail came onto the rim, a station wagon winked back light. Two figures were at the edge pointing out something down the slope.

"See those two?" Oliver said. "Those are some people I'm going to close a deal with. Mother won't like this deal, but by the time she finds out about it there'll be only two things she can do. She can repudiate it or she can accept it. She cares too much about the family name to do anything but accept it."

Swiftly he came down on them, and they turned with sun-whitened teeth, shading their eyes, Webber with his dumpy behind packed into whipcord riders, his chest fat in a gabardine shirt, a turquoise dangle at his throat, a Stetson pushed back on his head; the site man thin-shouldered in a loud sport shirt. They greeted him with respect. He was conscious that he had come on them out of the sun like an *hacendado,* like one of Burke Castro's cattle-raising ancestors, and that he sat above them high and powerful on a horse whose waltzing and bowing had them stepping watchfully clear. The site man had a big tube of blueprints under his arm.

"Gentlemen," Oliver said gravely.

CHAPTER 23

E
VERY TIME she came over, and she came nearly every day, she
brought something. Gifts for the children, and bed jackets and
baby presents for Barbara, he could take as natural manifesta-
tions of affection. When she arrived about dinner time bearing
boxes of hot steakburgers and fresh pineapples, those were the scrupulous gestures of one who wanted company but did not want to be a
burden; and when she brought plums, peaches, fresh vegetables, or
flowers from her mother's vast gardens, that was a neighborly sharing
of summer plenty. But he murmured when one day she replaced their
beat-up pots and pans with copper-bottomed stainless steel, and he
protested when she retired their old drip coffee pot and endowed them
with an electric percolator.

"What's she trying to do, buy our affections?" he said in bed that
night. "Tell her to lay off."

"Don't you say a word," Barbara said. "She's all unhappy and at loose
ends, and we're the only people she feels she can turn to."

"I'm flattered. But she doesn't have to buy us. You tell me she won't
use her money to buy herself a useful job, why can't she be that delicate
about us? Our friendship's free. Tell her no more percolators, please."

"I never knew you to be so sort of ungenerous, Leonard. She loves to
give things."

"I'm just wondering who's being most gratified," he said. "She's dangerous, she isn't responding to treatment. One of these days she's going to crystallize and go right through the cylinder head."

The next day when he came home Sabrina was there. Beside her chair was a new portable typewriter. She moved it toward him with her foot, saying, "I tried your old crock the other day and it's a wreck. Now you can save the world legibly."

But Leonard put his hands behind him. "It's a kind thought, but no."

"Take it, you idiot." She turned on the smile—not so frequent these days, and with the vertical line between her eyes still there to give her, even smiling, an eaten, discontented look.

He glanced at Barbara, sitting uncomfortably on a straight chair, and noted that she was embarrassed. She should be. "I'll just put it back in your car," he said to Sabrina.

"Are you serious? Really, you'd be doing me a favor to take it. Please. If you want I'll write it off as a contribution to the Greenbelt Committee."

"We're not deductible." He smiled—he felt he had to—and took the typewriter away. When he came back in Sabrina was still looking flushed and angry.

"I don't think that was very friendly," she said.

"I'm sorry. But look, it's got to be kept as even as possible, granted it's never going to be completely even."

"Even! Oh, damn people without enough money, they always make so much of a few dollars. 'You can't buy me! I have my pride!'"

"So?" Leonard said. His smile felt a little grim.

He discouraged the gifts, but there was no way, even if he had wanted to, of discouraging her talk. When she got dressed up in her hair shirt she asked ultimate questions and would not stay for an answer. She did not talk about herself; he had little notion about her relations with her husband and he knew nothing about the lover except that he seemed to be out—they both seemed to be out. What she talked about was the triviality of American lives, quoting a lady correspondent who had been in school with her in Switzerland before the war, and who now refused to live in the United States because American lives had no suffering in them and so no longer mattered. This Sylvia Morgan wrote stories about Iraqi girls gone blind from weaving rugs in dark basements, and she had one terrible one about a Palestinian refugee girl of no more than twelve, pregnant and syphilitic, whom she had found begging a public letter-writer in front of a mud mosque to write a letter to her parents. The letter writer had refused, finding she had nothing with which to pay.

"I agree, terrible," Leonard said. "But are we worse off because we have less of that?"

"Sylvia thinks so. Maybe I do, too. There's nothing to put iron in us. We grow up with too many of our wants satisfied."

"Oh, I heard that all through the war, and it makes me so mad," Barbara said. "Leonard never starved, and neither did I, but he was at Casablanca and Palermo and Anzio and everywhere."

"Neither blind nor syphilitic," Leonard said. "Did it ever strike you that your friend Sylvia might be a slummer with strong tastes?"

"Sylvia?"

"Where's she live when she's home?"

"London."

"East End?"

"Sloan Square."

"Weaving and eating crusts, I presume."

"No, really," she said, and slid out of his fingers without apparently knowing she had been trapped. "Really, don't you think we all live empty, stupid, selfish, undignified lives?"

"No. Some do. Some try not to. Some even succeed."

"Sabrina, you're hopeless!" Barbara said. "If there isn't any suffering in American lives, what's making *you* so unhappy?"

Sabrina was sitting on a hassock, having treed them on the sofa, and glancing at her reflection in the plate-glass window Leonard saw her handsome, frowning, unpainted face contract in an expression almost venomous. "Me?" she said. "An idiotic adolescent complication delayed into my half-baked middle age. It's probably about as important as a stubbed toe. Maybe that's why I feel so bloody American lately. There should never be a sentiment carved on an American tombstone. Not even a name. Here lies balloon, with the air out."

"Shyme, shyme," Leonard said. "You've been reading too much in the family papers."

It was true she read in them every morning, curled in a big chair with one of his pamphlet cases while he sorted and catalogued more of the scraps that family piety had preserved. She was an intent reader; somehow, watching her out of the sides of his eyes while she sat for two or three hours hardly stirring, he got a picture of her as a rather sullen girl, haunting solitary corners of that house with a book. Also, he watched her as she read because he was curious about her reaction. Having arranged and tabulated that bunch of eccentrics, he felt tender toward them: he felt half obligated to defend them against her scorn. Likewise, he told himself, in case she discovered in the family hell any variety of damnation that she thought completed her, he wanted to be around when she keenoed.

Once she said, looking up from Cornelius Wolcott's rather meager sheaf, "Maybe it was Great-Grandfather. I think he must have been such a money-maker that he scared them all. He worked to give them everything they wanted, and they got terrified because they couldn't think what it *was* they wanted, their New England consciences got all involved. There must have been *something* that would make a whole generation into ineffectual nothings. Do you suppose just the lack of a real father around could make four out of five of them old maids and another a matriarchal tyrant?"

"It was just plain lack of opportunity that kept Grace and Sarah unmarried, wasn't it?"

"That doesn't explain Bushrod and Mercer."

"Bushrod had the Harvard Club."

"Also he had the one job they all had to respect." Her eyes went back to the papers. "Whatever it was, the blessed Wolcotts nearly died out, do you know that? Whether Great-Grandfather scared them into impotence or not, he had five children and only *one* grandchild—Mother —and she came when Grandmother was past forty. They must have been panicked at the thought of all that money and all those things going to remote cousins or strangers."

On these studious mornings Sabrina had little of the frenzy of the absolute that agitated her in the evenings at Leonard's house. She reminded him of someone single-mindedly working on a term paper. "And then of course it happened again," she said. "Mother didn't get married until she was older than I am now. I was born when she was nearly forty. It seemed to be the fate of the Wolcott girls to be either sterile or desperately late."

"Procrastination," Leonard said.

But she would not laugh. He thought that when she simply opened her eyes wide, thinking of something besides how they looked, they were as beautiful eyes as he had ever seen in a human face. Then the thinking, sober look changed, the eyes narrowed, the corners pinched down in an expression irritable and gloomy. "How do we always get on the subject of sterility? Am I obsessed?"

What could he do but smile at her broadly across twenty feet of brown studious air?

Later, that morning or another, she lifted her thoughtful face to say, "Having that one precious child made Grandmother impossibly smug, you know? A she-buzzard with one egg, and that egg the last of the Wolcotts. She played matriarch to the hilt, she knew her importance."

"Well, there's a career for you," he said. "You too can be a matriarch."

"Ah?" she said. "I think they won't let you till you're a matron first." Maybe she *was* obsessed.

He dumped the great box of Mercer's photographs on the desk and spread them around: Mercer in a shepherd's plaid dress, Mercer in a tam-o'-shanter with a ribbon, schoolboy Mercer in Eton jacket, young-gentleman Mercer in morning clothes and in riding habit; Mercer bareheaded and in a soft sombrero, Mercer with curls, Mercer parted at the side, Mercer balding, nearly-bald, bald; Mercer bare-faced, Dundreary'd, full-bearded, gray-bearded; Mercer with setters, Chesapeakes, mastiffs; Mercer in knickers with a tennis racket, Mercer in gaiters carrying on his shoulder an unpersuasive ax and with his foot on an unresisting studio log; Mercer and a girl who was obviously Mrs. Hutchens at the age of a homely thirteen, sitting in a wheelbarrow in the grounds of what was probably the Nahant house, holding garden tools meant to deceive; Mercer as traveler, such a traveler as only the dedicated can become—in a tarboosh against a background of pyramids, in evzone skirts on the brink of romantic cardboard chasms with delphic grottoes; in knickers again, alpenstock in hand, upon a clearly authentic glacier, and in the same knickers, with alpenstock and rope and face of stern resolve, on the slopes of a Swiss photographer's painted Matterhorn. Here was Mercer in a punt on the Cam and Mercer in a sort of pirogue on the bayou-like waters of the Spree Forest and Mercer on a ferry-boat crossing some Dutch or Danish sound under a flurry of gulls. Here was Mercer on the Bridge of Sighs and Mercer rowing a gondola and Mercer inspecting an Arno flood from the Ponte Vecchio, Mercer looking out a ruined window of the Heidelberg Schloss, Mercer bracing one of Bernini's columns in front of the Vatican, Mercer acknowledging with squinted eye the superior height of the Tour Eiffel, Mercer with napkin on knee on a terrace overlooking what might have been Como or Garda or Maggiore.

Protean of costume and background, Mercer had been caught in the preservative lens in Salzburg, Paris, Rome, Venice, Chamonix, the Isle of Man, Boston, Falmouth, Yokohama; sometimes with sisters one or two or three, once or twice with brother Bushrod, once or twice with other travelers carefully identified on the back of the photograph. But mostly Mercer *solus*. Whatever the place or costume, however clothed or naked the skull, however undeveloped or grizzled the facial hair, always the eyes stared hopefully, with a look of questioning or of waiting, into the camera. Studying him as he lay spread through his whole life across the desk, Leonard decided that Mercer gave to the camera the face we usually give to no one but the mirror, and then not in company. I would as lief you would have someone see these pictures.

Sabrina had come and was looking silently over his shoulder. He had arranged the pictures as nearly as possible in chronological order, sometimes by dates on the backs, sometimes by the condition of Mercer's hair and beard. The sequence ran from a pensive eight-year-old in dresses and white stockings and curls, leaning against a carved table in the year 1861 and directing at the camera his girlish, hesitant glance, to a snapshot taken in the grounds of this Hillsborough house in June 1931—this last an old bald man whose mouth was hidden but not strengthened by a grizzled beard. He wore a peevish pucker between his eyes and the air of having been asked to answer something whose answer he did not know.

Contemplating him all the way from whining schoolboy to lean and slippered pantaloon, Leonard said, "He reminds me of Louise watching stars. 'Hey, Daddy, you can see him afterwards with your eyes shut.' "

"Can't you though," Sabrina said. Touching the photographs one after another with a finger, she moved along the desk, and without looking up at Leonard she said after a minute, "Isn't it a miserable transformation? Look at that little boy—it's a sweet face, actually; he must have been everybody's baby, especially his mother's. You can see it in the way she dressed him. And look how he comes on here, quite a handsome young beau, wouldn't you say?" Absently she raised two fingers to the slightly Roman arch of her nose. "The old Wolcott nose is really attractive on him."

"He looks a good deal like you in that one."

A sideward and upward flash of her great eyes, but no smile. What label for that expression? Somber? Hardly that dark. It was hard for her to look really somber because her eyes were so live. Pensive, maybe. Or maybe just an expression practiced in front of mirrors, part of the romantic actress's repertoire.

She turned a studio photograph so that Leonard could see it: Mercer and another young man posed across a chess table with the painted palaces of the Grand Canal in the background. "He looks as if he might be somebody, doesn't he? One of those young Bostonians who went to German universities and brought back learning by the boatload, or who spent years in England absorbing the knack of being responsible patricians. He might have gone on to assemble a great art collection, or found the Boston Symphony, or become a patron of letters or a writer of history who could be appointed Minister to the Court of Saint James's. One of the American Medici. Do you suppose Berenson looked any more promising when he set out for Florence?"

"Mercer did leave a sort of art collection."

"Toby jugs!" Her eyes, stretched wide, were like the great oval eyes he had seen in reproductions of paintings from the Ajanta caves. She looked sybilline; she might suddenly have begun to writhe three pairs of arms. "He was the saddest of the whole pitiful bunch," she said.

"Sarah and Grace were pretty sad."

"They never had anything but compensations and pretensions. Mercer might have had something, but it never got used."

"What do you think he had?"

Now her look was intense, a reading look of someone playing charades and guessing from slight hints. She threw her hands in the air. "I don't know. Whatever might have been asked of him. Doesn't it show in his face? He was ready for something, and nothing ever came."

"Still, he seems to have kept looking."

"Of course!" she said. "Of course. Look at all this ridiculous masquerade. He never in all his life found out who he was. He kept trying on different costumes to see if he'd recognize himself."

"Yes," he said, "that's intelligent. At least it's what I was thinking myself, so it must be."

But she would not be diverted. An odd, violent fling of the hand across the pictures, and "Look," she said. "There isn't a single picture of him doing anything real. Even when he has his picture taken as a country gentleman he has to borrow a gardener's rake and wheelbarrow and hoke it all up. He hunted himself around the world for sixty-five or seventy years and he never did find anything he was for."

Apparently he was being called on to compare her with Mercer as a collection of wasted talents. He felt like saying, "Remember my daddy? He was another. It's nothing unusual, and it's got nothing to do with money, if that's what you're driving at. It's only got to do with something like paralysis of the will. You've got as much money as Mercer had, and you're a hell of a lot better educated. Why don't *you* found a Boston Symphony? Or a San Mateo County Folksong Society? Or a little magazine devoted to genealogy? Or if it's wickedness you value, and hell you're bound for, why don't you go up to North Beach and disaffiliate, let your hair hang down, paint rings around your eyes and a target around your navel, and take to pot and strange unmade beds and make the *acquaintance* of vice, instead of sinning like a Victorian virgin and then running to the mirror to examine the horrid brand of damnation on your brow? Do any damned thing except gnaw your knuckles and cry how lost you are."

Instead, he opened his mouth and said something frivolous, and just then the white coat gleamed in the doorway and Lizardo said, "Lunch, Miz Castro."

Saved by the bell.

"Tell me," said Mrs. Hutchens over the crab salad, "how you are . . . getting on."

He sat, Odysseus disguised among women, with his left hand decorously in his lap. When he picked up fork or glass his little finger curled. Ha! Now and then it might be a good idea to spread his elbows and remind them that there were other ways, that an oilcloth-covered kitchen table had its manners as surely as this Heppelwhite. He said, "A day for flags and parades. As soon as I do Mercer's photographs I'm through."

"Oh, my goodness!" she said, as if he had knocked her wind out. "Oh . . . dear! Today?"

"I thought you'd be glad to have them all done."

"Oh . . . glad, yes . . . delighted. But it has been such a pleasure to see you . . . working with them every day and to help you as I could, and be . . . reminded of so many . . . things." Her trembling head scattered a distracted look around the dining room. "I'm so . . . *sorry!* Couldn't you then go straight through and catalogue some of the . . . collections?"

"Mother, you forget Bobbie's about to have a baby," Sabrina said.

Mrs. Hutchens did not look as if she liked the interruption. She kept her faltering and hopeful glance on Leonard, who lifted his shoulders. "I'm sorry. I'll only have about a month between the baby and school, and that's just about enough time to get Bobbie squared around. Christmas vacation I can do a little, if you still want me. But first I've got this tour of duty as a practical nurse."

She began getting ready to laugh, now, whenever she saw a certain expression on his face. "I imagine you are . . . splendid," she murmured.

"I like archiving better. Actually I'd have been through a good while ago except every time I tried rounding Mercer up he was off on a cruise."

"That was Mercer's . . . habit." Though she laughed, she did not look well. Her smile was vague and troubled, her eyes wandered past him and fell for a second, with palsied intentness, on Sabrina. She frowned quickly and lightly and said, "As you know, I am . . . terribly happy to have them done. It's always been a worry to me to have them so . . . disordered. Now I can . . . rest easy."

That mortuary note produced automatically encouraging smiles from him and from Helen Kretchmer. But before the old lady's regard was quite withdrawn from Sabrina, the dark blue eyes came up: for a moment mother and daughter looked deep into each other as if they shared a piece of not very pleasant information. Then Mrs. Hutchens drew a determined breath, wavered into a smile, and said, "Did you see the photograph of us all on the . . . Rhone Glacier?"

"Were you in that one? I didn't recognize you."

"Oh, yes. I was . . . thirteen. Mercer offered to take me abroad with him. Mother was to pay the bills. I didn't have a very . . . good time. I was homesick for Nahant and Mercer was a very fussy duenna."

Now it was Helen Kretchmer's turn to laugh. "Can you really have a bad time on a trip abroad?"

Mrs. Hutchens looked up as if pleased. "Oh, dear . . . yes. Why, I was born abroad, I never saw the United States . . . until I was six. My biggest excitement was coming back to Boston." Shakily she smiled, arch and fond. "Some day we must . . . see that you go. If I weren't so . . . decrepit we should both go instantly. It seems so easy, these days." The locket watch pinned to her shoulder began to shake, alarming Leonard with the fear that she was having some sort of seizure. But it was only laughter. "It was . . . most amusing," she said. "Mercer was to be . . . reimbursed at the end of the trip. But he never got around to presenting his bill."

The trembling of her mouth could not quite be stopped by the pressure of the napkin against it. "Finally he did present it . . . after nearly four years. I can remember how furious Mother was. He had charged her . . . six-per-cent interest for all the time he had . . . procrastinated."

Sabrina threw a devout look at the ceiling. Oblivious, chuckling, Mrs. Hutchens wandered on. "He was . . . remarkably close. He fearfully disliked being cheated, and he thought me . . . very extravagant. Still, he did let me take some lessons in . . . rowing a gondola. Did you see that picture?"

"Only one of Mercer rowing, not you."

"Pshaw," she said. "I did it . . . too, much better than he did. I wonder what's become . . ."

The Filipino brought a vast bowl of raspberries to which Mrs. Hutchens helped herself with excruciating slowness, berry by berry. With equal slowness, later, she spooned yoghurt out of the bowl that Lizardo held for her. "Those who have a sweet tooth may spoil their yoghurt with . . . brown sugar," she said. "I think it . . . ever so much better plain."

Dutifully they all liked theirs plain too, except Sabrina, who took no yoghurt at all.

"Isn't it astonishing . . . how one forgets," Mrs. Hutchens said. "I had not remembered about Mercer's attempt to . . . charge interest for years. But it was . . . terribly characteristic. As he grew older he developed a rather . . . jealous and grudging nature, I am sorry to say. He was . . . seldom on good terms with Bushrod, though Mother could always . . . manage them both. I remember once . . . Bushrod bought an especially handsome brass-mounted harness for his rig, and Mercer couldn't rest until he had got an even handsomer silver-mounted one. He was miserably envious when Bushrod . . . bought his special Rolls Royce, but he never . . . got around to matching it. After Bushrod died it always seemed to me Mercer had lost some of his . . . reason for living."

She murmured on, half-audible. Sabrina watched her, lifting raspberries to her mouth, shaking her head with a swift upward half-smile when Lizardo proffered the bowl again. Thinking what? Leonard wondered. Interested why? Still trying to gauge her own loose ends by Mercer's ravelings? Then he saw that Helen was watching Sabrina as closely as Sabrina watched her mother. What there? Envy, admiration, a sort of schoolgirl crush? Well, well, the currents that could circuit around one Heppelwhite table without a single leaf in, with only four people to lunch and one Filipino to serve them. Even the Filipino, prudent and impeccable by the sideboard, had one sort of expressionless face for Mrs. Hutchens, another for Sabrina. For Leonard and Helen he had the sort of expression he might have worn in the presence of the furniture. It was all like the complexities of an electronic hook-up, like the backside of a television cabinet. But for Leonard at least the picture tube was out, and only the sound went on, a broken murmuring, tuned low.

And what about that park? In almost a month, not another word about it, either from Mrs. Hutchens or from Sabrina. Well, he would not raise the question or bring the committee to call until she herself brought it up. Interfering with the family procrastination was a little too much like putting your finger in a worm gear.

A little later he stood with Sabrina in the front hall and watched Mrs. Hutchens go murmuring upstairs on Helen's arm. "I ought to get an apartment," Sabrina said, surprising him. "I'm not good for her."

"No? Why?"

"I upset her, and when she's upset she goes old on you. Did you hear her? She sounded as if she was all set to give up and die as soon as you make the last three-by-five card."

"Then I'd better string the job out."

"You'd like to preserve her, would you?"

"I would. I think she's great."

"She's a funny woman," Sabrina said. "There's some kind of need for justification behind all this family business. I wish I knew. I never knew her at all, I don't now. She used to get into such terrible, unreasonable, tearful, shaking rages with me about nothing—the clothes I wore, or my dirty fingernails, or people that I liked and shouldn't have. I hated her for twenty-five years."

"She doesn't seem very easy to hate."

"Not now," Sabrina said. "Not any more. I even catch myself thinking she likes to have me around, in spite of what I do to her."

One of those moments of awkwardness and embarrassment fell between them, and he said, perhaps making up for all the doubts that he expressed to Barbara in private, "It's been great for Bobbie having you around, I'll say that."

"Ah!" she said. "You two save my life every day."

The brilliant oval eyes touched him, and then her attention flicked away. Lizardo had come out of the drawing room with some letters on a silver tray. Between his eroded brown face and Sabrina's there passed sudden questions and answers. He changed expression without the apparent movement of a single muscle, the way a piece of sculpture or a mask changes expression when turned, and with a little nod he laid the tray on the hall table and went away. Indifferently, over her shoulder, Sabrina said, "Thanks, Lizardo."

But her neck had stiffened. She said something vague, focusing on the tray as if she could see through her shoulder blades, and when he said that he'd better get back to Mercer it was not clear that she heard him. She was already moving, or pouncing, toward the letters. From the cross hall, glancing back, he saw her grab them up and read one envelope, then another, then a third. Impatiently she flung them back on the tray, unopened.

CHAPTER 24

P REPARING for her nap, Mrs. Hutchens made a practice of lying on her back and relaxing every muscle of her body. It began, she told Helen, as a tingle at the roots of her hair, and spread through the rest of her rather like moisture through a blotter.

Helen, turning from drawing the drapes, saw her already at it. Her brow, which had been a good deal pinched and worried-looking lately —it was Sabrina Castro who bothered her, Helen was sure—was already determinedly serene. Relaxation flowed visibly past the eyelids, resolutely and tranquilly closed; down the cheeks which seemed to sag and loosen, dissolved by pure will; and so on down the shoulders, arms, body, legs. Under the violet mohair throw the feet tipped sideward with a little caving motion, giving up the ghost of tension.

From the part in her hair to the soles of her feet Mrs. Hutchens lay limp. She relaxed with ecstasy, she renounced her bones (which she thought must be hollow anyway, for she had found while swimming that she could float in any position, lying, sitting, on back or front or either side. "All this to-do about Great Salt Lake," she told Helen. "Is it so . . . wonderful that people can't sink? I could demonstrate it for them in my . . . bathtub.") But not while sternly relaxing. The effect of abjuring the bones was to make her heavier, not lighter. Her specific gravity increased by the second. She subsided toward her afternoon hour of rest as limp and heavy as a stocking full of quicksilver sinking in a pond.

Then unexpectedly her eyes were open, watery blue and white, fixed on Helen moving softly to the door. Under the deceitfully tranquil lids they had been as wide awake all the time as little chipmunks under roots. Helen stopped. "Here, here, you aren't even trying!"

A smile relaxed across Mrs. Hutchens' mouth and left her lips askew; her expression was at once anxious and sly. Still flat on her back, not moving body or limb, she said, "There are . . . things on my mind. I shan't be able to nap properly until I have settled . . . at least two of them."

As if suddenly recalling a duty, she began her eye exercises; she looked in agony. With her eyeballs rhythmically rolling right, then left, then right, she said, "I wish to do something . . . for that nice humorous young man. Do you think he would accept a little . . . gift? He and Barbara? Today will be his . . . last day. And they are having a baby. Do you . . . know how much his check will be?"

"I haven't figured it up. He's worked just over a month. Something like seven hundred dollars, I think."

"Please make it for . . . a thousand," Mrs. Hutchens said. "I'll sign it . . . with the others when I wake up."

A bitter little pod of disappointment broke under Helen's tongue. That nice young man had worked for a month, for twice his schoolteacher's salary. Helen Kretchmer, she felt like saying, has worked for seven, for a lot less than seven hundred a month. And been loyal to you in ways you don't know. Out of her mouth, quietly and warmly, came other words: "What a nice thing to do! You're terribly generous."

"He . . . amuses me," Mrs. Hutchens said. The awful eyeballs rested. A flicker like irritation passed over her face. Her arms and hands lay where relaxation had dropped them, and having wilfully sagged her cheeks she had not bothered to tighten them again. "I think I have never seen . . . such an original. And Barbara was always . . . like one of my own. Her father used to treat me for sinusitis."

The voice emerged as if out of a muted horn. There did not seem enough tension in her to move a lip, much less vibrate a vocal cord.

Her eyeballs flashed right and left and right again—Helen had the fascinated sense that she could hear them buzz like flies trapped in a window. There were wonderful things about this job, but the eye exercises were nearly enough to drive you from the house. She stood quietly at the foot of the bed and watched the lunging eyeballs come to rest. The freckled lids fluttered, but the cheeks remained serene. "There is . . . one other thing."

"Yes?"

Casual power lay soft in the bed before her. How easily a woman such as Mrs. Hutchens could change almost anyone's life if she wanted to! Could she have any idea what even a hundred dollars, the sort of gratuity she distributed as John D. Rockefeller used to distribute new dimes, could mean to someone like Helen Kretchmer? Could she even imagine that until lately Helen Kretchmer had never in all her life had so much as a hundred dollars ahead? And here went three hundred to Leonard MacDonald—a tip, hardly more.

She felt sure that the pang of disappointment had caught her smile back the way a dog's lip sometimes gets hooked on a tooth. Her lips were parted and dry. Without moistening them—she always wanted to be poised, and she was careful about the external stigmata of emotion—she brought them together. Her hand straightened the violet mohair over Mrs. Hutchens' feet. Mrs. Hutchens' pale lips had taken on the shadowiest of smiles. "You have a great . . . desire to travel," she said.

Helen found herself leaning too far forward. She laughed in a way she hoped was deprecatory and gay, and said, "Ah, my pipedream! The midwestern American with an itch for foreign culture. But I can't help it; it's what I dream about and save up for." She turned her lips down ruefully and laughed again. "Maybe sometime I can get a State Department job and get to work eight hours a day typing documents in Formosa, or work for an oil company and spend two years in a compound in Saudi Arabia or somewhere."

The old half-hidden eyes watched her from between sparse lashes. The long, soft, sagged face had assumed an expression that was—wasn't it?—doting and fond. She said, "My dear, I know how you have had to be so self-reliant and do . . . everything for yourself. You've had to . . . put off your own desires while your brother was growing up. I have thought . . . several times . . . it is unfortunate that I am not Auntie Grace, for then you would have . . . got abroad at least once before now.".

To the smile that wavered like the grimace of a baby's gas pain across the old lady's lips, Helen responded with a brave bright smile of her own. The frail old body lay quietly, as if waiting patiently for the tongue to pause and the eyes to stop their exercising and the mind to return and lie down.

"Please . . . come here," Mrs. Hutchens said. Feeling corseted, forcing herself to breathe easily, Helen went to the bedside. The freckled big-knuckled hand covered hers. "If it were not that I am . . . selfish and want you . . . here with me, I should send you at once," she said. "This is somehow a sad house, and Sabrina has not . . . helped it by coming home. It must be . . . confining for a lively young woman. But if you are willing to . . . wait a while, I shall try to make up for my selfishness."

The breathing that should have been even had become real labor. "I want you, my dear," said Mrs. Hutchens, "I want you to . . . draw yourself a check also, one that you can put in the bank and have ready for . . . when you go."

Abruptly Helen bent over and laid her face in Mrs. Hutchens' lacy bed jacket. She felt that she might cry; then she *was* crying. "You shouldn't," she said. "It's wonderful of you, but you shouldn't."

Tentatively the old arm came around her shoulders and then dropped away. "You have been so kind to me," the old lady said. "I have . . . come to love you very much." She chuckled in a strangling way. Though she could not yet lift her face to meet her employer's, Helen imagined it with a vague, wondering look on it, the eyes staring puzzledly with tears in them. "Now go and . . . draw yourself a check at once," Mrs. Hutchens said.

Dabbing at her eyes, laughing, Helen sat up. "But Mrs. Hutchens, you haven't told me how much!"

"Pshaw! I hadn't thought about it. I have no idea what it might . . . take, any more. Would you be able to have a . . . summer abroad for . . . say . . . three thousand dollars?"

"Three *thousand?*"

"Isn't it enough? If it isn't we can . . . see about adding to it . . . later. I must watch myself for fear I do something that Oliver would think . . . extravagant." Her smile stretched into a lewd grin. "Leave it at . . . three thousand for the moment. I shall think all the time I am napping what a pleasure it will be to . . . wake up and sign it."

She closed her eyes. The stern resolves of relaxation smoothed her forehead. "Now I must begin . . . all over again," she said. "Bother!" Helen watched it starting, the almost visible tingle at the hair roots, the willed loosening of all the little gathered-up nerves and muscles. But when she stooped and kissed the old lady she felt the dry lips pucker briefly at her jaw. The eyes did not open. The smile that lingered on the old blotched face was hardly a smile at all, but more like the final serenity.

Before the pier glass in the hall she quivered like a spear stuck humming in a door. She studied her blazing image for signs of magnification and enhancement, some extravagant metamorphosis. Her lower lip was caught between her teeth, her hands were clenched at her sides. She opened her mouth very wide and yelled silently at her reflection. The world hung before her nose like a ripe fruit, and she plucked it in one fierce gesture before she started down the stairs.

In the library, when she arrived, Leonard MacDonald looked up from behind a card file. His plaid shirt was incongruous against the satiny rosewood desk. Why didn't the silly fellow wear a suit and tie like other people? He wouldn't be unattractive, in a hairy over-masculine way, if he'd dress decently. But she supposed, with a small glow of condescension, that Levis and a J. C. Penney shirt were about what he could afford.

His bright eyes pried, and his eyebrows moved around. Then his brows and lips began to lift together, and he said, "All rosy and excited. What's up? Mrs. Hutchens win the Irish Sweepstakes?"

She smiled, but mysteriously. Inside her a gleeful child was chanting, "I know something I won't tell!" "Nothing's up," she said. "I came down to see how many days you've worked."

"Ah, that's it. MacDonald's leaving, oh frabjous day."

"It'll be pleasant to have the working persons out of the house," she said. "With a good airing it will be almost as it used to be."

Leonard said, "A man works his heart out"—he counted his fingers several times, his eyes on the calendar and his lips moving—"for twenty-three working days, and all he leaves behind him is a stale odor."

"Twenty-three," Helen said, and made a note on one of his file cards. "I'll make out your check and Mrs. Hutchens will sign it when she wakes up. Then we'll open the windows." She stood smiling at him. Smiling? Beaming. She felt extraordinarily pretty. She said, "You should know, Mrs. Hutchens thinks you've been wonderful."

"She does?"

"Oddly enough, yes."

"She's kind of wonderful herself," he said. "I came over here prepared for an eccentric old party and I go away persuaded she's a great lady."

"She certainly is."

He set the card file on the cabinet behind him, and turning, fixed her with his bright, inquiring, knowing eyes. "I'll pity you, going on working in the castle. That's what you're going to do, is it?"

She could see him thinking, How come no boy friends? How come no friends of any kind, and no interests outside the job? In seven months any girl, unless she's a real foul ball, ought to meet *someone*. How come she never seems to leave the place?

Scornfully she said, "I'm saving up till I can get a dolly that will cry and go to sleep and wet itself. After that I don't know."

It had been too reckless. He had suddenly got an unfamiliar glimpse of her. But she didn't care—she rather liked giving away the real Helen Kretchmer under the perfect secretary. And he wasn't as clever as he thought himself, for he was obviously fishing as he said, "Never get lonesome here among the mice and spiders of Chillon?"

"Never."

"No social sentiments."

"Not a one."

"Never write poetry on the walls, or send letters to Abbie Van Buren signed 'Wistful,' or 'Hoping'?"

"I'm so busy making out checks," she murmured.

"All work and no play makes Jill a pill."

"Thank you."

"It's nothing."

"As for play," she said, and felt the blood come into her face, "name me another job that provides a thirty-acre park with a tennis court and swimming pool, and golf every morning at the most beautiful and expensive club you ever saw, practically." *And* an apartment, she might have added. *And* board. *And* four hundred a month practically clear. *And* three-thousand-dollar bonuses!

"The fat of the land," Leonard said, watching her.

"Exactly."

"Well," he said, "I think you'll get your dolly."

"Thank you," she said tartly. "Thank you, I think I will!"

Back in her room she tore half a dozen checks from the big household checkbook and swiftly ran them through the typewriter: the monthly pay of Edelberto Lizardo, Bernadette Burger, Martha Daley, and Virgil Stillman. Oliver handled everthing except Mrs. Hutchens' immediate household. And what a break that she hadn't let him take that over too! Try to imagine any such gift out of Oliver—unless it was paid for. And if he had ideas like that, which he obviously did, he could revise them. She had not seen him since that horrible night at the pool, and she could stand to go till doomsday without seeing him. It had taken her an hour to get up nerve to open the dressing-room door and sneak home, and she had expected him behind every tree. And would she not be careful from now on! Around him she always felt as if she were wearing loose clothes around a lot of factory wheels.

Nevertheless, she said to herself, inking in the stubs, I guess I am a match for you, Mister Hutchens, sir.

An envelope for each check. Then a check for Leonard MacDonald, $1000, a fine fat sum whose writing gave her generous pleasure. Another envelope, another neat entry on the stub. Now her own paycheck, itself nothing to be contemptuous of: she looked at it with fondness. And finally the deferred thrill, magnified by deliberate delay. Pay to the order of Helen Kretchmer the sum of 3000 and No/100 dollars.

She laid it beside her paycheck. The zeroes were lovely. She looked down on more money than she had ever possessed in her life, or hoped to possess short of long saving or a lucky tip on the stock market. She had to close her eyes, get up, walk into the bathroom, look at herself in the mirror, walk back out again. The checks were still there.

From her desk drawer she took the red envelope containing her building-and-loan passbook. There were six entries, the first one a foot-in-the-door sort of deposit, the others solid: February 2, $50; March 5, $200; April 3, $250; May 4, $300; June 2, $350; July 2, $350. Not an indulgence or an unnecessary expense in seven months, nothing but the absolutely necessary clothes, a few personal articles, a set of second-hand golf clubs: she had seen at once that she could not walk up and down the fairways beside Mrs. Hutchens' gas buggy, attended by a caddy and sometimes a chauffeur and recognized by everyone, meeting everywhere those deferential or indulgent or merely amused smiles, with her old sack of rusty irons and ball-headed woods that had been her father's twenty years ago.

But nothing else. She had indulged herself only in the pleasures of accumulation and anticipation. Her hoard could not have been more real to her if she had carried it in a roll in the top of her stocking. Her mind held a vivid impression of her savings as worn bills stained and scented by human contact, smelling of powder and tobacco, patched with Scotch tape. She understood to its depths, with total pleasure, the lust of misers. Looking at the book that recorded her balance of $1500, and the checks for $3400 more that could be added almost intact, she said to herself, Helen Kretchmer, you little Scrooge, you!

All this came, incredibly, from two lyrical—and hard-earned—references, plus an introduction to Mr. Snell, plus *his* acquaintance with Mr. Cockcroft in San Francisco, plus Mr. Cockcroft's acquaintance with the Hutchens family. One break in a chain of accidents and she would be marooned in some stenographic pool among girls always looking over their shoulders, backbiting in the restroom, gossiping at lunch, trying to sleep their way to an advantage, trying to out-smart some middle-aged she-dragon of an office manager—good Lord. And a salary that would have gone, all but a few pitiful dollars a month, for a dreary room, skimpy meals, an occasional movie or concert, an occasional bottle of cheap wine to make the warmed-over pizza taste like

Italy or fool her into a moment's belief that the bargain lamb chops dressed up with paper frizzes on their ends were something out of the kitchens of Laperouse.

Instead, this. Lonesome, Levi MacDonald? she said in her mind. Oh, no.

It was fifteen minutes more until Mrs. Hutchens, who awoke as if by time signal, would open her eyes. Helen closed her door to keep down the sound, rolled a sheet into the typewriter, and banged away.

"Walt darling," she began, and smiled to herself because he *was* her darling, "if you weren't so utterly stupid you let the army catch you and stick you clear up at the North Pole, I would tell you something to make your eyes bug out."

When she had told him, and taken the pleasure of reading it all over and finding that the page corroborated her belief that it was true, she told him a few other things and certified them with x's. She told him she was *aching* for his discharge to come along. She told him of a dream she had had. She reminded him of some details of the week they had had in San Francisco before he flew up to the Aleutians.

Then she sat with her fingers quiet on the space bar, smiling softly and foolishly to herself and thinking, through the ambience of fortune and well-being, of not so long ago—Madison, and the years when she was earning her way through school and even trying to send something home each month. Every Saturday and Sunday for four years, those wretched mice to be inoculated; she had smelled of mice. And baby-sitting, all she could get of it, and no time for dates except when, in the last year, Walt sometimes came along and sat with her and they studied together. No more than three or four football games in four years, and no sorority because at first she had no alumnae backers and later she wouldn't take their little second-hand after-thought bids. Anyway, where would she have got the clothes and money to keep up with that crowd? Sometimes, seeing them all sunning themselves on the Mendota docks, some May day with hardly a riffle of wind and the sailboats drooping out on the blue water and herself on the way to the lab, she had hated them till her teeth clicked.

Spring was the worst time; it is hard to keep yourself uncomplainingly in prison in kite weather. But she remembered winter too, blizzardy mornings when she struggled up Bascom Hill sniffling and gasping, her nose red, her galoshes full of snow, her legs numb, and nothing to keep her warm except the old threadbare cloth coat she had worn for six centuries. You had to squint, coming uphill, because the wind brought flurries of drift and stinging snow down the slope; and the sidewalks underfoot, even when they had been recently sanded, had spots so slippery you never knew you had touched them till they brought you down. And then at the top, maybe, you looked up, and there waiting at the crosswalk, wearing only a leather jacket and with his shoulders up around his ears, his hands in his pockets and his books pinned under one arm and his breath spuming, Walt. She could see his nice white teeth, and his earmuffs, and his smile.

Bless him.

The air vibrated distantly with the strokes of the hall clock. It never struck the right number, but it struck punctually on the hour. Swiftly Helen added some more x's and a face with a beaming grin, licked the flap, tapped out the APO address. With the checks in her hand she went in to Mrs. Hutchens.

There was a wonderful moment when Mrs. Hutchens, with her Florentine portfolio on her lap, looked up communicating assurances and promises. Then she bent her head and drew her bird-claw signature onto the gift that emancipated Helen Kretchmer into everything she wanted.

Another sort of moment came later, when after a few minutes of hand and ankle exercises Mrs. Hutchens led the way up into the storage attic, and there from one of the hundreds of drawers and cabinets housing all that remained of Aunt Fanny and Auntie Grace selected for her a pair of elbow-length gray kid gloves. Her eyes were dewy as she laid them in Helen's hands. They were flattened and insubstantial as uninflated balloons, but Helen had the feeling that these, not the check, were the true proof of Mrs. Hutchens' affection. These came as if uprooted from her flesh.

Almost immediately Minna called and wanted her to play tennis with some of the children, and while she was in her room changing Helen could not resist working one of the gloves onto her hand. It went on only so far, and then it split like paper along the finger seams. Ruefully she pulled it off, folded the split fingers in, and smoothed the leather flat. She laid them in her handkerchief drawer, reminding herself that after all they had been bought seventy or eighty years ago. There was a lesson in them. You could no more leave it behind you than you could take it with you. If you were smart you first got a little security and then you began to enjoy it. She found herself wishing that all that awkwardness with Oliver hadn't come up. She would have liked to ask his advice about putting at least part of her money into one of those electronics stocks that were always doubling and tripling.

CHAPTER 25

ALMOST the first of August, and Sabrina sat where it seemed she had sat ever since her return, up to her neck in her mother's protected backwater like a disturbed patient in a tepid bath. Here it was warm, but out beyond the walls of the estate it would be hot. In an hour the bumper-to-bumper escape from the City would begin—had already begun for many—down Bayshore, El Camino, Junipero Serra. Ahead of the escapers, luring them through the milky traffic haze, would be the vision of a liberated hour or two of puttering in the yard, a beer in the patio, a plunge in the pool, whatever made the bedroom suburb dear. They would arrive, soiled, sweaty, grateful, and with their blood sugar low, at some inferior variant of what she had been fretfully enjoying all day, all week, all month, all year, all her life.

Upset with herself for the eagerness of her hope for a letter from Burke, she did not feel like going back into the library and watching Leonard MacDonald's absorbed archaeologizing among the family relics. It was time that job was ending—he had been literally fascinated, so much so that half a dozen times she had been on the point of screeching at him to get out and do something useful. That she had got him the job made no difference. That she had spent a lot of her own time digging in that junk heap made no difference. She should have known better than to do either.

For an hour she had walked in the grounds. And just now, coming onto the terrace, she had found her mother sitting with her writing portfolio in her lap, looking off absently across the garden. "Ah, my dear," said her mother. "Sit . . . down." She closed the portfolio quietly. Sabrina sprawled in a lounge chair and brooded out at the sweep of flagstones, the arc of the rose walk, the lawns.

In the gardens the air was neither the cool brown air of the library nor the milky smog of outside, but something stirless, growthy, at once stagnant and purified. (And why not? she could imagine Leonard MacDonald saying. You've got the trees to make your own oxygen. If the bulldozers peel the trees off the Peninsula for a few more years, and we keep getting a hundred new families a week in this county, and every hundred families keep on meaning a hundred and forty new cars, the rest of us poor dopes will be piping in our fresh air from Alaska.)

She was aware of the furtive turning of her mother's head, but she chose to pay no attention. She concentrated on how all the sun within her vision was filtered by oaks and cooled by lawn. It lay dappling, its force broken, over the greenish nest. She could see hardly any sky at all.

Not a note, not a call, not a word. From Bernard she had expected nothing—he was scared back into his Stonestown burrow, nursing his burned fingers and shaking when the telephone rang, and he would be a faithful and assiduous husband until next time he ran across some dissatisfied woman on a buying trip, and dared dispense again his easy favor of ecstasy. The contempt she had for him, the contempt she had for herself, could not quite overcome her sense of grievance. How he must have smiled, seeing her jump like a crazy terrier for his outreached doggie bonbon! It made her crawl—and yet thank God he could be recovered from, thank God he had shrunk to a nasty memory.

Yes? And what of Dr. Burke Castro, waiting coldly in Pasadena for her to come crawling home to bathe his feet with repentant tears?

Not a word! Not one sign. And here she sat, more tense and panicky every day, and she couldn't sit here much longer.

This garden was too inward turning. There was not a vista nor an allee in it to lead the eye outward; you couldn't see a gate, or a road leading away; you were buried at the heart of a green still wood. Sniffing, she smelled only a limy, dusty smell of gravel. Out on the combed rose walk a pink petal loosened and fell.

"Mother," she said, "would it be all right with you if I sent for my dog?"

Her mother lowered the book she had lifted close to her eyes, and with the predictableness of a recorded telephone response she said, "Oh, I wish you would not . . . ask that! It's so disagreeable the way they . . . spoil the shrubs and foul the walks. I always disliked it so when Mercer . . ." Her head turned in a sharp birdy gesture; her eyes changed. "Does that mean you are not . . . going back to Pasadena?"

Looking out into the roses, Sabrina lifted a shoulder. When a long time had passed without a sound from the other chair, she turned her head. Her mother was watching her with her mouth hanging helplessly open; in her eyes a sick intensity, a dawning, appalled certainty.

"Oh, Mother, don't throw a fit! It isn't the end of the world."

"It is . . . a disaster. Please . . . think what you are doing."

"It isn't all up to me. Two of us are involved."

The expression of wincing dismay did not pass from her mother's face, but deepened. "Is it so final, then?"

"I don't know. Maybe."

"I have not mentioned it because I hoped you might . . . think it over and decide . . . to make it up. It has been several weeks."

"Counting Mexico, two months."

"I didn't know Mexico was part of it."

"Mexico was part of it. And a long time before Mexico."

The still afternoon seeped around them. She watched the clustered gnats in the shade of the nearest oak. They hung in a tight mass, never still but never getting out of the bushel of space that they had for some reason chosen. What point in that unresting buzz? How did they

303

eat or breed? Did they just hang in their centripetal constellation until they fell and died? She heard her mother say hesitantly, "Couldn't you . . . go down, or telephone?"

"It wouldn't do any good."

"Someone has to give in."

"I gave in all I could."

"Oh! You are . . . to blame, my dear!"

"That's what you've always believed," Sabrina said.

"In being . . . unforgiving and . . . proud."

Sabrina moved her shoulders angrily.

After some time her mother said, "I always thought that . . . if you had had children . . ."

"Oh, you did!"

Without looking, she knew the expression of offended good intentions on her mother's face. They sat in huffy silence, and the afternoon like sluggish water closed over them again. She thought, Oh, why doesn't somebody call, why don't I get up the energy to go somewhere, why don't some of her cronies come over, even, why don't we read diaries! We can't sit around here forsaken in brocade like something in Amy Lowell.

They had the patterned garden paths; all they needed was the plashing of the waterdrops in the silver fountains. Toying with the idea of a swim, she gave it up because the pool would be full of Oliver's young. Her mother said in a voice that was placatory, almost apologetic, "I am afraid your rest hasn't done you . . . much good."

For the first time in minutes Sabrina looked fully at her. The long shaking face was surely trying to be kind. She threw up her hands and laughed. "No."

"If I could . . ." She broke off; her puckered mouth was rueful; she worked her hands in the air. "You see nothing of your old friends. You need diversion and . . . somebody to talk to." Her embarrassment grew, her hands fluttered. "If it would help to . . . tell *me*," she said.

And what a doubtful, peeping look accompanied that uncharacteristic remark! So far as Sabrina could remember—and her mother was undoubtedly thinking the same thing—she had never since very early childhood brought a trouble home to have it cured. She had learned young that it always turned out to be her fault that her knee was skinned or her dress torn, or that the child brought in to play with her was in tears. Anger, selfishness, untidiness, uncooperativeness, nastiness, these in her mother's eyes had been a Sabrina monopoly. "Why don't you ever take *my* side?" she remembered screaming once. How long ago? Twenty-five years at least, and yet the rankle was still there. Why not *ever* my side?

Oh, you are to blame, Sabrina! You're unforgiving and proud and spiteful. You will learn to curb that temper, my girl, or it will destroy all of us. Will you ever learn to be clean? Don't you know that the first rule of a lady's life is to be fastidious? Why, why, why do you do these things? It's as if you were determined to balk every wish I ever had for you. And learn to be civil, do you understand me? When you speak to me or any other adult. You're not too old to have your hands slapped. You're not too grown up to think things over in the closet. I wonder if there was ever anyone in our family who behaved as you do! I think you were sent as a punishment. And we will have no more words about it. And no impertinence.

Sent to her room to brood and sulk, Sabrina would have had an answer, a fierce one, before she learned the indifferent shrug and the insolence that stretched just over, but not too far over, a certain line. Her answer in those early years was something she hugged to herself: *You're not my mother! I don't belong here.*

There was something almost begging in her mother's eyes. "Nothing to tell," Sabrina said. "We've said too much to one another. It couldn't ever be the same."

"Said too much . . . about what?"

"About each other."

"How does Burke feel?"

"I suppose injured. Self-righteous."

"Self-righteous?" It was remarkable how her mother's expression of distress could have in it so much of corroborated expectation. And the question that she forced out was less question than statement. "He has . . . something to forgive you for, then."

"You haven't changed, Mother," Sabrina said. She looked out into the garden air, heavy as pewter.

"If you don't have anything to be forgiven for you are . . . most fortunate," her mother said.

"I've got plenty, and I won't forgive myself any quicker than he'll forgive me. But even so he might feel just a little guilty about the twelve years of decorative nothing he put me through while he developed the fanciest practice in Pasadena."

Her mother was shocked. "But . . . a doctor. He is dedicated to humanity."

"Some humanity. He's a society doctor, Mother, why not admit it? He turned out to have a face and a manner that rich women trusted. He was both attentive and socially acceptable—and that's something he owes *me*. He's always willing to come when he's called, and he's sympathetic to nervous ailments—in other people—and easy to get sleeping pills and tranquilizers out of. But there's not much medical missionary in him. His income's as big as mine, and that's one thing he's always wanted. He's always been as proud as Lucifer, and he's always hated it that his family had lost everything. He didn't marry me entirely for my face. I've been around for twelve years like a mountain he was determined to climb; he needed to plant a flag on my top, for some reason."

She said it in anger that grew as she spoke, and she was sure, or nearly sure, that some of it was true.

Her mother said, "And you speak of *him* as proud!"

"Oh, look, Mother—Ibsen slammed the door on that doll-wife thing seventy-five years ago. I might even have submitted to it, if . . . Oh, I don't know. If he had let me, I'd have loved to be a real wife. But I can't keep my own house—that wouldn't look well. I can't help him, either. Once when his receptionist got sick I filled in, and I loved it. I was part of the act. For a week and a half. After that he made me quit. How would it look, except just as a sort of temporary game, for his wife to go around in a white uniform and usher her friends into his office?"

"You wouldn't need to work in his office. You have . . . talents of your own."

"Even if they were legitimate talents I wouldn't go on perverting them," Sabrina said. "I wanted some of my husband, was that unreasonable? Any of my friends could get an hour of his time for a set of sniffles, but I couldn't even keep him through dinner. The wife he wants can shop, and play, and manage the servants, and dress well, and take little trips, and get her picture periodically in the paper. I've been abroad five times in eight years, every time alone, except that he flew over and joined me for two weeks once. I kept on suggesting that he turn some of his practice over to others in the clinic. No, people depended on him, they wouldn't accept substitutes. I begged him, and whenever we got into that stance he began to stiffen up the way he does. So finally I threw a fit, and then he tried to comfort me. You know what he said? He said I was so completely part of him that he unconsciously sacrificed my wishes as he would his own. Everybody else came first, in other words. Mrs. McKeever and her menopause hallucinations that any intern could take care of with a hormone pill was more important than his wife. I told him so—I suggested he *quit* sacrificing my wishes as he would his own, and he wanted to give me a tranquilizer. I told him to save it for Mrs. McKeever, and that's when I went to Mexico."

Surprised at herself, she stopped. Pouring it out to Mother. Now they would see if the gospels of family solidarity worked. If they did, there should be comfort, and reassurance, and healing. But her mother was staring down at her own bonily outlined knees. The light shaking of her head might have been dubious disapproval, or it might have been only her infirmity. Her hands, hanging loose by the sides of the chair, clenched once in a movement as apparently reflex as the flop of a fish on a wharf.

Lizardo came out with a tray on which was a glass of brown liquid. To fill the stretching silence after her outburst, Sabrina said, "What's that, Mother? Are you on some medicine?"

"Honey and vinegar," her mother said. "It is very . . . good for the joints. Should you like some?"

"No thanks."

"Orange juice?" Lizardo said. "Grape juice?"

"Orange juice, maybe." She met his eye and very slightly shook her head. If she had nodded, or measured on the air with thumb and finger, he would have dropped a slug of vodka in her drink. For nearly a month she had not nodded or measured. No drinking, no smoking. Ah, Mother, she thought, if you only knew how different July is from June! The image of Bernard was suddenly in her mind as still as a watchful eye, but examining herself for an emotion, she found none. Not in that direction. Remembered, but hardly conceivable.

Her mother sipped with puckered lips. "You should . . . try this," she said mildly. "You don't eat sensibly."

Sabrina let it go. Off in the green and gold subaqueous afternoon a quail called.

Her mother, shuddering pleasurably, put the glass down. Her eyebrows were raised so high that vertical wrinkles were pulled into the full upper lids, but even so her eyes did not open very widely. She said, "I expect that you do have something to . . . forgive him for, too."

"Well," Sabrina said. "Welcome to my side," and then smiled a brilliant diversionary smile because she liked neither the tone of her own voice nor her mother's half-lidded, appraising stare.

"But I don't therefore suppose . . . you are blameless," her mother said. "Much as I wished that, I have . . . never been able to. You must learn to recognize your weaknesses and . . . fight against them. You are your father's child."

Blink—and the sagging insistent face was a younger version of itself, still able to frighten and dominate, and it was contorted and mottled with fury. "Give me it! Give me it, I say!" She pressed with her thumb, and the little clam shell of gold clicked shut; the face was back in its darkness. Stretching out her hand, she laid the locket, with its thin falling chain, in her mother's hand. "Haven't you things of your own, that you must meddle in mine? If you haven't enough, I shall give you more. But I have asked you and asked you not to snoop in other people's things." For once, not the shrug and the silence that always infuriated her mother so; for once, defiance. "I wasn't snooping! I was looking at my father's picture. Is that so awful?" They stared hatred at one another. Her mother was recovering from the shock of finding her there; second by second she was coming back into control. From her gathering height she said, "Now

that you have looked at him, you may go and spend an hour in the
closet and remind yourself that you have seen a sneak and a liar."
"He was not! I don't believe it!" "I won't stand debating with you. Go
on now, go!" "Go where?" "To the closet." "What?" "Are you deaf,"
her mother said, "or only insubordinate?"

She broke her eyes away from her mother's, and her mind away
from the image that was shut like a locket-picture between valves of
time. The memory did not seem like much; it was not quite like having your father cut down by a madman with an ax, or run over
in the street before your eyes. Even my childhood traumata, she
thought, are trivial. I have nothing worse to remember than my
mother's face full of hatred. And yet 'tis enough, 'twill serve. She
took the glass of orange juice that was lowered before her, and when
Lizardo was gone she said, "My father's child? I don't suppose I can
take that as a vote of confidence."

"I have . . . told you he was not a good man."

"That's what I mean."

"But he was my husband!" her mother said. Her hand, hauling at
the chair arm, pulled her upright. "I have always been ashamed." Her
eyes looked wild; Sabrina had the impression that if she had been
within reach her mother would have taken her by the shoulders and
shaken her. "Not of him!" she said. "Not only of him. Of myself,
too."

Sabrina sat still. The quail hammered again at the pewter air. Her
mother's mouth shook so badly, all at once, that she sank back and
pressed her fingers hard against it.

"Why?" Sabrina said.

"He was involved in something that I thought I . . . couldn't forgive. I forgot all about his kindness and his beauty and the . . . hap-
piness he had given me. I wouldn't . . . forgive him. I should have
accepted him for what he was and what he had . . . meant to me.
I knew I hadn't either . . . looks or mind to match his, but I . . . let
myself freeze in my hurt feelings and pride. I should have remembered
only . . . how much he gave me."

Sabrina sat silent, watching the thin shoulders twitch, and thinking
of the flickering screen and the jigging, mugging figure made antic

by the camera's speed—a handsome face, a good leg in plus fours, probably the gift of gab, no character. How on earth a playboy should ever have married a Boston lady. Money, undoubtedly. In his careless good-natured way he would surely have expected the easy forgiveness of his weaknesses and vices that palaver and wheedling had always brought him. And instead he had run head-on into the puritan inflexibility, the grudge-holding God. I can't get sore, but I can sure hold a grudge, Burke used to say, joking. But it was no joke, it fitted them all, herself included.

She touched with her fingers the grayed, raised grain of the redwood lounge chair's arm. "I always thought you despised him," she said.

It seemed a time when she might have gone and put an arm around her mother's shoulders, and yet she found the act impossible. Gestures like that were possible only when the atmosphere was neutral, watchful, under control. Her mother touched her handkerchief to her nose, and looking away, said, "I did. I do. He behaved . . . very badly. But I despise myself, too." Her lips thrust out in a sharp pucker, her tongue clicked against her teeth. "I should never have listened to them, God forgive me."

"Listened to whom?"

"Mercer was a snob," her mother said, "but Mother was implacable!"

Seemingly very old, her dry hand clutching the arm of her chair, her scalp visible through the thinning hair, she sat erectly and would not meet Sabrina's eyes. Very old, and yet a long way from senile, as Oliver pretended to think she was. This was no vaguely smiling mind pottering around among the images of the past, but a woman scalded by emotions as hot and unreconciled as her own.

"Your father's child," she said, still looking away, "but mine too, mine too."

It was a long time before she moved anything but her puckering, trembling lips. Then she glanced across almost furtively, and her enlarged hand fumbled over the closed portfolio in her lap. "I was shocked at luncheon," she said, "to hear that . . . Leonard is so near the end of the papers. It made me realize that . . . everything is now on file . . . except myself."

"Yes?" Sabrina said.

"I have just been reading over some letters private to me. It seems that for the sake of the . . . archive they should be included, and yet they are . . . so personal and . . . humiliating."

"Ah," Sabrina said. "From father?"

Speaking as if unwillingly, with a curious effect of frail violence, her mother said, "I felt that in the history of the family these events . . . should be known. I thought that perhaps . . . now, in your own trouble, *you* should know them . . . that they might . . . help you. . . ."

She opened the portfolio and took out an unsealed envelope. It rested, lightly rustling, within the trembling of her fingers. "All right, Mother," Sabrina said. "If you want me to."

"I am somewhat uncertain. . . ."

"Whatever you say." Sabrina did not much believe in the melodramatics. She could guess that the letters contained some evidence of her father's infidelity, some lesion in his respectability—certainly something that she herself did not much care to know.

Her mother thrust the envelope at her. "Read it! Not here before me. I could not . . . bear it, I think. But read it and then seal the envelope and we shall . . . put it among the papers." She floundered up out of her chair. "Please read it and . . . imagine my feelings and my . . . regrets, and then seal it up. We shall mark it . . . Not to be opened until . . . What do you think? The year 2000? After my death? Oh my dear, I am so . . ."

She began to cry silently, while Sabrina stood ruefully watching, unable to touch her or make the conventional motions of sympathy or comfort. "I'll read them," she said. "I'll be glad to know, finally. But please be patient with me, Mother, don't think you can help. Nobody can. It isn't my decision now. He's got to make up his mind, and when he does, then I can. So *can* I send for my dog?"

"Of course, my dear."

"I'll keep him in the garage, if you want."

"Keep him . . . where you want him. He'll be company for you."

"That's nice of you, Mother. Is anyone coming for tea?"

"Only Helen and perhaps Minna."

"Not Leonard?"

"He said he had some . . . errands to do."

"I guess I'll skip it too, if you'll excuse me."

They were off on safe inconsequentialities. Her mother's eyes were only a little reddened; she looked, now, yearning and fond. My God, Sabrina thought, it's like mother and daughter.

Her mother said, "I'm glad you . . . suggested him for the papers. He's been perfectly magnificent. Once one forgets those . . . workmen's trousers he is . . . charming."

Out from the terrace the protected layers of the garden spread, daphne bushes, gravel walk, arc of roses, lawn, banked azaleas, oaks. The air was as silvery as if a metallic precipitate sifted through it. Sabrina felt all the drowning heaviness of being at the bottom of a pond, strangled and encumbered in weeds and slime, and all at once desolation throbbed and pounded in her head, she was bursting for air, and she said harshly, turning away, "Why shouldn't he be? He's the happiest man on earth."

After a few minutes, lingering, looking back, her mother shuffled inside. Her diaphragm knotted with passion and regret, Sabrina stood with the envelope in her hand. Lizardo came out and softly collected the glasses onto a tray. Softly he said, "You pilling okay now?"

"All right, Lizardo, thanks. Don't I look it?"

"Sim sad."

For a moment, as she sank back down onto the lounge, she summoned irony and a smile. "I'll survive it," she said. He went away, and she opened the envelope. Two letters only, both short, neither one dated.

Dear Emily,

I agree with you, it should be encouraged. I find his incessant affability rather hard to bear, and the less said about his mother's connections the better, but his father's family is at least respectable. Bluntly, I should be happier about the whole thing if there were some way of being assured of his fertility, but if we don't take this chance we shall probably have no others. After all, she is thirty-six years old. You must persuade Mercer.

In haste,
Bushrod

Sabrina folded the note and slid it under an ashtray and unfolded the other.

Deborah darling,
Is it a conspiracy? Or what is it? I can't believe you're in on it. In the last week I've been to your mother's house six times. I know you're staying there, but every time your mother meets me at the door and won't let me in. She says you never want to see me again. Maybe that's true, and maybe I deserve it, but I don't believe you said it, or if you said it you don't mean it. If I could see you and tell you my side of it you would see it was not the way the papers had it. I'd been drinking, yes, but that was all I had been doing. I've tried to telephone you but they won't put me through to you. Did you get the note I wrote you day before yesterday? I'll bet you didn't. This time I am having Elizabeth Crowninshield address the envelope so they won't think it is from me and tear it up. Call me at University 4664. I'm staying over in Cambridge at Donald's. I love you. If you lose faith in me I'm lost. If you won't see me again I don't know what I'll do. Kiss the children for me.

All my love,
Howie

Finely written in her mother's spidery hand along the top margin of this note was a three-line comment:

I did not see this till many years later, or receive his other letter, or *any* letters.
I never said I would not see him again. They told me he did not come.
I don't know what they told him to make him go away for good.

That was all of it, then. Out of all the paper-saving of the family, only two notes to commemorate the injury her mother had kept bleeding for over thirty years. At the heart of all the preposterous secrecy and suppression, only this for revelation: an undesirable suitor approved by the family when it was clear there was not likely to be a more desirable one; a despised but fertile son-in-law frozen out, locked out, lied to, threatened, eventually bought off, when he got into some kind of scrape that the family, with two heirs safely born, could elect to consider unpardonable.

It was not much of a story—ridiculous rather than pathetic, and so antique in all its details that it was hard to believe it had all happened in the twenties, that time of the hip flask and the Charleston and the Life of Realization. Superannuated grotesques, a domestic tragi-comedy as brittle as a minuet. And yet like her own low-voltage traumata, 'twas enough, it had served. She wondered which revelation bothered her mother more, the revelation that they had lied to him and conspired somehow to drive him away, or the revelation that they had approved him in the first place only for the possibility of heirs. The thought of what her mother had probably been like at thirty-six, nearly her own age, was painful to her: awkward undoubtedly, painfully shy, easily flustered, apologetic before her martinet mother and her aloof, eccentric, distant aunts and uncles; and before the young man burning, burning, and devoted, and strangling with impossible hopes, and hanging on that beautiful affability that Bushrod found so tiresome. Howie. Oh, good God. And when did she finally find out that they had used and abused her? When did she come upon the two letters that in any but a paper-saving family would have been promptly burned? At what point, and in what mood (angry repudiation? tears? injured dignity?) did she make that almost inconceivable break with Boston? Was that to escape the shame of her husband's disgrace and disappearance, or was it to escape Mercer, a snob, and her mother, implacable? Sabrina doubted that she would ever inquire. Anyway, it had been no real escape, for here came the total family inheritance, papers and all, pursuing her, and helplessly she embraced it.

What a pitiful little annotation, with the blubber of tears in it, and the nag of an unanswered question. "I don't know what they told him to make him go away." It was just as well she did not.

And the moral was what? Intended to be what? Forgiveness, was that it? Then her mother should have sent the notes to Burke, not given them to her. It was her mother's fate to be in the dark about almost everything that went on. What if she knew the fear that for days now had lain cold as a salamander, each day more coldly and surely there, in her daughter's mind? Just asking the question of herself, admitting by even that much her awareness, her unsleeping perception, of the fear, sent panic in a white flash clear to the soles of Sabrina's feet.

I'm afraid it's no help, Mother, she said to herself, and put the notes back in their envelope and licked the flap, with one moist sweep of her tongue sealing her mother's penitence and anguish away until the year 2000.

Then she went up to her rooms, picked up the telephone, and sent a telegram to Burke in Pasadena. Only the silent little fear with which she lived kept her from putting into it something affectionate and impulsive, something funny or whimsical, that would let him know she was only waiting for him to make a move, and that when he did she would come back gladly. A half dozen phrases formed themselves in her mind while she waited for the operator to get organized for taking the message. But in the end none of them was possible, not even "Missing you"; in the end she said only, "Will you please express Fat Boy soonest. Love."

Nevertheless sending the message cheered her. It was possible that even the word "love," even that characterless impersonal counter, would tip him from his angry coldness and bring her a reply that she could accept as the beginning of peace between them. She bundled that hope in with the secret fear, the two of them as incompatible as a flower and a spray of poison oak, and reconciled herself, though not patiently, to more waiting.

CHAPTER 26

H ELEN dreamed happily of money. She was typing a diary, and when she propped it open on the copying stand, old-fashioned yellowback bills slid from between its pages and wavered to the floor. She was up to her ankles in wealth. And waking up was only a slight disappointment, for she thought immediately of her checks and of her building-and-loan passbook.

Such a simple, lovely dream. But then, she said, I am such a simple lovely girl.

Pulling her knees up, she clasped them tightly and brought her nose down several times to each kneecap. When she stepped out of bed, her first act was to stoop, stiff-kneed, and touch her fingertips, then her knuckles, then her flat palms, to the floor. The day, she saw, was beginning under a mat of high fog. On the telephone wire outside her window a pair of linnets teetered and tilted and cheeped. The male, rosy-headed, edged sideways until he could touch beaks with the drab little female. As if ticklish, she skittered along the wire. And here he came sidling again, touching wing, touching beak, though nesting time was months past and the summer's hatch of nestlings would already be grown and gone.

Smiling, Helen watched them. Go wan, she said, don't come

316

palaverin around *me*. Off in the grounds another bird sang three sweet descending notes, a sound such as Eden might have heard.

She took her shower stiff and cold, without a hot preliminary; it was a way she had of not going soft. But she loved the big enveloping towel afterward. Some day she was going to have a closetful like it, thick as a bearskin and big as a blanket. And contour sheets with flowered hems, and pillowslips to match. And nice dishes, maybe not eighteenth-century Meissen like Mrs. Hutchens', but something nice, and enough of it to spread a whole party. If she and Walt did get to Japan as they had planned, maybe some Katani ware. And sometime a house with a patio where they could eat breakfast outside and hear the birds going it: she could see that pleasant table set with plates and cups as delicate as flowers.

Things. So many lovely things that she had never had. So many places she had never seen. She was giving her hair its hundred licks while she thought of them, and she made promises to her face in the mirror before she went downstairs to arrange Mrs. Hutchens' morning bouquet.

Going into Mrs. Hutchens' room later, she found the old lady lying wide awake in the frilled nightcap she had begun wearing since she had read about the dangers of chilly night air while the metabolic rate was low. She was convinced it was what had killed her father in Rome. And she was not inclined to take chances on the new viruses they kept discovering. It was her theory that bacteria lived on viruses, and that in destroying the bacterial diseases, doctors—she spoke of them as Science—had only made things pleasant for the viruses, the way men created a plague of mice by destroying all the owls. Whatever the effect of the nightcap on her health, she looked in the midst of that Brussels lace frill like some preposterous impersonation, like the wolf in Grandmother's bed.

Helen sang a greeting, "Good morning, good morning, good morning!" to the tune of the unknown bird's plaintive song. Holding the robe for Mrs. Hutchens to step into, she felt as fresh and cheerful as a bird herself. When Mrs. Hutchens had tottered off, humorously complaining, to her shower, she buzzed the kitchen and sat down in the bow window to look at the paper while Bernadette changed the bed. All over the back page, with maps and pictures, it said that a 380-acre tract in Woodside was to be opened by a group of developers, one of whom was Oliver Hutchens of Hillsborough, the land's present owner.

So Oliver had won that argument. But how, and when? If you were going to be of maximum service—and Helen aimed to be—you made it your business to know what went on. Yet this had happened so secretly and suddenly that she had had no hint of it. It piqued her pride that Mrs. Hutchens would not have told her.

But when the old lady hobbled in in a lavender wool house coat, her rabbit-fur eyebrows moving and her face mock-lugubrious, it was of something else that Helen spoke. She said, "I woke up this morning and had to pinch myself ten times before I believed what you did for me yesterday."

"Ah," Mrs. Hutchens said, "that little gift has been making me . . . have melancholy thoughts."

"What about?"

"I have been thinking that now you have the means to go abroad you will . . . leave me."

"Oh, not for a long time, not before next April," Helen said. It slipped out before she thought; she saw in her employer's face the shock it caused. Damn, damn. Sometimes words were as drastic as dishes that slipped and broke. Much as she liked Mrs. Hutchens, she hoped it would not come to the point, at the end, where she clung and begged. Because she could not give up her life with Walt, no matter how sorry she would be to leave. But what a stupid thing to let it out now.

"Not until . . . *April?*" Mrs. Hutchens faltered. "You do plan to . . . leave, then? You will surely go?"

"Oh, I'm sorry!" Helen said. "I'm to blame, I should have told you before. There's this boy, I mean we're engaged, he's up in a weather station in the Aleutians, he'll be out in April. So you see it *is* a long time."

Mrs. Hutchens, staring at her in something like horror, sat down, dropping the last few inches very solidly. "Oh dear . . . April. I had hoped for . . . something more, forever perhaps."

"You can't tell, maybe when we've had the trip we promised ourselves, and Walt has finished his degree, we'll settle down here and I can work for you again."

Trained to habit, Mrs. Hutchens' eyes acknowledged the flowers on the table. Her lids, skimpily fringed with sandy lashes, blinked with a premonition of weak tears. "Oh, dear," she said. "My melancholy thoughts were . . . altogether too true! Yesterday I was looking over some letters and things that should . . . perhaps go in with the papers, and they . . . made me sad. And I was so grieved when Leonard MacDonald left yesterday. It was such . . . fun to see the things being finally put in order, and now it's all over. And now you will . . . leave me!"

Helen put her arm around the old lady's shoulders and hugged her hard. "It's a long way off," she said. "And really, I hope Walt *will* want to settle here, I can't think of anywhere I'd like better."

"If it is a . . . position he needs, I could . . . Oh, pshaw, I mustn't be selfish, you will . . . want your trip."

"We'll work it somehow. And even Leonard isn't gone for good. He'll be back at Christmas." Shrugging and laughing and squeezing the frail shoulders, she added, "He must be feeling as wonderful today as I am."

"Mmmmm?"

"When he opened his envelope."

Mrs. Hutchens wiped her eyes and murmured unintelligibly into her orange juice.

"But he must be disappointed about the park."

"The park?"

"That you've decided to let Mr. Hutchens develop the land instead."

"Ah," said Mrs. Hutchens with a smile, "but I haven't. I have almost made up my mind to adopt Leonard's and Sabrina's . . . suggestion."

"But it says in the *Chronicle* he's going to develop it."

"It *what?*" Mrs. Hutchens sat forward suddenly and dribbled orange juice over her lip. With a moan of impatience she set the glass down and dabbed her napkin at her breast. Her hand reached out and

Helen laid the paper in it. The full, wrinkled lids drew down, the eyes narrowed and peered. "Where? Where does it say that? By the picture? Pshaw, I can't see. Read it to me."

Helen read it aloud. It said that 117 luxury homes were slated for the Woodside area. An association of four developers had yesterday filed with the planning commission of the town of Woodside a preliminary site plan for the development of 380 acres of hill land between Madrone Lane and the Old Merced Road. Plans called for lots of a minimum of three acres, on which the developers would build custom houses. Chester Webber, of Webber Enterprises, one of the associated developers, indicated that the houses, exclusive of land, would range between $60,000 and $110,000. According to Oliver Hutchens of Hillsborough, another of the developers and the man from whom the land was being purchased, the site plan was designed to make the most of the superb views and oak-dotted hills of one of the largest remaining tracts of raw land suitable for home sites in the county.

Helen stopped reading, catching sight of Mrs. Hutchens' face. The sagging cheeks were mottled red and white, the eyeballs bulged, the breath came hoarsely through the open mouth. When Helen stood up in alarm, she was waved back by a sidewise cut of the old lady's hand. She ran for a glass of water, but by then the fit was past. Obviously groping for a word, Mrs. Hutchens sawed the air. "My . . . reading glasses." Helen found them and helped her fumble the old-fashioned curled earpieces through the fringes of her hair and around her ears. She read the article all through and studied the photograph and the map. Then she lowered the paper and stared grimly out the window

"Is it some mistake?" Helen said.

"No. I . . . expect he said it."

Once or twice, especially when Sabrina Castro had said something that antagonized her, Helen had seen Mrs. Hutchens look formidable and unpleasant, but now she looked mean—for a moment she had a strong resemblance to her mother's portrait. Also she looked ill. Her eyes and temples were still flushed, her lips kept escaping from the teeth that tried to hold them still, and trembled into wordy shapes. This kind of upset could bring on another stroke, and if she had another stroke Helen herself would not know what to do, because she could not imagine herself leaving the old lady helpless and unhappy in the hands of some strange companion or nurse. Even while she bent anxiously with the water glass she was thinking that she had been right never quite to trust this Eden. It could become a trap.

"Will you . . . call him, please," Mrs. Hutchens said. "I wish him to . . . come over."

Dialing, Helen smiled reassuringly back toward the table and made drinking motions toward the orange juice. Mrs. Hutchens scowled. Then the connection was through, and she braced herself to speak coolly.

He came. "Hello?"

"It's Helen. Your mother wanted me to—"

". . . over your chill?"

"What?"

"Did you get over your chill, I said."

"Oh, yes. Completely."

"I'm glad to hear it. I never saw a cooler performance."

"I can't say I enjoyed it that much. Can you come over to see your mother?"

"Right now?"

"Yes."

"Has she been reading the paper?"

"Yes."

"Blowing a fuse?"

"It's nothing to joke about."

"So. Well, I'll be over. Keep your suit on."

Don't think I won't! she said into the dead phone. To Mrs. Hutchens, glowering across the breakfast table, she said, "You'd better have something to eat, it will all be cold."

With a shaky hand Mrs. Hutchens pushed her plate away. "Pshaw! He has . . . spoiled it for me. I couldn't eat anything." The flush at her temples had faded into mauve blotches, but in her throat there was still a redness like a rash.

"I guess I don't understand how this could happen without your being consulted."

"You do not know . . . Oliver," Mrs. Hutchens said. "He has been pressing me for weeks. Now he is . . . attempting a *fait accompli.*"

"What will you do?"

"I will not agree. I remember when I was quite young, Uncle Bushrod tried . . . something of the same sort with Auntie Grace and she . . . defied him. She said he could wait until she died."

"It's a shame," Helen said. "Promise me you won't let it upset you. It isn't worth making yourself sick about."

Frowning, Mrs. Hutchens looked at her knotted hands.

"Shall I ring? Are you sure you don't want to eat something?"

A quick impatient shake of the head. Helen rang. In an unaccustomed, comfortless silence they waited until Lizardo appeared in the door. Without comment he picked up the untouched tray and bore it off, and thinking that she had better escape before Oliver appeared, Helen rose. "Will you have any letters afterwards?"

Another shake of the head.

"Just your exercises and golf, then."

"Good gracious!" Mrs. Hutchens said. "Could I be in a mood for those?" The angry old eyes gleamed, swimming in their watery sockets, and then her whole face warped and softened, and she held out her hand, crying, "Oh, forgive me, my dear! I am . . . upset." Her voice quavered. She said, "I believe I . . . must return to bed."

Helen flew to turn down the covers. The frail weight tottered twenty feet leaning on her arm, and collapsed into the fresh sheets. The moment she stepped back, Helen saw the wisdom of that move. Propped among her pillows she looked twice as frail and twice as formidable. It was the best posture she could have assumed to resist Oliver or anyone else.

"There!" she said heartily. "That's better!" and saw Mrs. Hutchens' mouth, wobbling toward words, harden meanly and her eyes fix themselves on something beyond.

"Good morning, Mother," said Oliver from the doorway. "Good morning, Miss Kretchmer."

He filled the opening, and his smile was wide and polite. What a hunk of man, she thought hotly, and then as his eyes went all the way down to her feet and back up to her face she felt the blood warming her skin. Probably nothing had ever tickled him so much as to see her run squeaking through his damnable lights—nothing unless it was to stand here now and stare her down and make her turn red. Despising the heat of her face, she said to Mrs. Hutchens, "I'll be in the office if you need me," and started out.

At the last moment Oliver moved aside to let her pass, and she had the relieved feeling that he had already forgotten her before he moved over. He was looking toward his mother with an expression pleasantly and deferentially bland.

"You may . . . cancel it!" Mrs. Hutchens said breathily from the bed. "I will not . . . under any circumstances submit to it!"

She would have given a good deal to know how their talk went, and yet she would not have stayed if she could, for no matter how she side-stepped, she might either have to betray Mrs. Hutchens or anger Oliver. The buzzer might squawk any minute, the door could open and a voice call, and there she would be like a cob in a corn-sheller. Pretending to be occupied, she made her bed and picked up. On her desk lay the letter she had written to Walt the previous afternoon. The mailman passed the main gate about ten-thirty. If she happened to be out mailing a letter when the buzzer sounded, the debate in there might go on to its end without her. She picked up the envelope and went out.

The overcast had not yet burned away. She saw Virgil washing the station wagon and called to him that he need not have Mrs. Hutchens' car ready for golf this morning. All out the S-curve of the drive she dawdled, killing time trying to make sure what plant it was that filled the air there with a sour, mildewed smell. Coming back, she walked even slower, thinking, But honestly, Mr. Hutchens, how could I, in my position, presume to advise her on this sort of thing, even if she should ask me? I'm afraid you over-estimate my influence on her, Mr. Hutchens. I'm employed to look after her and do whatever she asks me to, not to give her advice. You yourself wouldn't want me meddling in her affairs that way. I'm sure you'll

323

excuse me, Mr. Hutchens, I'd feel presumptuous even to have an opinion. I'd like to do what you want me to, but you must see how awkward a position . . .

Almost as awkward as running naked for cover while that over-muscled beer-wagon horse laughed. Damn Oliver Hutchens, anyway.

Her watch told her that she had killed only ten minutes. Uneasily she went upstairs, to find that the door was still closed. Though she would have scorned to eavesdrop, she stood at her own door, listening. No raised voices, no anything; the house was too discreetly sound-proofed. She assured herself that Mrs. Hutchens, the real owner of the property, held all the cards: she could simply go on saying no, and there was nothing he could do. But that would not make him any easier to deal with when he came out. Because he thought she exercised influence on his mother, he would surely want her to do something.

Then she heard the latch click, and swiftly slid behind the desk. She was rolling a sheet of paper into the typewriter when he blocked her door, and she looked up brightly, prepared to be of service.

"What's this God-damned park thing?" he said.

"Park? Oh, you mean that idea about giving land to the county? That's never been more than a notion."

"Why wasn't I told about it?"

When she found it hard to meet the stare of his yellow eyes she shifted her focus ever so slightly and concentrated on the place where his eyebrows met in a double tuft of hairs. Even then, she had about as much chance of staring him down as a seal on an ice cake would have of staring down an icebreaker. "Why, there wasn't anything to tell. She's never done anything about it."

"How do you know about it, then?"

"Oh, at lunch, you know—just casually speculating to Mrs. Castro and Leonard MacDonald and me."

"MacDonald."

"Yes, but he—"

The tufts of hairs pinched together in a spasm, and she clung to her concentration on them in order not to have to deal with the furious irritation in the rest of his face. "Why in hell didn't you come

324

and tell me the minute you heard of it? I thought you were a friend of mine. I thought I told you I'd make it worth your while."

"I didn't know it was anything you'd be interested in—anything serious."

"No?" He put a cigarette between his lips but did not light it. His lips were white at the corners.

"I'm sorry."

"Oh, sure."

She did not insist, but sat with her fingers on the typewriter keys and looked between his eyes as pleasantly and directly as she could, not challenging him but not letting her innocence be put down, either. "Anyway, haven't you sold it?" she could not help saying.

There was a kind of smile in the way his lips stretched flat around the cigarette. "Bright girl. You'd have been brighter if you'd come and told me. What were you doing, getting even?"

Squinting up at him a smile as flat as his own, she was thinking, Some day, oh, some day let me be rich enough and secure enough to say exactly what I think to people like this one! Aloud she said, lightly blushing, letting her eyes be at last put down, "Of course not. But if I had you couldn't much blame me. You didn't give me much of a break."

The cigarette was motionless in the middle of his lips while he looked down at her. Then it wobbled, and he said, "Dreadful, was it?"

"Not very pleasant."

Now she blushed hard, and it made her mad. Oliver raised his eyes prayerfully to the ceiling. Her smile was stiff on her face, and she knew that hatred was nearly unmasked in her eyes. And at just the moment when she realized that his amorous interest meant nothing whatever, she realized that up to a point, and if the game got desperate enough, she had been planning to use it.

He snapped his lighter to the cigarette. "I suppose I'm a brute all around. You and Mother can console one another."

Smiling and smiling, she let that pass.

Abruptly Oliver's manner changed. He shrugged away what they had been talking of, he grew loungy and loose, and he said with a bright look from under his tufted eyebrows, "Who's been around at the philanthropic trough lately?"

"Hardly anybody."

"Not even old Krishna Lal?"

"He's been down in the Ojai all summer."

"No other causes demanding Mother's attention, only this park?"

"She's had very little time, she's been so wrapped up in organizing the family papers."

"Yes, I know." Seconds after he took a deep drag on the cigarette, smoke leaked out through his nose and mouth as he talked. "Nobody at all with his hand out? It hardly seems like Villa Mon Repos."

The buzzer exploded under the desk, and Helen jumped. Oliver said, "You'll find her surprised and displeased and angry, but more displeased than surprised and more angry than displeased."

"I hope you haven't upset her."

"Oh, I'm afraid I have. Once in a while you have to. Not everything in the world can arrange itself with the one purpose of not upsetting Mother."

She had risen, preparing to go, and now he leaned and crushed out his cigarette in her desk tray of paperclips. "Where's her checkbook? I want to take a look."

The entire implication, the total probability, stood in her mind like a theorem left demonstrated on a blackboard. She said stupidly, "Checkbook?"

But her manner was wrong, she knew she had muffed any little chance to put him off. His attention sharpened, his eyes became little bright halfmoons. "Checkbook, yes. I like to keep track of who's benefiting."

"I don't know," she said. "I wonder if I should—"

"Are you crazy?" he said. "Who the hell hired you? What are you trying to cover up for her now? Where is it?" Reaching around, he yanked open the center drawer of the desk, and the checkbook was there. He opened it and stood reading, turning back the stubs three at a time. Without glancing up he said, "You don't have to wait."

"I'd better."

His eyebrows peaked, he stared a moment and went back to turning

326

stubs. It was a new checkbook, and it did not take him long to run through them. His hand was brown and thick, with tufts of sandy hair between the knuckles. It paused with one round-nailed finger holding back the stubs to expose the last sheet, on which she could see her own neat handwriting. Her veins were running icewater.

Oliver seemed to muse. Half turned away as he was, he did not seem to have changed expression at all. Certainly he did not start, his eyes did not bug out, he did not roar. In the tone of commonplace he said, "What's this MacDonald check?"

"Seven hundred of it is wages for the work he did. The rest is a present—they're about to have a baby."

"I see."

The buzzer squawked again, three impatient burrs. Smiling, Oliver turned his face. "Aren't you going?"

"Get it over with!" she said.

"All right. What's it for?"

"It's a gift."

"A gift? A gift, why? It's not Christmas. Are you having a baby too?"

"I guess because she likes me. She wanted me to have a trip abroad sometime."

The quirk of his head to one side was the gesture of a man acknowledging the marvelous. "Just like that, she gives you three thousand dollars."

"Just like that."

"It was a nice surprise."

"Very."

Incipient dimples whitened again at the corners of his mouth. "Too bad she isn't in her right mind," he said. "Where is it?"

"I've deposited it."

"Not wasting any time. All right, you can write me your personal check."

"I'm not giving it back!" She did not care now whether she was white or red; she might have been either. She stared not at his eyebrows but straight into his eyes, and she would not be stared down.

"Oh, yes you are," he said.

"No, I'm not! It was a gift. I never asked for it or hinted for it or anything. I've tried to be everything she wanted me to be, and she likes me. She did it all by herself, and I accepted it."

"I could bring charges against you."

"For what? You just go right ahead."

Their voices stayed low—it was always difficult to speak loudly in that house—but Helen had let into her face all the hatred she had felt for him from the beginning. Kissing her by the swimming pool! Pawing her and trying to make her his stooge! Thinking she would stay there in the pool and let him come at her without any suit on!

He looked like a cool man killing a snake. Drily he said, "You realize you're fired."

She moved her shoulders furiously.

"By tomorrow night, say." He put the checkbook under his arm. "But leave a forwarding address. There will be certain legal papers following you."

Without answering she went through the door. "And if you know what's good for you, don't spend that money," he said.

She broke her eyes from his and hurried down the hall. Behind her she heard the buzzer again, loud and insistent, like a driver riding his horn.

CHAPTER 27

S HE HAD started downstairs to have breakfast on the terrace when Bernadette came heavily trotting from around the angle of the hall. "Oh Mrs. Castro, are you going out?"

"I was going to have breakfast outside."

"Mr. Hutchens wants to see you right away."

"All right. What's doing for lunch? Has Mother any guests coming?"

"Mrs. Hutchens isn't well, she's in bed."

"Really? What's the matter?"

"I don't know. She didn't eat nothing for breakfast."

Sabrina made some tentative connections between her mother's illness and Oliver's wanting to see her: there was generally something defensive or punitive about her mother's illnesses. If no one crossed her, she went on week after week hobbling and murmuring around, as healthy an organism as the country could show. She could probably wait. So could Oliver. But she herself couldn't. She must settle her mind soon, she had to know.

"I'll call him after while," she said; and to Lizardo, appearing at the foot of the stairs, she said she would like orange juice and coffee on the terrace. She was sitting out there brooding through the fog of a headache, and feeling more trapped by the minute as she watched the sun burn away the overcast and run in patches over the lawns, when Lizardo brought the tray. On it was an envelope that Lizardo's smile identified for her even before she snatched it up and looked. From Burke. So small a concession as that bald telegram had been enough, then; all he had been waiting for was for her to bend in the slightest.

Under Lizardo's eyes she could not show what she felt; the explosion of glad relief that like an expanding gas filled her until her skin was stretched with it. She could only make a wry and deprecatory face, wordlessly admitting that this was what she had been watching the mail for. Discreetly he went away, and she thrust her finger under the flap and burst it open.

Dear Sabrina,

I hoped that word from you, when you finally felt that you could communicate, would be a call or a letter about us, not a seven-word telegram about Fat Boy. I can't even begin to tell you how bitter this is to me. I am not made of brass—you don't have to make it any clearer. Robert is sending Fat Boy tomorrow by Railway Express. I am also instructing Pat Sherwin to start proceedings for a Reno divorce. I hope this will give you the freedom you seem to want—maybe with me out of your life you can be happy. Sherwin or the court will be in touch with you soon. The grounds, presumably, will be desertion. As plaintiff, I will put in the necessary Nevada residence.

Sincerely,
Burke

Her first reaction was a protest. If he had been there, she might have screamed at his pinched repressed face, Oh, that isn't what it meant at all! Then she felt a slow, sick subsidence, as if all the gas of gladness that had filled her skin were hissing out through a puncture. Then, with a deep breath, she told herself that now it was as bad as she could have imagined it, now she was finally face to face with it. Under the stiff control she imposed on herself, panic lay ready to jump and run. Her jaws clenched suddenly, her eyes darkened, she crushed the note in her fist and for a moment she simply hung on. When she opened her eyes, Oliver was coming toward her across the lawn.

She put Burke's note away. Like a drunken person trying to control the whirling world, she fixed her eyes and her mind in hard focus on the single fact of her brother; she gave him such attention as she had perhaps never given him in her life, and she saw him as sharply as if she were holding binoculars on him. If she did not see him that way, attend to him to the exclusion of everything else, she would go to pieces.

Dressed for the City in suit and tie and narrow-brimmed straw hat, he might have been any of the five thousand men who pour out into Montgomery Street at the noon hour. But the very clothes that reduced him in size and made him a type added something to him; he expressed the dynamism of a class and a society. He was what she had once told him he was—what, on one limited side, this civilization came to. In one controlled movement he straddled a lounge, skimming his hat into another. His face reminded her of old pictures before the war, when he had scowled out of the sports page from under a football helmet.

"Well, you're finally up."

"Betimes," she said. "Have some coffee?"

He waved it aside. Forcing herself, willing her hands steady, she poured a cup for herself. Then suddenly it shook and slopped in her hand, and what for perhaps a minute and a half she had shut in escaped her.

"Did you know Burke's getting a divorce?"

Oliver squinted at her silently. His face seemed made of some more durable material than flesh; it creased with a tough resiliency like rubber or leather. And thank goodness he was neither cynical nor protective, and she could see in his little thinking eyes no implications of blame. She felt better for having told him; in a way he was easier to talk to than almost anyone she knew. After a moment he said, "Well, I suppose that figures. How do you feel?"

She managed a jerky laugh. "I don't know yet. I just heard."

"Does Mother know?"

"No."

"You going to Reno?"

"No, he is."

"And leave his practice?"

"That's to shame me. He's entitled to his gesture."

In the quiet of late morning they might have been a friendly brother and sister making relaxed familial conversation in the patio. She wished they were: it would have been pleasant to have a brother. Or maybe they were, maybe he was. Already the mere act of telling him had steadied her. Over her coffee cup she said, "Bernadette said you wanted to see me."

She saw at once, in the way his eyes came back from an abstracted examination of the rose walk, how little her news had meant to him; it hadn't surprised him and it made no particular difference to him. "I did," he said. "Things have got to where I was afraid they might get."

And so it would be his problems, not hers, that they would after all discuss. Not entirely unwillingly, she acquiesced. "What things?"

"Mother."

"Why, what's the matter with her?"

"When did you see her last?"

"At lunch yesterday. She was exactly as usual, telling stories about Uncle Mercer and spooning up her yoghurt."

"I've been trying to tell you, just as usual means a little off."

"I'd believe that quicker," she said with a flash of venom, "if you weren't so hot to develop her real estate."

"When I do, she'll benefit, and so will you."

"*If* you do. Mother's thinking of giving it to the county for a park."

"Yes," Oliver said. "I heard your friend MacDonald made that bright proposal."

"I made it. She thinks it's quite a good idea." The brief moment of tolerance or rapport was gone. It was remarkable how fast the antagonism between them could harden. She said to herself that nothing mattered ten cents' worth to him except his own concerns, and he thought he could walk right over everybody.

"All right," he said, with less emotion than she had expected. "That lets me know where I stand. I gather you haven't seen this morning's paper."

Now, as he passed the paper across, his eyes were full of such scorn and anger that she half regretted challenging him. Did it matter, really? This morning, of all mornings, she should be able to find something better to do than quarrel with Oliver. Her headache lurked at her temples like a light turned low. Back in her mind, waiting for her attention, was the emotional explosion that she knew she had coming, and beyond that was the need for some decision about what to do with her life. Her dilemma screamed at her like a man pinned in a burning car, and Oliver discussed real estate.

She read only the headline and the lead paragraph before she put the paper down. "You can't," she said. "It isn't yours."

"So?"

"It isn't legal."

"No."

"I see why Mother's in bed. I was afraid it was on account of me. Did you really think you could bulldoze her that way? What did she say?"

"She says no. Very embarrassing, very bad publicity. Maybe a lawsuit."

He was looking at her with the air of humorous unconcern that she had seen him literally superimpose upon his scowl. Picking up the paper again, she read the story through. "Three hundred and eighty acres," she said. "It was sporting of you to leave her twenty."

"Those are for her park."

"I don't see anything in the story about any park."

"It was an afterthought," Oliver said, and smiled. "I just had it."

They sat eye to eye. Lizardo looked out from the tearoom and Sabrina shook her head at him and he disappeared. "What made you think you could get away with it?" she said.

"What makes you think I'm not going to?"

"Your signature's no good, you've got no authority."

"But if I can get it."

"How? You know by now how she acts when she's pushed around."

Now he sat up, or surged up. "Before I answer that I want to know about this half-assed park notion. Did you really, seriously, make that suggestion?"

So promptly and resistantly she came up to meet him, she felt like a defender of the faith. "Yes, I did!"

He appeared to muse. His eyes gleamed as if he wanted to laugh. "Our equity in this deal would be just about three million dollars," he said.

"Is that it? I hadn't computed it in dollars." Her headache made the sunlight pulse like the colorless throbbing of animalcules seen through a microscope, and again the things waiting in her mind made themselves felt or heard like people in a reception room scraping chairs, turning magazines, coughing. "Oh, Oliver!" she said. "For the love of Mike, of course I suggested it! I'd love to see this family do something, just once, that measured up to its opportunities. But that doesn't mean I ever thought she *would* do it. She'll procrastinate forever. Why can't you let her have it in peace? It'll only be a few years."

"Who the hell knows what will be going on in twenty years? You know the kind of haircut Opportunity is supposed to wear? Anyway, if I waited, I'd have to fight you for it. You're the one that wants to throw it away."

"*Give* it away. When that time comes we'll split it, how's that? You can develop your half and I'll make a park of mine."

His face, as he shook out a cigarette toward her, took one himself, and lit them both (and suddenly, she discovered, she was smoking again), was neither scowling nor artificially agreeable, but merely intent, and she admitted how really formidable he was, and how adequate to promote into action the kinds of ideas he could understand. "Look. She's in bed now. I've been brutal and unfeeling, I've threatened her security. But how's she going to feel if I do call this deal off and get us sued? I'm deep in this, you'd better remember. It would cost me—us— thirty or forty thousand just to back out. So I want you to save us all that money and embarrassment by helping me persuade her."

Almost respectfully he waited, while she sat tapping her thumbnail absently against her teeth. She said, "You planned all this in absolutely cold blood, didn't you?"

He gave her back her look. Obviously he felt he was involved in a crusade against the forces of weakness, sentimentality, and inertia. In his controlled voice he said, "A woman her age can't expect to run everything according to her own whims. I want her to be happy, and comfortable, and putter around with whatever pleases her, and have the best of care—do you believe me?"

"I suppose, in a way, that's how you feel, yes."

"All right. But she can't go on holding up the sensible administration of the estate. If she'd left me any other choice, I wouldn't have done it this way. I've been begging her all summer to let me do it right."

"But she wouldn't," Sabrina said. "Now what are you going to do when she refuses to sign?"

Oliver's eyes were as amber and steady as the eyes of some dogs, Weimaraners or border collies; they had no expression beyond an intensity of waiting. And he said what she had expected him to say. "Then I'll have to have the power of decision taken out of her hands."

He heaved his shoulder up, thrust his hand down into a pocket as if in search of something. But he did not move the hand, or bring anything out. He simply sat with one shoulder high, the hand thrust deeply down, an image of dominant, arrested power. "I suppose you find that unspeakable," he said.

"No. I just think it will kill her."

That brought an angry, incredulous, inarticulate sound out of him.

"No, really," she said. "You're a competitor, you always were. It probably drives you wild to see other people tearing down the track while you're tied to a post. And you've got an engineer's mind, which means you comprehend everything but the important things. No, unspeakable isn't the word I'd've used. From your point of view it's probably as logical to declare Mother incompetent as it is to have a contour survey just a necessary part of getting a job done. But I still think it would kill her. Because she isn't incompetent, she's only eccentric, like all the rest of us. And scared, like the rest of us."

"Speak for yourself, John."

"Oh, not you. Not Uncle Bushrod. But all the others, especially the women."

Now he softly withdrew his hand from his pocket, empty. His hard glance was retracted, he sagged back to an even stance. The forward weight of his arms, hanging down between his knees, pulled deep wrinkles into his coat where sleeves and jacket joined. "I haven't got time for genealogy," he said. "Since that story appeared, I'm on the spot."

"Who released the story? You created the spot and then put yourself on it."

"And so is everybody else on the spot," he said. "If you think a

335

guardianship hearing would kill Mother, then you'd better help persuade her to get rid of this useless land and settle back, not hurt one bit and a hell of a lot richer."

"Only posterity would be poorer," she said. "Or the public weal, or something."

"What?"

"Let it go," she said, "they're words you don't understand."

Through the shadow of her headache and the lurk of her own unsolved trouble she saw him as a rampant and impatient boy frantic at being balked from doing something momentarily more important than anything in the world. Probably he would wear out his building itch, and go on to something else, some new promotion, the way he went from sports cars to antique cars to water-skiing to skin-diving, but meantime he would create consequences both physical and human. His kind never anticipated consequences. His was the kind that left eroded gulches and cutover timberlands and man-made deserts and jerry-built tracts that would turn into slums in less than a generation. They got awards from service clubs and resolutions of commendation from chambers of commerce. They denuded and uglified the earth in the name of progress, and when they lay on their deathbeds—or dropped from the massive coronary that the pace of their lives prepared for them— they were buried full of honors and rolling in wealth, and it never occurred to the people who honored them, any more than it had occurred to themselves, that they nearly always left the earth poorer and drearier for their having lived in it. And yet what energy. What single-mindedness in their characteristic short-sighted causes. He had rigged this little deal, for instance, so that there was no comfortable way out except his own.

"Suppose something else," she said in a burst of impatience. "Suppose I won't help you persuade Mother?"

He had risen. Leaning one shoulder against the pillar supporting the patio roof lattice, he looked down on her steadily while he rammed short, crook-armed blows into the post. "Then I look bad in the papers," he said. "Maybe I get sued. So to protect myself, and protect Mother against her own foolishness, I'd have to move—in advance—to have a guardian appointed."

336

"How do you know the court would find she needed one?"

"Can you imagine her?" he said, steadily staring, ramming his fist against the post. "In some judge's chambers, answering questions? Fumbling, forgetting . . ."

"You're such a nice guy," Sabrina said.

"Yeah!" he said surlily. "This is if you don't give me any alternative. If I read you right, you'll fight these incompetency proceedings. So I'd have to fight *you*. There's a chance that your recent escapades around Tahoe, known to several but strangely missing from the gossip columns, might leak out. Mother, you say, would be killed by all this. I think she might. That's why we'd better avoid it. All you have to do is persuade her she can't keep four hundred acres of prime land stowed away like a bunch of old gloves."

Again they were eye to eye, will to will. She said softly, "Big Brudder, would you really blackmail me?"

"You're damned right, little sister, if I had to."

"What if I wouldn't blackmail? What if I didn't give a damn any more?"

"But you do."

"I give less of a damn every day."

His piston arm was still for a moment. "Then Mother would blackmail—as you call it—in your name."

She pressed her fingers against the skewer of pain in her temples. Out of a fretful impulse she said, "Oliver, wouldn't it be nice if in this family we felt protective about each other? Wouldn't you like me for a sister? Wouldn't it be good if we could be loving children in Mother's old age?"

His irony showed itself briefly and blandly. "Charmed."

"If you get your way."

He said with careful patience, "Once you think it over, you'll thank me."

"I doubt it. Anyway, what if she did fumble some questions before the judge? Would a court think she's senile just because she won't let you sell some land, and gives hundred-dollar checks to some dubious charities?"

His hands were deep in his pockets again. He went a half dozen paces down the terrace, swung back. "As to that, the evidence has accumu-lated."

"Something to Stanford or Mills? Some insane contribution to the Red Cross?"

"Seven hundred dollars for sorting the family papers. And when your friend MacDonald gets through she's so pleased to have them alpha-betized that she gives him three hundred for a bonus."

"She did? And he took it?"

"Are you out of your mind as far as she is? Of course he took it. One thousand bucks—for what? What earthly reason could anyone have for spending a thousand dollars to alphabetize that junk?"

"It sounds like a bargain to me. Even if it wasn't, what kind of evi-dence is that? She can sort the papers if she wants to."

"Yes? Then what do you think of a little check for three thousand dollars to La Secretary? Above and beyond wages. A token of esteem."

"Really?" Sabrina said, jarred. It was lavish, beyond precedent in her mother's carefully luxurious life. And it spoke of an affection that made her feel for an instant uneasy and ashamed. While her children discussed putting her under house arrest, she poured out her bottled-up love on her companion.

"That would have been just the beginning," Oliver said. "Little Helen was snuggled right up to the trough."

"*Would* have been? Why, what have you done?"

"I've canned her. Did you expect me to leave her there, with that tap running?"

"But Mother's devoted to her!"

"That's too bad. I'll get her three more, with a different kind of frosting. This one's out."

His thin-lipped rage astonished her. Then she thought she under-stood. "What's the matter, is she virtuous besides?"

She regretted the jeer the moment she let it go, not because of any concern for Oliver's feelings, but because the more she irritated him the less chance there was of controlling him. That she wanted to make him change his mind was perfectly clear. Helen had never been entirely to her taste—a little over-eager? a little too much the perfect handmaiden? It gave her the look of being on the make, though she quite probably was not, not in the sense Oliver meant. But if she went, what desolation in the apartment among the cushions. What a real emptiness in her mother's life, considering how she and Oliver qualified as daughter and son. And now other shocks to come. She felt the folded envelope in her skirt pocket, and said, "If you're deliberately setting out to drive her into incompetence, you've found the right way."

"She'll get over it. She has these spells to show you she's offended, and after a day or two she climbs out of bed as well as ever."

"You mean as senile as ever?"

"Come on!" he said angrily. "Are you going to help, or do we all go through the wringer?"

The pressure she was containing burst suddenly outward, nearly escaped. She clamped her jaw; her hands were shaking. "*God,* I wish we were a happy family!"

"We can be again in two hours."

"Again. Don't make me laugh."

"She couldn't buck the two of us. Give up that idiotic park and she will too."

"You should have caterpillar treads," she said. "They'd become you." She stood up into the gray shadow of headache; the sunny lawns, the dark oaks, swam for a moment in over-exposed planes and curves. "I'm not promising anything," she said. "But I'll talk to her and see how she feels."

"When? Right now?"

"My word, I've got other things to do too! I've got a . . . Is this the most pressing thing in the whole world?"

"Yes!" Oliver said.

But her anxieties would not assent to that, for Burke's note had applied red-hot iron to their infected relationship, and her own problem flamed with the urgency of seared flesh. Maybe it was better cauterized, she thought as she went inside—and yet, oh, damn him, if he had made one move, if he had understood one particle, given one inch, shown one grain of love or forgiveness, they might now be on the road to reconciliation.

Yes? she asked herself sarcastically. Now? If what she feared turned out to be true, it would take more than a gesture of good will to bring them together.

Would have taken, she thought, passing down the hall to the library through the dim cool interior air. Always keep the tenses straight, it's a form of honesty. Drearily, testing herself for nausea, she selected from the yellow pages the name of a gynecologist she did not know, and by simply being insistent with the receptionist, made an appointment for two that afternoon. For a minute she stood by the desk, feeling the room's emptiness since Leonard MacDonald was gone. From above the mantel the windless peace of Monet's lilies breathed down at her, a serenity, an untroubled blooming, a passionate intensity of quiet, something once perhaps possible, never to be found again.

She had botched it superbly, or he had, or they together had. And yet maybe not. Maybe this afternoon would release instead of condemning her, and she could . . . what? Yes, for God's sake, what? Start over? It was fantastic. And yet she yearned for just that.

She shook her shoulders and started upstairs, stopping by the drawing room on the way to snatch up a couple of cigarettes out of the visitors' box.

CHAPTER 28

ROM THE TURN of the hall she saw Helen Kretchmer softly closing her mother's door. The expression of the girl's face, turned in profile as she listened for sounds from inside, was still and sullen, but when she saw Sabrina it changed to the inquiring attentiveness of a well-trained store clerk.

"Is she asleep?" Sabrina asked.

"She's trying to relax. I got her to drink some linden tea."

"I've got fifty-seven varieties of sleeping pills if that's what she needs." Helen's smile was careful, almost patronizing. "It has to be natural."

"Yes, I suppose. How is she?"

"This morning she was very upset. Now she seems depressed."

Curiously studying her, Sabrina found the girl's eyes clear and steady, her face composed. She had no nervous habits with her hands, no apparent need for the nervous laughter that many girls in her situation would have been forced to. Simply as an exhibit in self control, she was admirable. "Does she know my brother fired you?"

She got her look back straight, without a waver. "I thought I'd better wait until she was feeling better."

That made one more unpleasant thing that her mother didn't know. If Oliver's power play was enough in itself to put her to bed, how would she feel if she knew how many other crises she had coming in the next few days? She had a right to be four times as depressed as she was.

"Yes," Sabrina said. "That was just as well. Right now I have to talk to her about Oliver's land grab, but later I'm going to see if I can't make him change his mind."

"Please don't put yourself out." Now the attentive mask was distorted just a little, the flush mounted under the perfect Visigoth skin. She was rather square-jawed, by no means unattractive, though she had the white eyelashes that Sabrina had always associated with Hereford cattle. Nevertheless admirable: independent and tough. Some girls would have been in spiteful tears.

"I *want* to put myself out," she said. "It's unjust."

"Yes," Helen said softly, enunciating very plainly as if she spoke to a lip reader. "Yes, I believe it is."

"Can I talk to you later?"

"Of course," Helen said. "He gave me twenty-four hours."

Well! Sabrina thought. Don't let me force it on you! Helen's eyes, cool and unappeased, locked with hers. Unappeased, she was still standing in the hall as Sabrina tapped at her mother's door and went in.

In the dusky room, behind drawn drapes, her mother lay querulous and wide awake among her pillows. As Sabrina entered she peered sharply, foxily, at the door. "Mother, how are you feeling?"

The shaking hands untangled the earpieces of the glasses and laid the glasses on the bedtable among a dozen pill bottles. By now the sun no longer shone against the windows, and the light was green-tinted, almost wintry. Braced back, the old lady glowered like an irreconcilable survivor.

She said she could not rest. She could not even relax, and she had growing pains in her feet—a sure sign of calcium deficiency. Sabrina found her a calcium pill and she sucked it while she complained. She was very strong against Oliver. If his position was awkward, it was all his own doing. She would not submit to having such an irresponsible and unfair trick played upon her; she would sign nothing. He had taken advantage of her earlier illness to get more power in his hands than she had meant to surrender. Oliver was not to be trusted with power. If he once managed to get control she would not trust him to spare even this place. Only a few weeks ago he had made the barefaced proposal to cut the estate up into little home sites. She thought it especially disagreeable for her children to be headstrong and unkind when she herself was unwell.

Sabrina, gritting on her untreated and untreatable problem as she might have ground on an aching tooth, sat frowning until the fitful murmur died down, and then said into the dry silence that succeeded, "You'll be wishing you'd given the land for a park when we first spoke of it."

"I have . . . already wished so." Her long face came up off the pillow, her bony Wolcott nose sniffed with fretful suspicion. "Do you know why I did not? Because I was afraid he would . . . fight it in the courts. I believe he . . . would have. Against his mother. And if I had merely put it into my will he would surely have . . . tried to break it."

Which was true, Sabrina admitted. But it was not the only reason why her mother had procrastinated. If they had all been at her, urging her to give the land, she would have hesitated just the same. "I suppose," she said. "Is your will in order, incidentally?"

"I fully believe so."

"Made when?"

"Last year."

"Before your stroke?"

"Yes." Mistrust gleamed from her lidded eyes. With a dry, unpleasant laugh she said, "Why . . . do you ask?"

"The earlier it's dated the less chance there is of breaking it."

"You mean it would be harder to demonstrate I was in my . . . dotage when I made it."

"That's how wills are generally broken."

"And how do *you* feel?" her mother said in a stronger voice. "Would you . . . help him try to break it? Do you think I am . . . in my dotage now? I am sure he does. Sometimes I have wondered if you both haven't . . . always thought so."

"Of course that's absurd," Sabrina said. "And of course I don't care what kind of will you write. Or rather, I do—I'd like to see you do something good with it, not just dump everything on Oliver and me. But that has nothing to do with this, because the park isn't *in* your will."

"Oh, pshaw," her mother said wearily and fretfully. Her momentary suspicious attention on Sabrina wavered away. She said, "It . . . distresses me to have the family quarreling over property."

"It isn't your fault."

"No, I believe it isn't. I have always felt that . . . wealth is essential for grace and . . . decency in living, but I never thought the *making* of money anything but unattractive."

"I don't know. I wonder if making it isn't a good deal of fun. It is for Oliver. Maybe it is for nearly everybody. Spending it can be fun, too. It's *having* it that can tangle up your life. The people who own their money badly or irresponsibly can be pretty unattractive. So can the heirs when they start gathering in a ring with their eyes gleaming."

"Is that the . . . situation we have now?"

"Oh, Mother!" She turned in her chair and looked at the shrouded windows. Accuse me of anything else, she wanted to cry, and it's probably true. But don't think I covet your money!

After a few seconds she heard her mother say, "Perhaps I have . . . offended you."

"Perhaps that wasn't called for. Your will isn't concerned in this." From her shirt pocket she took the cigarette she had picked up in the drawing room on her way upstairs. Her mother said, "Please . . . I must ask you not to . . . smoke, Sabrina. It irritates my sinuses."

Sabrina crushed the cigarette in her hand and dropped it in the wastebasket.

"I am sorry if I am . . . over-wrought and difficult," her mother said —martyred, Sabrina thought, by her own perception of her own impossible fussiness. "My sinuses have been . . . troubling me all day. Perhaps you would call Helen and ask her to start the . . . humidifier."

"I'll start it." She rose and found the switch. The enclosed stillness deepened to the hum of the fan.

"I had hoped you had . . . given up that habit," her mother said.

Sabrina sat down. "Mother, for heaven's sake, I came in here to see if

I could help you settle this land business with Oliver. Will you get it through your head that I'm on your side, and quit picking on me?"

There was, of course, an offended silence. Between them suddenly lay the fact of those letters yesterday, the unseemly revelations, the embarrassing intimacy, and on Sabrina's part the even more unseemly revelations to come. If there had been in her mother's voice, when it came, the slightest trembling toward the sympathy of the previous afternoon, Sabrina might have poured it all out. But her mother only said, stiffly, "If I have been . . . unreasonable I am sorry."

Business only, then. And anyway it would have been brutal to say all that. That was the trouble—it would always be brutal; she could not imagine a time when it could get said. "All right," she said. "What about Oliver?"

"Oh!" her mother said, sitting up straight in bed. "I have been so nearly . . . distracted! What am I to do? If I don't give in to him he is . . . disgraced, or so he says, and if he is, we all are. He knows how I dislike being . . . pushed. I can't . . . think why he would do it. It seems I am either to be dominated by my children or . . . involved in sordid squabbles with them."

"Child!" Sabrina said. "Squabbles with *him*. Remember me? I'm the one on your side. Let me ask you a question. Can you hold out, really?"

"I have told him I will . . . sign nothing."

"I know, but he still thinks you'll sign. Would the Wolcotts in Mount Auburn Cemetery welcome the publicity if he was made to look like a sharp dealer or a fool?"

"I don't . . ."

"Would *you* like it?"

"I most certainly would not."

"Then you may have to give him some land to play with."

"I have told him . . . no, and I meant no."

"You just don't know all the consequences," Sabrina said. In her skirt pocket she felt the stiffness of the folded note, and once again the flare of hopelessness, fury, panic, whatever it was, went through her clear to the soles of her feet; through its livid fading the petulant figure on the bed swam back into visibility. Helplessness had better recognize itself; in the end, no matter how many walls of pills and cushions it built around itself, it was only helplessness, and would give way or suffer consequences it could not even imagine. She said a little lamely, "He'd rather be nice to you than not, I think. His trouble is, he's energetic. I'm afraid you'll have to give him something for his energy to work on."

"And you are . . . on *my* side?" her mother said. "The park was partly your suggestion."

"I didn't say give him all of it. Maybe he'd let you alone if you gave him a hundred acres. Maybe it would take two, maybe he wouldn't be appeased with less than three. But if you don't give him some of it he's quite capable of being dirty and unpleasant. He thinks he represents Progress, he's combating the forces of foolishness, he's got his armor on."

"Nevertheless, he cannot do a single thing without . . . my signature."

She wavered an improbable look of deathless resolution from inside the frill of her cap. Between irritation and pity, swallowing back the gorge of her own fear and indecision, Sabrina thought, You're a lost cause, Mother. You don't know how vulnerable you are. The termites have been at your foundations till they're only shells. And it won't do any good to pebble your chin and put on that old patrician glare.

Then, lifting her eyes from the rug and meeting her mother's, she saw how wrong she had been. Her mother understood perfectly how lost a cause she was. The eyes were scared and pitiful, the mouth could not make itself firm.

The pang of gentleness, even tenderness, that moved her was a surprise. It had been her habit, at least up to yesterday, to think of her mother as peremptory or preposterous, but hardly pathetic. Held for a moment, touched, bemused, she had to grope for the place where their talk had broken off. "He's very energetic," she said again. "And single-minded. He never doubted himself in his life, and I suppose that's the most hateful thing you can say about anyone. He'd trample you down any way he had to, and when he had forced you to unconditional surrender he'd get sporting and pick you up and dust you off and give you the best of care, and think well of himself for his generosity. He's a very American character, your son."

"Oh," her mother said. "Yes . . . perhaps. But . . ." She lay back, with two fingers held trembling against her trembling lips.

And what am I doing this for? Sabrina asked herself, waiting. Is it just that I automatically oppose both Mother and Oliver, and so wind up mediating between them? Do I want some public demonstration of responsibility on the family's part, so I can feel better about what I am? Am I just hanging on, staying with this because I know as soon as it's finished I'll have the other, and I can't, can't, *can't* bear to face all that? Am I just for a change doing something wholesome, like a hard drinker going on milk? Or isn't there, hasn't there been for a long time, a certain tenderness toward that old tyrant in the bed? Don't I sort of half wish even Oliver could get a part of his desire, so we could remain, or become, a family? For a minute or two her mind was clear, she rallied herself to a clean formulation of possibilities. And then it began seeping up through her again, foggy and sad, the gray cloud of disenchantment to which she had awakened, and which had been made blacker, more threatening, more murky and inescapable, by Burke's letter. The wire of headache still skewered her from temple to temple like a reminder.

Her mother murmured, "If I remember correctly, Leonard said that . . . anything from ten acres upward would . . . be a public good. Then if we could save a hundred acres, it would be . . ."

"Magnificent, I think his word was. I'd rather see four hundred, but in the circumstances a hundred might represent peace with honor. Would you be willing to settle for that, if you had to?"

"Why . . . Sabrina, you seem so capable in these matters. . . . It distresses me so to think of . . . combating him again. . . ."

She faltered to a stop, the fan droned in the dusk, the air stirred faintly, from indefinable directions, with whiffs of coolness. "You want *me* to do it?" Sabrina said. "Mother, I *can't,* I've got a million things to do, I'm all tied up in . . . All right, I'll talk to him."

"I have felt so . . . dreadfully alone," her mother whimpered. "This morning I learned that Helen would leave me. . . ."

347

"You did? Who told you?"

"She did. She is . . . engaged to be married. I must look forward to losing her in April."

"Oh, well, but that's a long way off."

"But still."

"Yes," Sabrina said. Her relief that the knowledge was not immediate was tempered by her awareness that within twenty-four hours it would have to be. Again she was tempted to tell what she knew, and again she held back. Settle the Oliver business first—get out of the way, with relief, the least of the evils, and the others might be more easily borne. She stood up, aware suddenly, frantically, of the passage of time. All morning she had frittered away on ridiculous arguments about real estate, secretaries, all the unreal complications of her mother's life. Awaiting her were the ominous complications of her own. She must make up her mind whether to call Burke, or go down, or simply clench her hands and sit still. She wanted to talk to somebody, empty it all out —and that meant Bobbie. "I've got to run," she said breathlessly. "Don't you want some lunch now? Can I have Bernadette bring something?"

Her mother said, "Perhaps . . . you will ask Helen to come in. She often has good suggestions about things. I shouldn't like . . . I couldn't quite . . . oh, how could I eat!"

"You should, though." Hesitating beside the bed, she looked for some glint or spark of yesterday's sympathy and communion in her mother's face, but saw only petulance. Oliver with his pressures had forced that softer woman back out of sight. Nevertheless she could not help saying softly, "Mother, I read the letters."

A hard, twitching, suspicious look. "Oh, yes, the letters." As if she wished they could be covered over with dead leaves and forgotten.

"And I wanted to tell you," Sabrina said. "It wasn't that he wasn't fond of you. I'm *positive*. They lied to him and shut him out till he got furious enough to take their bribe and go away. They shut his mouth with money, but first they lied to him. I'm sure you shouldn't remember him with anger. I'm sure he—"

"What?" her mother said. "What? What are you . . . talking about? I hope you have had the sense to . . . put that envelope in the files."

Her eyes were diving, glinting off Sabrina's a moment and then gone, flustered and irritated and embarrassed as if what she had brought herself to say the previous afternoon were something shameful, and Sabrina's mention of it a breach of taste.

So, then. Sabrina managed a crooked smile. "Yes, Mother, I sealed it and put it away." Her mind stirred with a slow, incredulous exasperation. No wonder he had left, no wonder he had accepted the bribe and gone. She imagined him somewhat like herself, quick to anger, impetuous and outgoing, wanting the warmth of touch and the comfort of a human, not a Wolcott, response. Lord God, to go through your life asking for bread and being given a stone, and then to compound it by marrying a stone!

"That is . . . best," her mother said. "Will you please send Helen in?"

Her eyes would not hold, and after a moment Sabrina moved away. But could that irritable nag be hurt feelings? Jealousy? She put her head in Helen's doorway.

"Mother wants you."

"Of course," Helen said, promptly rising.

CHAPTER 29

S HE WAS thinking, as she watched Oliver coming across the lawn with his long, hasty walk, that what she had just said to her mother was unpalatably true. He had never doubted himself in his life. What he wanted he had always got, and his wants had never conflicted with any fine scruples. From the time he was sixteen, rumors of his girls had reached her; he had always been as cheerfully promiscuous as a rooster. So for punishment he had a submissive wife who gave him no trouble, five healthy children, and everything that his mind or his muscles wanted. And here she sat, who had hated him for his uncleanness, who had kept her sullen Victorian purity intact until it festered—here *she* sat. She carried to her lips the cigarette she had been crushing in her hand, and saw him, fifty feet away, dip a hand promptly into his pocket for his lighter. He came up to her with the lighter ready in his hand, but she scratched and cupped a paper match, and his arrival was obscured in a flare from the cigarette's shredded end.

He hooked an iron chair with his foot and sat down. "What's the deal?"

The impulse to punish him was more than she could resist. "No deal. She won't." Without visible sign he took that in; his thumb clicked the lighter on and off. "She thinks you should be sued, or go to jail."

Now he half bowed.

"Precisely what will happen when you tell them you have to back out?"

Dropping the lighter back into his pocket, he looked across the lawns with his teeth shining in a flake of sun. "I don't know," he said. "Confidentially, I don't plan to find out." And, as his eyes cocked up at her flintily from under his eyebrows, "What did you do, encourage her about that damned park?"

"She *wants* to give it, Oliver."

"Let her give the twenty acres."

"That's not enough."

"Oh, not enough! Woodside's already got Huddart Park. There are a half dozen beaches and redwood parks in the county. How many do you need, for God's sake?"

"You might as well get used to it," Sabrina said. "She doesn't think twenty acres are enough, and neither do I. Also I haven't got all day to talk, so you'd better listen. You can't force her to sign, and I don't think you'll succeed in getting her declared incompetent. If you're dirty enough to try."

"I'm still listening."

"I'll tell you what you'll do. You'll compromise. Isn't that a remarkable statement, coming from me? You ought to have to eat crow, but for everybody's sake I'll persuade her. I already have."

That brought his eyes around on her as hot as burning cigar ends. He coughed and put his big meaty hand to his mouth, watching her over it while the coughing spent itself. "Is it fair to tell me the details?"

"Fifty-fifty. Two hundred acres for your development, two hundred for the park."

His hands went on doing what they had started to do as soon as he took his palm away from his lips, the right fist knocking gently and regularly into the left palm, a controlled and casual patting as if he kept time to a band; but she could see his face grow darker and still darker and he seemed to have swelled in his light summer suit.

"If it was a five- or six-million-dollar deal before, it's still half that good," she said. "Your associates aren't going to throw away that much just because they can't get more."

"Maybe they'd take it," Oliver said, slapping his fist lightly into his palm, "but don't kid yourself for a minute that I would."

"Then we're all in for an unpleasant time."

"If we are, we'll know who to thank."

The wire of headache went thinly from temple to temple. She felt at once older and wiser than this recalcitrant she was trying to persuade, and impatient that he refused to be persuaded. Of all the days to get involved in something like this!

He had the lighter in his hand again, snapping it on and off. "A park won't hurt your tract," she said. "It'll double its value."

"Two hundred acres? What good is two hundred acres of poison oak and chaparral in the middle of a residential tract? I'll lay you a bet you can't get either the county or the town of Woodside to accept it. They couldn't afford to take it off the tax rolls. They wouldn't have the money to develop and maintain it."

"If I gave them an endowment they would."

He stared, looking for the clue to the joke.

"Why not?" she said. "I can afford it. I haven't lived up to my income for years—ever, maybe. I'm quite a well-to-do woman, thanks to my broker."

The lighter flashed silver, turning in the air, and he caught it and tossed it high again. "That's fine. It's too bad all that money couldn't have landed with somebody who knows what money's for."

"Lawns for children to roll on?" she said. "Bridle trails through the woods, for the time when the Trail Club trails are all under asphalt? A place to walk a good long way? Aren't those as good things to buy with money as anything else? Some place for the hermit thrushes and the hermits?"

"Very poetic," Oliver said. "Twenty acres, sure."

"The twenty acres still go to Mother, though I might borrow them and put up a summer camp for spastic children, or blind children, or poor children, or rich children, or some other kind of deprived children. But you'll have to give up enough for a park besides."

"Can you understand that the site plan's already made and submitted?"

"That's just a preliminary, it can be changed."

The flame in his hand leaped pale, a nearly invisible tongue in the sunlight, and vanished again. "No," he said.

For minutes she had had herself under control. Now the force of her containment burst her to her feet so suddenly that she saw she surprised him; his quick squinting look gave her just the slight pause she needed to clamp the handcuffs back on her cracking spirit. "All right!" she said. "Then depend on it, I'll buck you. You may be able to force that scared old woman into real senility, but if you do you'll never get my agreement to your contract. I'll be a lot tougher to handle than Mother ever was. I'll tie you up legally for the rest of your life."

He had a look of always coming at you; you felt you had to brace yourself for bodily contact. And his face had its old under-the-helmet scowl. But his voice was softer than it had been at any time during their interview. "Sister, I did you a favor a few weeks ago."

"At Tahoe, you mean?"

"At Tahoe. I hunted you down and I stopped you from making an even bigger spectacle of yourself than you already had, and I closed some mouths with money. If I hadn't, you might be hiding behind hedges when you saw an acquaintance coming."

"If you meant it as a favor, I'm grateful."

Snick, went the lighter flame. "You're grateful. That's nice."

It seemed to her that they were on the edge of something, that they teetered between hatred and affection. Their antagonism, though it had been all their lives the most intimate thing they shared, had never been quite enough for either of them. Perhaps he *had* meant to rescue her, not simply to forestall a scandal. But that didn't mean he wouldn't blackmail her if he had to. "You know what I wish?" she said. "I wish you really had hunted me up because you were fond of me, not so you'd have something on me that you could use for pressure when you wanted some quid pro quo. Do you believe I'd like to do something for you? Do you believe I'm trying to do something for you now?"

Oliver's mouth, tight as a razor cut, opened briefly. "No." He waited, saying no more. Off in the shrouded grounds some noon-singing bird, thresher or mockingbird, poured out an exuberant, changing gush of music. Now, she supposed, was the time when she should capitulate and earn a brother's love. It was all set up—bird song, nature's cathedrals, aspiration soaring heavenward, hearts united. And the cold certainty at the heart that was so ludicrous she wanted to guffaw, but that still was cold, that still made all this argument trifling. Perhaps it was that that made her want to be reconciled with Oliver; her trouble was of a sort that he knew all about. For the name of a good abortionist and other good and valuable considerations, I, Sabrina Castro, do hereby agree . . .

But she looked him in his hard amber eyes and said urgently, "Oliver, we've all got to have something to get satisfaction from. You can't have it all. So take your share and be a sport about it."

If there had been some infallible way of reading faces, some unchanging correspondence between muscular contractions and emotional meanings, she might have known what he was thinking. As it was, she couldn't tell whether he was half persuaded, inclined to smile, or restraining anger. Without inflection he said, "What's your final proposition?"

"Mine? You mean Mother's."

"Don't try to kid me she had anything to do with it. How big is your pound of flesh? Let me tell you before you open your mouth, fifty-fifty isn't enough."

"I wish you could let it be friendly."

His face was suddenly full of leathery ridges. "How much?"

Sabrina sighed. "All right. A hundred acres for the park and twenty for Mother, just for reassurance. That gives you two hundred and eighty."

"It doesn't give me anything. You and Mother benefit exactly as much as I do from every acre I develop."

"Don't think we won't all benefit from the park, too," she said. "Even from Mother's nest egg we'll all benefit. Think what a challenge it will be in the future to try to wangle that out of her."

The act of slapping his hat on his head transformed him into the Montgomery Street image, groomed and hasty. "Will she sign on those terms?"

She nodded.

"All right. Thanks for the favor."

"It *is* a favor, Oliver. You're coming out better than you had any right to expect."

"At ten thousand an acre we're coming out exactly one million two hundred thousand less than we could."

"Less taxes and costs and a lot else. Please, when you talk to Mother, try to act satisfied. She'd love to feel that it all came out in a way to please everybody. And if she scolds you, smile."

"Yes, Sister."

"One more thing, what about Helen? It's no good settling this land thing if you fire her. Mother dotes on that girl."

"That's one of the very best reasons she has to go."

"She's been good at her job, hasn't she?"

"How do I know?" Oliver said. "How does anybody even know whether she added an extra zero on that check? Mother with her eye methods can barely see the check, much less the zeros."

"I don't think she's dishonest."

"You and I can find quite a number of things to disagree about," he said. "That little tick is being washed out with kerosene before she gets her whole head buried."

At least for the moment, she gave it up. She didn't have the heart for fighting him any more that day, and after all, sooner or later her mother would have to adjust to Helen's leaving anyway. Maybe better now than later, when she might be getting really sick and really senile. For the girl's sake, too—Oliver was quite capable, if his mother defied him and kept Helen on, of making life utterly miserable for everybody. "I still think it's unfair to both her and Mother," she said. "But at least Helen will have the consolation of her check."

"Oh no!" he said. "That she's giving back."

"Oliver, no! If she agrees to go, you have to agree to let her accept that."

"Accept," he said. "You have an odd vocabulary." All in a moment he seemed to recollect the full burden of their talk, and began again to ram short hard blows into the pillar, staring at her steadily with his hot little amber eyes. "Take you all in all, it isn't only your vocabulary that's odd. What the hell part are you playing now? One day you're

Madame Bovary and the next you're a cross between a dutiful daughter and Robert Moses. I wish you'd decide who you are." His fist quit ramming the post and came down to knock once, with emphasis, on the patio table. "All right! She can take it. But she's out of here within twenty-four hours. And all right on this lousy deal you think is such a favor. I ought to charge you personally for the extra engineering and legal fees. And incidentally we'll have to decide where your pound of flesh comes off. Who's going to help cut it, you or Mother? Or will you send for your friend MacDonald?"

"Oh, lay off him, what's he ever done to you? I'll do it, and you don't need to worry, it'll be mainly sidehill and canyon. Where were you going to leave Mother her twenty?"

"Around the stables. Will that satisfy?"

"I should think so. It ought to join the park tract at some point."

"So eventually you can throw it away with the other hundred?"

"It'll adjoin your high-class development, too," she reminded him. "What a lovely bone of contention for us down through the years."

Unsmiling, his mouth still bitten in like a closed wound, he said, "Here's another thing. Mother will make me her representative with full powers in this. I'm not going to come running every time I want a posthole dug."

"That's reasonable. Then when we sign her up to that, you can sign with us in making the gift of the park, and get some credit. Won't that be nice?"

She smiled up at him while he hung in his most characteristic pose, leaning forward, the cigarette dangling still, the lighter suspended. His thumb moved and the blade of light awoke. "Just one favor after another," he said, and blew smoke and left her, walking fast around the corner of the house.

She found Helen sitting quietly in her office looking out the window, and again, as when Sabrina had seen her softly closing her mother's door, she noted the self-control—how a look that was brooding and sullen gave way to polite attentiveness.

"I'm sorry," Sabrina said. "I'm afraid I haven't persuaded him."

"It's all right. Thank you for trying."

356

"I did make him agree not to force you to give the check back."

And why should that get her a glance of hot scorn? Sabrina groped for something to say, but all she managed was, "I'm truly sorry, I think you've been good for Mother. Can I help, any way? Would a letter from me help you get another job?"

"A good secretary doesn't need to worry about finding jobs," Helen said. "I'm a good secretary."

Well, she was entitled to her pride. It became her. But hearing herself say, "I'm sure you are. Still, if you ever want a letter, please ask me," as if she were smoothing things over for a discharged servant, Sabrina was embarrassed, and hurried onto something else. "I don't know if I'll see Mother this afternoon. If I don't, you can tell her the land business is settled. Compromised, at least. She gets twenty acres for a sort of nest egg, and the park gets a hundred. Oliver will develop the rest. Tell her it was the best I could do."

Helen crossed to the desk, jotted the figures on a pad, and picked up a letter. She said, "I've been thinking how I'd leave. I know I can't tell her ahead of time, so I'll slip out tomorrow night after she goes to bed. Could I ask you to give her this?"

She had turned scarlet. Something in that unduly hot flush, and something in her expression, angry and hard and triumphant all at once, made Sabrina suspicious. "May I?" she said, and slipped her finger tentatively under the unstuck edge of the flap. Helen's mouth opened as if she were going to protest. Then she shrugged.

The envelope contained a note, and folded inside it the check for three thousand dollars, neatly typed, attested by her mother's illegible scrawl of a signature. "Giving it back?" Sabrina said. "Why?"

Helen's eyes obviously meant to be proud, aloof, and unconcerned, but they did not quite manage it. A sidelong, bottled up anger flashed out of them; her cheeks still flamed. Again she shrugged. "Oh—it seemed the thing to do."

Sabrina shook the unopened note by the corner. "What did you tell her?"

"Read it, if you like," Helen said indifferently, but the look of pride and anger shot from her eyes again, and she smiled a little smile.

Sabrina watched her a moment—furious, obviously, and feeling wronged, and with cause. She bent her head and read.

Dear Mrs. Hutchens:

I told you I was engaged, and that was a lie. I am married. When I first came, I didn't dare tell Mr. Hutchens because I didn't think he would hire me if he thought I couldn't stay a long time, and I desperately wanted him to hire me. I wish I had not lied to you. Now my husband wants me to join him in Alaska right away, and I must go. I'm miserable that I have to go so suddenly. You will understand why under the circumstances I can't accept your very *very* generous gift. But thank you from the bottom of my heart anyway. And please forgive me for running this way—I couldn't stand to say goodbye. I shall remember and love you always.

Affectionately,
Helen

For a moment she stood, frowning down on her headache, watching the blood rush up again hot and scarlet in the girl's face. "*Are* you married?" she said.

"Yes."

"Long?"

"We've lived together three weeks altogether."

"What are you doing, working and saving for when he comes out?"

"He wants to be an orientalist. We want to live a while in Japan."

"All planned out," Sabrina said. Standing stiff, Helen did not answer; in a quick glance she probed for irony or contempt in Sabrina's face. But it was not irony or contempt that Sabrina was feeling. She could imagine how well planned that life would be, and how consciously worked for. She had seen Helen play tennis, as aggressive, efficient, and determined as if reputation and dollars hung on every point. And once again, as so frequently lately with the MacDonalds, she met head-on a wash of tired, sad envy, as clammy and chilling as a wall of fog. A girl like this one had her whole healthy mind aimed like a gun. Her wants were real and realizable, her goals immediate and practical, her satisfactions could be earned, and therefore solid. For one day, she must have been put on the high pink top of a cloud by that check. Right now, underneath her affectation of indifference, she must be wild with disappointment. But enviable. That anything should matter that much, and that she could give it up without a whimper.

"Giving it back couldn't have been easy to do," Sabrina said.

"He left me a nice pair of alternatives."

"Had you thought of speaking to Mother directly?"

"She's got enough troubles. Anyway, she has to go on living with him, he's her son. I'd only be a source of constant friction."

"Yes," Sabrina said. "I suppose you're right." She folded the check back into the note, put them in the envelope, and handed them back. The girl did not quite understand.

"Please. I hoped you'd give it to her, and maybe help . . . explain."

"I don't mind explaining, but I won't let you give the check back."

"She'd think I took it and ran out. And I tell you something, Mrs. Castro, I like her too well to have her think that. The money would have meant a lot to us, but I won't take it if she's going to think I'm a sneak."

"I can tell her all about it, so she can blame the right party."

"No," Helen said, "I thought of that. But she's too old now to learn how to face up to things. She's run from everything too long."

And that was both perceptive and charitable. In fact, everything about this girl was so correct, honorable, intelligent, and self-controlled that Sabrina felt herself veering like a changeable wind, and wishing she would not stand there so self-consciously noble. She thrust the envelope at her, and Helen put her hands behind her back.

"Take it, you fool," Sabrina said. "Write her another note and tell her your husband cut his toe or something, it's an emergency."

"I won't lie to her."

"You were just saying she *had* to be lied to. This note lies to her, doesn't it?"

"At least if I give the check back she can't think *that's* the reason."

"Take it," Sabrina said. "I'll see that she doesn't think badly of you. I'll even lie to her if necessary—I'm used to it. But she wanted you to have that money, and so do I.

"And you don't think . . ."

She took the check with her characteristic lack of fuss, almost as indifferently as she would have given it up. She had remarkably clear, steady eyes, and the look she gave Sabrina now was less guarded, friendlier, a searching, wide-eyed curious glance of the kind she had been throwing her way all summer. It occurred to Sabrina that perhaps what had been offered her, and what she had rejected until it was too late, was an admiring younger sister.

"All right, then," Helen said. "Shall I write another note?"

"I would. She'll give you up easier if she thinks it's an emergency. For a while at least she can even be led to assume you're coming back."

They looked at one another, rueful. Light from the window behind Helen put a halo of pale gold around the edges of her hair. She made a funny little hunching motion of her shoulders, a gesture of half-humorous renunciation.

Sabrina looked at her watch. "Oh, my Lord," she said, and with only a hasty word left Helen standing there with her check in her hand. Within a minute, hurrying to get ready for her appointment, she had forgotten her entirely.

CHAPTER 30

FROM THE DOORWAY Barbara took one look at Sabrina's face. "Oh," she said, "what's wrong?" Over her shoulder she yelled until she had shouted down the clamor from the girls' room. "*Yes, it's Sabrina.* But just the same you're not to get up for another fifteen minutes. You *hear?* I'll tell you when. You stay down."

Steering her heavy front, she led the way out into the patio and shut both halves of the dutch door. "What?" she said.

"Burke's divorcing me, is all." From the plastic chair where she had flopped, Sabrina stretched her legs out into the sun past the hard-edged shadow of the overhang. The face she turned up mocked itself.

"Oh, gee!" Barbara said ineffectually, and sank to the edge of a lounge and felt the released ache spread upward from her feet into her legs. She rubbed the veins in her calf. "Why is he?"

"Why? Why do you think?"

"But that was . . . I mean, I thought you were the one . . ."

"Yes, isn't it comical? I thought I was making up my mind, and all the time he was making up his. It's what's called seizing the initiative."

Stretched at ease with mockery on her mouth and a vertical cleft pinched between her eyes, she lit a cigarette and threw the match on the bricks. "I brought it to a head when I sent for my dog. Evidently that was the unforgivable straw that broke the camel's unbending back."

Her voice was stagily husky, she lidded her eyes against the smoke like Marlene Dietrich being contemptuously and lazily provocative.

Rubbing her calf, full of sick sympathy, "Tell me," Barbara said.

Sabrina flipped a letter across; it fell on the bricks and Barbara stooped thickly to reach it. For a moment she looked at Sabrina, morosely staring into the fence corner with her finger tap-tap-tapping on her cigarette, and then she bent her head and read. "Sincerely," Sabrina burst out, almost before she had finished. "Isn't that a passionate nature? Sincerely!"

"But . . . *didn't* you say anything about the two of you? Did you just say please send Fat Boy?"

With a jerk Sabrina sat up; her eyes came around in a glance of scorn. "If I'd said anything I'd have had to say whether or not I wanted to come back. I was even thinking I might go, two days ago, but I wasn't going to write that to him. He should have come to me."

"Hutchie," Barbara said, "didn't he come to you, twice?"

"Oh, sure. Each time full of phony Christian forgiveness. He didn't want me, he wanted the gratification of thinking well of himself." Her cigarette dropped to the bricks, she stepped on it with a flash of brown leg, fished another from her purse, lit it, flipped the match, tilted her great eyes sideward.

"I should think you'd want to see him, or call him, and try to work it out," Barbara said. "I think he cares about you very much."

Looking up into the little acacia tree, Sabrina bared her teeth. "One consolation, I'll have pried him away from his precious practice for six weeks."

"You don't mean that," Barbara said. Her hand continued to rub ruefully up and down the distended, aching veins. One more child and she'd be having an operation on those.

"Don't I?" Sabrina said indifferently.

"Really, I don't want to mess in your affairs, but I don't see why you couldn't have written him, or write him now. Unless Bernard meant more than you said."

A spasm of disgust passed over Sabrina's face. Tap, tap, tap went her finger on the ashless tube of the cigarette.

Helplessly Barbara said, "I wish I knew something to say except I'm sorry."

"Ah!" said Sabrina, galvanized into a stocking-footed prowl up and down the patio. "If you knew all of it you'd be sorrier, or else you'd laugh out loud." For a second she paused, her lower lip between her teeth, studying the pattern of the bricks. She walked four or five toe-to-heel steps along a crack and teetered there, her smooth, brown, strong, well-kept fingers working against her palm as if rubbing off something sticky. She seemed to grope in amused bewilderment for the right expression to wear, and then she toppled off her balancing of the crack, and laughed, and said, "In your condition you should have lullabies, not stupid stories. I'll tell you after you've had this baby."

"I won't have to wait long, then. He's absolutely kicking me to death."

Curiosity, a steady, squinted look. "Can you really feel him that hard?"

"Oh, every few minutes. Here, feel." She took Sabrina's wrist and held her hand against her belly. They could not quite look into each other's eyes as they waited. Then a thump, a flop, of that life getting restless to be born.

"Yes!" Sabrina breathed. "My Lord, he's like a fish on a line." She took her hand away; her lips were drawn squeamishly back from her teeth. Uncertainly, vaguely embarrassed, Barbara said, "Maybe you'd like a drink."

"God, yes, could I? Don't move, I'll get it. You want one?"

"I wish I could. When you've carried a baby this long you'll do anything to get rid of it, but nothing to hurt it."

From the doorway Sabrina turned back. Her eyes were wide, blue and bright as some bright mineral. Very softly she said, "How about earlier?"

It took a moment for Barbara to comprehend. The baby twitched again; she thought he turned clean over; her insides rolled with an inevitable, queasy weight. Squirming, still rubbing her aching leg, she stared at Sabrina, hot-eyed in the shadowed door. "Hutchie, you aren't . . . you haven't got caught."

Nodding left, nodding right, Sabrina for some reason put on a prissy smile. "Guaranteed. I just got the report on the rabbit blood test."

"Oh, you've *got* to go back to Burke!"

"Can you imagine him accepting a child that's not his?"

"Couldn't it be his?"

"No. I wasn't quite a good enough planner to create an ambiguity. I seem to have been too abrupt, or too honest, or something." She laughed in a way Barbara did not like, and flung her arms wide. "Isn't it a dandy? It beats *East Lynn* all hollow. If I'd found myself pregnant two months ago, after trying for twelve years, how would I have felt, eh? No more doldrums, something to do, Burke and I reunited, hearts and flowers. But I manage it otherwise. Instead of being a sort of wife without children, I arrange to be a sort of mother without a husband. Out into the storm with me. Never darken his door again. Can't you see me with my head in a shawl and my babe clutched to my breast?" She knocked her knuckles against the doorjamb and produced a short hoarse bark. "If I don't lose it. Which would you do, if you were I? Pray to keep it, or make sure to lose it?"

The air was ripped by shocking screams. Half to her feet, lurching, Barbara saw the girls jumping around Sabrina, who held them against her legs and directed over their heads a shaky, complicated look. Only one thing it said clearly: Don't scold them. "Ah, ducks," she said with a laughing catch of the breath, "you really got me that time!"

"I ought to dust you off with the fly-swatter, you little devils," Barbara said. Shock was still pumping in her blood, and she felt her belly for the muscles that had been strained when she leaped up. "See if you can do something nice for Sabrina instead of scaring her to death. Go fill the ice bucket for her." They went, noisy as sparrows, and quarreled over the refrigerator door.

"I gather you won't contest it," Barbara said.

Sabrina, biting thoughtfully on her knuckles, spit out a shred of skin

364

scuffed loose by her knocking on the doorjamb. "Oh, how could I? I'm on his side. It would be a pity for him to get saddled with me again. Such a dedicated and selfless man." She spread her hands against the sides of the door in an exaggeratedly cruciform pose. "I've bitched everything," she said with a sudden lapse from savagery to self-pity. "Just out of some . . . You know what I should do? I should sell do-it-yourself crucifixion sets, no fuss, no bother, if you can drive three nails you can operate it, no home is complete without . . ." Her brilliant eyes blinked rapidly, a laugh came throatily up through the words. "I'm like the anti-Semitic Jew in Germany," she said. "Remember him? He went around wearing a sign saying 'Down with Us.'"

Later, when the children had quit hanging around and gone rather brattishly to play down the street (they expect gifts, Barbara thought; every time she comes, they expect something; it *isn't* good for them), Sabrina said, "I don't know. I could go abroad and have it, I suppose. Or I could go away and get rid of it. Certainly I couldn't stay here. Mother, for one thing. And imagine sometime walking down a street in the City, all bulging, and meeting Bernard."

Barbara said curiously, "He doesn't mean a thing to you, now."

"When I got involved with him I was sick," Sabrina said. "Would you stay around somewhere where you'd stuck your finger down your throat?"

They were sitting in the patio again. The casual afternoon sounds of Greenwood Acres belled in the summer air. It was noisier with children than it would be in an hour, when the television programs came on. Barbara had set a sprinkler to going on the bank of shrubs in the corner of the fence, and a pair of linnets and a towhee were ruffling their feathers in the spray. A big dark oval of wet spread up the grapestake fence, the pittosporum leaves gleamed like varnished leather. It was very peaceful and neighborhood-y, and she did not like to think of Sabrina taking her trouble off to bear it alone, since it was hatred, and not love, that was fertile inside her. Once she would have thought it marvelous if she and Sabrina could be pregnant together, and compare notes, and help each other get ready, and have little

365

private jokes. Now it only made her sad. She said, "You wish the baby wasn't his."

"I haven't thought much about it. It shouldn't matter—it isn't the baby's fault."

"It might be hard to love a baby if you didn't love its father. Or maybe—I don't know."

"Maybe there won't be any baby anyway. I haven't demonstrated myself so fertile I can guarantee to pull it off the first time."

"Don't you sort of hope there is?"

Sabrina looked at her queerly. She was, thank goodness, much calmer. "That's your answer, is it? You'd try to keep it."

"I can't imagine not trying to." Barbara shivered a little, pleasurably, thinking of some secret office where a silent nurselike woman might let you in and get you ready, and a man whose face you would not want to see, somebody surgical and heartless and perhaps not even clean, would clean you out like taking the seeds out of a cantaloupe. Ugg. Thump and flop inside her. She said to herself fiercely, Don't be smug!

As if reading her mind, Sabrina said, *"God,* I envy you, Bobbie MacDonald! If this had happened right, do you think I wouldn't be delirious?"

Job's comforter, she could think of nothing but comforter's words, and Sabrina had never been one to love Pollyanna. Her way was to anticipate the worst and then treat the worst as beneath contempt. She went inside and fixed herself a third drink, and when she came back carrying bottle and ice bucket and glass, she said gloomily, "I always did envy you, you know. I don't understand why I ever liked you."

"Me?" Barbara said in her most comic squeak. She looked down at her swollen front and held out handfuls of her disordered hair.

"Even when we were little. You never wanted anything, you were so blasted unselfish, but you always got things anyway."

"Name one thing. Except maybe Leonard."

"That's a considerable exception," Sabrina said. Her mood had turned back to humorous savagery. "Mother's in love with him, did

I tell you? She positively twitters when he's around. We all do. Yesterday when he was quitting she felt worse than if somebody had taken away her diet or her exercises. . . . What?"

"I said we almost died when we opened Leonard's pay envelope. He called her up, thinking it was a mistake. It was the sweetest thing for her to do, we're going to put it in the bank for the baby."

"But Leonard isn't the only thing," Sabrina said, undiverted. "Ever since the very first summer I knew you, in that camp on Fallen Leaf Lake when we were eight or nine. Remember? Who worked like a fiend for four weeks to win the Good Camper Medal? And who did win it?"

"Oh, that was robbery!" Barbara cried. "You earned it twice over. I think I cried when they gave it to me, it was so unfair. I wanted you to win it."

"Yes, but I didn't. Remember?"

Remember? How could she forget that place, wanting her children to know it when they got a little older. It was a spot sweetly elegiac in her memory, a place all brown. She could see it simply by closing her eyes—even without closing her eyes, for it was there now, behind what her eyes were looking at, as if a color transparency had been twice exposed. Right before her Sabrina's face, the sharp sun and shade, the wet green of the fence corner with a fragment of rainbow afloat above it; and beyond those, wavering and faded, the nostalgic vision in sepia: brown shade, air as brown as tea, a brown grove pierced by a slant of sun that touched chestnut-colored on a sugar pine and sorrel on an incense cedar. And in this and through it, protectively colored, the brown tents and shingled cottages, and the little brown people like creatures hatched out from under toadstools on the brown forest floor.

Sabrina was looking at her through a brown glass. She said, "After a quarter of a century I can still tell you exactly how I did in that competition. I got ten points for winning the swimming race, and eight when you and I came in third in girls' canoeing—"

"If you'd had a decent partner you'd have won it."

"And I got nine for my natural-history collection. That really made

367

me mad, I had more tree funguses and salamanders and cones and pressed leaves and flowers than anybody, but because it wasn't put up neatly they only gave me second. And I got seven points in the fishing contest." She turned her lips inside out. "And *four* for neatness and bed making."

Barbara giggled, rather surprised that the brown leg in the chair six feet away did not have a Band-Aid on it somewhere. Sabrina had always loved the visible evidence of wounds. And the face that looked at her amusedly over the glass could be made with only a slight narrowing of the eyes into that other face, just as vivid, thinner, more eager, not less proud and scornful, with its camp pigtails so tight that the eyes were pulled Chinese. The demon camper. She had bossed their tent like an Irish foreman, everyone had been afraid of her will. And being her best friend had been a distinction next door to beatitude.

She giggled again. "Remember the flies?"

"Ah," said Sabrina, "there was nobody even close on flies. I wonder what brain thought up that idea for a competition? Probably the idea was to teach us how to avoid typhoid and filth diseases, mmm? So I sit in the tent every spare minute with a nice wet newly licked sucker and catch flies on it, and when it dries out I lick it sticky again. I had whole envelopes full of flies all stuck together. And I stood over that Miriam Hodge like a polls inspector when she counted them."

The giggles came as irresistible as hiccups; as soon as they got control of themselves their eyes met and they burst out again. Barbara, wiping away tears, supposed that there must be some alcohol in Sabrina's amusement, and some relief in her own. Yet the very thought of that intense little girl sitting idol-still in the brown tent with her fly-trap sucker clenched in her fist made her explode all over again. Sabrina, just taking a sip of her drink, blew spray and bent over groping for a handkerchief.

"Mosquitoes!" she said. "I won hands down on mosquitoes too."

"Yes, and I never understood how. I swatted every skeeter I saw, but you had millions more than me."

"Mosquitoes don't raise welts on me," Sabrina said. "I had a real ingenious idea there. I turned myself into bait. Remember the swamp down by the mouth of the creek? Three or four mornings I went down there before anybody was up—"

"Oh, that was cheating!"

"Cheating, nothing. I sat there in the cold, chattering my teeth out, and let mosquitoes settle down and sink their stingers into me so deep they couldn't get away, and then I swatted them ten at a time and picked their corpses off into my little envelope. Cheating my eye, I earned those mosquitoes."

Barbara was pressing both hands against her stomach, holding it in and gasping for air. But something odd happened. One minute they were in a giggling fit, both of them wet-eyed, crying, "Remember? Remember?" and the next there was Sabrina back in her ironic, challenging temper, saying, "And *still* they gave it to you. Still you beat me. You stayed up close on measly little points for neatness and tooth-brushing and tent-sweeping and deportment. . . ."

"They over-rated all of those. You should have won it."

Sabrina was sliding her upper lip along the edge of the glass. "You know what won it for you. I was so full of envy and hatred I could have drowned you. You won it because when we were all going on that overnight hike up to Desolation Valley, and old stupid Sally Stearns got sick, you volunteered to stay home with her."

"Did I volunteer? I don't remember."

"Of course you volunteered, and of course you remember. I'd never heard of anything so stupid. Everybody in that whole camp thought she was the dopiest thing alive, she had three left feet, she couldn't do *anything*. So you give up that marvelous overnight and stay in camp and read *Little Women* to her, or something."

"She cried, she wanted to go so. I suppose I felt sorry for her."

"I suppose you did. I suppose none of the rest of us did, one bit. She could have had cholera and I'd have cheered. But if I'd known there'd be *points* for it, I'd have been Florence Nightingale. I was going to use that hike to comb the mountain for more natural-history specimens and cinch ten points. So you feel sorry for old

Stearns and stay home with her and in the end they give you ten *extra* points for unselfishness above and beyond the call of duty, and you win the Good Camper Medal."

She laughed through her nose into the hollow glass, set the glass aside, stood up, took a handful of Barbara's hair and twisted it hard, and harder. "And should have," she said. "They were quite right. You always did know how to love people." On Barbara's upturned, protesting face she dropped a grimacing smile, and twisted the handful of hair another turn. "It looks as if I could use some of your knack." The grimace widened. "Down with us!" she said, and dropped the hair and went on in to the bathroom.

Later the children came home, with three others in their wake, all of them dressed up in suits and dresses and with vast adult shoes tied on their feet. Sabrina was enormously surprised when they revealed who they were. She found some candy in her car and distributed it (Oh, *no*, Sabrina, Barbara felt like crying. Not right before dinner!) and they tottered and strode off again, headed for television at a neighbor's house.

"Look at them," Sabrina said a little thickly. "That's the real pleasure of childhood, you can be anybody you want to. You can be Mama just by wading around in high-heeled shoes, and Papa by snipping a mustache off the dust mop. When you grow up you get stuck with yourself."

The bottle, which had been nearly full, was down to the halfway mark, but she did not seem drunk—only talkative, and intent on drawing self-destructive morals from reminiscence. Barbara sat uncomfortably, moving when she was kicked hard enough; she did not feel especially well, but she would not lie down as long as Sabrina was upset and needing to talk.

"I mean, childhood's wonderful for *children,* it's wonderful to have the capacity to be anybody, so long as you know very well you're you. But suppose you grow up scared you may not be anybody, or are somebody it's disgraceful to be. Mmmm? Leonard and I were looking over Uncle Mercer the other day. He had that kind of no-identity nightmare all his life, and he never married or had anybody to reassure him he really *was* anybody. You know what's the danger of having money? It makes you too free."

"That ought to be good."

"There isn't anything worse. Trying to be human in an atmosphere of absolutely free choice is like trying to sharpen an ax on a cake of soap."

She rocked a little. By her eyes she was not yet at the stage when argument became a whip in her hand, and she went flogging you around in circles with a mixture of logic and paradox, but she was on the way. Barbara, shifting for the hundredth time that afternoon, would have given a good deal for a drink herself. She wished Leonard would get back.

"We're a wild species," Sabrina said. "Darwin said that. I was reading him up in old Charlie Grulich's doghouse. Nobody ever tamed us or bred the wildness out of us. And we evolved in an atmosphere of Necessity, do you see, with just enough blind chance to keep us awake and enough free will to keep us encouraged. Take away Necessity and we begin to huddle and squeak and run off at all angles. I'll tell you what Original Sin amounted to. The Greeks invented it, not the Jews. We began to control our environment, and we lost Necessity. Once you lose that you aren't innocent any more, you're only responsible—guilty and responsible. Do you believe that?"

"If you say so."

"I say so. We used to be able to blame something outside ourselves, God or luck or fate or circumstances, when things went sour. But everything that happens to somebody like me is probably her own fault, and did you ever think what that means? When there's only yourself to blame, all alone out there?"

"You didn't choose your genes, did you?"

"I've been prowling in that alley. Leonard even said Mercer looked like me, and I hoped for a minute I had inherited all this. But Mercer never did anything like what I do, he just went around looking, he stayed a haunted child. He was like all the other Wolcotts, his trouble was that there was no purpose or climax or catastrophe in his life. That's not my trouble. I know who I am, and who's responsible."

"Oh, Sabrina, let yourself up! You haven't done anything but make a painful mistake. You're not envious, or evil, you're the most—"

"I'm the most," Sabrina interrupted. In her eyes the tiny capillaries had begun to be engorged with blood; her eyeballs had a reddish shine. Red-eyed, she went hunting among her self-destructive ideas with a feral eagerness, and she would have no comforts. "Since we're on the fascinating subject of me, let me tell you what I am. Did you ever have the feeling that your thoughts were absolutely vile, a regular witches' brew? Did you ever feel like committing some awful crime— not just one of those unmotivated literary murders, but something really monstrous? I wonder what it would feel like to be somebody the whole human race shrank from? Maybe that ghoul in Wisconsin who dressed out his murdered women like beeves and hung them by the heels in his shed?"

"For heaven's sake!"

"How about cannibalism?" Sabrina said, and fixed on her a brilliant, baleful glance. "Does it tempt you? I've heard people—especially women—say they'd eat human flesh if they had to to stay alive, one of those Donner Party situations. I always wondered if I would. But I can imagine myself eating human flesh just to be horrible."

"You know what you'd do?" Barbara said, and stirred half in anger. "You'd be the one in the lifeboat who volunteered to be eaten."

Sabrina, suspending her harangue while she examined the notion, threw upward into the little acacia one of her patented smiles. For a moment she was youthful, unmarked, untroubled, as fresh and perfect as a leaf just formed, hardly dry; and she shook like such a leaf in a ripple of—what was it? Delight? Pure pleasure? It was what Barbara had always, a little awed, worshiped in her. She could sometimes give you the sense of pure blissful *being,* without a care. Then the smile went askew, the mockery showed under it. "The idea has its attractiveness, at that," she said. "But it isn't horrible enough. No, I'll tell you what I'm like. You remember a psychopathic gray kitten that wandered into the grounds once? The cook and I tried to catch and pet her, but we never laid a hand on her. She'd sneak back after we were gone and eat what we put out. I *anguished* over that damned animal; it was a personal insult that she wouldn't let me pet her. She was around a long time, and when she grew up and got in heat and groveled on the ground the way they do, I called the vet in a panic, I thought she was dying. Then later it began to be plain she was going to have kittens. See how it all fits?"

"You're absolutely crazy," Barbara said, not amused.

"I fixed her a box down in the greenhouse," Sabrina said. "Would she use it? Not she. She had her kittens in the woods somewhere like the wild animal she was. Then I kept hunting *them* so I could tame them, but she'd hidden them too well."

Her eyes never left Barbara's face while she fumbled an ice cube out of the plastic bucket and reached to tilt whisky into her glass. "One day I saw her eating something down by the cutting garden. She ran off, but I found what it was. Know what? One of her kittens, with the head chewed off."

Barbara felt a stir of weariness and exasperation and a squeamish qualm of revulsion, and because her feeling seemed a disloyalty, she made an exaggerated comic face. "Yik," she said. "Sabrina, what a story."

Musing, Sabrina took her fingers from her glass and examined the wet prints they had left. "I had nightmares for a week," she said. "I kept seeing that filthy beast crouched over her kitten, gnawing on bone with her head turned sideways. So I had one of the gardeners catch her in a net and take her to the animal shelter to be chloroformed. Then for a while I kept hoping a kitten or two would show up, looking for food, but none ever did. I guess she'd gnawed *all* their heads off."

"And this is you," Barbara said, beginning to smile. "This cat."

"You're not supposed to smile. You're supposed to grit your teeth and look at me with loathing. Because God knows I *am* that cat. The cat that sits behind Judas at Last Suppers, that's me."

At least there was a prospect of relief in the very violence of her exaggerations. Sooner or later she would make herself laugh. So Barbara cracked her own face with smiling until she forced out on Sabrina's a response of humorous disgust. "All right, Chessy Cat. The loathsome is always laughable, I suppose. What got us started talking about me? Let's talk about you. Are you comfortable?"

"Not one little bit."

"Can I do anything?"

"I wouldn't trust you."

"You're right. Isn't it about time for Leonard? How about me starting dinner? Tell me what you're having and I'll put it on and get out of here."

"Oh, please, you're going to stay, aren't you?"

"You don't want me around every night."

Barbara winced and held still, pressing both hands against the violence in her body. She felt blown up like an inner tube about to burst. All afternoon she had had trouble breathing. When she came out of her brief self-absorption and caught Sabrina watching her with reddened eyes, she made a face and said, "Excuse me, I seem to have a visitor. Of course we want you to stay. Tonight especially."

"All right," Sabrina said. "At least we can celebrate the end of the period of indecision. And you know what else I'm going to do? While you're in the hospital I'm coming down here and cook meals and look after the children."

"Oh, Leonard's a good cook, and he won't be working."

"What can he cook? Spaghetti? I'll bet he can't even boil frozen vegetables. No, I want to help. I won't eat the heads off your children, it isn't horrible enough. It's only my own I'd eat the heads off."

"Don't," Barbara said without smiling. It was an effort not to show how much that kind of talk upset her; she was feeling worse by the minute, and her face could not be forced through all the expressions of sympathy and agreement that Sabrina wanted. And the girls would be back any time, and she could hardly bear the thought of their noise. Heavily she put a hand on the arm of her chair and heaved upward.

Aghast, she stared at Sabrina, her body frozen, half forward out of the chair. The warm wet spread beneath her like a shameful childhood dream. She heard Sabrina say, "What is it? What's the matter?"

With the realization that there was no pain, the paralysis left her body, but the fear remained. Swift and sharp she twisted to look under herself and saw with inexpressible relief that it was not red. But then she felt shame rising up her neck and face, and she said, "I'm all wet. It's all right, I guess—it isn't blood. I'm just . . . Oh, my goodness, isn't physiology a messy, dreadful. . . . I'm ashamed, Sabrina."

Sabrina had stooped and put her drink down. Sharply, with an edge like anger in her voice, she said, "Who's your doctor, Pendleton? What's his number?"

Before Barbara could answer, or get out of her shameful chair and go to the bathroom, the front door opened. "Leonard," she heard Sabrina say, "what's the doctor's number?"

Instantly he was outside and bending over her, and she managed a shamefaced smile. "It isn't anything. I'm just incontinent, I guess. Isn't that awful?"

A look of quick question and answer, anxiety and corroboration, passed between him and Sabrina. "Poo," Barbara began, "don't *worry* about it!" But Sabrina said, "It could be the water sac. If it is, they'll want to bring on the birth. I think you'd better call."

He pushed Barbara down as she floundered to rise. "Don't you move," he said, and kissed the top of her head. "Stay where you at." His cleats squeaked on the asphalt tile inside. Sabrina, her eyes glittering, picked up her drink. "Is your bag packed?" she said, almost gaily. "And if I sit with your children till Leonard gets back do I get ten points?"

CHAPTER 31

Leaving the hospital grounds, Leonard opened the car window. Fagged and wrung by the labor of male childbirth, he drove with the night air cold as ether on his arm and face. When you had three children the novelty should have worn off, and yet his mind moved on tiptoe, oppressed with the wonder and indignity of what it meant to be born. To be repudiated into separateness by the mother flesh, or else to be dragged as this one had been, headfirst or butt-first or by the foot or with a doctor's thumb hooked in your jaw, onto an operating table smoking with light, and there, helpless and bloody, wrinkled, sightless, still voiceless, to be caught up in rubber-gloved hands, dangled by the heels, slapped, snipped, circumcised, washed, tagged. A patch on the navel, a slosh of silver nitrate against the possibility of your parents' indiscretions, a diaper against the certainty of your own, then a blanket, a nurse's nylon arm, and out you went one way, on the road to becoming one of the world's three billion identities, while your twilight-sleeping former home, your dark warm wounded refuge, was wheeled out another. By that time you had learned to bawl.

It was nearly three in the morning, and for a minute or two, perhaps the only such interval in the whole twenty-four hours, El Camino lay wide, straight, utterly empty, blinking its amber signal lights. Not a parked car, not a pedestrian or drunk or policeman, not a prowling cat, not even a statue or a monument, broke the perspective-exercise of white-marked lanes. El Camino lay like a road excavated from under the rubble of centuries, like a thoroughfare in which the automatic signals had outlasted humanity and its traffic, and gone on endlessly blinking into the blind ashes, and been dug up still blinking. It was a street that powerfully suggested questions of direction and destination —and what was one man alone doing on this reach of asphalt made for the wheeled millions? He glanced in the rear-view mirror, hopeful of lights behind him. A yellow blink, and a half mile farther back, another, and that was all. Along both sides of the royal highway, across empty sidewalks and entrances into which the wind had stirred overnight accumulations of paper and dust, the bright store fronts grinned their skull's grin.

At such an hour, on such a street, a man walking home alone, not drunk enough or sleepy enough, or merely full of night-sadness and night-loneliness, might see himself strange as a vampire or pitiable as a lost child. The sound of his own heels on man-made adamant could start his heart pounding. The thought of a barren room, an unshared bed, could bring him to a stop to knock his head in desolation against some wall.

Into this, like hunters who lead a pup to the mouth of a bear's cave and tell him "Sic 'em!" he and Bobbie had just brought forth seven-odd pounds of human consequences, the product of their joint effort to escape the inescapable. Each alone was only a self, and a self was the most desperate of all things to be. It might be flattered by accomplishment and praise, anaesthetized by play or by one of the opiums, tranquilized by friendship, transcended after a fashion in art or religion; but unless you were lucky enough to be an artist or scared enough to accept one of the organized religions, there was not even a partial or temporary cure for yourself except biological love and the tenderness, the gratitude, the willingness to suffer for and with, that at its best accompanied it.

Bromides, banalities that it would have embarrassed him to say to anyone. And yet they moved him. Back in the hospital, in the beginning

377

of another identity, was the start of another hopeless search for what was lost when love's growing-together was parted again. Driving up empty El Camino through the blink of warning lights, Leonard thought, There's nothing higher than this, this is as human as you ever get.

He heard the sound of an irregularly worn tire: wheels out of balance again. And the old Chevvy was throwing more and more oil. After ten minutes she smelled like the pit at a motor track. Well, onward and upward, one thing at a time. God bless Mrs. Hutchens and her bonus. Once, in his prickly youth, he would probably have refused it. With a wife and three children, and maybe a little sense, and definitely some friendliness for the giver, he would do nothing of the kind. Bobbie and this baby were as good a cause as any of her other charities. He must call her tomorrow and announce the arrival of a son.

It seemed that the world would go on, patched with string and baling wire and visited occasionally by fairy godmothers. One job finished the other day. Coming up, all that business of night shifts, formulas, bottle heaters, colic, gas. Pretty soon the first staff meeting; pretty soon after, themes on every chair and bookcase. In the midst of it Barbara, safe and serene as one of those Chinese junks that ducklings were supposed to crawl up onto in the evening.

Slightly slowing for a yellow blink, he saw in his mind the little waif, hurt in being born, being brought to Bobbie for the first time and laid beside her warmth that was radiant without being thermostatically controlled, and how the gown would be opened and he would find a little consolation for the outrages that identity had brought him.

Man, Leonard said, translating himself into the vernacular, it's a rat race.

He climbed out beside the gray convertible in his driveway and stood looking at it with respect but without envy. It had been left with its top carelessly down; his finger, swept along the top of a seat, left a streak of wet. Well, he should worry. He supposed that people like himself should be grateful to anyone who did his duty by the American standard of living and consumed at least one new car each year. If it were not for those stalwarts, how could the economy go on cantilevering itself out over empty space? Sabrina, who said she hated being a consumer, did pretty well at it. She should get a big gold star, Heroine of the American Way of Life; Heroine of the AWOL.

A late moon was resting on the eaves of the house next door. Silvery light fell like an invisible sediment on roofs, the neat lawn of his neighbor Sloan, his own ragged ground-cover of beach strawberry. (Sloan, not so delicately hinting, had offered to pitch in and help, some Saturday, when Leonard got ready to plant his own lawn.) He stood looking, and some tick of Time went past—a moment or a thousand years—and he squeezed his tired eyes shut and looked again, and the night hung silent around him, the invisible silver was still falling, the moon was already lower on Sloan's flat roof.

Quietly he went around the carport. The entrance was dark, but the long narrow window beside the fireplace shed a yellowish dusk along the walkstones. Still up, debating her dilemmas, beating her breast, plucking her crazy flower petals eenie meenie minie moe; still running around like a child in a snowstorm grabbing for flakes and crying when they melted in her hands. And blaming herself furiously all the time and doing her best to live up to her own bad opinion of herself. Poor Sabrina. With every possible advantage and every privilege that a most privileged life could give her, she managed to make everything come out wrong, or persuaded herself that she did. There should be a permanent stool for her down at Packy's Park Inn, where the disinherited, disgruntled, and disenchanted sat all night nursing coffee mugs and keeping a desultory conversation alive with the barman.

He walked the zigzag stones and laid a hand on the doorknob, but drew it back. She might be asleep on the sofa. He couldn't exactly walk in on her in her shift; on the other hand he would look silly ringing his own doorbell. If she were a high-school girl baby-sitting, he assured himself, he would walk on in; nevertheless he did not want to now. So he tapped lightly on the door and at once squatted down, yanked up his coat collar, hunched his head between his shoulders, twisted his face upward, and began to twitter and scratch.

The door opened, her eyes jerked downward, she stepped back with a yelp. He hopped around, a thirty-inch dwarf, scratching himself on the chest and mewing. "You ass," she said, "I ought to kick you."

Leonard stood up and stretched and yawned and edged inside. In the pantomime of his entrance he got a good look at her: stocking-footed, rumpled, her eyes what his mother had used to describe as "two burnt holes in a blanket." And not sober, a good way from sober. He said, "Kicking permits issued only on Saturdays, one to a customer."

"You're pretty sassy," she said as she closed the door. "Is everything all right? I know it's a boy, because I called—and what happened to the call *you* were going to make? I waited two hundred years, in here with your blank windows staring at me. Why don't you get some drapes so all the owls and bats can't look in? How *is* Bobbie? It seemed to go on forever, and they'll never tell you anything. I called three times before they'd even give me that 'mother and child doing well' routine. Is she all right?"

Without waiting for an answer she slid down the bare asphalt tile of the hall and closed the door of the girls' room. Her eyes as she came back looked enormous and too light for her face. And what was there about her that always made it difficult to talk to her? She was a Halloween cat with her hair on end; invariably she got him sparring and assuming a Big Kidder pose.

He said, "Did you ever try to borrow a telephone dime in a maternity ward at one or two in the morning? Besides, they had to give me twilight sleep and three transfusions for my couvade. Drapes we don't have because we don't care who looks in, owls or bats or whoever. Our family life is an open book, banned in Boston. But yes, in reply to your question. Everything seems to be okay. For a while there it wasn't. The baby got hurt some, and Bobbie had a hell of a time."

He saw their figures coming side by side around the bookcase and moving toward the black plate glass, and outside in the patio the fat yellow shape of the plastic wading pool Sabrina had brought the girls one day. It had never before occurred to him that those un-draped windows were unpleasant, but he supposed that if you were jumpy you would imagine all sorts of eyes. And she had been there a long time.

"I was afraid of that dry birth," she said.

"*And* breech. A fine traumatic entrance." Suddenly tired to death, he sprawled down on the sofa, and blowing out his breath he said seriously, "I'm sorry about the call. At first I was too busy holding her hand." He held his own hand in front of his face and flexed it, remembering the bird-clutch of her fingers, the wet forehead and clouded eyes: she hadn't been able to see him half the time, she had just hung on. Then he looked up under his eyebrows and saw Sabrina watching him with her lips drawn back in the expression of a child who sees a fearful bug. Imagining herself having a child? He said, "After they took her to the delivery room I was in too much of a sweat to think of anything else. It wasn't very decent of me. I'm sorry."

Used up as she was, haggard with highballs and lack of sleep and all her self-induced anxieties, she could still be transformed into something extraordinarily attractive by the lifting of a few small muscles of the face. The smile lasted only a second or two; then she raised her hands and began pushing backward with her fingertips against her temples, smoothing out what might have been a headache or might have been only nerves and muscles knotted with strain. Her fingertips moved in circles, and at each movement her eyes were elongated, and just at the moment when they were most slitted, the exposed whites glittered. Then the rubbing fingers brought the eyes back to their normal shape, and instead of a Halloween cat with slit pupils and greenish light-reflecting eyeballs there was Sabrina Castro looking softer than usual, tired, intent, almost tender. Her lifted arms tightened the yellow dress across her breast. She was very well made; her round upper arms were evenly tanned; she gave the impression, in spite of her haggard eyes, of indestructible health. Then the rotating fingers drew the skin backward, the narrowed eyes glittered at him.

Still with her fingertips pressed against her temples, she said, "I haven't congratulated you. Which I do. The father of three." She laughed and dropped her hands. "But next time I'll send along a roll of dimes, and if you don't call once an hour I'll eat your children."

"A werewolf." He yawned and cracked his jaw. His legs were ticking away their tension the way an over-driven car ticks away its heat. "Did they behave? Or *did* you eat them?"

"Not this time. They're angels, as you bloody well know. I suppose the new one will be another of the same, and be a monster of virtue and beauty, and graduate top of his class."

"It's me genes," Leonard mumbled. "Best damn genes in San Mateo County." To evade her eyes, he inspected the sole of his shoe and removed something fictitious from between the cleats. He wondered if she meant to stay on the rest of the night, and if he would have the character, eventually, to point out that he needed some sleep even if she didn't. By going to bed right now he might manage at most four hours. Not with joy, he heard her say, "You need a drink. We have to toast this heir."

Unwillingly he stood, saying, "Let me . . . if we've got any." But she had already slid stocking-footed into the kitchen. Through the pass-through, ducking so he saw her white-ringed eyes and the part in her dark hair, she said, "When I'd put the girls to bed and been alone one half hour in that glass cage I took the liberty of having some delivered."

Promptly Leonard reached for his wallet, remembering too late that it contained nothing but two one-dollar bills and Mrs. Hutchens' thousand-dollar check. He sat holding it, feeling foolish, while Sabrina cracked ice out of a tray. "Put it away," she said, stooping. "I was the one who sat here all afternoon and drank up everything you had in the house."

"And then sat here with the kids while we took off to the hospital. At least we ought to provide the baby-sitter's whisky. All the best houses do."

"Let the sitter buy this one." A soda bottle fizzed open. She came carrying two glasses. "To parenthood."

"Ah, parenthood!" Their eyes touched in a glint of meaning. He supposed she would know that he knew about her—you could cover a lot of conversational ground between labor pains. He drank. The drink was cold, smooth, faintly rusty-sour; he felt it all the way down like the silvery tube of a thermometer with a bulb at the bottom. Lowering his glass, he said, "That is not a MacDonald-type whisky. That one has been cooled a long age in the deep-delvèd earth."

Sabrina had sat down and sprawled out her stockinged feet. Her head rolled against the back of the chair as she canted it to look at him with incredulous mockery on her mouth. "A quotation for every occasion."

"Break, break, break," Leonard said, a little annoyed.

"Do you memorize all these little phrases, or do they just stick to you?"

"You've heard of the human fly. I'm the human flypaper."

"I wonder if I ever knew anybody who so loved his wife and little ones, and his job, and was so full of little capsules of wisdom and poetry to be taken like vitamins. Don't you ever sit around like other mortals, and stare at your wretched image in the glass, and devour your own liver?"

He sipped his drink, he furrowed his brow. Inanely, shadow-boxing, he said, "Liver? I thought you only ate babies."

"The liver is for iron. God forbid I should be an anemic werewolf."

He agreed that an anemic werewolf would be an abomination.

Violently unladylike in her posture, her hair loosened and beginning to sag from its smooth coil, her expression theatrically grim, she looked at once as vivid and as ominous as a lit fuse. "Answer the question."

"Was that a question? I thought it was an assertion."

"It was both."

"What is it you want to know?"

With an exclamation she sat up straight. "How do you manage to be so damned satisfied with yourself?"

Softly he said, "I kind of like being alive, if that's what you mean."

"I hate to see people I like sink into this middle-class quicksand and never send up even a bubble."

Leonard studied the palm of his hand, telling himself that this was Bobbie's oldest friend, that she was in a disturbed state, and that she had always, in her way, been helpful and generous. But he could not keep his voice from going brittle. "What is it I'm supposed to want? To improve myself, as they call it? Take a Ph.D. and get a university job and publish articles in the PMLA?"

"At least that would be better than being stuck in high school."

"Maybe I'm doing more good where I am."

"While you stagnate."

"I read books," he said. "I listen to music. I have some friends. I find out something new every now and then."

"I do you the honor to respect your brains. I think you could do something, if you'd try."

He almost laughed, the phrase was so exactly what he might have said about her, but he had not lost his irritation at being attacked senselessly at the crack of dawn. "What'll you have?" he said. "Poetry? Music? Architecture? Is that it, art? I'll tell you a secret. You need a talent and a conviction, you make art out of what is a gift or a curse, or both. I do what I can do. I try to help keep the world half-way livable. If science was my racket I'd be red-hot to retrack the moon or find some smaller particle or a deeper sea bottom, and then you'd say I was doing something, probably. But literature's my racket—the tradition, human wisdom, all that. These days, my job is nearly all conservative. I want to keep reminding myself and my captive audience what it means to be human."

"You're so ambitious," she said.

"Yeah!" he said, and he was really angry now. "So maybe I'll teach everybody to be as fat-headedly satisfied as I am, assuming I am. So art dies out of the world because nobody's tormented enough to produce it any more. All right, I'd buy that too. But don't worry about me being that successful. I guess we can depend on the torment. Meantime I do what I can do, not what I know I can't."

As he talked her face had gone perceptibly slacker; a line sagged from the corner of her mouth down toward her jaw. Apparently she had been attacking him without reason and was not listening to his huffy replies. Her eyes were vague and unfocused. Something warned him, Walk soft. "Of course," she said indifferently, "it's none of my business."

"When it comes to that, you're quite right, but since we're talking about beliefs, I'll tell you what I believe in. I believe in human love and human kindness and human responsibility, and that's just about all I believe in. Old T. S. Eliot talking down his high-church nose at the decent godless people! I'll accept the godless if I can manage to be decent. I don't want any liver. I just want to try to touch little matches to little bunches of human kindling. The political revolutions will blow us all up at last, probably, but I'm not working for any. The only revolution that interests me is one that will give more people more comprehension of their human possibilities and their human obligations."

Vagueness remained in her half-averted face. Trying to challenge her eyes, he had the impression that even the vagueness might be artificial and acted. Her eyes moved until she was looking at herself in the reflecting window. She said, "Oh, Leonard MacDonald!"

Abruptly she jumped up. Retreating into his drink as into a hole, he watched her move around the room. She picked a thread from the rough fireplace bricks and dropped it in the grate, and spinning around upon him she said, "You knew my husband is divorcing me."

"Bobbie told me. I'm sorry."

"You shouldn't be. He's entirely right."

"Even if he was, I'd still be sorry. And I never saw anybody entirely right."

Turning quickly, she slopped her drink, and as she stooped to mop it up with a paper napkin she turned sideward at him a face that was strained, venomous, and old. She said, "It's Bobbie's fond belief that I've been having a sort of rebellious fling and sooner or later will go home and patch things up."

"Are you sure she isn't right?"

"What I've been having isn't a fling."

Because she demanded it, he had to ask, "What is it, then?"

"It's a disintegration."

"Oh, come on!"

"You think not?" The way she turned in her stockinged feet and went into the kitchen made him remember that in the days when she had intensely pursued painting and literature she had also taken a turn at modern dance. She moved like Katherine Dunham or somebody—but he wondered if Katherine Dunham moved like that when she was offstage. Dangling his glass between his knees, thinking unhappily about what time it was, he heard her pour another drink.

"Listen!" she said, "if this is a fling, I'm tired of it. You know what I did about ten o'clock tonight? I picked up the telephone to call Pasadena. And I couldn't make myself do it, it would have been too dirty and unfair."

"Maybe he wouldn't have thought so."

As if he had brushed a switch and set loose a horrible blast of amplified sound, she went into a high, scratchy shout of laughter, looked at him where he sat uncomfortably nursing his drink, caught her breath, and was off again. It was like some play whose action has led toward a confrontation or revelation, and the revelation comes to the accompaniment of maniacal mirth, hysterically catching and pouring out again, screech after screech, with omens of disaster and breakdown in it, peal on peal convulsing some rocking character as the curtain comes down; and after the curtain you hear it still there, not so much stopping as running down gradually from lack of wind and strength, dying out into dark sobbing before the house lights come up. But here there was neither curtain nor houselights, and he could only wait, studying the ice cubes in his drink, until she got over it. And oh, God, it was nearing four in the morning, and the girls would be awake at six.

Abruptly the laughter was over. She said intensely, "He thinks so. I'm a horror to him."

Collared by a confessional or weepy drunk at a party, you could spot someone you knew, or have to go to the can. Here there was nothing to do but sit smiling and let her bend his ear, the weariness and boredom of listening complicated by an honest liking for the fool woman. There was a good deal to her, if she could ever quit being the leading lady in her own melodrama. She challenged life to be worse than she anticipated, or treat her as badly as she deserved; and if she kept it up she would harass and higgle it into being and doing just that.

"Why shouldn't I be a horror to him?" she was saying now. "Name me a deadly sin I'm not riddled with. Pride? I'd have cut my throat before I'd go back begging. What are the others? Lechery? Well what do you think?"

"I don't think anything."

"No, you'd be in your neutral corner smiling your middling smile. What *are* the others? Wrath? My God, I'm always furious about something. Envy? Don't I envy you two your grubby self-satisfied little life till I'm burning alive with it? Avarice? Gluttony? Well, I don't know. . . ."

"The verdict is for acquittal. On those charges there is no evidence."

She gave him an oblique, wandering look. The burst of argumentative heat had already passed; she looked depressed, sick, dead on her feet. Vaguely she said, "There's another, that's only six," and slapped a hand at the air. "Anyway. Whatever it is, I've got it."

"Who hasn't?" Leonard said.

"Not as much as I have."

"Well, it's a funny thing to be vain about, but if you insist."

For a second the silence of the house was all around them; her assertive specter mimed and postured over his submissive one in the obsidian window, and remembering placid Barbara and the new wounded identity in the hospital, he felt a compassion for all fouled-up or suffering humanity, and especially for this frantic woman threshing like a moth in a web and steadily spinning out of her entrails longer and longer filaments to entangle herself. There was something pathetic and generous in the way she always managed to deceive herself to her own disadvantage. And she knew a good deal about herself without being able to forgive herself for it; so she went around demanding forgiveness of others, or else forcing them to listen to her running herself down.

"Sabrina," he said, "why didn't you pick up that telephone? I think it would have worked."

She was incandescent, she came up like a flame turned suddenly high. "Yes?" she said huskily. Her eyes, which had seemed too light for her face when he came in, seemed now very dark, a deep, somber, sulky midnight blue. "Yes? Well let me tell you. A half hour after I almost called him, he called Mother's, and Lizardo directed him over here."

"So you did talk to him."

"I did," she said with an insolent upward flash of eyes, "And it *didn't* work."

"But he wanted it to? I mean, he called wanting to patch it up?"

"Yes, that's what he said."

"And you'd been going to call him up with the same glad word."

"Yes."

"So you both wanted to heal it. Why didn't you? Did you knock yourself to him somehow? Show him your sores? Insist on your wickedness?"

Her shout of laughter went up again, short this time, a sardonic convulsion that spent itself in a single bark. "Marvelous!" she said. "You do have a sharp eye, don't you? No, we were just honest with each other. He told me he'd been thinking it over, and felt he had to make one more try. So I told him *I'd* been thinking too, and was about ready to come back, but he should know I was pregnant and the child wasn't his."

"Just like that, right in his teeth."

"I had to be honest," she said resentfully.

Under Leonard's foot the asphalt tile was sticky with something. He tried it several times, pressing his cleats down and pulling them tackily away. A vast, irresistible yawn rose up from his deeps and pried at his mouth till his jaws ached and tears popped into his eyes. Honest? Yes, in a way. But challenging, too, probably. He could imagine the tone in which she would have said that: "I'm pregnant. It isn't yours." Straight at his head like a beanball, brushing him back before he could get set. Don't think you're going to offer me any charity. I'm coming in with my flags flying, wearing my sidearms and carrying a token from my lover, or I'm not coming. Honest enough: but a kind of boasting in it, a taint of arrogance. He couldn't be blamed for bristling—and anyway the mere fact of the child would have been a jolt to him. No man would enjoy seeing a casual trespasser make a crop in a field where he himself in twelve years hadn't been able to raise a dust.

"What'd he say?" he managed to squeeze out past the yawn. It would be politer to sit up and pay attention while poor Sabrina told the unhappy climax of her private soap opera, but he was too tired to do more than blink a token interest. His bones were of rubber, his muscles of slack string, his lids kept dropping over his eyes as if they had sinkers on the lashes.

"He seemed to think I'd *planned* it," Sabrina said in her husky, cracking voice. "First he said I sounded as if I was glad of being pregnant. I said how should I sound, and he said ashamed. I said I *was* ashamed. He said why did I present it to him as an ultimatum, then? It would be a little bit more appropriate if I *asked*, on a thing like that. And so on and so on. It would have been an easy piece of dialogue to write. His principal worry seemed to be that I insisted on dominating him. *Dominating* him, can you imagine? Trying to make him into something contemptible. He thinks it's all a personality conflict and it's bad for my soul or my character or something if he gives in. He said he gave in three times this summer, and came back on his knees wanting to patch things up, and each time I gave him something nastier to swallow. He wondered if there would ever be an end to it, or if I was just intent on seeing how much he'd take. Etcetera etcetera etcetera. *Ahhhhh!*" she said violently, "he's the coldest, stiffest . . . !"

Leonard finished his cold, smooth bourbon, shook the ice cubes, lifted a look at her passionate, discontented face. "Well, at least you've settled your mind on that."

At once she broke from her leaning, pouncing stance above him. Soft-footed, high-arched, she took a turn up the room and back. "No," she said, and now her forte had become pianissimo, a husky whisper. "No, he did try. He tried three times, as he said. I might even have been unconsciously testing him with all this business. But it wasn't to dominate him. *It wasn't to dominate him!* I wanted to be . . . noticed, maybe."

"Well, too bad, too bad. I'm sorry. But doesn't the baby sort of help? I mean, *aren't* you sort of glad?"

When he started speaking, she was standing with clenched hands in a pose of arid desolation. Before he ended, she had erupted in scorn as hot and sudden as a grassfire. "Can you imagine me letting him be born? Without a father?"

"He'd have a name. You're still married."

389

"Nevertheless."

Okay, nevertheless. It was her funeral, or her lying-in, or whatever it was. He supposed it would have to work out that way in her self-destructive syndrome: want a child all her married life and abort it when she got one. Aware that he was not being as sympathetic as was perhaps proper, he said, "It kind of throws you back on your old problem—nothing to do."

She flicked him a look of suspicion or distaste that made him instantly antagonistic; he promised himself that if she didn't go home in five minutes he was going to bed anyway.

"Because look," he said, "we've been over this before. There are a million things to do. If you don't know how, you can always go back to school and learn."

"Can you see me making up one unit of the Average Daily Attendance of a high school evening class in Creative Crockery or something?"

"So you're convicted of the deadly sin of pride."

"You're damned right."

"Nothing attempted nothing gained, as the man said."

"You're so right."

It had got past any stage of sense. Even her speech had dropped into the stereotypes of boredom. She went walking around the room, carrying her glass and rising every step or two onto her stockinged toes. Humming to herself, she bent to examine a photograph of Louise and Dolly framed on the wall. "Speaking of things to do," she said, "you and your committee will have a few. Mother's giving you a hundred-acre park."

"She *what?*"

"As a monument to the Wolcotts, I imagine. You owe it all to your interest in those ridiculous papers."

"Why, good hell," he said, in an excitement as real as if he had been in shape to sustain it. "You don't have to worry about something to do. You've *done* something. Talk about Mercer and the American Medici, do you know what you may have done for the next fifty generations of people on this peninsula? You—"

She turned, and her face was full of contempt. "Oh, quit it!" she

390

said. "My boils won't respond to that kind of high-school-adviser medication. The hell with the foolish park. I'm riddled, can you get that through your head? I'm the kind they just sew up again."

Closeup—blazing eyes, gritted teeth. HOLD, then gradually UP theme song, "I Faw Down Go Boom," as we FADE.

But in his eagerness for sleep and release he was premature in his closing of the episode. She wasn't through yet. There she still stood, the linen dress creased across from hipbone to hipbone; it was almost the only time he had ever seen her when she didn't look like a fashion plate. She was staring at him as if she hated the sight of him. "Listen, Leonard MacDonald, stay away from me, don't come around me with your unasked advice. I'm ugly, I truly am. I've got running sores. I've always had an ulcer in place of the affection anybody ought to find in her family. I've got a cyst where my father ought to be, and now my husband turns out to be a . . . a what? A *fistula!* All the time I was a child I hung around asking for love from my mother and instead I had it impressed on me that I was something dreadful, like hereditary syphilis, that had got injected into the Wolcott bloodstream. And with all that money I was as visible as if I'd been painted bright yellow. I couldn't so much as blow my nose in an unladylike fashion without putting the whole family in jeopardy, and if I broke loose out of that jail all I did was prove she was right in being scared of me. So I learned to fester. I festered into marriage and I've just festered out of it, and I won't be cured by your Greenbelt Committee praises or your Boy Scout advice."

With a finger he drew on the air the sign of the cross. "Fester in peace."

He started to stand up, but some motion of her hands stopped him. Her hands were long, smooth-skinned, well kept; they impressed him then as useless hands, untrained, unskilled. And how in hell had he ever got the idea she hated being a woman? She *wallowed* in it. Now her smooth hands pressed down her hips, smoothing the creased linen, and her eyes gleamed with a red, stubborn insistence that made him groan for the lovely cool quiet of his solitary bed.

"I might join the search for a father," she said. "Burke was always making those little third-grade Freudian suggestions. Do you suppose that's why I act the way I do, some dirty little grubby father cathexis? Is it possible that all that's the matter with me is penis envy?"

"Penance envy is the modern form," Leonard said, a little jolted. It was one thing to hold such a conversation as this in ordinary circumstances, but another to have it flung at you by a haggard-eyed handsome woman in front of windows that reflected back an inescapable two-ness, and at past four in the morning.

"So I married a father substitute and that didn't work, because he really *was* my father, he thought he was obligated to train my character; and then I had an affair with another father, and that didn't work. Isn't this the way stupid people apply psychology to their lives, trying different pieces of formula till they fit? Who am I to hold myself higher than the other stupid people? The stereotype says penis envy leads to frigidity and nymphomania, isn't that it? Well, hooray, it gives a girl a nice orderly program, and Burke could hardly say I was doing it to dominate him."

With one of those incomparably double-jointed movements that only women can manage, she reached back and jerked the zipper from the back of her neck to her waist. The dress fell open and she shrugged it forward till it fell around her hips; her body emerged like a brown vegetable from its pod. In a glare of vision, though he never dropped his eyes from hers, he saw the division of her breasts where they swelled into the brassière, and the molded hollows of her shoulders. She was tanned all the way down, and she stood there like an adolescent daydream, going through motions that at thirteen or fourteen he had taken pains to imagine, and that he could still imagine, given a little prompting. He knew that off to the side their mirrored images faced each other in the black window, and it was all he could do to keep from turning to look. The suddenness of her act had taken all words from his mouth. His heart thudded in his ears.

Then she dropped the straps of her slip and reached back to the hooks of the brassière. "Unh-unh," Leonard said. "Take it easy."

"Don't you want to see my sores?" Her hand stayed back, cramped so that her right shoulder was thrust forward.

392

"You're drunk, or sick. You wouldn't like yourself tomorrow."

"Not as well as tonight, you mean?"

"Cut it out," he said. "Put it back on."

He saw her fingers push at the hooks, and he grabbed her wrists. It took him a second to capture them, and in the twisting and wrestling he touched her bare skin and inhaled her smell of whisky, tobacco, scent, clean hair. She was laughing as she struggled with him, and her laughter made him mad. Good God, what if somebody *was* looking in that window! He wrenched her around and got one wrist and then the other, thinking, We look like the cover of some paperback. Then he had her tied up; she quit struggling; she glared at him out of her great eyes vitreous with tears, and bit her lower lip harshly up between her teeth.

"Jesus, are you nuts?" he said. "What are you trying to prove?"

Biting down on her lip, she stared at him.

"Nymphomania?" he said. "I never saw it done clumsier. Or wickedness, is that it? Trying to demonstrate how biblically evil you are? Good God, any fourteen-year-old in Redwood City probably knows more about that kind of wickedness than you'll ever know. Most of them even know enough not to call it wickedness. I wish I could help you, honest to God I do."

"Then take me," she said. "I'm frigid of course, but I know how to pretend." Her face was twisted, the swim of tears in her eyes broke and ran down her cheeks. With his arms around her, his hands holding her wrists behind her back, he couldn't keep his face from coming close to hers, and he was never sure from second to second whether she was going to kiss him or bite his nose off. "Take me!" Of all the . . .

"I ought to slap you, you know," he said. "I remember, even if you don't, that Bobbie thinks you're the greatest thing in the world." Her eyes skidded away from his, her tongue licked a quick tear from the corner of her mouth. "Is that it?" Leonard said. "Is it just *because* she's your friend? Are you just so hell-bent to bust something?" He let go of her, and she staggered. "Boy, it beats me," he said. "Come on, I'd better take you home."

Sabrina stood looking down. Absently, as if thinking of something else, she pulled the slip straps up and put her arms into the sleeves of the dress and lifted it on. Just at that moment a look that was furtive and questioning slipped out the corners of her eyes. "No, I can go by myself."

"It's too late, and you're in no shape to drive."

"How would you get back?"

"I can drive along behind you and at least see you get there."

"And leave the girls?"

"They'll be all right for twenty minutes."

"No," she said again, dully. A ragged breath caught in her throat, and she made something like a smile. For the glimmer of an instant it transformed her, even in that state, and he thought, If she'd come at me smiling instead of brandishing herself like an ax I could have got hurt. "Please," she said, more strongly. "I'm all right now. I want to go alone."

He watched her zip the dress together, but now she seemed less double-jointed, and there remained a four-inch gap. With a look from under her brows she turned, and he zipped her together and hooked the little hook. Her lips trembled at him, he shook his head, she bowed her forehead against his shoulder and he put his arm around her. Female enough—too much woman, it seemed to him, to be going to waste. "Forget it," he said, and started her toward the door.

Halfway, she broke loose from his arm and slid back to where her pumps stood by a chair. For a moment she was immobilized, squeezing her heels into them, and then she came past him and through the door. As he started out after her she closed it in his face. "Please," she said from outside. She seemed all right, and he let her go, but he opened the door and stood in it while the car started. The entrance lightened as the car backed into the street, and when it started forward the glare blazed in his eyes. He wondered if she was looking back. Watching the tail lights diminish up the street he said to himself, "Brother, how tangled up can you get?"

The feel of her skin was still on his fingers. He wished he had thought to at least go out and wipe the dew off the seat for her.

CHAPTER 32

S HE TURNED the key, the whispering motor died, a spring sighed toward quiet. Five o'clock in the morning. Back above where the driveway left the sky open, the light of San Francisco burned coldly on the overcast, but there was no murmuring from that hive. Soundless the City, the Bayshore, El Camino. Too early for the industrious, too late for even the most riotous. But Ah, she said, *I'm* still up.

Down her back her dress was soaked; her hands were wet from the wheel. Her arms and back ached, her mouth was dry, her mind lay sullen as a sick dog, but clear—too clear. There was just enough light to show her the dark lines of half-timbering on the garages and bring her the dull shine of the greenhouses, but she could not tell whether morning was coming on or whether the light in the oak by the tennis court threw illumination this far. By leaning, she could see it there among the leaves, livid as the night light in a morgue.

Her shoulders contracted. She hated the place, inside and out, when everything was this still. When she liked it most was in a big winter storm, when the trees moaned and creaked, and the light swung the shadows of limbs, and big sycamore leaves skated along the ground on their turned-down points, walking high like tarantulas, sounding a dry threat, and then in a gust were swept away, and smaller leaves sailed past, and the tennis-court fence sang and the air turned obliquely silver with rain. Within minutes you would be clawing the wet hair out of your eyes, and looking upward you would see the storm coming in nearly horizontal among gray limbs and threshing leaves.

Once she had run out into that kind of storm after a quarrel with her mother—that locket business, and the preposterous demand that she go stand in the closet. Out of the closet she had burst like a whirlwind, and now, standing shivering beside the car in the cold predawn dark, she remembered in her very skin the feel of that exposure—clothes soaked, hair drenched, health endangered, pride upheld, protest registered. Had she really, as it seemed now, been expressing her resentment against other things as well, against a whole lifetime of rejection? She was only recently back from Lausanne, where she was sure her mother had sent her to get rid of her, and where she had had brooding occasion to compare her mother's letters, infrequent, stiff, and hortatory as if taken out of Grandmother Emily's resolutions, with the warm long incessant letters of some parents. Anyway a tornado of protest and anger and wrong. Hugging her elbows and chattering, she had walked up and down the flooded lawns watching with satisfaction as lights came on in different parts of the house where they searched for her. Somebody came and stood in the doorway looking out. After a while Lizardo and a couple of gardeners and a maid—not Bernadette, an earlier one, May—had converged with raincoats and umbrellas and flashlights, and hunted and called until, after they had got good and wet, she had let them find her.

That storm had expressed her; it spoke her mind. And she had gone back in unallayed and unappeased, giving in to nothing and accepting nothing. Fatherless, and now motherless; for her mother had not come hunting. She had sent the servants. There was neither surrender nor reconciliation in going back. And yet a pang of regret, too; buried somewhere in that memory was the tag of a daydreamed alternative ending in which her mother had come flying out, appalled at what she had done, unmindful of her own clothes or health or the need of propriety before the servants, and found her, and they hung onto one another in the gale and were washed with rain and tears.

Ah, ah, ah. For the space of a shivering sigh she was frantic for childhood and a rescuing hand, for the figure to forgive and be forgiven by, and she thought of Burke, icy and self-righteous, saying in a voice gone shrill and tight with anger, "Where would it ever end? Have you considered that? Where is the point where you'd have me enough under control to satisfy you? Do you think I'm only made to speak and roll over when you snap your fingers? It's as if you needed to kick me and tramp on me and flog me just for some perverted pleasure you get to see me come crawling and lick your hand. . . ."

He had no more understanding or feeling than a rock. With one gesture, one word, he could have made it possible.

But then she saw what she was beginning to do again, and the sick dog in her snarled. What a sneaky thing the mind was, how it could twist and turn, looking for any roadside where the garbage of blame could be thrown. Let it be an offense to any one, and to ordinary decency, so long as *I* am rid of it! Just once, she told herself, stand up to it. *It?* You know who. Plug all the secondary holes, wait at the rat's front door and see who appears.

None of that escaping—Mother never loved me, I never had a father, I had too much money, I was smothered in ancestor worship for a bunch of ridiculous fossils, I was brought up to live in nineteenth-century Boston rather than twentieth-century Hillsborough, my husband never let me have a place in his life, but kept me an indulged and excluded child. Escape holes, all of them. Plug them and wait, and what twitching nose came cautiously into view. Saying what? Squeaking, "Love me!"

It seemed to her she had never loved anything in her life. Love in her had been a demand, an anger, a hostility, a challenge, a greed. Burke was right, it was an ultimatum she had presented him with. A spoiled brat with a temper tantrum: she had known it all the time, ever since Mexico, known it at Tahoe and known it tonight. And knowing it she had flung herself straight at Leonard, not only reckless of consequences but asking for them, screaming for them, the worse consequences the better.

A greed, never a gift, never the sort of love that came out of Bobbie as naturally as perfume came off a flower. Bobbie, she thought, do you

397

understand at all? Can you? I think maybe Leonard does, a little, in spite of everything. If anybody decent can, you can.

She listened, turning her head sharply. Deepest silence, and only enough seepage of starlight or floodlight or earliest morning to make the dark swim. A flash of weakness went down her legs, the kind of flash she often got from too-vivid imagining of an accident: how the bus could loom disastrously around the blind corner, how the knife could slip and the appalling wound widen. She put her hand on the side of the car and felt it clammy as a wet corpse, and was afraid.

She must go inside. She wanted to talk to Lizardo, who would demand nothing and never blame her. And then she remembered that Lizardo was in the City on his night off. His room would be empty, the key would be on top of the door where he left it for her in case she wanted a drink. And the possibilities that suggested themselves were so instant and logical and completely visual that she turned away from them with another weak flash down her legs, and went walking off unsteadily through the grounds.

Three times she met what she did not want to see. The first time, passing the greenhouse, she saw it only as the faintest reflection in the glass, a movement of darkness upon darkness, and she fled it. The second time, as she stumbled along the gravel road at the edge of the pear orchard and crossed under a light at the corner, it sneaked up behind her and appeared suddenly, puddled and foreshortened, at her feet; and then as she hurried it scissored and grew tall, lapped over a hedge, threatened a tree, and merged with the dark. The third time, she stood on the coping of the swimming pool and saw it inverted, hugging its elbows, staring up at her from the dark shine of the water. The image was dim, but seeing her it knew itself. There was a stern justice, the fulfillment of a deserved anathema, in the fact that it was upside down, like the images of conquered kings on the temple of Monte Alban.

Behind her the wistaria arbor wept slow, heavy drops. Across the pool a bird awoke with a startled squawk, and was answered by a chorus of sleepy twitterings. Birds were coming awake all over. At a distance something—chickadee? phoebe?—sang three long, pure, quavering, descending notes. Without her noticing, the dark had given way to pure gray twilight. The image stared upward at her, and she felt again how, given the slightest chance, it began to demand, began treacherously to plead for itself.

Somewhere along her walk she had picked up a handful of gravel; she found it dented into her cold hand under her arm. Reaching out her hand, she dropped the shattering shower into the reflected face, and then quickly, before it could re-form, she backed away.

Daylight was so close on her heels that she had to resist the impulse to run. What happened when such as she were caught out? Did they evaporate? Dry up? Go blind? Were they exposed in all their loathsomeness? Shape-shifter, witch, or vampire, she did not wait to see. But inside the front hall it was still night, and with her back against the door she thought again of Lizardo's room. In a moment she was out of her shoes and on her way. Dark as smoke, her shadow coiled ahead of her down the stairs.

The basement corridor was as livid as an Utrillo street; she felt at her back the vacuum emptiness of the great room where the clothes lockers were, but nothing in that mausoleum of shed or fictitious personalities pulled her toward it. Softly on the blue-bordered gray carpet she went to the door at the corridor's end and found the key on the ledge above it and went in. The door shut behind her; her fingers, groping in the blackness, found the light switch.

On the white wall of the little cell General MacArthur's face leaped out, reduplicated many times, as if she saw him with the multiple eye of a fly. Below him was the desk, and in the desk the drawer, and in the drawer the gun, exactly where it had been stored in her imagination ever since she had stumbled on it while looking for a pencil. It was marvelously smooth and cool and heavy in her hand. She moved past the cot and into the L that gave on Lizardo's bathroom, and in the mirror on the bathroom door she faced it again.

There with a surrealist intensity, the hateful image glared back at her; when she raised the gun and saw the face over the dark hole of the muzzle, it still glared. The flash of weakness went through her legs again; she saw the image shatter soundlessly, the mirror split and ray outward from the bullet hole, the long triangles of glass drop from the rocking frame. One. Now the other. The muzzle still wavered there in the smashed glass, and she looked deep into her death. Naming over the names of people she had wronged beyond forgiveness, she named everyone close to her, and then named herself. The black hole spun, there was a light inside it like a flashlight in a cave.

She thought, Is this the way? Is this truly the way? One little act of justice and it's over? Close out Mother's fears by showing them all justified? Free Burke, and relieve poor cowardly Bernard, and remove myself from the MacDonalds' garden the way you'd stamp a snake? Is this all there is to it? The touch of a finger and it's over before you hear a noise?

And the child? It goes too, in its womb-tomb? All unsuspected, unless Burke or the MacDonalds tell, or unless they cut me open and discover with satisfaction what they think is the cause of this.

The room was composed in her mind like a painting, how they might find it, how poor Lizardo might find it when he came back. On his neat couch the slumped figure with the gun in its hand, dark blood down the serape cover and puddled on the floor—and in the mirror glass the hateful image like the face in Veronica's handkerchief, but shattered, cracked, slivered, with a hole between its eyes.

She was on the edge, or over the edge, of hallucination. Before her eyes the shattered mirror fused and ran, and her throat contracted in a hiccup of terror, for now there was no reflection of herself at all in the glass, it was as blank as a window in a fog. She sank down onto the floor and put her face close and searched for herself and saw only a slowly churning, ominous mist, and only after long staring could she bring back the image, and reassure herself that the mirror was neither shattered nor empty, but as it always was, always would be. There glared back at her the intact face, distracted, open-mouthed, narcissistic, contemptible; and here outside she herself swam between dream and waking, between fascination and loathing, dizzy and half drunk but with her stage sense fully aware of what she was doing. What she had done all her life—faking, posing, staring at herself in a mirror and despising and being despised by what she saw. She hiccuped, and the image mocked her.

She saw it, bleak and strained, its hair loosened and all but falling, bow downward with a crying mouth, and when after a while she brought her own face up from her knees, the searching, damned, hated face was rising to watch her, its great eyes alert to catch hers. It hiccuped.

Hopeless, hopeless. Disgust, contrition, terror, despair, were rising in her like black water filling a well. The haggard thing in the mirror, with its face convulsed, raised the gun. She saw the wavering, circling black hole steady toward her own eyes. The throat jerked in a hiccup, the lips moved in vindictive words: *First you*. She saw the thumb move on the butt, searching for the safety.

The explosion shocked her deaf and blind, obliterated her. For a second she was wiped out, as dead as if the bullet had plowed through her skull, and a white terror that was like the instant of death glared in her mind, blinding everything. Then she heard a last, delayed tinkle of falling glass and an irregular clicking that she discovered was the chattering of her teeth. She opened her eyes.

No face looked back at her. The mirror lay in slabs and splinters all around her, blasted completely out of the clamps that had held it to the door. In the wood where it had hung was a climbing line of holes. Dully she counted them: seven. Then the awkwardness of her body made itself felt, and she found that she was on her knees with the gun held in both hands nearly above her head, the muzzle pointing at the ceiling. The recoil ached in her wrists. Promoted by the memory of things flying past her in the moment of the shot, she looked to her right and saw cartridge cases scattered on the rug. The whole clip, then. She had pushed something wrong and it had fired a whole burst.

And that burst, shocking people awake at dawn, that detonation of disaster from the bowels of the house, would have them all out like disturbed ants, her mother whimpering, Helen calling the police, Bernadette peeking down the basement door, gardeners coming . . .

She listened, motionless, holding her breath, like a sneak thief who had knocked over something in the dark. The whole room smelled of gunpowder. Still cocking an ear to the stillness, she thought, Now there's no bullet for me. It did not seem a thing about which she should have feelings, one way or the other; she took it only as proof that she could not stay here. She saw that her arm was bleeding, pricked by flying glass. Her eyes came around and up, seeking the mirror and the woman who would be crouched there listening, with a thread of blood on her arm. The dull surprise of not finding her there swelled into panic. She must get out of here!

Snapping to her feet, she opened the bathroom door to see what damage the bullets had done. Nothing but a series of lead-stained pits in the concrete foundation wall. She stepped through the shattered glass to the desk, put the gun in its drawer, and shut it away. A memo pad with a forgotten shopping list lay on the desk, a pencil beside it. With panic growing in her, her legs running almost as she wrote, she scribbled DON'T SAY ANYTHING, S on the pad, and was out the door. The switch dropped Lizardo's room back into dark, the key turned with a click and went up above the door. She listened for sounds: nobody yet. In her noiseless stockinged feet she fled to the stairs and up them, cracked the hall door, looked out into somber brown daylight, saw no one. Noiseless, she ran up the curving staircase, down the empty hall, in her door. Breathless and safe and grateful, she leaned on the door and listened. Not a sound. It had happened so deep down that it had affected the house no more than a rat's stealthy rustling among cartons in an empty storeroom. Like the tree that fell in the forest where no ear could hear it, it might not have happened at all. Gasping for air, letting her heart shudder back to a slowing pound, she half felt that it had not happened; already it had the improbability of hallucination or dream. And that left her right where she had been before, where Burke's final rejection had put her.

But on that she shut her mind, clamped it fast and locked it. It was definitely light outside; she heard the plaintive three-note bird. It must be six o'clock. For a while, as she lay in bed jack-knifed and shivering, with her hands between her thighs to warm them, she maintained her watchfulness over her mental processes, deliberately keeping her brain as blank as a washed blackboard, sweeping the eraser over every random image that tried to appear. Later, surprising herself, she yawned. Shortly the blankness began to buzz and drift with the images of on-coming sleep.

CHAPTER 33

S HE WAS out driving and stopped to listen to a woodpecker in a tree. But the woodsy lane where she had paused fused smoothly with a freeway jammed full of traffic and barred by barricades and lanterns, and when the woodpecker sounded loud and close she saw that it was a young workman, stripped to the waist, breaking up the pavement with a jackhammer. The surface cracked and buckled under his drill; his braced arm muscles vibrated; the concrete caved, and fissures radiated across it dangerously close to where she was stalled. There was water underneath, she felt the car tilt and slide, inexorably sinking, while the demonic jackhammer drilled on. She cried out to the workman. For answer, he smiled knowingly, and in front of everybody halted there, blocking her in back and front and sides, he exposed himself. The pavement was buckling under her wheels, she was locked in beyond any chance of escaping him. All she could do was spit at him in disgust, whereupon he smiled wider. She opened the door to run, and found herself naked under hundreds of eyes. "Pardon me," she said, squeezing through, pretending all was as usual, "Pardon me, may I get through, please?" But her skin quivered like a horse's skin under the swoopings of a horsefly, and when someone stood in front, refusing to let her through, and looked at her accusingly and asked her for her license, she broke into the cold sweat of panic and said it must be in her purse, and she didn't have that with her. She could hear the jackhammer man laughing, she was surrounded by unfriendly faces. Your license, they said. Where's your license?

Gasping, she came up from a long way down, and the dream faded and she was aware of the curtained light of her room, and of something sick in her that was worse than the dream. Someone was tapping lightly on her door.

With her face twisted out of shape in the pillow, the corner of her mouth wet, she lay and listened. The tapping came again; someone cautiously tried the door and found it locked. Sabrina sucked at the corner of her mouth and felt her eyelashes scrape against the pillowslip, but she did not move.

Tap-tap-tap. Still, lie still. *Tap-tap-tap* again, persistent and timid. Then nothing more, a lengthening absence of noise, unheard departure and descending stillness, curled eyelash butterfly-kissing percale, gray light avoided, back turned on it and face into the pillow deep and absorbent, and down the curtains, down, down.

When she awoke again she came clear out of the protective envelope knowing what she had lain down with. Her mouth was as dry and tainted as her thoughts, and skewered from temple to temple was the wire of headache that these days she hardly ever quite lost. Lying still, she pinched her brows down upon it, and upon the images that broke and flicked through her mind, corroborations of a dreadful self-knowledge. She lay like one who has fallen a long way, and regaining consciousness explores the extent of his injuries. And looks up from examining his own bruised body and sees sprawled around him the bodies of those whom his recklessness has brought down with him.

Burke was a wincing pain in her mind, for though she admitted his imperfections and weaknesses—his ambition, his social climbing, his dancing attendance on rich neurotic women when he might have been out curing more legitimate and more painful ills, most of all his stiffness and touchiness and pride—the wreck of their marriage was her fault, not his. It had been a marriage better than many; it could have been better yet if she herself had tried to make it so, and given more and demanded less. It touched and saddened her to think how far his pride had actually bent. Three times—and the first time he found her barely cool from the arms of the lover, and the second time cold and apparently unrepentant over that vulgar pickup from Petaluma, and the third time insistently, boastfully pregnant. No wonder he had finally, in a strangling voice, said, "I can't take any more of this!" and hung up. She remembered him as she had last seen him, up at Grulich's, his eye twitching, his face tightened down on its bones, his whole expression aghast with incredulity and outrage. Like being bitten by a shark, he had said.

Oh, it had hurt him—and the flood of sad warmth that went through her at the thought made her acknowledge how much a part of her intention that had been. Pique, and pride, and anger, and finally unforgiveness, were the weapons she had used against him; and having forced him to concessions she had demanded more and still more, unconditional surrender. It was she, not he, who could have cured it more than once with a word, and who had not spoken.

And so her child, if she retained it, would have not even a pseudo-father. But then neither had she. Neither, for different reasons, had her mother; neither, to all intents and purposes, had her grandmother and the great-aunts. It seemed a Wolcott prerogative.

She wondered if there were some Emersonian compensation that filled her womb at the same time it destroyed the whole fabric of her life, and that was so mystical it made her grimace. Then she found herself wondering what night, of the many possible nights, this child had been conceived, and the memory was so ugly to her she gritted her teeth and shut her eyes. Everything that her mind found to deal with was ugly to her, and yet, with everything collapsing in hysteria and ruin, she had slept last night, and from the look of the light had slept late. Peace after frenzy? All passion spent? She supposed that when you jumped off the Golden Gate Bridge you should be content when you hit the water: that was the climax you bought and paid for. She remembered Jerry Mollar in Pasadena, who always sat on the floor at parties, on the theory that from there it was impossible to fall off. But having fallen, as she had, what now? Gutter out? Crawl away with arms and legs dragging, on some agonized journey toward help? Sit here and wait for rescue?

The remarkable thing, she discovered by degrees, was that she did not feel totally shattered, not even by the clear recollection of last night. She only felt sobered and awed, as a reckless driver may be cooled down by a narrow escape from death. She might almost have smiled at the memory of her theatrical destruction of her own image, the gravel in the swimming-pool face, the bullets in the mirror, if her self-contempt had been only a little less acute. And the business at Leonard's house filled her with passionate shame. Insufferable. Her guilt crawled on her like a loathsome legged thing. And yet under the frantic consciousness of having polluted and disgraced herself there was a quiet, speculative little voice that asked, Did you mean any of it? Weren't you just driving recklessly in some show-off tantrum? If Leonard hadn't had sense, wouldn't it maybe have turned out that *that* gun didn't have any bullets in it either, you'd have somehow cheated on your own recklessness? Histrionic gestures, not despairing ones; bruises, not fractures. She wasn't healthy, but she could crawl.

She held her watch under the bed lamp and forced her eyes to focus and saw that it was nearly one. He might still be home, getting the girls' lunch. Call him now, get it said. She lifted the telephone over onto her stomach, and propped in bed, frowning with headache, dialed the MacDonalds' number.

Louise answered, sounding younger on the telephone. Sabrina loved her little inquiring mew.

"Hello, ducky. How does it feel to have a baby brother?"

"How did you know? Who is this?"

"You mean you don't recognize me?"

"Is it Sabrina?"

"It certainly is."

"You sound funny."

"I wouldn't be surprised. That's from staying up late waiting for your brother. Have you been to see him yet?"

"Daddy's going to take us at three o'clock. His name's Ian."

"Ian? That's pretty fancy."

"It's Scotch."

"I guess it is. Did you and Dolly sleep late?"

"No. I woke up early to see if the baby was here, but they kept him at the hospital."

"They always do, honey. What time *did* you get up?"

"About six, I think. Or five."

"Poor Daddy. Couldn't you have let him sleep?"

"We wanted to find out about the baby."

"I suppose so. Is he there?"

"No, they kept him at the hospital."

"I mean Daddy."

"Yes."

"May I speak to him?"

"I guess so. Are you coming over? Will you go with us to the hospital?"

"Maybe. But let me talk with Daddy now, will you?"

She kissed the mouthpiece and heard the alarming smack in return. The receiver clanked down, there was a crash that sent waves of pain pulsing along the wire between her temples. She held the telephone at arm's length and waited, hitching the pillows behind her with the other hand. The deep breath she drew made her dizzy. Then the breathless little-girl voice said, "Here he is!" and Leonard, hoarse and croaking, said, "Hi."

"Hello, Leonard. You sound the way I feel."

"I was all right till that sheepsfoot roller went over me about 6 a.m."

"If I'd had any sense I'd have brought them home with me last evening. Wouldn't it help you to let them stay here while Bobbie's in the hospital?"

Evidently he did not hear her. His voice, almost unrecognizable with a cold or a summer allergy, or perhaps simply with sleeplessness, croaked at her:

> "In short, the well-known firm of Krupp
> By shooting cannon at a pup
> Could scarcely more have used him up."

She had to laugh. "Still there with an apt quotation."

"Semper fidelis," Leonard said.

There was quite a long silence during which she could hear the girls jawing in the background. "I called to say I'm ashamed," she said at last.

He let that rest a while, too, before he replied in his neutral croak, "No need to be."

"Oh, yes! I'm ashamed to be calling like this, too. I hate people who call up the morning after a party and say delightedly, 'Oh, was I just *awful?*' I know I was awful. I was vile, I was out of my mind."

"Forget it."

"I wish I could. When I woke up a while ago I realized that for two or three months I've been deliberately acting as cheap and stupid as I know how. Why, do you suppose? I ought to have more sense than that. I ought to have more control of my emotions. Whatever could have been the matter with me?"

Still incorrigibly neutral, giving her nothing, he said, "Troubles, I suppose. It's not so strange. If they're better this morning, fine."

"They're no better. They're just the way they were. But I think I might be able to look at them differently. I seem to have waked up clear-headed about myself. Last night seems to have done that for me, at least."

"Good."

"Leonard." She waited for a word, an encouragement to go on, but heard only the voices of the children at a distance. "After I came home I thought about killing myself, Leonard. I had the gun in my hand."

A long, a very long silence. She started to break it, to tell him about the fusilade through the mirror door, and stopped after one inarticulate "Uh . . . ," realizing that she couldn't tell that to him or to anyone, that showed her too plainly at the pitch of her hysterics, and she wanted him to know no more about those than he already knew. She hung on the receiver, fidgeting, until he said, "Oh, no, you wouldn't want to do that."

Leaning forward, hunching over the telephone drawing breath for a new rush of words, she drew back before the dry skepticism of his tone. Depressed, she said, "My God, I'm still at it, aren't I, like a fifteen-year-old hashing and rehashing herself over the telephone. Am I really that kind of self-deceiving stereotype, Leonard? Do you suppose I have to have it both ways, and enjoy both the sin and the repentance?" She barked out a hoarse laugh. "You'd think it was bad enough already without me starting to drink for the hangover."

"I expect the hangover is realer than the sin was."

"The hangover is real, all right. My God, Leonard, I hope you—"

"Well, that was what you wanted, wasn't it?"

"Oh, damn you!" But his growl had loosened something, the way sound waves might loosen the tied-up joints of an arthritic. She combed her hair back with spread fingers and said, "I *am* ashamed, and that's the last I'm going to say about it. How's Bobbie? Have you seen her yet this morning?"

"She's all right."

She hesitated. "Did you tell her about last night?"

"Why should I? You see any reason to?"

She burst out, "I was crazy! I was out of my mind! I can't imagine why I'd—" Every mucous membrane in her head was swollen tight. While she groped on the bedtable for a Kleenex she heard his neutral croak. "Sure."

"I'd like to be your friend," she said.

"That could probably be arranged."

"I'd like to stay Bobbie's friend too."

"I expect you have."

"You treat me better than I deserve," she said. "Listen, will you let me do something?"

"What?"

"Let me come down tonight and fix dinner for you and the girls."

Now the silence was as complete as if water covered them. A brief distant outburst from Louise, and more inundated quiet. Finally Leonard said, "Oh, we'll make out."

"But I'd love to. I promised Bobbie I would."

In the distance Dolly began to cry, and Leonard spoke aside to her. When his voice came back it said, "I guess I think it's better you don't."

"Ah, you're punishing me!"

"No, I just think you hadn't better."

She was rubbing the Kleenex back and forth across her dry lips. "Ever?"

"I don't know about that. Just for now."

"Can I have something sent over?"

"Please don't bother."

"It's no bother."

"Just please don't, then."

"I'm sorry."

"So am I."

"You've got every right to punish me," she said. "I've earned it twenty times over."

"Oh, for God's sake, quit beating your breast!"

For a moment she was furious; then she accepted that too. "All right," she said. "*Live* on spaghetti. When are you going down to see Bobbie again?"

"Around three, I guess."

"Would I be in your way if I went down early, right after two?"

"Look," he said, "would you mind not, just for a day or two?"

"Oh, you *are* angry," she said, and then, stiffly, "All right, I deserve it."

"For God's *sake*," Leonard said, "for once it hasn't anything to do with you. I'm sorry to get—oh, forget it. But you ride it into the ground. Bobbie's got her hands full, that's all. She could do with a few days of quiet."

"Something's wrong!"

"Not with her. But the baby's got a bad mouth and can't nurse. Also the foot they thought they twisted getting him born is a club foot. They operated on him this morning."

"Oh Leonard, you didn't tell me!"

"I didn't know till I went down today."

"Oh, poor Bobbie!"

"She's all right," Leonard said. "She's got what it takes. But she's got her hands full, she's a full-time comforting machine, and this nursing business is tough on them both. So I don't want you going down there and confessing some fictitious sin and fouling her up."

"I wish it was fictitious."

"It was fictitious," Leonard croaked. "You're the phoniest maenad I ever saw. You're a good deal better at self-flagellation. But give her a day or two, eh? And no God-damn repentance." Click, he was gone.

Under his interdict there was nothing she could do for him and the girls, but flowers for Bobbie she could manage. She telephoned and ordered them, vastly. And books, though she had paid so little attention to anything all summer that she had no idea what was new or good or talked-about. Getting the bookseller's suggestions for a random half dozen brought home to her how absolutely the summer had been blanked out. Turning her eyes obsessively inward she had isolated herself inside her own skin, she had spun in the minuscule nebula of her own gaseous emotions the way she had seen gnats hover in a cluster under oak trees; and holocausts could have happened, missiles could have wiped out San Francisco, men could have landed on the moon and found naked footprints in the ash by a crater—she would not have known; she would have been inside, absorbed, picking her navel, nursing her grudges, galvanized by the alternating current of unforgiveness and guilt, which are only the two directions of the same thing.

No God-damn repentance, Leonard said. Could she remember that lesson? No more mirror-staring, because, stare as she would, she would never bring out in the glass any face but the old one, never another and better—and that, she supposed, was what she hated most. The very fact that she was always watching herself was constant proof of her own depravity; she could see the hateful and demanding pride in that face the moment it came sidling around the mirror frame into view.

Stop it. Think of health, think of trees, think of the happy accident of mother's park, think of Leonard's decency and Bobbie's warmth, think of trouble like this club-footed child, the pain, the expense, the anxiety, the successive operations. When she had been nursing a secret contempt for Burke because he did so little charity work and seemed so much less interested in cureless human pain than in the self-induced or boredom-induced ills of rich old women, had it ever occurred to her to do something herself? Outside the Junior League, whose charities she subscribed to and worked for with an indifference tinged by that same snobbish anti-snob contempt, what had she done? She made up her mind that the MacDonald baby would walk straight if she had to fly surgeons in from Vienna every second Thursday. She daydreamed a plan to borrow her mother's twenty acres in Woodside and on them to create a summer camp with riding and swimming and hikes and health, and maybe Good Camper Medals too, for children on whom life had laid handicaps. She was still planning it when the light, tentative *tap-tap-tap* that had first awakened her sounded again on her door. She knew at once who it was. Lizardo. Poor devil, he had probably been in a sweating panic ever since he came home.

"Just a minute," she said, and jumped out of bed—too quickly, for the room reeled and she had to put a hand against the wall. Tying the belt of her robe, she unlocked the door and opened it a few inches. Lizardo's brown face was there a little below her own, his eyes liquid and doglike and asking, his mouth and throat working. In a hoarse whisper he said, "You okay?" Then his eyes widened at the crust of blood on her wrist and hand, so that she swept the cuff of the robe up to her elbow, exposing the scabbed scratch. "It's nothing. A sliver of glass. You saw my note? It was last night, I was down having a drink and I got playing with the gun and it . . ."

Before his steady unhappy look she faltered. He did not believe her, he knew what she had been down there for. Yet she did not think it was hurt feelings at being lied to that tormented his wrinkles into a crying mask; it was dismay, a shattering and appalled and total dismay that she should even have thought of destroying herself. Maybe dismay too that she should have thought of doing it in his room; as he thought it over during the morning, before he could waken her and reassure himself, he must have had visions of what he *might* have found in his room. And yet it was a compliment, of a sort. Didn't people always go where they felt safest to kill themselves? Maybe, too, there was a little dismay in poor Lizardo that his gun should have been involved, the gun that he kept loaded against shadows and dreams but had never intended should be fired.

Through the crack in the door she put her bloodied hand on his arm. "I'm sorry I worried you," she said, and found that she could smile. "It's all right now—really it is. Don't worry a bit. Does anybody else know? Has anybody said anything?"

He shook his head.

"Will you call a repair man? Get yourself a new mirror, or a new door? Plaster up those pits in the wall? And see that I get the bill, not Helen."

412

The knot of anxiety was loosening in his forehead, he tilted his head doubtfully and stared at her with his brown devoted eyes and said, "You all right? You not hurt, or . . . sick?"

"I think I'm better than I've been all summer."

"I belieb maybe," Lizardo said, and now at last he smiled too. His smile kept pulling his lips wide and he kept straightening it back over his teeth and it kept pulling away again. They stood whispering and smiling in the doorway.

"Maybe it'll teach both of us not to dramatize our lives," Sabrina said. "Let's just get it patched up and forget it, Lizardo."

"Okay. You want breakpast? Lunch?"

"I don't know. Something, maybe. Which is most appropriate? Is Mother still in bed, or will she be lunching downstairs?"

"Sims better today. Downstairs, I belieb."

"I guess I'd better have a tray up here. I don't feel much like conversation."

"Okay," Lizardo said. "Oh, I porgot, you dog is come."

"He is? Oh, bring him up!" she cried, and pushed him off down the hall, flapping her hands after him as if shooing off a fly. But the exertion sent such waves of renewed pain through her skull that the room darkened, and she groped her way back to bed and lay wincing and smiling at the open doorway until he appeared, an explosion of affection, pawing the air and dragging Lizardo halfway inside after him. He panted and groaned and whined, frantic with love, and she said, "Oh, old Fat Boy, old talking-dog Fat Boy, did you miss me, did you miss me that much, did you? Oh, let him *loose,* Lizardo!"

He hit the bed, a hurtle of solid weight and gray whiskers and gobbling tongue. His impact knocked her head against the headboard, the covers flew as he leaped off the bed and tore around the room and came piling up on the other side. When she got hold of him, took handfuls of his hair and hide and held him, he shook and whined and drove his nose toward her face.

"Oh, such a talking dog!" she said. "Such an old loving talking dog! Did they put you in an old box and shut you in a baggage car? And did you miss your mudder?" She put her face in his doggy hair and hugged him. Her head was pounding, she felt her voice scattering out of control. Fat Boy crouched and panted in her arms, and when she loosened her grip on him he drove his tongue in her ear. She found that there were tears in her eyes, and looking past him she saw Lizardo discreetly closing the door.

"We're a disgrace," she said. "We embarrass people."

Later she invited him in while she took a shower, but he remembered those too well. He hung in the dressing room and groaned and wagged his apologetic tail, and when she meanly said the plain word "bath" he sneaked away. But he would not completely leave her, either, and so he lay in the doorway with his hind legs sticking out behind and his chin on his front paws. His eyebrows curved over his eyes in a four-inch plume that twitched as his eyes followed her. Getting dressed, she talked to him, mostly compliments.

"You're a fine looking schnauzer, you know? Oh, a magnificent schnauzer. What a fine head, eh? And splendid whiskers, and a nice dark eye, if it wasn't under all those eyebrows. And don't you have a solid barrel on you, and forearms like Popeye, eh? And don't you just naturally goose-step, with a name like Bernsdorff von Bernsdorff. You think so?"

The dark eyes followed her as she dug out stockings. The eyebrows moved, tilting like a quail's plume. The stub tail moved, stopped, moved again.

"Oh, you old mutt, do you adore me that much?" At her movement, his legs gathered, he was ready to leap up. "Not yet, not yet," she said. "But do you know why I'm putting on jeans? So you and I can take a good long walk. Shut up all night in a box! Did anybody come and exercise you, or give you any water?" She moved, and he moved six feet and dropped again, watching her. "How did you and Burke get on?" she said. "Was it lonesome in the house?" A lonely, regretful pang went through her, and she shivered. The tail moved; the eyes, upturned, showed each a new-moon of white below the dark iris. With her moccasined foot she rubbed his head, producing a faint, soft, infinitely nostalgic jingling. "I don't know why I didn't send for you right away, or bring you in the first place. I might have kept my sanity with you around."

Each time she went back and forth between rooms he rose and followed her, until the sight of his devotion made her squat down and pull his ears. "Fatty, I think you love me. Is that it?" She pulled his ears back until his eyes were slits with long curved eyelashes. "You know what I am, pup? What I am too much? I'm a zoophile. It's supposed to be something shameful. For some reason psychologists think you should love people better than dogs." Squatting, she thought that over. "I probably can't do it," she said. "Maybe I can learn to love some people as *well* as dogs." She stood up. "And I can't expect them to love me the way you do," she said.

He had a bad breath. "That old box," she said. "Just wait, you can try every bloody tree and bush in this park. For once it's going to be good for something."

CHAPTER 34

I F SHE had been doing what her feelings most urged her to, she would have been moving, with gifts under her arm, down the corridor of the maternity wing on her way to Bobbie's room. Even thinking about it made her aware of how complicatedly affection and pity were entangled in envy—for a moment she coveted a crippled child of her own, as being more dependent and demanding more love—and she had long since comprehended that envy, if she had luck and continued to carry this baby, could be replaced by a smug sense of membership. She visualized the propped doors and the cranked-up beds and the repetitive shrines banked with offerings of candy, fruit, flowers, books, and could almost smell the unspeakable self-satisfaction that emanated from every cell of that temple. The thought of being in one of those beds, looking out with her face painted for company and her proud smile turned on, made her feel qualmish—or was that only her altered physiology evidencing itself, the bud sickening the tree? Into her mind, like a page from one of the anatomy books she had sneaked looks into at twelve, leaped an anatomical model with its pelvic organs sectioned, and in the uterus a comma-shaped foetus: shame, portent, mystery. First she, then another. In the lexicon of her mother, where words like adultery and unfaithfulness and respectability had currency, it would be called fulfillment.

She had let Fat Boy pull her around four entire circuits of the grounds, and her legs were tired. But the headache was gone, and she felt—did she not?—steadier, more capable of doing from minute to minute and from day to day what must be done. She had facing her, for instance, the problem of Helen's leaving, and the necessity of babying her mother through that bereavement that as yet she didn't even suspect. It occurred to her that she had planned to try once more to get Helen reprieved, and she walked for five minutes considering arguments and pressures that could be used on Oliver and only slowly realized that she did not want Helen reprieved. She liked Helen a great deal better since her misfortune than she had before it, and yet as long as Helen was in the house it would be she, not Sabrina, who played the part of daughter. And for some reason the part of daughter was a role that Sabrina found she wanted to play.

Then Fat Boy surged hard against the leash and she stepped quickly out of the drive before the crunch of tires, and looked up into the sharp, dark, lively face of Leonard MacDonald.

For a second she was ready to run. She stood at the edge of the grass with her arm stretched out to Fat Boy's leaning weight, and he sat still in the old blue Chevvy with his elbow on the door and examined her with his quizzical, prying, amused smile. She could see in his face no contempt, surliness, or blame; he did not appear to be laughing at her or disgusted with her, and she said, blinking, shifting her feet with a jingle of bells, "Well, hi. What are you doing over here? How's Bobbie? How's the baby?"

"Still fighting the battle of the breast," Leonard said. "Right from the beginning he's one of those who don't know what's good for them."

It seemed fair that she accept that as an allusion to herself, and she so accepted it, laughing out of a sense of difficulty and strain, and letting Fat Boy stretch to sniff the car and the hand that Leonard hung down for him. "How's his foot?"

"I don't think it bothers him much. They cut the tendon and braced the foot around. He'll have to have a string of operations."

"I know," Sabrina said. "And I want to . . ." She stopped herself in time. Promises of help would sound to him like one of the forms of self-indulgent repentance. "Will he be all right eventually?"

417

"They tell me he'll be running the four-hundred-meter hurdles in the 1980 Olympics."

"You take it very well," she said, and meant it as a sincere compliment. But he clowned away her sincerity with a rubbery distortion of his whole face, saying, "Daddy told me a man should try to be as good an anvil as he was a hammer." The flattening sun was in his eyes, and she moved so that her shadow fell across him. "Ha!" he said. "What took the light betwixt that star and me?"

Grinning, untouched, untroubled, he regarded her with what she hoped was friendly interest. "I dropped by to see your mother for a second and give her the news," he said, "but I was hoping I'd run into you. How's it go?"

"All right. Better, much better."

"Were you kidding about last night?"

"You mean, the gun? No, I wasn't kidding. I was going to." She let her eyes flash upward—she wanted to catch in his face the dawn of appalled belief, but he only looked wise and foxy and alert.

"Why didn't you?" he said, so bluntly that she searched his face for the jeer that must lie under the words. For heaven's sake, this is my life we're talking about, not some movie I decided not to go to! she said to herself, and rather sharply, covering her antagonism with a shrug of self-deprecation, she added, "Why? Several reasons, probably. Incompetence, mainly. I shot the mirror off Lizardo's bathroom door."

And that reached him; she saw awaken in his mobile face and in his prying brown eyes the belief she had wanted there, the concern. "You did?" He pursed his lips, she expected him to *t-t-t-t* like a shocked grandmother.

"Also," she said, "I guess I decided at the last minute that I'm not a tragic heroine."

"Trivial thing like me," Leonard said. With his head cocked on one side, his breath hissing a thin whistle between his teeth, he regarded her with an air of comprehension that she found insufferable. "Well," he said, "I'm glad you changed your mind. I hadn't figured your strangulated conscience would be that bad. It shouldn't have been. You definitely all right now?"

418

"I've finally come to agree with you that there's nothing wrong with me except I'm self-obsessed, naïve, silly, and ridiculous."

He did not contradict her. "Good," he said, and stepped out of the car. "Is your mother home?"

But Sabrina did not want the conversation to end there; the more infuriating his air of omniscience was to her, the more she wanted to tell him what had been going through her head all day. "She's probably about to have tea. But don't go in there yet. Come on and walk me over to the tennis court and back. Because first I want to tell you how grateful—"

"Nah," Leonard said. "No gratitude, no repentance. But I'll promenade you, nothing loath."

He offered his preposterous low-comedy arm, and she took it with a laugh, appeased. "What are you going to do?" he asked as Fat Boy towed them across the soft nap of grass. "Going to take a trip, or get a house somewhere, or stay here, or what? Bobbie was wondering."

"Would it seem queer if I told you I want to stay here?"

"Queer? No."

"And bring forth my illegitimate child in the bosom of the family?"

"He isn't going to be illegitimate."

"Mother will put two and two together and guess he is."

They must have walked fifty feet before he answered, and she studied him as they went arm in arm across the great sweep of grass. He was the hairy, muscular sort that ages early; though he could not be more than a couple of years older than herself, the skin of his neck and face was weatherbeaten and coarsened, the hair on his crown was thin. He walked looking at the ground, his lips thrust thoughtfully forward, the comic mask for a moment off, and it seemed to her, in a rush of gratitude and liking, that she knew exactly what Bobbie had fallen in love with: there was a steadiness in him, a responsibility, a decency and goodness all the more remarkable for coming from an unlikely, uneducated, and insolvent source. His mouth, even, when you saw it in profile, and when he was not clowning or shadow-boxing, looked sad. She said to herself, If he can do something like that with himself, just by an act of will, so can I!

"Beautiful dog," Leonard said, with his eyes on straining Fat Boy, and she understood that he was not going to comment on what her mother would think of her child. He probably thought she was asking for sympathy; he probably felt that if she feared her mother's reaction, she shouldn't expose herself to it; he perhaps thought it ridiculous to borrow trouble in advance. So thinking of herself, she praised Fat Boy.

"That's just about the best schnauzer in California," she said. "Maybe *the* best, if I'd take the trouble to show him more."

"He's got style, you can see it."

She stopped. "Leonard, I want to read you my future and see what you think. Will you tell me, honestly?"

He squatted with a creaking of tight Levis and began rubbing gently behind Fat Boy's ears. He picked a foxtail out of the eyebrow plume and smoothed the wiry fur down the dog's back. Squinting upward, smiling painfully— Was that embarrassment? Did she bother him that much, with her problems?—he said, "I may not have any thoughts, but shoot."

"This is where it started," Sabrina said, and the moment she began on it she heard the passion shake in her voice. "All that falseness and play-acting and pride and unforgiveness. Do you think I could stay here and simply wear it out, make myself over? Do you think, for instance, I could manage to get closer to Mother at this late date? She's told me a few things lately, I think I understand her better. If I made every effort to accept her and be an affectionate daughter, do you think I might get her to accept me? And the baby? She's not a bad woman, I find. She's very generous, even. If she had any help from anybody she could be that responsible patrician we talked about once. If somebody were around to advise her how to give, and where, and to whom, she could make her money do quite a lot of good. I think maybe between us we made a start on it with this park. But there's more than that, it's more personal than that. Except when her old Wolcott grudge-holding is stirred up, or she's scared, she's naturally affectionate. I never knew that at all until I watched her this summer fall in love with you and Helen. Leonard, I want to get in on that! I'd like to learn how to love people the way Bobbie does, just the way the sun shines, and I can't think of a better place to start than where I first started failing. What are you smiling at? Oh Leonard, I *mean* it!"

"So mean it, it's a fine program."

"But you don't think I can do it."

"It doesn't quite take care of your whole life, just being a sacrificial and devoted daughter. She isn't going to live forever. Then what?"

"Of course she's not. That's why I want us to get closer together now. I want her to accept this baby, too, guilty as he is. I don't want him fended off the way I was." She saw the thinking twitch in his smile, and said, "Is that some more self-pity? Maybe it is. Maybe it isn't, too. Listen! While this house is still here I want to keep it as it is, for her sake, but I want to bring something into it besides all the *things* she's had to live by. You're quite right, it won't be long. She'll die, or have another stroke and be bed-ridden, and Oliver will come panting to liquidate the old white elephant and erect a tract where it stood. You know just how it will be—or do you? First museum directors and antique dealers will be down examining and appraising and putting on little tags, and somebody like you or Helen will spend days with lists and receipts and certificates of genuineness and old books of check stubs, and we'll discover that for thirty years there has been a Georgian pine or a Tudor oak room, complete with wrought-iron staircases and Adam fireplaces, that Mercer or somebody shipped from England and stored in a warehouse and never uncrated—acres of such stuff, here or in Boston, that everybody's forgotten all about. Maybe a few things, some silver or glass, the family portraits, the Monet, the jewels, will get set aside for Oliver or the children or me, and the rest of it, the whole packrat's nest of it, will end up in antique stores or—after we've taken care to get it vastly over-valued for tax-deduction purposes—in museums. Then I suppose Lizardo or Bernadette will hang around unhappily caretaking in this empty old barn until the wreckers come, and do-it-yourself home-builders will drive up in their pickups and station wagons to get a few doors or a crystal chandelier or some good seasoned redwood lumber, and finally Oliver's bulldozers will start smashing down the wall and uprooting the oaks, and I'll have to stay around just to see that he maintains some minimum responsibility, and doesn't split it up into little hundred-foot lots for the fastest and biggest profit. Isn't that a thing worth doing? You've always been telling me about all the useful things to do. Isn't it worth something, couldn't I maybe justify myself a little, if I try to save Mother from all that change until it doesn't matter any more to her, and then try to see that change when it finally comes isn't too ugly?"

He was crouched below her, his hairy brown hand stroking the dog's neck. His upward glance questioned whether she was going on. Then he said, "Yes, that's a sound, aggressive, do-good-and-love program."

"Oh, go to hell!" she said angrily. "I thought I could talk to you. Also, remember, I'll be having this baby. And I'll be trying to give him love but not too much love, and not the wrong kind. Do you recognize *that* quotation?"

She dropped, almost flung, the leash across Fat Boy's back, thinking that when a person really tried, she deserved something better than mockery and doubt. She let her eyes blaze at him, and his lips curved in the faunlike smile.

"You wanted me to tell you what I thought."

"Leonard, it seems to me you're the most inconsistent person alive. Those are your own sentiments I've been giving you back. Now you seem to think they're funny."

"No," Leonard said, and squinted off across the green blaze of grass. From the distance Sabrina could hear children yelling in the pool. "No," Leonard said, "I think those are good things to do. I couldn't suggest any better, for a fact. It's funny how many different kinds of things you can make a halfway decent life out of if you believe in them and work at them. Likewise it's funny how no combination really turns out to be exactly the Kingdom of Heaven, you know? I think you'll do some of those things, sure. But I don't think you're going to emerge out the other end clothed in white samite. You're a little like my old Chevvy."

"A crock?" she said. "Thanks very much."

"You do well to take it as a compliment. She's an old and faithful friend. But sometime this summer or fall she's going to quit, there'll be a big sound of marbles in the transmission and blam, she's dead. Then I'll take her all apart and put in a new rear main bearing, and while I'm at it I'll grind the valves and give her a ring job and clean the carburetor and the gas lines and pack the front wheels and change the plugs and check the timing and the points, and when I'm through she'll run again. But she'll still be a 1954 Chevvy, she won't be a new car. And nobody should expect her to be. You dig me?"

In the warm shadow of the oak they stared at one another. A breeze came from somewhere and she saw the light undersides of the grape leaves on the tennis court fence riffle whitely and then come back to their sober green. Fat Boy started away and she stepped on his leash with a faint tinkle of bells. "Heel, boy," she said, and he came and put his nose against the back of her left knee; her fingers just reached to his ears and his curving plume. "You don't believe in conversion," she said to Leonard. "You don't believe there's anything a person can do."

"I believe in repairs," Leonard said. "Until they arrange a trade-in system it's the best we can manage."

Watching him, saying nothing, she started toward the house. At the front door she picked up Fat Boy's trailing leash. "All right," she said. "I'll brood about it. You go on in and see Mother, I'm going to go upstairs and change. She has a fit when I run around in jeans and squaw boots. Can you stay for tea?"

"I've got to get back to the kids."

"Well, go ahead then. Mother'll be glad to see you."

"In my jeans and squaw boots."

"I think you've been educational for her," Sabrina said. "Maybe for all of us. Guru MacDonald. Can I go see Bobbie tomorrow?"

"Why not?" Leonard said. "She needs affection, too."

CHAPTER 35

IT WAS a half hour before she came down again, still with Fat Boy on his chain. A look out the door showed her no blue car in the drive. It was just as well; she did not want to feel again, so soon, the mixture of helplessness, inconsequence, and stupidity that he had left her feeling. He was so right, she simply fell out of one pose into another, incurable. And yet she had a resolution hardening in her to prove him wrong. Watch me, she felt like telling him. Give me a chance. Let me try.

She turned from the door, enclosing herself in brown twilight, and instantly she was aware of them hanging over her, staring down from the damask walls. In amused dismay she thought, Lord, *nobody* should ever have her portrait painted! Great-Grandmother Wolcott was a bony, patient stare; Grandmother Barber's bituminous glower had in it no more glimmer of softness than the caricature of a prison matron; her mother simpered out from among the organdy meringue with such affectation that she looked imbecilic. As for the scowling child on the landing, with her look of hot question, who was she to criticize? She had done, if anything, worse than any of them.

Nevertheless, as she held Fat Boy on a short lead and gave them back their looks, one after another of them seemed subtly to alter. Something sad crept into them—had perhaps been there always, unseen until she let herself see it. It was there in the downward corners of her great-grandmother's mouth, in the ridge between her grandmother's eyes, in the look almost of panic with which the gray-blue eyes of her mother stared through the simpering mask. The faces of prisoners—hers too, the face of a child grown up in hiding, peeping at the world through cracks and skylights. Any of Uncle Mercer's photographs showed the same thing. Grace and Sarah could have joined the gallery without altering its tone in the least.

Something was missing from their inheritance as pigmentation was missing from the genes of albinos; they lacked it as white cats were inclined to deafness. Leonard, telling his apparently unfeeling story while the stars fell, had been right. It was not laughter they forced you to, but pity.

So return to it, go down smothering among the cushions, turn herself into a spook at thirty-five? That was not what she meant. Return to it, maybe, but not to sleep. Bring something else back with her, something she had refused to possess before. Turn a wall into a window, let some light in, make that idiotic telescope in the tearoom point at something? It tempted her.

In the gray light by the stairs the tall clock, older than any of the portraits or the people who had sat for them, went on steadily measuring time. Measuring time? Measuring the distance of its pendulum arc. If you tore off its hands, its brass bob would continue solemn as a pelican in flight, its portentous ticking would still sound as if it had a meaning, its striking of thirteen, or of three when other clocks said eleven, might still carry persuasion to prisoners who heard it in the night. The family must have kept it to corroborate their pretense that time was circular or elliptical, and that it did not pass, but returned.

She gave it a good look as she went past toward the library. It was as stiff as a cigar-store Indian; its hands hung around its face like bedraggled feathers; it said three-fifty five. A glance at her watch assured her that by another and better measure it was actually five-thirty.

Coming down the hall, she heard voices in the library, and when she looked in the door she had a moment's dizzy feeling that the hands had really been torn off, and that time really did revolve around a changeless center. There was the unaltered setting, the gleam of rubbed wood, the ranks of fine leather bindings touched with soft afternoon light, Monet's lilies so still that she might have seen a water skater move on the magical surface. There were the three women, prisoner, crony, and companion, preoccupied with poking back among old papers for meanings and justifications and regrets. Her mother had one of the pamphlet cases in her hands; there was a gap in the shelf of files that Leonard had left.

Fat Boy growled. "Oh, good gracious!" her mother said, peering through her glasses, leaning forward, interrupted in some exposition. Sue Whiteside, with one of her exaggerated gestures, threw back her head and opened her mouth wide in silent greeting. Helen Kretchmer directed at the door a straight, sober look. So time was linear after all: tomorrow when her mother awoke, her life would have been changed —would never be the same again. Though she did not know it, she had already lost her independence, which had been a fraud from the beginning, and was about to lose some of what she had called her security. It was a moment like the breaking of something fragile and prized, but not after all very valuable. You felt sorry not for the loss of the thing itself, but for the person who mistakenly valued it, thinking it essential to her contentment. And you tried hard—no repentance! no God-damn repentance!—not to feel sorry for yourself.

It passed and was gone in the space of a second, while she stood snubbing Fat Boy close in the doorway and the three of them raised their faces toward her. "Hello, Mother," she said. "You're feeling better than yesterday. Good. Hello, Mrs. Whiteside. Hello, Helen. Mother, this is Fat Boy. He's come to sleep on your satin sofas and dig up your rose bushes."

She led him around to each in turn. Mrs. Hutchens cringed away from his investigative nose, Sue Whiteside reached out a hand to pet him and drove him mistrustfully off, Helen with knowledgeable casualness let her hand hang knuckles forward until he sniffed them, and then she scratched behind his ears. That seemed enough for the moment. Sabrina made him lie down under the desk, where he moved now and then, a hairy intruder, sighing and dragging his chain, and rumbled omens.

426

Her mother's eyes on Sabrina were meaningful, burdened with a question or a shared secret. Significantly she pulled the contents from the folder she held, and Sabrina saw the sealed envelope she herself had put there two days before. Understood, then. Not rejected as yesterday morning, the very notion of such shared intimacy repudiated. Back where they were in the patio, trying to reach across. She had the feeling that her mother would never again mention those papers, but the act of showing them, and of now with raised furry eyebrows acknowledging what she had done, had perhaps eased something between them.

"I was telling Sue and Helen that I have a . . . few things not yet to be added to the . . . archive," the old lady said. "For the moment it did not seem quite . . . modest to have Leonard sorting your baby pictures, for instance."

Her eyes begged laughter; she shook, and unhooked one earpiece of the glasses from her side hair, and fumbled the glasses off. She swung her head and body back and forth—restoring, Sabrina supposed, the natural vision that the cheating glasses had impaired. But even in the process of swinging, the pale eyes touched hers with an urgency: Shall we be . . . jolly, now? The silent shaking of laughter lasted only a moment, and she was saying, "There is even a diary that I myself kept . . . for a short time. I have never shown it to anyone. It is not a . . . very happy document, I'm afraid."

Out of an accumulation of feelings Sabrina said, "Is a diary, ever? Any more than a portrait is ever a happy picture?"

That fixed the attention of all three; they stared at her painfully; they thought she had something to tell them. "Are you saying," her mother said with a glazed, distressed look, "that . . . no life is happy?"

All of them looked a little glazed, trapped in sober meditations that none of them wanted to indulge. She was tempted to ask them in that heightened moment what they thought of Sylvia Morgan, for whom American lives no longer mattered because they had no suffering in them. How about it, Mrs. Whiteside? How can you and your schizoid husband matter when you have always eaten well, had the best of medical care, and been able to afford the weekly chamber music? How about you, Miss Kretchmer? You look strained and half sick, but what have you lost? A job, some daydreams. Has either of you seen a son or brother dragged off to the gas chambers, or patriots shot down in the streets? Mrs. Hutchens, you? You lost a husband? Can you pretend that being frightened into self-indulgence and lovelessness is anything serious? Can I pretend that what I've been putting myself and others through is worth more than an incredulous snicker?

Their eyes were bright, watching her. The library was gray and cool. Under the desk Fat Boy groaned and dragged his chain and thumped his chin down on the floor. She saw the crescents of white under his pupils as he looked up at her, and she said to the argumentative ghost of Sylvia Morgan, who was at least partly herself, that if the world treated you so badly that you had no really dreadful hurts, you must make the best of those you had. Solve the problems of pain, hunger, and injustice, and behind them would be the paler, less consequential, and totally incurable problems that were not supposed to matter. And if you didn't even have those, you would invent them.

"Everybody's lost something, or wants something he can't have," she said. "It doesn't have to be reasonable, or just, or important, he can still be unhappy about it."

And to those who found themselves nearly content with their lives, they sent a club-footed child as a reminder.

Her mother lifted her dewlapped face and twitched her hands in her lap. "Wouldn't it be splendid," she said. "Wouldn't it be splendid if everybody . . . could have exactly what he wished! But of course you are right. Few if any do." She turned the rings on her fingers and scattered over Helen and Sue Whiteside a shaky, wincing smile. "I wonder if I have ever . . . told any of you about my balloon?"

They turned questioning, smiling faces.

"In the Boboli Gardens in . . . Florence," Mrs. Hutchens said. "I must have been six, I think. We were on our way back to Boston from Rome and had . . . stopped to visit friends who had a . . . villa on Bellosguardo. I think it must have been on that trip that mother sat for her . . . portrait to Frank Duveneck. He was very fashionable. But that has nothing to do . . . You see, on this day mother had let the nurse go, and I had my . . . own mother to look after me, as I . . . seldom had. It was . . . perfectly splendid to walk with her holding onto her hand. She seemed so much more . . . stylish and wonderful than a nurse."

She paused to chuckle and glance around in her way of asking a story to be amusing. Her eyes touched Sabrina's and held a moment, broke almost embarrassedly away. "If the truth was told, I was always a little . . . afraid of Mother. She had a way of seeming . . . terribly remote and stern, and she believed quite rightly in being . . . firm with me. But on that trip she was . . . jolly and full of fun. I think she was happy to be returning to America after . . . more than seven years. She had not even . . . gone back when my father died. This day she took me in a *carrozza* to the gardens, and we had a . . . splendid walk. It was spring, the weather was lovely, a perfectly . . . glorious day."

"Weren't you excited, too?" Helen said. "About coming back to America?" She said it, Sabrina assumed, more to urge on the slow wheels of the story than for any other reason. Her mother limped through stories in short, slow stages, like an old lame person climbing a hill, and she needed periodic encouragement.

"I looked upon . . . Boston as fairyland," Mrs. Hutchens said. "They used to laugh at me, I spoke English with a German . . . accent, because my nurse was a Swiss. I desperately wanted . . . to speak correctly. Aunty Grace on one of her visits had . . . given me that ambition, I think."

"Tiss-you," Sabrina said. Her mother's rabbity gray eyebrows moved upward in pleased recognition.

"But . . . the balloon. We were walking in the gardens, just . . . my mother and I. You know how the gardens . . . fall in those terraces down toward the Pitti Palace, with a view of Florence below." She looked around for confirmation. Sue Whiteside and Sabrina nodded, Helen Kretchmer pulled down a lugubrious and untraveled mouth. "There are many . . . cypress walks and esplanades, and small grass plots where children were playing, and benches where nurses and . . . mothers were knitting in the sun. It was a beautiful . . . day, with puffy white clouds and blue, blue sky. And then a man came . . . selling balloons, and Mother bought me a lovely pink one, the loveliest pink I ever saw, a beautiful pink balloon on a string." She touched her fingers to her lips and shakily pulled them. "I think I was never so happy as to be . . . walking in those beautiful gardens with my . . . own mother, on my way to Boston, on such a beautiful day, with a . . . beautiful pink balloon tied to my finger."

Sabrina, watching curiously, saw her mother's chin pebble and quiver. The pale eyes swam with sudden unbelievable tears. "Oh, pshaw!" she said angrily, and squeezed her eyes shut so that drops fell into her lap. "Pshaw! Of course it . . . got away. I remember I stood there crying and crying, while my pink balloon . . . floated off over the heads of children and over the balustrades and the . . . cypresses, and off into that blue sky and . . . away out over Florence. It seemed to go as high as the Duomo or . . . Giotto's tower, and finally it was only a . . . speck, and then it disappeared. I cried so that Mother grew angry with me and . . . wouldn't buy me another. She said it was my own fault that I had lost it. Oh, oh, it was the most . . . dismal day of my life!"

Sue Whiteside was laughing, wheezing out clouds of smoke. In twenty years of intimacy she had never discovered that Deborah Hutchens disliked smoking. Helen frowned, a quick tight frown, and looked down at her hands. But Sabrina met her mother's eyes fully, and those old washed-out eyes were rebellious and totally unreconciled. In a strong, bugling voice Deborah Hutchens said, "If there is one day in my whole life I would not . . . want to live over! If there is . . . one day that sums up everything!"

"But a balloon," Sue Whiteside said. "'You're joking."

Mrs. Hutchens bit down on her shaking lip. "They say you can drown in two inches of . . . water," she said. "I have drowned several times . . . since, but never more thoroughly."

Her eyes, still wet, focused toward the doorway, and Sabrina turned to see Lizardo there with the tea cart. At once her mother's brows drew down, and she said in the ominous level tone of a hundred remembered reprimands, "But I didn't . . . ring, Lizardo." Then at a groaning sigh from under the desk they looked that way. Sue Whiteside guffawed. It was Fat Boy, plumping his chin down on the bell in one of his stretching sighs, who had rung for tea.

Mrs. Hutchens gazed around as if astonished to see them all there. She motioned to Lizardo to bring the cart in. "Why," she faltered, "he makes himself . . . right at home. Perhaps he will take over and run the house."

She busied herself behind the cart. Pouring tea was a thing she did with pottering grace. The spirit lamp under the urn fluttered a blue, almost invisible blade of flame. In the silver sides of urn and pot, the reflections of faces, arms, bodies, advanced and retreated, enlarged and diminished, in a ghostly saraband. Lizardo went around with a plate of sandwiches as perfectly shaped as if they had been made by a lapidary.

"Speaking of taking over the house," Sabrina said, "would it be all right with you if I asked the two little MacDonald girls to stay here while Bobbie's in the hospital?"

Her mother paused with the pot held wobbling over a cup. Her lips thrust out and then drew in; it came out nearly as a smile. She said, "I was so pleased to hear of their baby. As for having them here, are you sure you have not already . . . asked them?"

"Not exactly. Sort of."

Now was a cool interval, a suspension of everything like the winding and resetting of a clock. "They are very welcome," her mother said, and poured and set the pot down. "I only wish you had . . . thought to inquire whether I was . . . well enough. Yesterday, you recall, I was unwell. Fortunately now I am . . . better."

Lizardo carried cups to Sue Whiteside, to Helen. Mrs. Hutchens said with her slow wobble of humorous complaint, "My children have suddenly acquired the habit of presenting me with . . . *faits accomplis*. Just yesterday I was . . . living a contented quiet life and now today I find myself . . . developing land and giving away a public park and entertaining . . . dogs and children."

"You needed to be smoked out," Sabrina said. "I'm going to make it my project."

Now for an instant there was a confrontation, a glance of question and answer that passed between them. As clearly as words her mother's eyes said, It's final, then? It's divorce? and Sabrina made a little mouth of regret and admission that she hoped communicated her sense of responsibility without slipping off into any blame or self-pity or self-indulgent guilt. Their eyes held only a moment, but it was a look of sympathy and communion—at least it seemed so to her. She wondered how it looked, or what it meant, to Helen Kretchmer, who with her customary way of noticing everything had intercepted it. Sabrina's eyes, turning from her mother's, touched Helen's sober blue ones in another sort of look, with another sort of tacit understanding—and *that,* probably, was noticed but not understood by her mother. Well, there were revelations to come, and adjustments for everybody.

Their images, stiffly unmoving for the space of a breath, moved again in the fat silver side of the urn—her own, her mother's like a bulbous idol with a very long neck and a tall headdress, and Helen's. They shone there distorted, and around them and behind them the library stretched out like a Dutch interior, even to the little window showing the sky, even to the laddered wall of books and the frame inside which glowed Monet's lilies.

"You do not . . . believe me about balloons, perhaps," Deborah Hutchens said with a halt and a catch and a laugh. "If you do not, it is surely because you never . . . had a pink one."

Sue Whiteside guffawed again, reassured that it was a joke after all. But the three tied together by their complicated triangular glance of understanding and renunciation were not laughing, or even smiling.

"I believe you," Sabrina said.

"So do I," said Helen.

They sat within time, suspended or circling. Sabrina had a moment's clear vision of the two of them, her mother forty years younger, herself forty years older, transposed within the unchanged room, chatting through repetitive teas in gray or golden afternoon light shed on them from the window beyond whose protective glass the sky moved and marbled, gray and white and blue and sometimes remotely starred, but always far-off, never with a promise in it. Was that what she was submitting to? Was all her meaning inside here? She acknowledged the possibility, at least as real a possibility as her resolution of a half hour ago to turn walls into windows and let air into the old crypt of a house.

Helen stood up to set her cup on the cart. To Mrs. Hutchens' inquiring, fond motion with the pot, she shook her head. The inquiring

432

gesture extended itself to include Sabrina, and Sabrina reached her cup for more. Her mother, still wearing the soft, fond smile, gestured for her to hold it closer, and she leaned. As she did so she saw her reflection swell forward up the rounded urn toward the elongated headdress of her mother, while the face of Helen Kretchmer withdrew.

FOR THE BEST IN PAPERBACKS, LOOK FOR THE

In every corner of the world, on every subject under the sun, Penguin represents quality and variety—the very best in publishing today.

For complete information about books available from Penguin—including Puffins, Penguin Classics, and Arkana—and how to order them, write to us at the appropriate address below. Please note that for copyright reasons the selection of books varies from country to country.

In the United Kingdom: Please write to *Dept. JC, Penguin Books Ltd, FREEPOST, West Drayton, Middlesex UB7 0BR.*

If you have any difficulty in obtaining a title, please send your order with the correct money, plus ten percent for postage and packaging, to *P.O. Box No. 11, West Drayton, Middlesex UB7 0BR*

In the United States: Please write to *Consumer Sales, Penguin USA, P.O. Box 999, Dept. 17109, Bergenfield, New Jersey 07621-0120.* VISA and MasterCard holders call 1-800-253-6476 to order all Penguin titles

In Canada: Please write to *Penguin Books Canada Ltd, 10 Alcorn Avenue, Suite 300, Toronto, Ontario M4V 3B2*

In Australia: Please write to *Penguin Books Australia Ltd, P.O. Box 257, Ringwood, Victoria 3134*

In New Zealand: Please write to *Penguin Books (NZ) Ltd, Private Bag 102902, North Shore Mail Centre, Auckland 10*

In India: Please write to *Penguin Books India Pvt Ltd, 706 Eros Apartments, 56 Nehru Place, New Delhi 110 019*

In the Netherlands: Please write to *Penguin Books Netherlands bv, Postbus 3507, NL-1001 AH Amsterdam*

In Germany: Please write to *Penguin Books Deutschland GmbH, Metzlerstrasse 26, 60594 Frankfurt am Main*

In Spain: Please write to *Penguin Books S. A., Bravo Murillo 19, 1° B, 28015 Madrid*

In Italy: Please write to *Penguin Italia s.r.l., Via Felice Casati 20, I-20124 Milano*

In France: Please write to *Penguin France S. A., 17 rue Lejeune, F-31000 Toulouse*

In Japan: Please write to *Penguin Books Japan, Ishikiribashi Building, 2–5–4, Suido, Bunkyo-ku, Tokyo 112*

In Greece: Please write to *Penguin Hellas Ltd, Dimocritou 3, GR–106 71 Athens*

In South Africa: Please write to *Longman Penguin Southern Africa (Pty) Ltd, Private Bag X08, Bertsham 2013*

If you're interested in reading more about this author . . .

THE LIFE AND LEGACY OF THE
PULITZER PRIZE–WINNING NOVELIST,
TEACHER, AND CONSERVATIONIST

WALLACE STEGNER
His Life and Work

Jackson J. Benson

"The west does not need to explore its myths much further; it has already relied on them too long."

—Wallace Stegner

Wallace Stegner's life stretched from the horse-and-buggy age of the last homestead frontier to the information age on the edge of the Silicon Valley in suburban California. In this magisterial new biography, Jackson J. Benson traces the trajectory of Stegner's prolific and highly influential career as author of endless literary treasures, including the Pulitzer Prize–winning *Angle of Repose* (1971), National Book Award–winning *Spectator Bird* (1976), and the best-selling *Crossing to Safety* (1987), and teacher of Larry McMurtry, Robert Stone, Ken Kesey, and Ivan Doig.

Jackson J. Benson is the author of *Hemingway: The Writer's Art of Self-Defense* and *The True Adventures of John Steinbeck, Writer*, winner of the PEN-West U.S.A. award for nonfiction.

Look for literature available from Penguin's Pulitzer Prize–winning author Wallace Stegner

☐ **ALL THE LITTLE LIVE THINGS**
The sequel to the National Book Award–winning *Spectator Bird* finds Joe Allston and his wife in California, scarred by the senseless death of their son and baffled by the engulfing chaos of the 1960s.

ISBN 0-14-01441-8

☐ **ANGLE OF REPOSE**
Stegner's Pulitzer–Prize winning masterpiece—the story of a century in the life of an American family and of America itself.

ISBN 0-14-016930-X

☐ **BEYOND THE HUNDREDTH MERIDIAN**
John Wesley Powell and the Second Opening of the West
A fascinating look at the old American West and the man who prophetically warned against the dangers of settling it.

ISBN 0-14-015994-0

☐ **THE BIG ROCK CANDY MOUNTAIN**
Stegner portrays more than thirty years in the life of the Mason family in this harrowing saga of people trying to survive during the lean years of the early twentieth century.

ISBN 0-14-013939-7

☐ **COLLECTED STORIES OF WALLACE STEGNER**
Thirty-one stories, written over half a century, demonstrate why Stegner is acclaimed as one of America's master storytellers.

ISBN 0-14-014774-8

☐ **CROSSING TO SAFETY**
This story of the remarkable friendship between the Langs and the Morgans explores such things as writing for money, solid marriages, and academic promotions.

ISBN 0-14-013348-8

☐ **JOE HILL**
Blending fact with fiction, Stegner creates a full-bodied portrait of Joe Hill, the Wobbly labor organizer who became a legend after he was executed for murder in 1915.

ISBN 0-14-013941-9

□ RECAPITULATION
Bruce Mason returns to Salt Lake City not to perform the perfunctory arrangements for his aunt's funeral but to exorcise the ghosts of his past.

ISBN 0-14-026673-9

□ REMEMBERING LAUGHTER
In the novel that marked his literary debut, Stegner depicts the dramatic, moving story of an Iowa farm wife whose spirit is tested by a series of events as cruel and inevitable as the endless prairie winters.

ISBN 0-14-025240-1

□ A SHOOTING STAR
Sabrina Castro follows a downward spiral of moral disintegration as she wallows in regret over her dissatisfaction with her older and successful husband.

ISBN 0-14-025241-X

□ THE SOUND OF MOUNTAIN WATER
Essays, memoirs, letters, and speeches, written over a period of twenty-five years, which expound upon the rapid changes in the West's cultural and natural heritage.

ISBN 0-14-026674-7

□ THE SPECTATOR BIRD
Stegner's National Book Award–winning novel portrays retired literary agent Joe Allston, who passes through life as a spectator—until he rediscovers the journals of a trip he took to his mother's birthplace years before.

ISBN 0-14-013940-0

□ WHERE THE BLUEBIRD SINGS TO THE LEMONADE SPRINGS
Living and Writing in the West
Sixteen brilliant essays about the people, the land, and the art of the American West.

ISBN 0-14-017402-8

□ WOLF WILLOW
A History, A Story, and a Memory of the Plains Frontier
In a recollection of his boyhood in southern Saskatchewan, Stegner creates a wise and enduring portrait of a pioneer community existing on the verge of the modern world.

ISBN 0-14-013439-5